# *Risk*
## *of*
# *Change*

## by

# Kathleen Collins

2012

Spinsters Ink
P.O. Box 242
Midway, FL  32343

Printed in the United States of America on acid-free paper
First published 2012

Editor: Katherine V. Forrest
Cover Designer: Sandy Knowles

ISBN 13: 978-1-93522-653-6

# Acknowledgments

I would like to thank my friends who have continued to believe in my work as a writer through many years including Lucy Field Goodman, Patsy Rogers, Carol Ogg, Douglas Goetsch, Lou Gaglia, Morton and Vera Leifman, Ellen Ensig-Brodsky, Jan Angelo, Beth Heyn, John Gavriluk, Felice Levine, Lil Hara, Hal Lieberman and the late Maggie Black and Judith Anderson.

I thank the Virginia Center for the Creative Arts, Cummington Community for the Arts, the Northport/East Northport School District and the Open Meadows Foundation for their support.

I am deeply grateful for grants allowing me time in which to write from my close friends Irene Fast, Lois Smith, and the late June Larkin, Zita Attinson and Ruth-Jean Eisenbud.

I thank my children, Stephen, Thomas, Anne and Mary who have always been steady in their support of my writing.

I owe Katherine V. Forrest a special debt for her warmth, insight and boundless care of this manuscript.

And I thank the staff at Bella Books and at Spinsters Ink who work behind the scenes.

## Dedication

For the women
who have given meaning to my life
with my love
and for women like them everywhere

## About the Author

I started on a farm in Redmond, Washington, had a wonderful English teacher in a Seattle high school and went on scholarship to Barnard College where I had two amazing women teachers. While married and raising children, I lived in Washington, Oregon, California, Greece, Delaware and New York. I have three grandchildren. My oldest granddaughter is in the Peace Corps in Benin working in a women's health clinic. My partner of fifteen years, a renown printmaker, Judith Anderson, died in 2008.

For twenty-six years I have lived a few miles from the north shore of Long Island where I swim in the summer and walk in the winter. I am a fierce supporter of Obama.

I was teacher of the year in 1991. I started a club in my public high school to stop bullying and to fight all bias, including racism, sexism, anti-semitism, and heterosexism. We changed the climate in the school. As a writer I was unable to go public at that time and so used a pseudonym for *Lovers in the Present Afternoon* and other lesbian work. Now, retired, I can be open about my lesbian writing. *Risk of Change* deals with both society and the private lives of two women who love one another in our time and dare to take the risks that love requires.

# PART I

# CHAPTER ONE

*September 1995*

The lifeguards leave on Labor Day, storing away their towers, taking in the buoys that warn off boats and Jet Skis and keep the kids within bounds. All summer Meg swims farther out than most, to avoid the floats and flying Frisbees. She alternates stroking leisurely on her side with floating on her back for at least an hour every day, savoring the quiet beauty of the summer sky above her, broken only by the shifting shades and patterns of the clouds above the Sound and the drift of gulls.

After the guards leave, Meg, knowing that at sixty-four she has endurance but not power, swims closer to the shore, where a few walkers come and go, and in the late afternoon a fisherman or two cast from shore for the blues that run in the fall. It is as though the whole of Long Island Sound is hers alone. On this Wednesday after Labor Day the sky is a sharp clear blue and as Meg sidestrokes parallel to shore she can see several fair-sized fishing boats, with gulls trailing over them, sailboats out farther, and far across, the blue outline of

Connecticut. They should have gotten my letters by now, Meg thinks. It's been a week.

And why did you even bother with the one in Alaska? Meg chides herself. A pilot/teacher. Another teacher in Texas. Psychologist in Maine. Artist in Oregon. Of the hundred or so self-descriptions in the pamphlet of lesbian personals for women over fifty, they had been the most likely.

A bush pilot and Meg? Maybe not! Maybe none of them will even write you back. Go home and finish that chapter. She checks her water-resistant watch. Thirty-five minutes and her hands and feet are already cold. Not like August when she could swim forever. You're never ready to get out, she thinks, laughing.

Floating on her back she scans the blue/white sky, tracing the flight of two black-backed gulls soaring on the wind, then kicks once and curves upward, forward, lifting her head out of the water, letting her legs drop and kick back under her, launching her body, turned dolphin, into a long, smooth glide, as she strokes parallel to the deserted shore, then turns and leaves the water. She pulls on her sweatshirt and heads home.

Two miles away from the beach, past streets lined with oaks and dogwood, still thick summer green, in a neighborhood of upgraded summer cottages built in the forties mixed in with newer, larger houses all set on half-acre lots or larger, Meg turns into the long driveway of her home, a small house with log cabin siding, on an acre of shrubs and trees thick enough to hide the house from the road in summer. She stops the car after the turn and leaves the engine idling, while she takes her mail from the roadside mailbox she herself recently installed on its heavy post. She stands, flipping with a slight flutter of expectation past the telephone bill and the local *Yankee Trade*r, but there are no envelopes from her publishers and none from the women to whom she has written. She gets back in the car and heads up the driveway, and it is then that she notices the beat-up orange Chevy and two little boys running up and down the overgrown pathway to the front door.

Parking, Meg runs her hand through her short hair, still damp from swimming, puzzling about who they are. She walks toward the Chevy, notices Washington State plates, and sees the dark-haired girl in jeans, sitting sideways on the hood, blowing smoke rings into the woods. As Meg gets closer, she looks again up the path and meets the dark brown eyes of the older boy, perhaps five, as he stops cold to inspect her.

"Hi," he says.

"Hi," Meg answers, smiling, prompting the girl on the hood to leap down and the little boy up the trail to freeze.

"Hey, Grams, it's me. I'm Shannon."

"Well, hello," Meg says, letting this information work its way into an understanding. Shannon is Angie's oldest kid. Angie is Meg's oldest daughter, who has been in Alaska for twenty years. The boys would be Angie's grandchildren! While she is taking this in, her arms go around the girl in a bear hug.

"Mack and Dylan," the girl says, pointing to the boys, mostly hidden by the wisteria that covers up the path they have been exploring.

Smiling, Meg kneels, holding out her arms to the boys, who stand, undecided for a moment; then Mack, the older one, twists quickly in and out of her welcoming hug and Dylan, three, settles in against her, trusting and warm. "I'm still wet, huh?" she says to Mack, who is inspecting her in her swimming suit and sweatshirt. Mack nods.

"So come on in," Meg says to Shannon, "and tell me how you got here!"

"We took a boat from Ketchikan to Seattle, and I bought the limo in Seattle and drove and drove!"

"Get yourselves something to drink. There's milk and maybe some root beer in the fridge. I need a shower quick! I'm freezing! I'll be right out."

Disappearing into the bathroom, Meg calls to Shannon, "There are some chocolate chippers in the cookie jar. Help yourselves!" As she starts to strip, she realizes that she can't run naked from the shower to the bedroom as she does every day. She pulls her wet suit up again and ducks into her bedroom, grabs her jeans, a shirt, clean underwear, and shivering by now, goes back into the bathroom to leap into the shower, for a moment thinking of nothing, exulting in her body's glow under the warmth of the streaming water.

*** 

By bedtime Shannon has brought their baggage in, and Meg has arranged the little guest room off the living room for the boys, with a sleeping bag for one and the single bed for the other, and opened the futon in the living room for Shannon. Meg has flipped automatically into a quick run for milk and cereal from the A&P, pizza for supper, ice cream for after their baths. She's hauled up toy soldiers that once belonged to her sons, Jimmy and Tim, from the basement, for these boys to play with on the deck.

They've called Angie in Juneau to tell her the kids are safely in New York. Meg has called her youngest daughter, Liz, who lives only twenty minutes away, to tell her that Angie's family has arrived. "Careful, Mom. Shoo them out or they'll settle in. That Shannon's not trouble-free, you know."

"Umhm," Meg says, thinking, I'll just give her time to find a job. She seems like a good kid. "Here, say hello." Meg hands Shannon the receiver.

It's then, with the girl's voice in the background, with Angie's voice still in her mind, that Meg, standing inside the screen door between the sunroom and the deck, watching the boys move the soldiers across the worn, cracked planks, finds Mack's dark brown eyes looking steadily up at her as he asks about the bird working its way up the maple, "Is that a woodpecker or a nuthatch, Granny Meg?"

As she answers him, Meg is seized by the presence of her son Tim's ghost. "That's a woodpecker, Mack," Meg answers. "Tomorrow we'll get out the bird book and make sure."

When the boys are asleep, Shannon and Meg sit talking on the deck, Meg with her tea, Shannon with a Bud she brought in from the car. "I've been working in a cannery in Ketchikan ever since Brad disappeared. He was a trucker," Shannon says, as though that tells Meg everything.

Meg nods. "When was that?"

"Dylan was about eight months. He cried a lot. I wasn't getting any sleep and Brad hadn't ever planned on family life." Shannon laughs and Meg recognizes Angie's laugh, amused, resigned, from the time of Arlo Guthrie singing "Alice's Restaurant" twenty-five years before.

"Do you ever hear from him?"

Shannon shakes her head. "It was over, that's all."

"Hard on the boys."

Shannon hesitates. "Dylan couldn't care less. It was hard for Mack though. It was."

"I'll bet they get up early. We'd better get some sleep."

"Thanks for taking us in, Grams. I'll get a job quick and find a place to live." Shannon stands up and stretches.

In jeans and a T-shirt with a grizzly on the back, the tall, thin girl looks about fifteen, Meg thinks. But she must be what? Twenty-five? Maybe not even. "I laid out towels. The shower has a glitch. If the water goes cold, just turn it off a minute and start over. It'll work that way."

Shannon goes down from the sunroom to the yard to bring up another suitcase. As she comes back in, she stops on the stairs to examine the snapshots on the stairwell walls. "Hey, there's Mom! You and Gramps! And is this you and your mother?"

"Umhm. That's almost fifty years ago," Meg says, smiling.

"Oh my God!" Shannon says, leaning close to the frame as though to decrease the distancing of time.

The phone rings. It's Liz, inviting them all for supper the next night. Meg accepts, hangs up, notices the answering machine is blinking, and automatically punches the play button on the machine. The voice that comes into the room is a stranger's voice, slightly guarded, but beautiful. "My name is Joanna," it says. "I thought I'd call and say hello. I liked your letter and…"

Shannon calls from the stairwell, "Who are these women on this side? I don't recognize them from Mom's album."

"Just a minute, Shannon," Meg calls back.

Shannon comes up the stairs, saying, "Oh, sorry. I didn't know you were on the phone."

Meg pushes the play button again, to hear what Shannon's voice blanked out, knowing too late that she doesn't want this call to be shared with Shannon, not knowing how to turn it off without wiping out the message. The voice arrives again. "My name is Joanna," it says as before, "I thought I'd call and say hello. I'm the printmaker in Oregon, the one riding the bike and playing tennis." The voice laughs and the laughter ripples like waves across a lake. "I wondered where I could buy one of your books. My number is …" Meg is writing down the number, ignoring Shannon's curious glance, ignoring the blush she knows is spreading across her cheeks as she hears this Joanna telling her to call, or write, to let her know.

***

Later, when Shannon is asleep, Meg closes the door between the kitchen and the sunroom and replays the message, listening again and again to the stranger's voice, trying to discover what this Joanna might be like. Too late to call her back tonight, she thinks. I'll do it tomorrow when Shannon is out looking for a job. And the boys? Oh, just go to sleep. It's not an emergency call, you know. You've got these kids to help right now. Other things can wait. No way, she thinks, as the stranger's laughter resonates in her ear.

Once in bed, Meg thinks, I'll write the woman a note. Better, I'll send her a copy of my short stories. With a note attached? Yes! That settled, Meg reads awhile and then turns out the light. Strange to have Angie's daughter here, she thinks: Tim's niece. And my great-grandsons. Wow! Sweet of Liz to bail me out with dinner tomorrow night. I'll haul up some more toys for them tomorrow from those basement cartons.

Dozing, Meg remembers her swim in the afternoon as something done long ago and far away, before the orange Chevy erupted like a benign volcano, spewing the smell of pizza and old suitcases, the perpetual motion that is children's hands and feet, the unfocused energy of this young woman, wet towels, milk glasses and beer cans left half-empty on the table, the mumble of boys' voices talking their way into sleep in the guest room, the cans of smoked salmon Shannon hauled out of her suitcase to stack on the table, the unfamiliar sense that in the morning there will be cartoons on the TV and Mack and Dylan running to the deck to play with the toy soldiers where they left them in little lines, all spilling like lava across the usual calm of her daily quiet space. It'll be fun to have them for a little while, she thinks, smiling. They're sweet kids.

Halfway asleep, Meg feels moments from the seventies hover and then replay: Angie singing "Where Have All the Flowers Gone?" and herself at the kitchen counter packing lunches for Jimmy and Angie and their friends to take on the bus to Washington for a protest march, while Meg stays home with Liz, too little to take along…cookies and apples and sandwiches and squares of gauze soaked in water to use if they should be maced, thinking it's like sending children off to the Civil War must have been.

Meg tries to slip into real sleep or to wake, to check on Mack and Dylan, but instead she's back in 1972, hearing the knocking on the door of the house she'd rented after the divorce. She had opened the door on that ordinary Tuesday afternoon.

The young men had stood, speaking in military English, and all Meg could think about was that they were as young as Tim and that the one with the dark brown eyes like Tim's was still alive.

"Where does your mother live?" Meg had interrupted.

Confused by the question, he was slow to answer. "Missouri, ma'am."

"I never knew anyone from Missouri. Do you have brothers?"

"Yes, ma'am, but they're too young—" He blushed, thinking it was wrong to say to her, then finished, "—too young to have to go."

"Would you like some coffee? There's a pot already made. Please do."

"Thank you, ma'am, we'd appreciate that if it's not too much trouble." The older of the two was acting out of protocol, the younger following his lead.

Meg set out cake and cups and then turned again toward them, asking, "Would either of you rather have a glass of milk?"

The boy from Missouri hesitated and then nodded and it was as Meg poured the milk into a glass that she began to cry, that the words that they have said began to sear her flesh like lightning, the pain radiating through her like a heart attack, and the tumbler fell, shattering, its shards gouging the linoleum, the white of the milk clouding the blue of the kitchen tile the way the rising tears forever blurred her vision.

# CHAPTER TWO

Joanna's voice goes straight to heaven. Standing in the back row of the lesbian chorus she lifts her head to sing skyward, her face radiant with delight. She sings with the same single-mindedness that she works with at her etching press. Whenever she is actively generating beauty Joanna is free of the self-consciousness that secretly plagues her daily life. Planting tulips, sketching, carving, all transform her. Now sunlight strikes through the stained glass shepherd with his flock above her to shimmer amber on her hair, while, unknown to her, the women around her soften their own singing to let her voice be heard as the resonant center of the piece.

The church has let the group perform as part of Portland's annual arts festival. They are singing a mix of ballads and feminist songs they have written for themselves. Joanna herself wrote one, in memory of an old, close friend, the woman Emily was named for, based on *The Ballad of Sir Patrick Spens*: "Last night I saw the new moon lying/With the old moon all in her arms."

"Beautiful. Haunting. Mourning personified," their conductor wrote about it in the photocopied program notes.

The audience is laced with familiar lesbian faces but Joanna does not notice anyone in particular until the concert is concluded and there is a final round of applause. For the first time she checks them out and near the back she sees Theresa, shouting, "Brava!" and waving both her hands as though she's holding castanets. For me? Joanna wonders and an abrupt mix of joy and doubt twang together in her chest as the chorus files out, up the aisle, through the doors, down the stairs, to the reception.

It's been three months. Standing alone against the wall Joanna sees Theresa with her curly blond hair, Guatemalan blouse, tight jeans, cross the room with that slight swing of the hips she always has, to pick up a cup of punch and head for the side door to have a smoke. Joanna, commanding herself to stay with the others in the chorus as they laugh together over their false start in the second song, finds she is racing across the room after Theresa. "Hello, Theresa," she says, once out the door. Her voice sounds to her ear like a note gone flat.

Theresa, who is sitting on a low brick wall, facing away from her, turns at her name. "Oh, hello, Joanna," she says, as though surprised, as though she didn't know that she was there.

"Did you wave to me?" Joanna asks, knowing as she asks it that Theresa will deny it.

"No, no, I didn't see you. Were you singing then?"

Joanna nods. "I thought you might want to come by the house. I've missed you."

Choking on her pride, Joanna has repeatedly dialed Theresa's number, her fingers throbbing to touch Theresa's flesh, her lungs cramping, determined to breathe in the same space with her, not to be alone, not to feel the jagged air that is the open-ended lost in space black hole. Every time she has hung up before Theresa could pick up the phone.

"No, Joanna. No more tries. It's over."

Her face is a mask. There is nothing there that Joanna can recognize, nothing that she can connect to the woman with whom she played tennis, ate Thai, watched erotic videos and made love for two months in the summer.

"Better to walk unshod in the desert. I think so." Theresa grinds out her cigarette and leaves it, a bit of ash, a tiny piece of paper, bent and scorched.

***

Never again! Joanna pulls into traffic, gripping the wheel as though she swings from it out over all of space. I will do my work. I've got a steady job, can pay the mortgage, buy the food. I've got what I need—my trusty stallion—she pats the dashboard, envisions herself galloping over the plain; and my work. That's the important thing. And if I ever look at another woman may the goddess blind me with briars—whoops! Mixed metaphor! "—binding with briars our joys and desires!" she says out loud. Though she tries to smile, it is not laughter but tears that struggle to erupt as she reruns the encounter.

Why a desert? Why unshod? Because Theresa's crazy, that's why. She did wave to me. Maybe she didn't even know that she did though. Let it go, Joanna, just let it go. Oh to hell with every woman on the planet!

So you get used to solitude. Be a nun. A secular nun. My studio my cloister. Abruptly, an image that will be part of a new etching rises in her mind. It emerges from a mist, as though she is walking toward it through a fog along the ocean and it is a stone structure on an island just off shore. Her hand craves a pencil with which to sketch as she begins to see height and the circular base comprised of giant stones, oval, square, in varied hues of gray, wedged together and overgrown with moss. Suddenly angry that she is not within reach of her sketching pad, Joanna zooms around a slow truck ahead of her. Enraged with herself for having followed Theresa outside, for having spoken to her, Joanna says out loud, "A vow of silence then? Christ! I've most of my life talked to no one but myself in any language approaching that of intimacy." Oh fuck it all! I think I'll go get drunk.

Knowing she won't. Knowing alcohol can't touch it. Never could. Alone is alone inside alone, like those little wooden dolls inside dolls inside dolls. On the outside you can't tell. Can't see the inner hollow, the final hollow, the last secret on the inside, the hollow too hollow for anything to be within. That's what I am. A Russian matryoshka. Stiff like that. Unfeeling like that. But charged with love, cursed with love. Ignominy sweeps through her, its vertigo forcing her to pull off the road. Joanna puts her head down on the steering wheel. Her hands still grip the rim.

To hell with every cruising lesbian on the planet! And that includes this writer in New York. I should not have phoned her. Probably she writes lesbian romances. Or half-assed goddess tracts. Joanna hoots with the thought. Just let it go. She probably won't even call me back. She's off in Hawaii with the bush pilot from Alaska. We're all crazy!

   With an angry laugh, Joanna snaps her head up and gets out of the car, lights a cigarette, leans against the fender taking deep drafts of the smoke. Its tendrils touch her flesh within, wind inside the inner carved out space, warming that final emptiness, for that minute soothing the chafing of nothing against nothing.

# CHAPTER THREE

Meg falls cheerfully into her new routine with an immediate familiarity. This morning Shannon has a job interview at a diner. Meg goes grocery shopping. The boys are strapped in the backseat, Mack with a handful of soldiers, Dylan with his constant bear.

Underneath the way the days glide by there is in Meg a fluttery expectation. She is waiting to hear the reaction of the artist in Oregon to her book of stories. Will she phone? Write? Or doesn't she read? Will the book be laid aside? Will she dislike it? Since she was ten years old and began to write letters and poems to the teachers she loved best, Meg has waited with this excitement for readers to respond. To her words. To her words on paper.

"In the bag! I'm a workin' woman!" Shannon swings in the door, a bag of heroes in one hand, Cokes and a six-pack of Bud in the other. "Eat up, men! We have arrived!"

"Congratulations!" Meg calls from the deck where she's gathering up her suit and towels. "We're going swimming. Want to come?"

"Grams! It's September!"

"We've got a few more days of it! C'mon!"

In the car on the way to the beach, Mack says, "Mom, we can call her Granny Meg."

Shannon nods. "That's good, Mack. I like the sound of that."

"But she's your grandmother, not ours," he adds.

"Yeah. Granma is yours."

"Will my Granma be at the beach?" Dylan asks.

Everybody laughs. Dylan hurls his bear at Mack who throws it back. Dylan starts to cry. They arrive at the beach and get the kids out and on the sand. "It's okay, Dylan," Shannon says. "No, your Granma won't be at the beach. She's a long, long ways away, in Alaska."

"Why?" Dylan looks up with tears on his face.

"That's where she lives," Meg says. "But I live here in New York. Let's go get our feet wet, Dylan."

Shannon sits on the sand, watching the boys who are running in and out of the waves by the shore, and digging with the shovels and buckets Meg found in the basement.

Knowing she isn't responsible for the kids, Meg swims out a ways and floats, enjoying the interlude of solitary peace. No letter yet, she thinks. But this Joanna just got the book. Takes time to get to Oregon. You could call. No, not now. I can't do that. Not until she's had time to read it. And why are you hooked on this unknown artist in Oregon? She probably paints china, for God's sake. No, she's a printmaker. Meaning what? Photocopying collages of sunsets?

"Teacher in Texas" is off the list. She wrote back that, in truth, she would never leave her hometown. Meg is relieved to hear it as her second letter also talked of bridge and taking tours of historic sites, of enjoying Mardi Gras and dining out in Houston. While floating, Meg gives a sudden downward kick and arches up and forward into a sidestroke. She names for herself the women she has seriously partnered in her life: Four. Like parsley, sage, rosemary and thyme in the song which drifts through her head as she floats, watching the light clouds waft across the turquoise sky.

"Hey, Grams, are there any jellyfish?"

Meg lifts her head to yell back, "No, Shannon. Too cold!"

Maybe you should quit when you're ahead. Swim. Write. Enjoy the grandkids all. Meg flips into her sidestroke, checking out the kids and Shannon on the shore. She's getting cold. She checks her watch. Have to get out in a few minutes, she knows, too cold to last much longer.

\*\*\*

Back at home the boys watch cartoons while Shannon catches up on laundry and Meg does her accounts. Later Meg finds Shannon, her ubiquitous can of Bud beside her, on the old chaise lounge on the deck reading ads for apartments. "My God! They want a fortune for a place to live!"

Meg sits down across from her on the one usable deck chair. "Here's what you should do, I think. Stay here a month. You're welcome. Chip in on the food and save the rest. Then in late October, find a place. And move in on November first."

Shannon stares down at the newsprint for a long minute and then looks up with a big smile. "You sure?"

"I'm sure."

"Well, thank you, Grams!"

"You're welcome, Shannon."

After the boys are asleep that night, Shannon calls her mother in Alaska to tell her she's found work.

Meg also talks to her. "Hey, Angie, we're having fun down here. Any chance of your coming for a visit?"

Angie laughs. "Not right now, Mom. I'm working round the clock trying to get funding for this fieldwork."

Shannon and Meg settle on the deck. "To celebrate bringin' cash home again!" Shannon says, lifting a Bud to Meg.

"To celebrate!" Meg answers, lifting her cup of tea.

"Like payday at the cannery. That's where I learned to drink."

"You and Brad didn't party?" Meg conceals her surprise.

"When I first met him we did. Kid stuff. Brad had a pickup and we'd drive out in the woods and park. He'd bring a six-pack or two. But I didn't really get into it."

Shannon opens another can and walks back and forth by the railing, looking out into the woods. Meg thinks it's hard to imagine her looking any younger than she does now.

"I got pregnant. Like right away. Brad and the other kids thought I should have an abortion, but I didn't want to. The teachers were always saying we were too irresponsible to have babies, that we'd party and not eat right and how that was terrible for the baby. So I decided I'd show them by God and I didn't party, not even once, while I was pregnant or nursing." There's pride in her voice.

"At first Brad was really into being a daddy, you know. He quit school and got a job driving and we moved to Ketchikan. He'd take Mack and me around and show us off."

Shannon tosses her empty beer can up in the air and catches it with a snap of her wrist as it falls. "After Dylan was born he changed.

He wasn't ready to settle down. One day he just took off. Mom said
I could come back home. I didn't want to go back home. I had a
neighbor who did day care in her house so I got the job at the cannery
instead. Every Friday was party time and then I really got into it, you
know."

Meg nods and finishes her tea.

\*\*\*

Shannon starts work. They enroll Mack in kindergarten. A bus
picks him up and drops him off at the end of the driveway. Dylan stays
home with Meg who takes him shopping with her in the mornings.
Afternoons they go to the beach if it's a nice day and stay inside if it's
not. Shannon's shifts vary and Meg simply suspends her work on the
novel.

They boys are playing in the yard. Meg is making spaghetti in the
kitchen. Shannon pauses on her way up the stairs from doing laundry
in the basement to ask Meg more about the photo gallery that lines
the stairwell. "How long were you married, Grams?"

"Twenty years."

"Was it all bad?"

Meg laughs. "No, sweetie, of course not. The first ten or eleven
years were fine. We had babies and that was fun and we were dirt-poor
but we didn't care about that." Long gone, Meg thinks, and Franklin
scenes fade like cave drawings lived with long ago, now glimpsed
through a darkened opening in a distant mountainside.

"You married young?"

"Umhm. Just like you."

"We had fun too at first."

"I'm glad."

There's silence for a while as Shannon ranges back and forth in
front of the snapshots. Then, "Mom and Uncle Tim were like twins,
Mom said."

Meg smiles. "Very close." She stops chopping onions and stands
still, knife poised above the cutting board. "When Tim died in
Vietnam, it broke Angie's heart. She ran away to Alaska. She was mad
at the government for the war." And mad at us, Meg thinks, for not
keeping Tim safe, remembering her arguments with Franklin.

"Canada would be safe," Meg had said.

"He'd always be ashamed. He'd be in dishonorable exile."

"Vietnam is not an honorable war." Meg had read Jonathan
Schell's series in the *New Yorker* and realized that this war was not like

World War II when the United States fought against fascism, when it was the good against the bad.

"Give it up, Meg," Franklin stated. "I went to war. It's Tim's turn now."

"Tim had been drafted," Meg goes on. "His father was a veteran. Franklin and I fought about it. There were lots of other causes, but that's when the marriage blew up."

Shannon goes out on the deck, where she can look down to check on the boys, and coming back in, leans in the kitchen doorway, watching Meg continue to chop the onions and garlic.

"Mom likes living up there though."

After Angie's angry divorce, Meg had sent her enough money to go back to school. Angie graduated into a government job doing ecological studies of unmapped terrain.

On her way back down to get her clothes from the dryer, Shannon calls again. "Hey, who are these?"

Meg leaves tomatoes half washed in the sink, and laying the knife up out of reach, goes to see. Shannon surely knows. Angie must have told her, Meg thinks. Yet there is a sudden gulf of silence on the stairwell. So maybe not, Meg thinks. Just maybe not.

The silence is now a fact that words don't change. Meg decides that information may make it easier to get past. "They're women I've lived with; they're all gone now."

Shannon is not looking at Meg but staring at the wall of women as though they have not been there before this day, as though Meg has unexpectedly conjured them up to confound Shannon, who was until this moment doing familiar laundry in a normal washer in her ordinary grandmother's house. Shannon rests her finger on the glass of a large frame which holds a dozen snapshots of Rosalyn.

"That's Rosalyn," Meg says, "she was very special," and walks back up the stairway to the kitchen, picks up the knife and cuts up a tomato for the salad. She can hear Shannon going on down to get her clothes. Shannon comes back up, carrying the basket full and goes into the guest room to put them all away.

"When did you know?" Shannon slides behind Meg in the narrow galley to take a beer from the refrigerator. "I'll set the table in a minute. I want to check on the boys." She leaves to go out on the deck without waiting for an answer, as though there'd been no question.

When she comes back in, Meg says, "I didn't know when I was growing up. I didn't know when I was married. I found out when I fell in love after the divorce and the person I fell in love with was a woman. That's when I knew."

# CHAPTER FOUR

Driving home from work, Joanna curses as the rain begins. She's determined to mow the lawn on Saturday. At least it didn't rain last weekend when we were at the cabin, she thinks, remembering the mellow time at the lake with Greta and Marlene. She never feels odd man out with them, safe in the presence of their long-time certainty as a couple.

Joanna parks the car in the garage, goes back to take her mail from the box by the street, notes the acceptance of a print in a show in Chicago, and checks out the sky above the scrim of falling rain, thinking it's not too dark and may clear up by morning. Walking up the short walk to the porch, key in hand, she sees that Jack, their mailman for twenty years, has left something inside the screen door, leaning against the wide, red front door. Red, she tells people, so it's easy to find her house on the long street of similar two-story family houses, most with white siding, all with a small patch of lawn, a single car garage, and two or three trees. Hers are a maple and two plums. The real reason she painted the door red was to announce to herself that the house was hers, not Walter's and hers, but hers. The red was a flag of rage turned into triumph, fury transformed into a celebration. She'd done it twenty years ago on the day of the divorce, by which time she'd found the job in the bookstore and knew she would survive as a single woman with three kids to raise. Her youngest daughter, Emily, had burst into applause when she came in from school and saw it. Will hadn't noticed. And Miranda, in her deliberately trashy jeans, a cigarette defiantly dangling from her mouth, flashed a look of scorn, saying, "You're kidding, right?" and went up to her room.

Seeing the package propping the screen open, Joanna knows instantly that it is the book from the writer in New York. I could just mark it Return to Sender, she thinks, with a wicked grin. And probably should. Bending to pick it up, she knows that she can hardly wait to read it.

Joanna, who reads half a dozen books a week, and rises to one that pleases her like a trout to the perfectly cast fly, settles with her after dinner decaf and a chocolate bar in her favorite chair and begins to read. At first, she's disappointed because it's a collection of short stories and not a novel. Still, after a few pages she knows she will write back to Meg. Joanna reads into the night. Excitement rises in her like stage lights coming up around the characters. At midnight she takes the book to bed with her and reads until she falls asleep.

Saturday morning, back in her chair, she settles to read with her coffee and cigarettes. The sky is Oregon gray, but there is no rain falling. Her body is set for a long day of yard work before the winter rains lock in. Her legs nudge her toward motion. In a minute, she thinks, I'll start that in a minute, knowing nothing will keep her from reading on. About twenty pages short of finishing, she closes the book, not wanting it to end. I'll mow and do the chores and save the last story to have with my after dinner coffee, she thinks, dreading the stab of desolation that comes as she closes any good book for the final time.

As a child under the covers had been her cave.

"Are you still reading in there?" Her father's suspicious voice crisscrossed the room like the spotlight from a guard tower. He stood, framed in the dim light from the hall, undecided. Then he walked toward the bed.

"No, sir."

The book was hidden where it always was, between her body and the wall. The flashlight was wedged between the mattress and the wall. He stood peering down at her. He put his hand on the bulb in her desk lamp, found it cold to his touch. "See that you don't. It's too late. Do you hear?"

"Yes, sir," she mumbled, making her voice sound sleepily obedient. "And tomorrow clean up this room."

When he was long gone she kicked the book up closer to her chest, stroked it with her hand, but did not dare begin again to read. She recited to herself one of the last paragraphs she'd read and as she turned the page in her memory to read another, fell asleep.

In the garage Joanna oils the heavy lawnmower and hauls it outside to the lawn. The leaves, beginning to turn, remind Joanna that autumn is upon her, closing in with death and darkness. Even now, in the forenoon, she can hardly discern the line of the roof where it meets the curves and nearly straight lines of the branches of the trees under the dark cold clouds that are about to unleash a heavy rain.

It's not that there are so many storms. It's the gray damp cold that locks in under a gray sky. The Inuit have many words for snow, she thinks. In Oregon you need that many words for rain. The space between the heavens and the ground is filled with gray, sometimes streaming down in a heavy rain, sometimes such a light moisture you could almost call it fog—falling fog! Joanna smiles grimly at the phrase.

Snow would be easier, she thinks, lucid, transforming everything it graces into beauty. But this gray: elongated gray. The days like blotters soak up the rain and become themselves masses of gray as though rain itself joins the hours in some grotesque symbiosis, a natural bewilderment that has forsaken the bright time statements of the sun. Assessing the grass, dampened the night before, Joanna decides it's dry enough to mow. She gets the motor going and starts her rounds. One more week of this, she thinks, and then she'll let it go while the leaves fall. End of October she'll rake.

Reluctantly, Joanna sits on the porch to rest. It was a lot easier when Sandy was around to help. They weekended back and forth for five years, took out trees, put in a patio for Joanna, a fence for Sandy. Until their last exchange:

"You're sleeping with Renee, aren't you, Sandy? Her car was at your place all night."

There was no more denial, only a leaden silence before, "Oh, I'm sorry. I don't know why I'm doing this. I don't want to lose you, Joanna, but I can't stop."

"There's nothing left to say."

Joanna grinds out her cigarette. Like a litany the lines intrude from three years before, "I can't stop. There's nothing left to say," coming in even strokes the way the fall rains sometimes begin, intending to stay, intending to soak through all the leaves into the grass, through all the grass into the ground, a heavy cold waterlogging of the whole yard, leaving it barren and devoid of joy. Joanna works fiercely, still bewildered that Sandy would secretly make love with someone else and enraged that she would conceal it for months.

As Walter had always lied. Certainly Walter didn't even think adultery was a sin. But that was the way of men, not women. Becoming a lesbian, Joanna had thought she was free of sexism, free of power games, free of deceit. The lesbian chorus wrote new songs so they could sing the truth. New friends lent her books by lesbians who were truth tellers.

"Then does everyone lie?" Joanna mutters, parking the mower, taking the clippers and the edger out to finish up. Maybe I'm the only one who still persists in thinking that lying is a sin, and she snaps angrily at the tall stray grass.

"Yo! Anyone for bikin'?" It's Hildy, sliding to a stop at the curb.

Joanna smiles eagerly but her body aches. "Not this minute, I guess. I've been fighting a damp lawn all morning."

"Want to come over and do mine for me?" Hildy dismounts. "So offer me a glass of water." They go inside together, laughing, talking. "Show me the sketch you did of the new model," Hildy demands, headed for the basement. "Marlene says it's a regular Michelangelo!"

"Yeah, right!" Joanna blushes, shaking her head, but follows Hildy down the stairs and gets out the pad she uses when they meet for their life drawing session at the college.

"My God! That's great!" Hildy leans over the sketch, studying the charcoal lines.

"Want some lunch? I've got peanut butter!"

\*\*\*

After supper Joanna lays a fire and sits with the last pages of Meg's book. She has, on purpose, barely thought of Meg all day but now her new presence is like unexpected flowers, out of season, suddenly delivered on no special day, a brightness in the room, her written words singing in Joanna's brain.

As she closes the book cover Joanna jumps up and goes quickly to her studio. Once there she fills a large mailing envelope with photographs of her work and the commentaries she has written about these pieces. She composes a letter to the writer, telling her how much she likes the book she has just read. When the flap is sealed and the envelope stamped, she puts it by her purse to mail the next day.

***

Meg in New York responds with a letter in which she says she has set the photographs all around her study/bedroom so she can "ponder" them. She sends an unpublished manuscript for Joanna to read. It is an account of her own experiences with her son's life, first as a child, then as a student, then as an opponent of the war in Vietnam; and last of herself as a grieving mother of a soldier who dies there. Joanna closes it with an odd wish to take Meg in her arms.

The way the leaves whirl down in the winds of October, their letters cross the country. They begin to call back and forth in the evenings. Joanna sends more photographs of her carvings and homemade lesbian cartoons in which she photocopies women from art magazines and commercial ads, draws conversation balloons and writes in funny dialogues. "Lonely here," says a Titian nude lying on a bed surrounded by angels overhead. "Is she afraid to fly?" asks an angel.

Give it up! If you can't have successful relationships with people who live right across town, how could you connect with someone in New York? Joanna asks herself and hears her own voice saying on the phone, "Adrienne Rich is giving a reading on campus. Why don't you come to hear her? You could stay with me, of course."

"She's my favorite poet."

"So will you come?"

"Let me think about it."

***

Greta, Marlene and Joanna swing into Joanna's driveway on their bikes. "Now tell us all!" Greta plunks herself down on the porch.

Joanna laughs. "She's coming for a week."

"A week? Are you absolutely crazy? You haven't even met her!"

"We talk on the phone all the time. And I've read her books!"

"Yeah, Stephen King writes books too but I wouldn't want him to come to dinner, let alone stay a week!"

"Tell you what! You and Hildy can come to lunch to meet her and vote. Okay? How's Tuesday?"

"That's a deal. Secret ballot?"

"Secret!" Laughing, they hit the palms of their right hands together in the air.

# CHAPTER FIVE

The jet noise magnifies as the plane gathers speed down the runway at LaGuardia. In her daydream Meg wraps her arms around the sturdy young hippie on his motorcycle and leans into the wind. She feels the bike curve up the ramp onto the freeway, feels the rider ease up the gears, tightens her hold on his waist and enjoys the wind in her face. Not until they are airborne and circling west does she look down at the Hudson, savor the view of the harbor, and let herself know it's a plane, not a bike, and that she is traveling alone.

Meg knows she looks younger than her sixty-four years. Her light brown hair is short and curly with too few gray hairs to show. She is wearing black slacks and a long-sleeved turquoise blouse with matching earrings, silver and turquoise. She is smiling, playing peek-a-boo with the lively three-year-old in the seat in front of her as she and her slightly older sister pop up and down.

In her inner vision, Joanna takes Meg's hand as they walk underneath the maples with their overhanging branches of red and yellow leaves, leaf shadows blowing in the moonlight. As they walk toward the house from the car after the poetry reading, Joanna starts to turn Meg toward her.

Meg considers for a moment the Joanna collage she carries in her mind: a smiling face framed by the flowering branches of a plum tree in the only snapshot Joanna has sent; the resonant beauty of her voice singing a solo with the lesbian chorus on a tape; the startling power and beauty of her etchings, which Meg has seen only in photographs; her lyrical hooting laughter on the phone. Meg stops imagining what might happen when she lands in Oregon.

The plane hits turbulence. By the aisle a teenage girl is crying, frightened by the plunging of the plane, fingers white from gripping her purse. As young as Shannon when she had Dylan; or you yourself, when you met Franklin, Meg thinks. "It'll calm down in a little while," Meg says with a smile across the silently reading boy between them.

The girl can hardly speak. "I never flew before. Did you?"

Meg laughs. "Sure, but not when I was your age! Pretend you're on the roller coaster!" This elicits a quick sideways smile from the boy. Meg leans across him to give the girl the novel from her own lap. Not a lesbian book, she thinks automatically and so okay to share. "Just read a little while and we'll be there. Right?"

The boy ducks deeper into his own book and nods. Boys of a certain age have necks like colts, Meg thinks, and would bolt away if you reached out to stroke them. Lightning stabs against the clouds. And if we crash and I die, it's not that I'll be with Tim, get to listen to him playing his guitar; it's only that I won't be here where I still miss him. That's what people mean about going to join the dead. We can stop missing them when we die in the same way that we stop hurting from the body's pain. It's a double negative, she thinks, with a wry smile. But two wrongs don't make one right.

Meg closes her eyes against the lightning that makes a jagged maze between the clouds. After a few minutes she dozes, wandering down path after path that dead-end in impenetrable brush although she knows there is a clear meadow of sweet-smelling clover just beyond where there is bird song and what might be the notes from a boy's guitar…

The plane jolts in the turbulence, startling Meg awake. Again she thinks of Tim and then with determination she dodges away from memories of the past but not quite in time to avoid hearing just out of earshot Rosalyn's tender laughter, nor to miss a flashing memory of them together on a flight, their hands connecting them with such an intensity of love that Meg thought their aura must be lighting up the night, glowing as though the moon had risen inside the plane.

Meg reaches into the bag at her feet and extracts an envelope of photographs of Joanna's work. She is particularly moved by the animal and human figures. They have a subtlety and clarity that make it hard to believe that they are not alive. They seem etched in mid-motion, caught in mid-feeling. Power. Beauty, Meg thinks. Amazing. That streak of reverence, that intuitive feeling for the beautiful in nature, music, art. Rare. This Joanna has a soul, Meg thinks.

Meg has memorized them all. Flipping through them, she stops at a favorite: four shots of a bone carving, circular, like a napkin ring, of a woman with a whale's tail. A mermaid? A whale mother? Unspeakably beautiful, Meg thinks, touching the glossy surface with her finger as one would touch the living woman in the grace of her breathing arc.

Again Meg sees lightning stab against the clouds. Soon then I'll meet this Joanna woman. She must have warmth. Humor. Not need me to keep her afloat. We must fall in love.

The sky is dark now. There are no stars. The plane is tunneling through heavy clouds. And just who do you think you are? Meg asks herself. If she is the perfect one what makes you think Joanna will have you? And don't wait for the goddess herself. You'll still be waiting when you're ninety-nine. Better to stay waiting, peaceful and alone, than take on someone too heavy to carry, she retorts. All I'm saying is you've turned down woman after woman since Rosalyn walked away. Your Rosalyn is not coming back in a different form with a different name. *Rosalyn, like Tim, is gone,* Meg snaps angrily at herself and drops, as though hitting an air pocket, as the plane moves smoothly on toward Portland. In front of her the three-year-old laughs and tries peek-a-boo again, ducking down beside her father. Meg laughs back at her, suddenly missing Mack and Dylan. Should I tell Joanna all about them? She doesn't know Shannon drinks too much beer. She doesn't know she told Shannon they could stay for a month.

Meg opens her purse and takes out her only snapshot of Joanna. The sun glints on her glasses. The blossoms of the plum tree seem to be blowing in the wind around her face. What a lively face, Meg thinks. What if she's femme? Neither of them has asked or even hinted. Doesn't matter, Meg thinks, and feels herself cringe at the denial. Erotically, she feels an absolute aversion to every femme. Good friends. But not lovers. This Joanna has this really curly hair. Could she possibly have a permanent? Meg balks at the idea and touches the snapshot lightly with her finger, trying to know. She wishes it were a butch haircut. She wishes Joanna's personal had said, "Soft butch."

At least I'm standing free, she thinks. I've never left one woman for another. If I had to leave, I left, stood alone in open space before

I found another. I'm free to meet this Joanna. Joanna of the lesbian chorus, Joanna of the carving, Joanna of the etching press, Joanna who please God will not be wearing lipstick and that kind of clinging perfumed blouse!

Meg checks her seat belt clasp and retrieves her novel from the now smiling Shannon-girl by the aisle. Watching the ground rise up Meg reminds herself like telling beads: I already know Joanna's work is wonderful, her voice beautiful. I know her soul through her work.

The wheels touch down. "And I know she laughs and here I go again," Meg whispers to herself with a quiet smile. It is eagerness, not reluctance, not caution, but simple joyous reckless eagerness that propels her down the ramp and into the waiting room.

# CHAPTER SIX

Swinging her car into the parking garage at the airport, Joanna panics. I've invited her for a week? Visions of herself cornered by an indecipherably oppressive woman smother her. She lights a cigarette and heads for the terminal. "Fool!" she mutters. Meg writes amazing books, she answers herself back. So she writes. Writing, dumkoff, is not loving. And writers are the most notorious liars of them all! Not this one. She writes like a woman who cares about the truth.

The spring returns to Joanna's step. She takes two last deep draws on her cigarette just outside the door, carefully grinds it out in the giant rock ashtray, and goes in, almost at a run. Which gate? Which flight? She pulls a slip of paper from her jeans pocket, checks it, checks the board, and finds her place near the great windows that adjoin the dock. The plane is taxiing in. She's seen a snapshot of Meg, a grandmother holding a newborn. Without the baby in her arms will she be recognizable? I'll know her voice: that beautiful mellow voice. Phones may distort. What will it feel like to be in the car with her, that close?

The scenario that disappoints collides with the scenario that makes her heart race in a dark interior explosion that rains shrapnel down on Joanna as the door opens and the miscellaneous bodies come flowing through. That one? Oh, I hope not that one! Maybe that one? Joanna grabs for a cigarette, remembers where she is, carefully puts it back inside the pack. She is looking down, gently wedging the cigarette in among the others when Meg walks in.

\*\*\*

A few minutes later, Joanna swings Meg's suitcase into the back of her old Honda station wagon and unlocks the passenger door. Her smile is a sideways, private smile as she walks around the car, gets in and drives out of the huge parking lot and onto the highway. They begin to tell one another where they've been in their lives and what they've known as if they're in a canoe, as though each dips a paddle in a familiar rhythm driving their bark between a river's banks.

Joanna's house is an old frame house, with bright blue trim and a front door which, she points out, is bright red. "Makes it easy to find," Joanna says, smiling, turning in the drive.

It is a dark and rainy day and the front yard is gray, spattered with rain puddles across the small winter weary lawn. Once inside the house, the world turns bright. Joanna's own work and the work of others hangs on every wall. The carpets are white, the furniture old and simple, mostly wood: heavy kitchen chairs, a low round coffee table, a worn and polished kitchen table which is clearly the only place to eat.

Meg follows Joanna up the stairs, holding her breath for just a minute, hoping she won't be led into Joanna's room, thinking how to ask for separate space if she is. Joanna takes her into a small room with a single bed in it. "Once my daughter, Emily's," she says, smiling, "and still her decorations," gesturing at the skeleton and anatomical diagrams among music posters on the walls.

"Where is Emily now?"

"Medical school in Maine."

Meg gestures toward the skis leaning in the corner. "Yours or hers?"

"Mine. I do cross-country though not downhill anymore. And your children?"

Let's not get lost in family histories, Meg thinks, answering succinctly. "Jimmy in California, Angie in Alaska. Liz's divorced and lives near me with her kids."

Joanna takes a minute to check her memory, reconciling the smiling grandmother she's seen in the snapshot Meg sent to her with the physical presence of this lively woman. "The baby you're holding in that snapshot is hers then?"

"Yes. That's Jonathan. He's three now."

"How did that Angie get to Alaska? I thought England and Maine were as out of reach as they could get!" Joanna laughs ruefully and then abruptly takes the topic away from children, asking, "Could you use a glass of wine?"

Relieved, Meg doesn't start in about Angie, let alone about Tim or Shannon and her kids. "Sounds good. I like to fly but I'm glad to touch ground again."

Meg perches on a tall kitchen stool while Joanna cooks. From time to time Meg wanders through the living room, hall, study, family room and back into the kitchen, studying paintings, sculptures, photographs. Unlike museums and galleries which make Meg claustrophobic after a short while, Joanna's house feels comfortable to her. She can ponder at ease. In spite of the abundance of artwork, there is a simplicity, an openness, a farmhouse welcoming in these rooms. Meg stands in front of each etching for a long time. The majesty of the work overwhelms her. Seeing it in the photographs was compelling and interesting but seeing the original is entirely different, like meeting Joanna face-to-face after seeing only a snapshot.

"Your work is beautiful," she says. "Powerful and beautiful."

"Oh, well, thank you," Joanna says, blushing as she fills their glasses again. "Want to swing the lettuce?"

Meg does a double take. Joanna is handing her a closed wire colander. Seeing her confusion, Joanna says, "C'mon," and heads out through the hall to the front door. Standing on the porch she grips the colander firmly and then swings it around and around like a lariat.

A cowboy, not a femme, Meg thinks and laughs as the water spatters her, glistening in the sunshine of late afternoon. Shadow, coming with Siamese grace toward the steps, pauses and retreats. Joanna, grinning, hands the colander to Meg and goes back inside calling over her shoulder, "The onion's burning!"

Meg stands, twirling the lettuce, feeling transposed not only from New York to Oregon, but into a different era, in which this striking woman who does the most amazing work runs a sweet and simple kitchen and dries the lettuce by hand, outdoors. Smiling, Meg swings the colander around and around even after the water has stopped spraying out.

While they eat chicken pilaf and garlic bread, Joanna reiterates how much she likes Meg's work. She especially likes the manuscript about Tim's life and death. "I don't know how you wrote that," she says, putting down her wine and giving Meg a deep clear look that Meg has not seen before.

"I wrote to survive."

"Well, yes, but I don't know how you found the strength."

Meg thinks about Joanna's work, much of it dark, touching on war, on death. "Your own work is very strong."

Joanna shrugs in a self-deprecating way. "I haven't had to face anything as hard as losing your son."

They talk late, wake early. The heavy skies clear by noon. The wind is moving the last light clouds swiftly away.

"Want to go out? The day is actually clearing up."

They drive up along the Columbia River. They pull off at several overlooks, each with a view more beautiful than the last, with the river stretching unbelievably far from bank to bank way down below them and evergreens as far as they can see. Mt. Hood rises with its pastoral majesty nearby and in the distance the Cascades, precursors of the Rockies, already hold their early winter snow.

"Want to walk?" Thank the goddess, Joanna thinks, for a clear day.

"I'd love it."

They park at the bottom of a trail and walk for an hour up the mountain. Their time continues to be like canoeing, their language balanced, their conversation the stroking of their paddles, now shallow, now deep, but always gauging one another's thrust, never throwing off the other's pace. They see rabbits, small birds, a woodchuck. They stand a moment, resting, before starting down again. "See?" Joanna points to two birds circling the nearest crest.

"Hawks?"

"Eagles, I think. We have lots of hawks down lower. I see them on my way to work almost every day." They walk in a leisurely way down the trail. "I'm glad you came," Joanna says, giving Meg an open appreciative glance.

"So am I." Meg smiles, thinking how beautiful Joanna is out here with the wind in her silver hair.

"Shh!" Joanna's hand touches Meg's arm and Meg freezes, puzzled, then sees the deer walking quietly out from an alder grove. They stand together watching as three does make their way across the steep slope.

A young mother with a baby strapped on her back comes up the trail toward the two women in blue jeans and jackets. "Hi," she says, nearing them, not having seen the deer.

Joanna silently lifts her hand to point. The young woman smiles, nods, continues up the path. The first deer lifts her head with sudden knowledge, turns and followed by the others, leaps lightly into the woods. Meg feels Joanna's fingers, still on her sleeve, press lightly for a moment against her arm before they go down the trail, step matching step again.

*** 

That night they hear Adrienne Rich read. The familiar lines resonate between them like a long known and remembered song. Walking out, Joanna stops to introduce Meg to Greta and Marlene and Hildy who confirm their lunch date for Tuesday. Several other women smile at them as they pass.

Once home, they get out the volume of Rich and read their favorites to one another on into the night.

*** 

Sunday Joanna takes Meg downstairs to her workspace in the dark cellar to show her what she's working on, what she has stored away, including some early paintings, done before she chose printmaking as her medium. Meg, fascinated, struggles to absorb the range of Joanna's art, its beauty, occasional humor, occasional political focus. She is increasingly impressed by its strength. "It's wonderful. Beautiful and amazingly powerful."

"I'm glad you like it." Joanna laughs. "Some women take one look and run away!"

"From what?" Meg asks, genuinely surprised.

"The Medusa! Anger scares some people off. I'll bet the same ones wouldn't read all your stories, either."

After dinner they settle on the family room floor while Joanna digs out old photographs from the bottom drawer of the sideboard. There is a glad eagerness to her movements that appeals to Meg.

"Oh look!" Meg exclaims, seeing Joanna as a three-year-old. Her heart does an odd clutch at the sight of the little girl running toward her mother.

"I have another drawer of more recent snapshots upstairs. Or is that enough?"

"I'd like to see more."

Joanna rises and Meg follows her upstairs. In the bedroom Joanna takes out a big folder from a bureau drawer and lays it on the bed.

There's no other place to sit. They sit on the bed with the folder between them. Reticently Joanna holds out snapshots of herself and her former lover. "This is Sandy. We were on a trip to the Grand Canyon."

Meg looks carefully at the two hikers, in jeans, boots, denim jackets, posing on a high rock slab, arms entwined, smiling. "You look happy."

"I guess we were."

"What happened?"

"No one fell, if that's what you mean!" Joanna laughs.

Meg waits for her to speak again. Joanna's voice is carefully calm. "She found another woman. Younger."

"That's hard." At least that never happened to me, Meg thinks.

Joanna hands her a stack of snapshots. Meg leafs through them, thinking how odd it is that women tell one another all about their former partners right away as though that is the crucial part of their vita, something to be gotten out of the way before they can go on.

Meg smiles, holding out one of Joanna and a laughing woman. "Same jeans, boots, denim jackets." And everybody's butch, she thinks, bemused. Now that she sees Joanna walk and watches her handle her work in the studio, it is clear to Meg that Joanna, curly hair or not, is no femme!

Joanna gives a hooting laugh, thinking how much she likes Meg's smile, the way her blue eyes light up when she laughs. "And you?"

Meg looks a moment longer at the couples, then hands the snapshots back to Joanna who slides them inside the folder. Start from the beginning, she thinks, reluctantly.

"I fell in love with a woman right after the divorce. First lesbian lover for each of us."

Meg speaks quickly, wanting to know more about Joanna, not to summarize her own familiar past but fair is fair, she thinks, and begins to recite. In love, free of the disillusioned anger of the marriage, life had seemed on a true course for happiness. But Vietnam took Tim. The darkness is like scar tissue after surgery. Somewhere inside her body there is still a small rough hollow, a space shrinking into itself, that as it contracts sends tremors of pain radiating out through the adhesions into the healthy cells that now surround it. Joanna has read her stories. Meg hears herself moving forward in time. "She would say I wasn't available for her anymore."

Joanna studies Meg, asks quietly, "And you would say?"

"When people asked me, I said, 'Our relationship just didn't survive after Tim's death.'" Secretly, Meg lost respect for Martha who didn't stay beside her, as though they'd been flying in tandem in a war zone until Meg's plane was hit; Martha looped away into safe airspace, leaving Meg, wounded, to come out of her downward spin all by herself.

Joanna listens, tipping her head questioningly, liking the way Meg's hair curls around her face, the way her eyes change when she is serious. Abruptly Joanna swings up from the bed, saying, "Why don't we get out of here? There's some work of mine in a gallery downtown. It's open late!"

"Fine with me."

\*\*\*

They planned to go up the Columbia again on Monday morning. At breakfast they decide to go out for picnic supplies. Without discussing it, Meg has been trailing Joanna through the house as she does her chores. Joanna goes upstairs and Meg follows, talking as they go. In Joanna's room, Meg sits on the bed while Joanna rummages in her closet for her jacket. Meg looks up, seeing the sunlight frame Joanna's face and without thinking, with a rising gladness and surprise, knows what they are about to do.

Joanna turns, puts out her arm. Shoot the rapids, woman, flickers through Joanna's mind. At the touch of Joanna's hand on her shoulder, Meg stands, rising to an embrace.

Joanna's lips touch Meg's and it is Joanna who guides them downward on the bed where they lie, kissing, as they pull off their own jeans and one another's shirts. It is as though their canoe has been gently beached on a sandy shoal. The sun is shining down on them as the waves lap against the sand and their hands discover one another's flesh, their lips open to one another's tongues and all their conversation yields to the awakenings of first touch.

\*\*\*

Monday night it begins to rain. Except for Tuesday lunch with Greta and Marlene and Hildy, and a trip to Blockbusters to lay in a supply of videos, including Whoopi Goldberg's *Ghost* and Cher in *Moonstruck*, old favorites of Joanna's, and at Meg's suggestion, *Shadowland*, they stay in the house. The rain has settled in, constant and steady, encompassing the house with its muted drone. Lying together, it is as though Meg and Joanna are being held in the palm of a tender and windless storm.

On Wednesday they read two acts of *King Lear* out loud and bring in Chinese for dinner which lasts until Friday when they order pizza. "Shouldn't we be going to museums or concerts or something?" Joanna asks, Friday night, laughing, her mouth full of pizza.

"No and not," Meg says, mimicking her grandson, Jonathan, age two, when he announced a negative.

\*\*\*

Saturday morning the rains let up. "Let's drive up the Columbia again and picnic in the car," Joanna says. "Everything's wet but the sun is out, the sky is clear."

Seeing the river with Joanna for the second time, listening to Judy Collins singing "Both Sides Now" on an old tape from the glove compartment, Meg reaches over to hold Joanna's hand.

"Can't, I need both hands for these curves," Joanna says.

"You know what?" Meg says.

"What?"

"It's like we grew up in the same neighborhood, isn't it?"

"I don't remember you down the street. Was I too busy climbing trees?"

"Not geographical," Meg says, smiling. "Judy Collins. Adrienne Rich." Meg thinks of their laughing together at Whoopi Goldberg and adds, "Films. Did you see *Bambi*?"

"First film."

"Me too. That's what I mean," and as Joanna parks on an overlook, Meg takes her hand again. "I didn't understand about the silver screen. I thought that forest fire was real!"

\*\*\*

The last night of the visit, they are still awake at three a.m. At last too tired to make love any longer they say good night. "Seriously now, we have to sleep," Joanna says.

"Right."

After a few minutes Meg realizes she is kissing Joanna's shoulder. "That's not the way to put me to sleep, you know," Joanna says, rolling over to return the kiss.

"We're too tired to sleep," Meg says, laughing.

"I know. But I really have to sleep."

They lie quietly for a while. Outside a truck passes. "Lord, it's morning!" Joanna says without opening her eyes. "It's the garbage men!" She pauses. "It's my friends come to find out if I'm okay? Missing lesbian sought by anxious dykes?"

Meg begins laughing uncontrollably. In the midst of it, to her absolute surprise, she is saying, "I love you. I love you," laughing with delight between the phrases.

It is as though Meg has long been trapped on the ocean floor in a sunken steel maze that was once a ship in which she sailed the Caribbean with her lover, Rosalyn, long ago. Suddenly the maze is flattened to patterns on the ocean floor obscured by the shifting sands. Freed from the twisted wreckage, Meg drifts up toward the sunlight, breaking the surface into the bright light of dawn surrounded by the myriad rising bubbles of her laughter.

"I love you, Joanna. I really do."

"Oh, Meg, give me a little time. It's been so fast, so fast." Joanna speaks and then abruptly is asleep. Meg smiles and lies beside her, watching her quiet breathing, until she too falls into a deep and peaceful sleep.

***

They agree to take a trip together in April when Joanna has to go to California for her son Will's wedding, but even as they make that tentative commitment they both know they are spinning faster than they can say. On the plane Meg writes Joanna a brief note and quotes, "Oh Western Wind, when wilt thou blow/ the small rain down can rain/ Christ that my love were in my arms/ and I in my bed again" and with that deep skittery fearful joy which she had thought she would never know again, mails it the minute the plane lands.

# PART II

# CHAPTER SEVEN

"Liz! Are your lights out?"

"No, are yours?"

Meg laughs. "How'd you guess?"

"How long have they been out, Mom?"

"They were out when I woke up. I'll call the light company."

"Need anything?"

"No, thanks. I made my breakfast tea on my little propane camping gadget. Everything okay over there?"

"Yeah. Cash flow problems but nothing new. Call me when the power's back, okay?"

\*\*\*

Meg hears the truck from the electric company as it pulls into the driveway and goes out to meet the repairman.

"This ever happen before?"

"A power failure?"

"No. This is just your house and no one else's. Let me look around."

Meg goes inside to clean up the kitchen while she waits. Could the kids…They moved out on the first of December; one month had turned into two but Shannon eventually found a one-bedroom apartment in the basement of a house in Rocky Point that wasn't too expensive and was near the diner where she works. Meg misses the boys but is relieved to be back at her own work. No, they've been gone two weeks. It's nothing to do with them. Could it be the Christmas lights?

The man knocks on the front door. "Could I check the fuse box?"

"It's in the basement."

Meg can't start work until the current comes back on. At least with the old typewriter you didn't need electricity, Meg muses, sorting a stack of mail waiting to be answered, writing checks to pay a few bills. When he comes to the door again, the repairman seems perplexed. "Try your lights."

Meg clicks the porch light to check and the little bulb by the door goes on. She smiles and nods. "Power's on!"

An older man, he looks around the yard before he speaks. "Fine place you've got here. Out of the way. Hard to find them anymore." Meg waits. He rubs his hand through his hair several times, looking around the porch as he does so. "It was that light you've got out by the driveway."

There are no streetlights in this neighborhood. Meg has always loved the country dark. There is an old lamppost halfway down the driveway and Meg leaves it on sometimes when she's coming home late at night. "What was wrong with it?"

"It shorted out. Someone rewired it so it would."

Meg hesitates before she speaks again. The pattern of her neighborhood events, like a familiar country road with known signposts on it: from broken to fixed, from power outages to the normal flow of electricity through the myriad wires of the landscape, has just washed out.

"You don't mean on purpose?"

"Definitely on purpose."

Meg remembers her high school students writing stories about their own exploits that included various kinds of mischief: knocking over mailboxes, doing 360s that wrecked someone's lawn. "Are kids doing this sort of thing this year?"

He shakes his head. "No, this is the first time I've run into this." He smiles wryly. "You having a feud with any of your neighbors?"

Meg laughs and shakes her head. "Nothing like that. Will it work now?"

He nods. "I fixed it for you. Not supposed to though. Come along, I'll show you."

One summer when Franklin was in graduate school on the GI Bill after Korea, Meg worked night shift at a plant that made aircraft components. She soldered tiny wires, color coded, to the correct connecting post. She recognizes the little colored sheaths, knows how you can cut the sheath to strip the wire before you solder it. What Meg does not recognize is the language of deliberate malice. She looks questioningly at him but does not know what to ask.

He looks up at her with an odd and thoughtful glance, then closes the cover of the panel and stands. He shakes his head. "I've no idea," he says to her unspoken question. "But you might want to write up a report down at the precinct."

***

As Meg walks through the familiar evening quiet of the house, the event recedes. She stands on the deck, checking out a rising storm. By the time Joanna phones for their good night talk, Meg has decided not to mention this to her. No sense in scaring Joanna, Meg thinks. And thinking that, it registers on her that she herself knows full well that she could easily be on some list of gays and lesbians with a star beside her name, meaning some group or individual might seek her out to harass her or to bring her harm. Nonsense, she tells herself, it was some neighborhood kid who picked that light at random because it's hidden underneath the trees.

Watching the leaves roiling past the window, the trees bending in the tough nor'easter, Meg gathers her house around her like a shawl. Fierce, the wind whips the branches of pine and cedar in a frenzied dance. The bare oak and dogwood do not bend as far, do not sway in wild swathes. Alone is good, Meg thinks. Alone in this house was absolutely right from the moment I discovered it.

The week she signed for it, Meg had brought her old friend, Sarah, to see it. "My God! You conjured it!" Sarah said, laughing with delight. "It's your dream house! How?"

"I cruised this neighborhood all spring. Realtors told me I couldn't afford to live here but I kept my eye on the old ones, the small ones, and kept hoping, and when this one looked like it was going to be for sale one Friday afternoon I grabbed it."

"Meg, if you need a loan, just ask." Sarah's eyes darkened with her concern. "Herb and I each have our own discretionary account and I'd be very glad."

"Thank you," Meg said, "but I'll be okay."

In addition to her regular high school classes, Meg taught in night school, tutored after school, gave in-service writing workshops for faculty, and taught summer school. With a big mortgage on it, the house was now hers, entirely hers.

Watching the evergreens thrashing in the wind, running her eye over every tree and bush the way she might run her finger over a favorite piece of polished wood, savoring its feel, Meg thinks, "Mine, this house is mine." And she retorts, "Be careful, woman. Watch your step. You don't know this Joanna that well yet."

The letters flow, longer and longer. Joanna sends Meg another tape of her own singing, including her own song based on the *Ballad of Sir Patrick Spens*, and Meg sends Joanna a tape of herself reading a number of Adrienne Rich's love poems and ending with Yeats' "The Lake Isle of Innisfree," as though to say that this is how it will be when they have a beautiful and quiet place together near Long Island Sound.

Listening to Joanna's resonant voice that night saying she can't wait for April to arrive, she's counting the days already, Meg answers, "So am I!" and when they've talked the hour which they've agreed is their limit and are ready to hang up, it is Meg who is the first to say, "I love you." When she wakes, restless, she cannot remember what it was she dreamed.

# CHAPTER EIGHT

*The board is narrow and Joanna can feel its spring as she moves forward on it, walking lightly, surely, until she stands, poised, flexing her knees three times in preparation for the thrust forward and slightly up in the arc that flows into the dive. In midfall she is grabbed by doubt. What is the depth of the water here? Has she asked? Does she know? Should she pull out into a shallow entry? And the water smacks her belly as she tries.*

Joanna wakes, gasping for breath, arm in midstroke, to stare into the darkness of her bedroom. She turns her eyes to the window in search of moonlight, always a comfort for night sweats. There is no light. The sky all day was solid heavy clouds sometimes breaking to let rain begin to fall; in the night the heavy storm-gray blocks out all light from moon and stars. Sometime before morning there will likely be heavy rains. Joanna hates the uncompromising gray, yearns for rifts in the cloud cover that would let even a glimmering of starlight through. Meg has promised more light, blue sky even in December.

Still close to the dream Joanna senses all her friends behind her on the beach as she walks out along the board; everyone is staying there, on land, as she alone climbs up to make her dive and as she leaves the board, as her feet relinquish their grip on its smooth steady surface and go into the air, she hears its motion shiver through the air and knows that she will not again have anything she knows beneath her feet but only air through which she falls and falls toward an unknown expanse of water there beneath. "Are you insane?" she whispers to herself.

Like a strobe light she moves her thoughts in search of Meg. Her arm reaches out; sensors on her skin flicker on alert. But there is no flesh against her own. The sheets are indifferent and cool. Even Shadow, the cat, is curled against her feet, not at her shoulder where she could feel her warmth. Joanna starts to reach for her but knows if she moves nearer, Shadow will wake, yawn, stretch and likely as not choose her own space again and Joanna could not stand to have her move away, not still be near. I can't do it, she thinks. I cannot leap off into unknown space. I wouldn't have anything. I wouldn't have anyone. I wouldn't even know my way to the goddamn grocery store.

Belly flop, hell! The wrench would break my back.

*Meg walked from the shower to the bed, her body barely dry, her skin giving off that glow, that clean body odor already charged with sex. Joanna opened her arms and Meg's body came against her own, length to length. Joanna savored every cell that touched hers, every tiniest hair that twined with her own along her inner thighs, her arms, the rich mat of pubic hair from under which the sweet strong smell would rise, sifting upward when Joanna put her fingers on those lips, slid one finger gently in, moved her face to touch, her tongue to stroke and probe.*

*Joanna kissed Meg's cheek and then her lips, first gently and then, as Meg's lips opened to her own, more forcibly until the slightest suggestion of a brushing by Meg's tongue excited her past restraint and her own tongue lunged past Meg's lips to fill the warm cavern of her mouth. Thrusting her tongue, Joanna moved her hands along Meg's shoulder, thighs. She stroked her breast, relinquished her mouth to suck her nipples, pulling gently one side, then the other, until she could wait no longer and slid downward, letting her own breasts graze the dampened space, letting her mouth find its place, her tongue coming home against Meg's clit, circling, lapping higher, probing deeper, coming back to seize it, lift it, take it, until Meg gasped and screamed.*

I'll go to her, Joanna thinks. I must.

***

Eating lunch together, Hildy asks, "Will you two visit back and forth forever?"

Joanna shakes her head. "We don't know yet."

A quiet panic laces Hildy's words. "You won't leave Oregon, will you?"

Joanna stares into her sandwich. "Meg wouldn't leave New York. She has grandchildren near her. And now some great-grandchildren, too! But she's young, Hildy, she seems very young. She lives right between the ocean and Long Island Sound. I've checked the map." Joanna hears her voice running on, persuading Hildy of something she hasn't herself yet chosen that is already carrying her along like a raft down rapids. "And she loves her house. I've never wanted to keep mine, you know." To clinch her argument with herself she ends, "And there would be light there, Hildy—not this—" lifting her hand toward the gray sky.

"You're going to move there, aren't you?" Hildy's voice mixes shock and recrimination.

"Maybe not."

"Yeah, you are. Lock, stock and barrel. When?"

Joanna stares at her. "I don't know. I could leave the bookstore and go on Social Security when I'm sixty-two. That's in a year and a half."

Hildy looks at her askance. "You have a wild streak in you, Joanna. I could no more start a whole new life like that than fly to the moon."

They empty their trays in the trash can and walk out of McDonald's and down the street toward work. Joanna watches two squirrels chasing each other up and down a huge old maple. A kid goes by on a skateboard. She can feel his body flash by, that close.

"My God, you'd have to sell the house, pack everything—AND you'd have to pack up your press!" Hildy hoots. "That'll stop you. No way you'll ever get THAT done!"

That night Greta calls. "Rumors are flying, Joanna. Calm me down."

"About what?"

"Hildy says you're moving to New York. Truth or lie?"

"Who knows?"

"Why in the name of the goddess would you leave your press, your friends, your house, your WHOLE BLOODY LIFE of thirty years? Why, Joanna, why? And don't tell me you're in love—that's an in and out thing and you just can't stake a whole fucking LIFE on it!"

"I can't live without her." Joanna is surprised to hear herself put it so simply. She doesn't add any other words and Greta changes the topic and rambles on awhile about an upcoming art show in which they will both have work.

When the conversation ends, Joanna grabs a sandwich and settles with her tools to work on the ring she's carving from a steak bone (since she chooses never to use ivory) to give Meg when they meet in San Francisco. She plays folk songs on a tape and the steady certain movements of her hands shaping the bone bring peace back into her body.

# CHAPTER NINE

Meg gets up to use the bathroom at four a.m. The light won't work. Walking quietly, knowing her way by heart, she goes to the front door and clicks up and down the switch which should turn on the driveway lamp which she thought she had left on all night.

Meg stands very still by the door, checking to make sure it's locked. She goes carefully from one window to another, checking that they're closed and locked. Her bedroom windows are always open; she likes to sleep year-round with fresh air blowing through. Cloudy but no wind, no rain, she notes as she lowers the sashes, turns the locks. Should I call the police? she wonders. And answers herself, No, not until morning. Then I will. First my electrician. She smiles wryly. The light company won't do it again for free.

She goes to the front window in the living room and looks through the bare branches of the oaks at the neighbors across the street with their all night driveway lights ablaze as she had known they would be. Meg stands in sudden isolation, in a pit of darkness that reaches upward toward the dark winter sky. This is not the familiar sharing of the power shortages which regularly come with storms or excess heat, giving everyone a sense of sojourning together, laughing at the inconvenience of candlelight and camping stoves, neighbor the more connected with neighbor for being together in the temporary hardship. In this darkness she is alone.

I'll read a while now, Meg thinks, by flashlight. I'm too wide awake to sleep. Or watch TV. No power, stupid. As in, it's the power that's out. No TV. No cup of cocoa either. With a flicker of fear, Meg wonders if the phone still works. She makes her way through the kitchen to the sunroom where she picks up the receiver from the phone on the table. Dial tone. That's a good sign, she thinks. He didn't cut the cable.

The electrician comes before lunch and confirms her diagnosis. "Cute," he says, "really cute."

"Are kids doing this sort of thing around town this year?" Knowing she'd asked the repairman from the light company, Meg tries again, wishing this fellow would nod and say, "Damn kids—what will they think up next?"

Instead he shakes his head, says, "No, I've never seen anything quite like this. You say it happened once before?"

Meg nods, recognizing now that this is a thing that will happen again and again.

The police say they will come sometime in the next few hours. Meg is wearing old sneakers, jeans, a rust-colored flannel shirt and a jacket. She sits on a chair whose back has broken off long since, in the open garage, sorting out fifty years of papers stored in cartons, move after move. She's cleaning it all out to make room for Joanna who might be leaving Oregon, might be coming across country to live with her when she retires and goes on Social Security. They haven't worked out any details but this is the direction their phone calls have taken; this is the house into which Joanna would come and Meg has determined to clear the way.

Meg is surrounded by high stacks of debris, carpet remnants, blue and sand, a roll of linoleum hardened into curves, litter boxes, long unused, stacks of musty hardcovers. She's put out cartons of paperbacks for recycling—too mildewed to give away; they were soaked in the once flooded basement of an earlier house, and Meg had kept them out of nostalgia and a refusal to see the damage. She doesn't know yet if the truck will take hardcovers, intends to call. Clothing lies in piles: a '70s Led Zeppelin T-shirt of Angie's, a Scout bandana of Jimmy's. She finds her father's World War I canvas army bag, one foot square.

***

The policeman is young. Meg watches him walk up the driveway from his car. The cars, the uniforms, always seem unreal to Meg. A movie set. But not a real dark-haired boy bending his head down as he talks to her about a real lamppost. He goes inside with her, looking around, checking out the walls of the stairwell where all the snapshots hang, as they walk up to the sunroom.

"Grandchildren?" he asks happily.

"And great-grandchildren, would you believe?"

"No kidding?"

Meg smiles, saying, "I'm sixty-five." She's used to ticket takers not quite believing she's a senior.

He sits at the table in the sunroom, glancing around, saying, "You've got a real nice place here," before opening his notepad.

He runs through the routine questions: Neighborhood feud? Neighborhood kids with a bad rep? Anyone particularly mad at her? He sizes up her age reflectively and skips the next few questions. Then he gets to her occupation, family. Finally he says, "Think about it. Anyone who might want to make you trouble?"

Meg shakes her head. "No. I liked the kids. After twenty years I could count on one hand the bad kids I knew in that high school."

"One is all it takes," he says, as though she's missed the point. The young man studies her, stares out the window at the squirrel running across the deck after another squirrel. "Once, okay," he says. "But twice, no. It's unusual, is what. You had any hang-ups lately? Any heavy breathing? Threatening calls?"

Meg shakes her head again. Now, she thinks, is when I explain to him what I'm thinking. He's six feet tall, very clean-cut and too young to be a policeman. He's thinking I'm like his grandma, Meg thinks, chicken soup and all. He starts to put his notepad away, looking puzzled more than worried.

"There's one other thing," Meg says, as he stands up. He stands still, waiting. Could offer him milk and cookies, she thinks. Reluctantly, Meg goes on, "I give workshops on bias. How to fight racism, anti-semitism, sexism and heterosexism."

He listens with the blank face students wore when they were unsure what was happening next.

"It could be there is someone who hates gays and lesbians and decided to pick on me."

The young man smiles, surprised. "But, why? Ma'am, *you're* not gay."

Meg laughs. "Well, yes. I'm a lesbian. And there are people out there who hate us all."

He is reassembling his thoughts and looks, she thinks, like a kid rebuilding a complicated LEGO set. "You don't look like a lesbian," he says, smiling down at her.

That's *not* a compliment, sir, Meg thinks. Save the speech, she checks herself and smiles back. "You might make a note," she says. "If you hear of any hate crimes around here, let me know."

"I will," he says. "Seems unlikely though."

Meg thinks that what seems unlikely to him is that she is a lesbian, not that it would be unlikely for there to be men who pick on gays. "You don't come across hate crimes much around here, I guess."

"No, no, we don't. Now and then a bar fight—racial stuff, you know—but not much else. A few years back we had a lot of swastika graffiti over in Commack—actually still have swastikas turn up—not right around here though." He pauses, still realigning this situation. "You're not Jewish, are you?"

Meg smiles at his confusion and shakes her head as he goes on. "And you've got no graffiti here—no broken windows—nothing like you usually get when somebody's really on a drunken rampage. But you couldn't even do a delicate thing like that—" He gestures toward the lamppost in the driveway below, "—if you were drunk. Do you think you could?"

When the policeman has left, Meg thinks that now she really should tell Joanna. By phone? No. Maybe in a letter. Make it casual. Tell her the police weren't worried. Lie a little. Just a little. Tell her you're not worried either. Don't tell her you're sleeping with the windows closed and locked. Don't tell her that.

Meg goes back to work. Several boxes later a red pickup pulls into the driveway. Meg knows immediately that she doesn't know the driver and that whatever is happening means trouble. Shannon gets out, slams the door behind her, and walks up the driveway, Bud in her hand. The truck backs out, honking, and is gone.

"Hi, Grams," Shannon says, with a silly smile.

"Hello, Shannon."

"I need a little help, I think," Shannon says, half falling, half lowering herself to sit cross-legged on the cold garage concrete near Meg.

"I can see that."

"Could you...would you...should you?" Shannon starts to giggle. "Do you have any peanut butter? I'm so hungry, you wouldn't believe!"

"Yes, I have peanut butter." Meg sorts, making order of what is happening. "When are you supposed to pick up Dylan?"

"Mack's okay. Don't you worry. Mack's just fine." Shannon tries to stand up and failing, settles down again. "Dylan's bus comes home... no, Dylan comes home with me...his bus doesn't come home...his bus doesn't come at all!" She starts to laugh again and succeeds in standing up.

"*Shannon!*" Meg shouts at her. "When does Mack's bus get to your apartment?" Meg checks her watch. Three-fifteen. "Shannon?"

"Yeah. Well, I guess. Should you?" She laughs. "No...but would you? I'll bet you would."

"Come on! Let's go meet Mack at the bus stop, and then we'll go get Dylan from day care."

"Oh, Grams, that would be so fine, just very fine."

"Let's go."

"I need my peanut butter sandwich first."

Meg does not want to leave Shannon alone in the house. Neither does she want Dylan to see his mother as she is right now. She chooses to protect Dylan. "I'll go get the boys and be right back. Do not turn on the stove, Shannon."

"No, no, Grams. I will not turn on the stove. I want peanut butter. Don't want soup. Peanut butter, Grams."

"Shannon. Drink milk. There's some in the fridge. Then go to sleep."

\*\*\*

Later, after she's given the boys their supper and let them watch one of the Disney videos she got for them while they stayed with her in the fall, Meg wakes up Shannon and takes them all back to their apartment. By that time Shannon is drinking a gallon of orange juice and apologizing. It was her day off, she says. "It won't happen again, Grams, I assure you! Thank Granny Meg, boys, and say good night."

\*\*\*

At bedtime, trying to sleep, Meg, to escape the wire cutter and the thought of Shannon's drinking, sets herself to remembering time with Joanna. Thinking about an evening in Oregon when they read Shakespeare out loud together, Meg drifts off.

*We brought in wood and laid a fire earlier in the day. We light it now and sit beside the hearth, about to read Lear. You touch my hand, lean to kiss my lips.*

*Your voice works its way into me the way the flames enter the wood, first tracing its shape, then taking it from within. When Gloster recognizes the King's voice, we stop. "Let's not get into the Cordelia part tonight," you say.*

*"Let's not." I close my book and move to sit on the floor, leaning back against your knees. The flames flash yellow, orange, red, lapping between the logs. You stroke my hair. Your hand moves to my shoulder and then to lightly graze my breast. Delight shivers through me like a breeze.*

*"Tell me when you're ready." You've left Lear on the heath. Your voice is your own again. I nod, savoring the warmth, the light of the fire, the leaping of the shadows against the sides of the brick cavern and up the chimney into the smoky dark.*

*The last log shudders, drops, scattering ashes, the flames flaring up in a sudden burst, a myriad of sparks. I turn my head toward you and our lips meet, letting you know I'm ready to find our way into our bed, to hold one another, hands dancing our way together into love and sleep, under the down comforter, listening to the snow-gentled wind among the cedars and the last quiet cracklings of the blackened oak as the final flames transform it into white heat, then lingering flickerings of rose, and then the quiet softness of glowing embers relinquishing their light.*

# CHAPTER TEN

Everybody does it. The idea of retiring and moving away is nothing new. Snap out of it, Joanna tells herself severely. Yeah, well, three things are different for me, she defends herself. First, I'm doing it alone. Mostly, retired people are coupled when they move. "Second," she mutters, "I've lived in this house longer than most people stay anywhere. It's thirty years worth of stray snapshots and misplaced parts."

Joanna rummages in a drawer for the screws with which to attach the highchair tray before giving it to the local women's shelter. They are there, all right, in a little envelope, rolled up in a rubber band and labeled. He would have done it that way. Whatever else, and there was plenty else, she thinks grimly, Walter had been neat. Joanna pauses, lights a cigarette. Better scrub it before putting it together. She takes the Murphy's off the shelf and goes to work.

And third? she challenges herself. Third, she hesitates, breathing the smoke out slowly with her lower lip extended. Isn't any third, I guess. It's no different lesbian or straight. Oh? Since when? Joanna laughs out loud, a hooting self-deprecating laugh. Okay, so third, I'm lesbian. And so is Meg. That's good, she retorts sarcastically, it would be awkward if I were moving away from my entire and total world to live with a straight woman.

There aren't any lesbians in Oregon then? You had to go two thousand miles back east?

***

"April is so far away," Joanna says to Meg, her voice gone unexpectedly flat and low at the end of their good night call.

Meg's chronic reassurance floats back across the plains, over the Rockies, and filtered through the steady drone of the thick February rain in Oregon, falls dull as a tennis ball gone bad on Joanna's court.

In the pause that follows, Joanna takes a long draft on her cigarette. Like the blaze from a Roman candle unfolding in her mind, she knows the extent of what she does not know about this stranger who lives so far away in a house that Joanna has not seen, on a street in a neighborhood in a town where Joanna has never been, with friends and family whose faces, bodies, clothing Joanna has never watched, whose voices Joanna has never heard. She cooks foods Joanna has never tasted in a kitchen whose odors Joanna has never smelled.

"This isn't working, Meg," Joanna says.

Meg plummets silently in shock.

Joanna allows herself two more draws on the cigarette before she speaks again. "Are you free next week? I'd like to come to New York," —to find out what the hell I'm doing before it is too late, she finishes her thought. That's what's wrong about April. April will be in California. What will that tell me about Meg? Not enough. She's seen my house already. Met my friends. I don't know beans about this woman named Meg.

"Great!" Meg says. "Yes, if you're coming, I am free! What a wonderful idea!"

***

As the plane circles in over Manhattan Joanna cannot imagine where it will set down. She wishes she had asked to land at Kennedy where the ocean provides spaciousness and there is no sense of danger from skyscrapers. She knows LaGuardia is there somewhere among the buildings and Meg is there somewhere among the crowd but

Joanna does not want to be where she now is, in a plane groping for a runway, in what feels like a dive into tumult.

Meg, waiting in the terminal, hardly recognizes the anxious woman hurrying down the ramp, head down in confusion. "Hey, there, Joanna," she calls as she starts past her.

They have a perfunctory embrace. "Got bags checked?"

Joanna nods and Meg leads her down the stairway to the huge room into which the many moving belts deliver luggage. "You point. I'll grab!"

As soon as they're out the door, Joanna lights a cigarette and once they're in the car and on the highway, she looks over at Meg and tries to smile. "Well, hello there!" And this is New York, she thinks, mayhem and hurtling cars.

After an hour on the freeway they turn off. "I'm sorry it's not spring yet!" Meg says. "It's so beautiful in the spring. Just wait!"

Joanna sees that they are now in wooded neighborhoods. As abruptly as the descending plane had found its runway and taxied to a stop, Meg has found her way to quiet tree-lined streets. The deciduous trees are winter bare but there are more evergreens than Joanna would ever have expected. The yards are about like the yards in Oregon and the houses are a similar mix. They drive for almost an hour on quiet roads through pleasant neighborhoods.

"I didn't know there were so many trees on Long Island," Joanna says.

"Wait till you see the beach!"

Joanna gasps as they go around a sharp curve and are three feet from the water in a lovely cove. A few large fishing boats are anchored there. "Won't they get locked in by ice?"

"Not here. I've only seen this frozen over once. There'll be ice around the edges off and on in January and February. Some years not even that." Meg drives around the cove, out on a spit where there's water on both sides, and parks in an empty lot on the Sound side. "Come on, just for a minute." Meg gets out and runs the few yards to the water.

Joanna follows her. Whitecaps sparkle in the sun and low waves crest and wash ashore. A variety of gulls drift overhead or sit, all facing north. "See Connecticut!" Meg waves toward the north.

Joanna sees the low blue stretch of land far across the Sound. There isn't another person at the beach. The large parking lot is empty. Joanna takes Meg in her arms for their first real hug. "Hello, hello," she says, kissing her, and thinks, it is Meg. It is my Meg.

Meg drives a few miles up the road and turns into a neighborhood that could be in Portland. Then she turns into a long driveway with trees, half evergreens, on both sides of it, and stops in front of a house with log cabin siding. "Welcome!" Meg says.

They go in the back door, up a stairway, and are in a room with windows on three sides. It's a narrow room with a graduate-student-type door-set-on-files for a desk and a beautiful cherry table in the other corner.

"How lovely!" Joanna says.

There is a vase of daisies and iris on the table. Meg, puzzled, sees the card beside it. "With my apology and thanks, Grams—love, Shannon."

"Beautiful!" Joanna says, leaning to smell them.

"My granddaughter left them," Meg says, smiling, leading Joanna through the small galley kitchen which Joanna notes with considerable alarm. A one woman space, she thinks. And barely that!

Beyond that is a living room with a fireplace in the center of the outer wall. On each side of that is a bedroom. Meg puts her suitcases in the smallest room. "But you'll sleep with me!" She points to the queen-size bed that fills the other room except for a word processor and printer on a desk wedged into the corner by the windows. There is a small bathroom off the living room.

For a moment Joanna looks around to see where the rest of the house might be. Upstairs? None. Downstairs? "There's a basement full of junk I'm clearing out!" Meg laughs with embarrassment. "I've moved so much I never got everything unpacked! There's a washer and dryer down there too. And a Ping-Pong table. Do you play?"

Joanna nods. Truth is this is a summer house. Meg lives year-round in a summer house! Joanna remembers a summer she spent as an art student in a shack on Cape Cod. But I was a kid, she thinks. How does she fit?

Joanna walks to the front door and onto a small covered porch. She lights a cigarette and looks around. Huge, ancient rhododendron—their leaves rich green. A big bird feeder hangs from a pole with a brilliant cardinal perched on it that flies away at her approach. Meg follows her out, her face shining with pride. "You can hardly see the neighbors in the summer! It's an acre of woods."

They go through the house again, and out through the sunroom to the deck which is a story high. "What's under here?"

"A garage. And look! The land goes way back there. I own to that fence. And to their driveway! No one can ever build anything that will change the way this is. And I'm not near any road they'll ever widen or put a shopping center on! It's safe!"

Joanna looks at Meg, whose face glows in the wind, whose blue eyes are bright with excitement. "Let's go inside. It's wonderful. I want to kiss you, Meg."

"Before supper?"

"Yes, even before supper." Going through the kitchen to the bedroom, Joanna breathes in an odor from a bakery. "You baked?"

Meg nods. "For breakfast though," lifting a dish towel she has used to cover pans set on the counter. Joanna smiles, recognizing a favorite—fresh cinnamon rolls.

***

In the morning, waking first, Meg leans on her elbow, studying Joanna's face. She finds it beautiful. Serene, she thinks. Awake, Joanna is determined to be lively, even vivacious. She moves with alacrity, is quick to prompt laughter. But asleep there is a trusting openness that Meg adores. She gets up, pulls on her bathrobe, picks up her pen and sits by the desk while she scribbles a short poem.

Waking, Joanna smiles as she studies Meg who is intent on her writing. We'll make the house bigger, she thinks. I'll clear up the yard which you've let run wild. I'll build myself a real studio. We will both do our work. And Meg-o'-my-heart, we'll be a happy pair of lovers, you and I. When Meg lays down her pen, Joanna speaks. "Hey, you old poet, come say good morning."

Joanna, who draws weekly from live models at an artists group on campus, casts an approving eye as Meg strips before lying down with her. She's best without her clothes, she thinks. Meg pays no attention to her wardrobe, dresses in jeans and blouses, sweatshirts and sneakers. But nude, she has an unconscious grace, a beauty of line that Joanna treasures. Sometime I'll sketch her, she thinks. Oh, yes. And she reaches out to enclose her in her arms, to stroke the smoothness of her thighs, the skin oddly resonate to her touch. Is it because she swims so much? Joanna wonders; does the salt water keep her young? She moves with the authority of a ballet dancer when we're in bed. Yes, that's it. Completely without self-consciousness. And then Joanna stops reflecting and joins in the deep kissing in which they both delight.

***

That evening they spend alone. A light snow drifts down on the evergreens. Meg has a candelabra with a dozen little candles in it whose flickering flames are like chimes reverberating in the many windows of the sunroom where they eat. They sit after dinner, talking over coffee.

As Joanna lifts her cup her hand begins to tremble. Setting it down, it clatters against the saucer. Meg, watching, tips her head slightly, lifting an eyebrow, and waits for Joanna to speak.

"You've noticed," Joanna says, blushing and laughing. "It's nothing. I've had this shaky hand for years. It used to be called a familiar tremor. Now they call it an intentional tremor. It's not! Intentional that is!"

"Does it interfere with your work?" Meg is not smiling.

"No. No, I don't know why but my hand is always steady when I'm drawing."

"Then it doesn't much matter, does it?" Now Meg smiles at her.

Joanna is staring at the space between Meg's head and the wall behind her, as though all time has gathered in this moment to spin before her eyes like a fragile mobile spun from glass, and she sees only its crystal curves, hears only its gentle chimes.

"You like that?" Meg asks, gesturing at the wild horses in the print of a cave drawing that hangs by the window, seeing Joanna looking there intensely.

"No, no, it's not that. I was just thinking. This is only our second visit and you already know me better than anyone ever has." Joanna's words are tinged with surprise.

Meg takes Joanna's hand. "I love you," she says, smiling across the table, wondering if it's too soon to give Joanna the ring she has waiting in her bureau drawer.

***

The next night they go out after supper to meet friends. Music is playing as they walk into the lesbian bar with pool tables in the back. Sue and Yvonne have gone ahead, claimed a table, ordered beer. Joanna, to her own surprise, takes Meg in her arms in a slow dance feeling as though they've been a couple all their lives. When the fast music comes Joanna remembers that she isn't good at dancing and leads Meg over to the pool table.

Over a glass of wine, Joanna remembers the fifth grade. The girls whirled the ropes in double loops and Joanna could not run in. She watched them from a distance, admiring the pattern of the twirling as the sunlight struck the braided colors of the ropes, the bright patterns of the skirts, the gleaming of their long dark hair. They thought she disdained jump rope, preferring softball or soccer with the boys or even marbles out behind the shop. Only she knew that it was a thing she could not master, not able to comprehend the rhythm of the beat the turners set in their unspoken conspiracy. Only she knew that her stumbling feet within the confusion of the rising, falling ropes matched her feelings whenever she was within a bevy of girls, wanting to be admired, desiring the adoring looks that they turned toward distant boys instead, not even knowing that herself, knowing only that she does not know quite how to move, talk, laugh, tell secret jokes, or toss her hair the way the other girls seem to know by definition of their being girls.

But I can dance with Meg and not miss a beat. She smiles as they do that once again.

***

On the last night of the visit, they go from the dinner table straight to bed. "Let's skip the dishes," Meg says.

"You ever had a dishwasher?"

"Nope."

"Want one?"

"I don't know. There's not much room in the kitchen!" Meg laughs. "I don't miss it."

Joanna lies on the bed, anxious about packing and flying, her body stiffening as though she's already in the terminal, running for the gate, as though she's certain to be too late.

Meg lies beside her, kisses her expectantly, feels the distance that has come between them. "Turn over," she says. Joanna turns a questioning glance on her. "You need a little massage, I think."

Joanna turns over. Meg moves her hands along her shoulders, down her back, up again, kneading the tightness out of her shoulders. She ignores the arthritic pangs in her hands doing what she has done for friends for years. Eventually, Joanna turns over and takes Meg in her arms. "Thank you," she says. "You are a wonder."

"You're welcome," Meg says.

Joanna moves her hand over Meg's breasts, smiling. "I do need time to collect my things and pack. But first things first." She moves her body over Meg's as their lips meet.

***

Later, after Meg has cleaned up the kitchen while Joanna packed, Meg asks Joanna to come in by the fireplace for a moment.

"I really do need to go to sleep," Joanna says.

"Come here just for a minute. I want to give you something." Meg holds out the little box that holds the ring she's chosen. It's an amethyst in a double circle setting. "I wanted to get you rubies, but I couldn't."

"I like this better," Joanna says. "It's beautiful."

"I love you. Is it all right? I mean, it's not too soon?"

"It's not too soon." Joanna feels a flash of confidence, as though something—she can't quite remember what—that had required her attention has been completed and she can go back to Oregon, having accomplished whatever it was she had set out to do. "I'm glad I came. We'll work out the ways and means by phone."

***

Back in Oregon, a week later, Joanna picks up the ringing phone with the Murphy's rag again in her other hand. Meg's voice comes like a flute across the miles. "So how's it going?"

"I called three realtors today. I told them I can't move until fall but I need to know what they think, when it should go on the market." An hour later they say good night and Joanna falls into bed. Her alarm is set for six. Meg's voice fills her like music.

Joanna drifts toward sleep and finds herself remembering Isabelle's bunk in music camp. As a senior counselor, Isabelle shared a cabin with one other counselor who often slept in the director's house. On those nights Isabelle invited Joanna to come play flute duets with her after campfire time. After the duets there was always a goodnight hug and kiss. Gradually the hugging went on longer and one night Isabelle led her to her bunk where they lay hugging and kissing on into the night.

Isabelle's lips moved like nothing Joanna had ever known before, as gentle waves when floating in the lake, as wind through the grasses by the shore. Her own lips seemed to move without moving against Isabelle's and Isabelle's tongue glided along like a flute note until it almost entered between her lips.

Joanna dared not breathe, not to frighten Isabelle away, as though she were a great blue heron poised on the edge of flight, her whole body, rapt with joy, about to be lifted up with the spread of those great wings into a radiance of motion beyond her ken.

# CHAPTER ELEVEN

"Hey, Mom, could you keep the kids tonight?" Liz's questioning voice is underlined with the happy assumption that Meg will be free and glad to see them.

"Can't! I have to give that bias workshop in Huntington."

"Tonight? Oh damn!" In the second of silence Meg can hear Liz shifting her thoughts around to accommodate this news. "I forgot! Well, I hope it's a smashing success!"

***

"The baby who is born Black or Jewish or female will also grow up as a member of a minority group," Meg says, "but from the moment of birth the family, the community, celebrate and love this kid, raising him or her as an insider, special, one of their own.

"Not so for the baby who will grow up to be gay. There's no welcoming committee because the child at birth is not yet known to be gay and who would buy the champagne if the baby was labeled: designated gay?"

As she goes on, Meg is checking out the audience the way she would have checked kids the last week of school. Usually there was nothing but balloons or ticker tape dropped off balconies. Still she knew how to scan a room, recognize furtive looks or giggles.

"It may be a delightful discovery: I'm in love and it's the best thing that ever happened to me! Or a despairing suspicion: I'm attracted to the wrong gender.

"Discovering that we have the ability to love should be a moment of fulfillment that gives promise of a life of loving and being loved. If I can love another, then I will find someone to love me in return. There are more songs and poems written about love than anything else."

Meg looks around the room. Her glance hovers on a glowering man whose wife is smiling at Meg, then moves on to a kid with his arms crossed, wearing a backward baseball cap. Could one of them have short-circuited the lamppost? she wonders with a strange, deep shiver.

"I'd like you for a moment to think about the first time you ever knew that you loved someone. Not when you told them; you may never have told them; or you may have told, dated, even married him or her; but I want you to think only about that moment when you felt your heart come alive because you were in love…"

Meg watches as the men and women, the majority middle-aged straight couples whose son or daughter has come out to them, think back. "Take your time." She waits until the silence and the distant look in their eyes tell her they have found their way. "Hold yourself there in that moment." She gives them a long minute of silence in which to savor the wonder of first love.

"What if at that magic moment instead of hearing love songs, instead of having your parents affectionately tease you for this major step in growing up, you were told, *NO!* you're mistaken; it's just a phase; ugly; a sin to feel that way; revolting; you're a disgrace, sick, bad. Change yourself. Delete."

The room stirs with discomfort. A woman sitting near the front wipes tears from her cheek. One of the few youngsters, a boy of seventeen, perhaps, gives a harsh, shrill laugh. Meg knows she's scored.

An older man, wearing a dark business suit, calls from the back, "Are you a lesbian?"

There is a buzz. Several heads shake in disapproval. Meg goes on red alert. Is he the one? "Yes, I am a lesbian."

"You're a damned hypocrite!"

Meg speaks clearly, forgetting her anxiety in the rush to truth. "No. The kids didn't need to know that I was lesbian. They needed to know that if they were gay or lesbian, that was absolutely fine."

"Your club was recruiting kids to be gay."

"No, it was not. My club was fighting bias. One year we had skinheads harassing Jewish kids and faculty. That's why I started the club."

***

As she walks swiftly to her car, a younger woman follows Meg, and looking around anxiously, says softly, touching Meg's arm, "I'm a teacher. How did you have the courage?"

That's the simple kind of scared. The other scared? Scared they'd fire you.

First year. Tough class. Jimmy Tomkins. Back row. The only drug dealer you ever had in class. Or knew you had, Meg corrects herself. Cold eyes. One of the few bad kids in twenty years. Lied. Stole. Let other kids take the rap.

They had just read a short story in which a girl was pressured into having sex. The discussion was intense. "What do boys say when they want a girl to have sex and she says no?" Meg asked.

The answers came from around the room with embarrassed laughs or angry glares:

"C'mon, give it to me."

"Put out!"

"Don't you love me?"

"It won't hurt you none."

"I guess I know a cunt who will."

Jimmy Tomkins was looking straight at Meg. Behind him two boys were sitting on the window ledge, kicking their feet, talking to one another. Next to him a girl was combing her hair. To Meg's right Debbie said softly, "What are you scared of?"

A second girl thought Debbie was asking her a real question and snapped back, "Of getting pregnant, asshole!"

Jimmy Tomkins, still staring right at Meg, said, loud and clear, "Are you a lezzie?"

Meg was not ready for that one. She answered him with a deadly voice of absolute incredulity and command: "Are you talking to me, Jimmy?" Not knowing what to say if he said yes.

The coldness of Meg's challenge stopped the class. They'd never encountered that from her before. The silence stretched around the room, electrically expectant, just short of a chaos she'd never experienced with her students.

Jimmy Tomkins met Meg's eyes, calculating. Habit defeated him. They weren't in his alley, not inside his van, not in a dark place where no one would ever know. It was a classroom in a school and he wouldn't escape after attacking a teacher, even if he left her bleeding and for dead. It would be, he knows, a wasted act. No profit for him in it.

"Naw," he said, with mock surprise. "I just meant guys say that to a girl who won't put out. 'You must be a lezzie,' they say. Right?"

"Right," Meg said. Relief surges through her. She could breathe again. "So how can girls say no and make boys understand?"

The discussion raged until the bell cut it off and Meg was left with the four minutes between classes in which to recover. As the kids left the room, she walked to the window to look out, put her hand on the ledge. As though she'd touched a live wire with her open palm a spasm passed through her body.

That night Meg rehearsed a careful speech. If a student in class were ever to ask her if she was a lesbian, she would answer that she does not ever ask them in class about their private lives and neither may they ask her. And if he should pursue? She challenged herself. Then I'll add, "For instance, anything sexual is private. I would not, for example, ask you, 'Do you masturbate?'" This, she knew, would silence any adolescent boy.

In twenty years none ever asked and as time passed it mattered less and less. Both students and faculty respected her as she respected them.

*** 

Meg drives home over the same route that she took on her way home from work during the last six years she taught. The car, which now has a hundred thousand miles on it, knows every turn. Her mind drifts back and forth over the decades. Years later she heard from an ex-student in the post office that Jimmy Tomkins was upstate in prison.

Alone in her car, Meg confronts herself: so you are scared. You do think the lamppost events were dangerous. She checks her rearview mirror to make sure that there is no one behind her.

She thinks of Joanna's lovely face in sleep as she stretched out her hand toward her and then to Dickinson's love poems and then to the moon rising over the trees on her left to a flight of the car in a familiar orbit between school and home and circles up and over the moonlight in the branches behind the black pickup and out and over the wind-roughed water of the bay and with a jarring wrench of her hand snaps suddenly alert, resolutely pulling the car to a stop beside the road, next to a church underneath the dark branches of some oaks.

Meg opens the door and gets out, stretches, walks back and forth on the path beside the road. Can't do that, idiot! she chastises herself. My God, it's as though the sheathing is wearing thin between the levels of waking thought and dream. She explores this with both curiosity and fear. Too close to falling asleep at the wheel. Can't have that. Stay focused, woman, get home safe. At which word she looks around, checking for lurking or angry men. She is alone by the side of the road with trees and moonlight and an occasional car passing down the road.

Okay? Awake? Okay, go drive. And no more reminiscing. Just drive the car, okay?

# CHAPTER TWELVE

On the way to Will's wedding in San Francisco Meg and Joanna meet for a visit to Meg's old therapist and longtime friend who has retired to Santa Barbara. At eighty-eight Sarah uses a walker as they go from her condo to their car on their way out to dinner. "So Joanna, you have a daughter studying medicine?"

They eat at a restaurant on the coast, watching dolphins swim by. Sarah wants to know everything about each of them. They share a chocolate cake with coffee and take their time. It's late when they drive back to the condo where Sarah's husband chose to stay, reading in his study.

They walk from the car to the door and then abruptly stop. Sarah fumbles with the latch and then rings the bell. "I forgot my key," she says, ringing it again.

No one comes to the door. "He doesn't hear well, you know," she says, laughing. "And he might have gone to sleep already."

Joanna is standing a few feet away from Sarah. She nudges Meg and mouths to her, "I have to pee."

Sarah turns away from the door. "I'll go around to the side door and knock there. Maybe he'll hear me then." She limps away.

"I really do have to pee," Joanna repeats.

"Well, you can't right now," Meg says, laughing.

Sarah returns, shaking her head. "And besides," she says, "I need to pee."

Joanna and Meg start laughing and Sarah joins in. "Probably you do too, hmm?"

Sarah begins to pound on the front door. They are all laughing and Meg and Joanna join her in knocking. Eventually, Sarah's husband opens the door.

"Don't you have a key?" he says crossly. "I was asleep, you know."

"I forgot my key," Sarah says, moving past him and straight into the bathroom.

"Thank you," Meg says, but he has turned and already disappeared into their bedroom.

Sarah comes through again. "You girls get a good sleep."

"Thank you for the dinner," Meg says.

"Weren't the dolphins fun?" Sarah, using her walker, goes off to her bedroom.

Meg and Joanna go into the professor's study where a sofa bed has been opened for them. When they are both in bed they turn into one another's arms to kiss and snuggle.

"Meg." Joanna hesitates, then fills in the silence. "I do have to pee more often than you'd think. I always have. When I was a kid they teased me about it at slumber parties—especially if I'm laughing."

"So I shouldn't make you laugh?" Meg smiles at her in the dark.

"No, that's okay." Joanna smiles back.

"We almost had to sleep on the lawn," Meg says.

"The professor was not pleased," Joanna answers. "Cranky old guy, hmm?"

Meg nods, then, laughing, says, "Let's trash his study!"

Joanna giggles and Meg joins in as they pull the covers over themselves to muffle their howls of laughter.

\*\*\*

At breakfast, as Joanna starts to pour herself a cup of coffee, her hand trembles too much to do it. Meg, by now completely used to this, automatically leans to help her, taking the cup and the coffeepot from her hands.

Sarah, already sitting at the table, watching, chides Meg, "Let her manage things on her own."

It's an echo of some old dialogue in their long-ago therapy hours and Meg pulls back, startled. Then she rallies and turning her back to Joanna, says quietly to Sarah, "Joanna has a tremor. It's not Parkinson's. It's an intentional tremor. She's had it checked out."

Sarah does a double take and apologizes. "Oh, I'm sorry, Meg. I should have known you knew what you were doing!"

Joanna has seated herself by now with a cup half full of coffee.

"Want me to fill that cup?" Meg asks.

Joanna blushes, shaking her head. "No, thanks. This is fine."

Meg, feeling protective, passes a plate of pastry to Joanna.

"I heard you girls giggling in the night," Sarah says, smiling. "You'll have to come our way more often. And next time I'll remember to take my key!"

They laugh together.

***

"We can duck out by eleven or so," Joanna says, smiling and letting her fingers graze Meg's cheek as they dress in the motel.

Meg laughs. "We're worse than teenagers! We'll see how it goes. You can't leave before the bride and groom, you know!"

Joanna folds her in her arms and gives her a long, deep kiss. "We're not the bride and groom? Could have fooled me."

Meg laughs and straightens Joanna's collar. "You want a double ceremony? Can't. You're not wearing your tux and tie!"

On the steps of the church, Joanna is surrounded by her son Will's friends who have come from Portland to San Francisco for the wedding. The bride's family say a strained hello and the music begins. They are escorted down the aisle and seated near Joanna's ex-husband, Walter, and his wife, who nod without smiling in response to Joanna's polite greeting. Meg sneaks a cough drop and offers one to Joanna who shakes her head, amused. Meg, who doesn't have a cold, whispers, "I'm scared I'll cough."

Watching Will stand beside the minister, waiting for Celeste to walk down the aisle, Joanna sees Walter thirty years before. But Will's not like him, she thinks, thank God. Really not. As the vows flow around them like the tune of an old and tired song that these young ones are making new, Meg wants to hold hands, but contents herself with pressing her arm against Joanna's.

***

The first two days after the wedding Meg and Joanna glide from bed to bed, driving their rented Corolla up the coast toward Portland, stopping early and leaving each motel at check-out time. "I'm sorry, love," Joanna says, kneeling at the foot of the bed, lifting her face from between Meg's thighs, "but that's the maid in the room next door. We're out of here!"

"It's okay," Meg manages to say. "Tonight will come."

"Actually, it's you who'll come." Joanna grins.

In the car again, Meg asks, "Do you think we'll ever make Portland?"

"I do. And furthermore, tonight we're camping out. And there's no check-out hour in the morning!"

They've borrowed Will's tent and sleeping bag, which they'll ship back to him from Portland. They sign into a park on the Oregon coast early in the afternoon. Driving through the park they find most of the sites are already taken. "Oh damn! We may need to go into the wilderness!" Joanna says.

"We'll find one," Meg answers, driving slowly up the narrow, winding, bumpy old dirt road.

"I spy!" There is an empty place on a bluff overlooking the Pacific. "Oh yes!" Joanna shouts and takes the sign-up slip back to the ranger's station.

"Like 'Cortez silent on a peak in Darien!'" Meg says.

They stand in silence taking in the unending magnificence of the Pacific. Meg breaks the silence. "We won't fall in, will we?"

Joanna laughs, shakes her head, and they pitch camp, Joanna directing Meg where to put the stakes, how tight to pull the line. Once the tent is tied and steady, they lay out the sleeping bags inside it, zipping them together to make one big bed. "Come here," Joanna says, pulling Meg down into a long embrace.

"I love you," Meg says and they make love, the sun dappling the canvas over their heads, the ocean far down, directly below the bluff, surging rhythmically toward the shore and out again, over and over, before they hike down to the beach in the late afternoon.

"My God, look at those waves!" Meg says, as the water crashes on the rocks and sand in great rolling barrages, assault after assault. "Are those kids down here alone?" She points to three youngsters climbing on the rocks.

"Probably. But they're okay."

"Not if those waves get any bigger they're not!" Meg eyes the darkening sky, the height of the gathering waves off shore.

"Okay, they're not yours!"

Meg walks down the beach, stands by the boulders where the kids are climbing. "You been here before?" she calls up to them over the roaring of the surf.

"No! We're from Oklahoma!" the youngest shouts back. He's about eight, she guesses.

"Your folks know you're down here?"

The kids don't answer. "You'd better go back to camp and ask them if it's okay. The tide's coming in pretty fast and those rocks you're on will be under water in an hour."

"Yeah, I guess," the oldest answers, sounding unconvinced. Just then a huge wave smacks their rock high enough to drench them with its spray and the kids shriek, half with delight, half with fear, and sliding down, head back toward the trail up to the bluffs where all the tents are pitched.

The wind is rising and the incoming tide thrashes against the shore in crescendos of silver spray and darkening waves. Above them on the cliffs pines bend before the wind. Meg licks the salt from her lips. "You think it's gonna storm?"

"Could be."

"God! It's magnificent!"

"I'm starving. Let's go find a pit and do our beans and hot dogs."

After they eat, they walk along the bluff. It starts to rain and they dive into the tent, laughing. "Got towels in that there pack?" Meg asks. "I don't think I brought any."

Joanna throws a towel her way and stands by the open flap, pondering the weather. Then she ties the flap shut and changes to her pajamas. "If we lift off in the night, wake me up!" she says, crawling inside the sleeping bag.

\*\*\*

Hours later, they awaken. The wind smacks against the canvas and the waves below the bluff pound on the boulders and against the cliff in great resounding collisions that seem to rock the bluff itself. Abruptly Joanna pulls herself away from Meg, stands, unties the flap and sticks her head out. Almost without pausing she goes out, yelling back, "*C'mon! Hurry!*" As Meg follows her out between the flaps Joanna is already turning back in to collapse the tent pole. "*Lie down!*" she shouts into the wind.

Meg stands, confused as to where to lie. "*There! Lie down!*" Joanna yells again and runs to pull up stakes as Meg stretches on top of the wildly pulsating canvas. As the stakes are pulled up, the wind lifts the flaps which fling the canvas and ropes at Meg, smacking her arms and face.

Joanna is grappling to hold the whole tent from blowing off the bluff. Meg feels about to be carried off into the surf below, knowing the tent has become a giant kite belonging to the wind. The wind rips it out of Joanna's hands. She shouts, "*Drag it! Drag it, dammit!*" Joanna is hauling it away from the edge of the bluff before Meg is even standing. "*Get off it!*

Meg trips, trying to stand, falls flat, fights against the wind and finally stands. She stumbles off the canvas and grabs hold to help pull it toward the car.

It takes what seems to be hours. Eventually they get it between the car and the woods where they can win against the wind. "We have to get the sleeping bags and our stuff out of there and then we can roll it up!" Joanna is still shouting although it's no longer a necessity.

They put their gear into the car and roll the tent, stow it in the back, and then climb into the car themselves. Inside it's oddly quiet after being in the open wind. Joanna is breathing hard. She lights a cigarette and takes a long, deep pull on it. Meg puts out her hand, expecting Joanna to take hold, but she does not.

Joanna smokes in silence for a few minutes, then says, "I should never have pitched camp there! That's why it was empty for Christ's sake. Everybody else knew better."

"We're fine. No harm done." Meg smiles reassuringly at Joanna who now reaches out to take her hand.

"Could have hauled us right off."

"Not your fault. We're fine. I think we'll just lean over and sleep here," Meg says. "It'd be hard to find a motel; you can go a long ways out here without anything but woods!" Meg rolls down the window to hear the wind, to get back into the moment.

"Hey, better keep that shut! Lock your door and put your head down in my lap."

"Maybe we can tip the seats back?"

"Before we do that, I have something for you in my pocket." Joanna smiles.

"In your pocket?"

"Umhm."

Meg puts out her hand to stroke Joanna's thigh and hip. "I don't feel anything."

Joanna laughs and lifts herself up a bit so she can take an envelope out of her hip pocket. She gives it to Meg.

Meg turns on the flashlight. Pointing it down at the envelope, Meg looks for writing but sees none. She opens the envelope, expecting a letter, a poem. Inside is a baggie. Inside the plastic Meg can feel something small and hard. She looks at Joanna with a puzzled smile.

"Go ahead. Open it."

Inside the baggie is a ring. Meg takes it out and in the flashlight's beam she can see that it has an exquisitely perfect Celtic design carved into the polished bone.

"Try it. It should fit."

Meg slides it on her ring finger. Like a small electric charge, a shiver passes through her. "I love you," she says. "It's beautiful, Joanna. Thank you." She turns to kiss Joanna, clicking off the flashlight as they embrace.

They fiddle with the seats which do tilt back and eventually, with their coats thrown over themselves, they sleep. By morning the wind has died down and other campers are up early to hike or pack up and move on. "Well, partner, what do you say? Drive on just a little ways and be sissies and check in early to a nice hot shower and a motel bed?" Joanna blows smoke and looks her way.

"Could be a plan. Shall we start with breakfast at the first diner that we see?"

"And how! I'm for a stack of pancakes and a side of ham!"

Meg laughs and starts the car. "Go for it! I'm a muffin type myself. With jam!"

The storm has blown the beach clear and as they drive on they see the stunning blue of the Pacific cascading upward in sunlight like hundreds of unseen waterfalls all landing right there before their eyes. "Love you," Meg says.

"Love you too. Want to try sailing out there?" and they laugh together.

# CHAPTER THIRTEEN

Stark awake Joanna curses, needing sleep. Outside somewhere a cat howls into the late spring night. Beside her in the bed Shadow stretches, alerted by the yowling, purrs a minute as Joanna strokes her long black hair and then leisurely jumps down from the bed. She orders herself to think about Meg, about being with her, about lying together in the motel the day after the storm, that close together. Joanna can almost feel skin against skin until she hardly knows where Meg's breath, lips, hands begin and her own end. But Meg is not here this night. Only emptiness lies next to Joanna in this bed. Joanna is alone in the long expanse of minutes that comprise the wakeful night, that stretch like desert sands interminably between this dark moment and the first moment of the dawn. Almost worse to think of Meg at all. Better not to feel the lack.

Like the day after Joanna's fourth birthday. They'd had leftover cake for dessert, served on the little flowered plates her mother painted long ago. Joanna had the daisies. She was sitting on her mother's lap as she did every night after dessert. Her mother's hand was stroking her hair. Her mother's voice was making warm air on her ear when she spoke.

Her father was about to speak. Joanna felt it like the air before the wind—cold air, harsh wind. She felt her mother's expectancy stiffening her arms.

"She is too old for this, Helen."

Joanna was not sure what he might mean. She waited, not breathing quite.

"What are you saying?" her mother asked, her voice lilting slightly as it sometimes did, her arms tightening their hold around Joanna.

"She is not a baby anymore."

"She's not all grown up just yet."

"You are not to hold her after dinner any longer. She may be excused with Peter at the conclusion of the meal and then you and I will have a few minutes of adult time with our coffee."

"But..."

"That's all there is to it," he said, "and it begins tonight."

Rage against her father curled through Joanna like an acrid wisp of smoke. She yearned for her mother to fight back, to use the strength in those warm arms to resist him with a sword, to shout out the words she believed must be forming in her mother's throat.

Joanna felt her mother's arms go slack and knew there was no hope. Her mother gently pushed her down from her lap. "We'll have other times," she whispered in Joanna's hair, relinquishing.

Joanna in one quick glance surveyed her mother's placid face, slightly flushed, the stern demeanor of her father in his chair where he sat like the cast iron curls in the fence in the churchyard. Then I will fight him for her, she thought, tightening her right hand as though around the handle of the sword, placing her left arm behind her as she raised her right arm, hearing the steel of her blade crash against the steel of her father's as they clashed. Silently she left the room. Alone in her bedroom, desolation had snaked through her body like a chill.

Confronting her wakefulness, Joanna again rises, lights another cigarette and goes to stand by the open window. Moonlight delineates the big maple right outside, exactly like the maple by her childhood house. Joanna, still raging at her wakefulness, goes to the kitchen for a cup of chamomile. And where is Shadow? She walks the downstairs rooms in search of her but finds nothing but silence in the dark. Suddenly remembering the new etching she is working on, Joanna goes to the basement to check it out. The plate is about a foot square which is much smaller than her usual prints. Her working sketch is of a nude woman, somewhat Rubinesque, yet startling, moving forward as if about to engage another. The woman is more impressionistic than her usual realistic figures. Joanna thinks she will title it "DELIGHT!" She has just begun to etch in the background.

I could phone Meg, she thinks, craving the warmth of her voice. Now there's an absurdity. Even if Meg were here, asleep, I would not wake her up.

Turning out the lights, Joanna goes back upstairs to bed. The landslide of memories will not let up.

Age five. Outside the house, after a beating, Joanna lay hidden in a fern hut at the edge of the neighbor's lot. Thor's body pressed itself warm against her. Thor nuzzled her. His warm tongue lapped her arm, her face, and Joanna looked down with an unguarded gaze. There was no one else to trust. It was only Thor whose eyes saw Joanna's eyes unshielded. It was Thor's tongue that soothed her flesh, Thor's paws that begged her to stroke him in return, Thor's tail that evidenced pure and unguarded delight without the criticism her father found an ever-present necessity, without the anxiety always lurking in her mother's eyes, without the unpredictable lash of vindictive violence that Peter carried side by side with his tree climbing boyish dares.

Shadow is on the bottom step. Bending to pick her up, Joanna thinks: that is the final memory. I'll lie down and snuggle Shadow and go to sleep. My God, it's three o'clock. Joanna goes back upstairs, carrying the cat. She looks at a snapshot of Meg on her bureau. She lies down carefully. Now, mind, go blank, she says and begins to count backward from one thousand.

***

Her brother, Peter, calls late one night. "He's gone, Joanna. You waited too long. You could have come to see him, you know. But anyway, the funeral will be on Saturday. That way you won't have to miss work. It will be at eleven. I didn't know if you would come up Friday night or not so I told them not to make it too early. You can drive up Saturday morning if you'd rather. Or Friday. There's not much left to do. Some papers in a strongbox. He left an old will with his lawyer's office. He was out of it. Not much left, once you can't move around. He's been bedridden now for months but you probably weren't cognizant of that. Did he even recognize you the last time you were here?"

"No, Peter, he didn't. Peter, I'm not going to be there. You go ahead."

"Oh, you have to come. By tomorrow morning, once you've reflected on it and felt mortality in your bones, in your dreams, Joanna, felt the pulse of time thundering in your ears, that old scythe in the grasses by your door, you'll change your mind. You'll regret it all your life if you don't come. It's one thing to—"

"Peter, I'm not coming." Joanna takes a deep, deep breath as she always did when their father lifted his arm, determining that she would not flinch, would not betray herself beneath the fury of his assault.

Nor, in this case, beneath the flurry of drunken words that Peter heaps on her in long, convoluted phrases that do not resolve into sentences but cycle back into themselves like Faulknerian prose gone mad, allowing itself no periods, no colons even, only the onward rush of self-absorption, only the pseudo meaning of high sounding prose. "You have to," he intones, "have to…"

"I'm not coming, Peter."

Peter rants and flails longer while Joanna resists the impulse to hang up on him. Eventually she manages to interject that she has work to do and does hang up.

On the morning of the funeral, Joanna thinks of her father's death; it is not as a passenger of Charon across the river Styx that she envisions him, but rather as head down against a storm, plodding, as John Bunyan has Christian at his death, taking heavy steps, trying to cross that final water.

Before she could even read, Joanna was allowed to look at anything she found in the family bookcase. The volumes were wedged in so tightly that she could scarcely pry them out. Crouched in the shadow of the bookcases, she studied the bindings as she would a tall showcase of jars of penny candy, choosing with care which one to tug out from its hiding place. Their backs, like tablets decorated with hieroglyphics, were a mix of green, gold, and flaking brown bindings, some made of thin leather, some of what seemed like musty cardboard.

Her mother, who sent her for piano lessons, showed her how to paint flowers on china plates, tried in her own ways to run, smiling, beside Joanna in a mountain meadow filled with daisies where larks sang, but their house was not a meadow and Joanna's father did not countenance random joy. On his way in from work he moved through the house turning off laughter in the same way he turned off an unused lamp, pontificating about wasting electricity, about the many hours of work it took to earn the money that it cost to raise a family.

Joanna finds herself again remembering the bookcase in the living room when she was very young, the way she ranged the books around her where she sat. They were the castle wall, the flow of their words the moat he did not cross. Safely encircled, she escaped. They included Shakespeare, Ivanhoe, Longfellow, Poe, Dickens, a beautifully bound Bible filled with almost transparently thin pages edged in gold, and *Pilgrim's Progress*, which had the most compelling illustrations of them all.

It was to these illustrations that Joanna went again and again, fascinated with every shading, every detail of every figure, tracing with her finger the carefully etched lines. As though the illustrator's hand held her hand as she moved it across the page, she felt flow into her body the ability of the artist to transcend daily experience. She memorized with her touch the terrifying power of the forms that he had drawn. Giants in motion crouched and leapt, rivers flowed. Her mother had read Joanna fairy tales. She knew that words could entertain, could transport her into worlds beyond her own. But in these drawings, the artist transformed her world itself, carrying her not as a witness to the events of others as the words in fairy tales did, but altering the world itself around her. Tracing the lines with her own touch, Joanna felt the flat and vacant time/space of the house be transformed into the vibrancy of life. She felt her very flesh respond, leap into life, as her fingers touched the artist's hand, held out to her as God's to Adam in the Michelangelo.

***

Late in the day, Joanna goes to her studio. She works into the evening on the new plate, not satisfied with the woman's hair. Tomorrow, she thinks, I'll work on it more and then I'll take a proof. When I start printing, I'll pack one and send it off to Meg. I think she'll like it, she muses, though she may blush! And Joanna smiles broadly as she goes upstairs to sleep.

# CHAPTER FOURTEEN

"Can't have beer at the beach, Shannon," Liz says decisively, taking the six-pack out of the cooler that Shannon is about to carry out to Meg's car for their beach picnic.

"Whoa! Who's to notice?"

"The kids." Liz's voice is laced with disapproval.

Shannon angrily leaves the kitchen, hurling back, "With friends like you, who needs the cops?"

Liz flushes, says in an aside to Meg who's making tuna sandwiches, "She's headed for big trouble, Mom."

Med nods and wraps the sandwiches, calls the kids to get their shovels and buckets ready.

"We'll talk about it later," Meg says, dodging, having no answer.

***

Walking down the driveway, shaded by the thick oak leaves overhead, seeing the heavy July foliage where the undergrowth covers the ground as in the Northwest of her childhood, Meg savors the richness of summer. When they lived in California there were no seasons. At Christmas there were still poinsettias blooming underneath the palms. The dry San Bernardino mountains stretched stiff and bare year round. Sometimes a rare rainfall left a trickle in the riverbed and people took their children for a ride to see. "Look! There's water in the river," became a family joke. Meg loves the rhythm of the New York seasons, the waning and waxing of each, the cyclical promise that each leads forward and will itself return another year. The earth is turning and circling.

Taking the mail from the box, Meg walks back toward the house. Since the incidents began, the lamppost interrupts the landscape the way strip mining might. Staring at the silent post, ripped ivy, scratch marks in the metal where the screw driver slipped, Meg closes her eyes and sees, against the background of the summer woods, those slight metal slashes, as she would see the shattered sun on her closed inner eyelids after inadvertently staring for a second directly at its light.

Meg runs to answer the phone. It's Angie, calling from Anchorage. After they chat awhile, Angie says, "Hey, have you seen Shannon today?"

Meg goes on red alert. She has not seen Shannon since Sunday at the beach. "Why?"

"Have you?"

"No. What's up?"

"Is she drinking, Mom?"

Meg is trapped between wishes to protect: Angie from worrying about Shannon; Shannon from getting caught; Shannon from drinking by enlisting an ally, even one three thousand miles away.

Simple truth wins out. "I've seen her drink too much a few times, Angie. I don't see her regularly enough to know exactly…"

"Oh Christ! Are the boys okay?"

"They seem fine." Meg starts to tell her about Mack taking good care of Dylan and stops, knowing this is something Mack's learned of necessity that will only make both Angie and herself feel worse if they start to talk about it.

"This apartment she's got. How near to you is it?"

Meg describes the one-bedroom apartment, in the back of a house in a quiet neighborhood in Rocky Point. She does not tell Angie about the broken rusty swing set that can't be used that fills up the tiny backyard or about her own hesitation about buying them a new set, not knowing how long they'll be there.

"And her job?"

"She's been waitressing."

Meg can hear the questions Angie does not ask. Would you keep the kids if Shannon gets in real trouble? How much financial help will you give them? Are they eating enough?

After the call is over, Meg tries to get back to the work of sorting out the cartons in the garage. The sun sifts through the trees above her. She's thinking about her most recent exchange of letters with Joanna in which they've begun to work out the details of Joanna's move. Once Joanna's house is sold, Joanna will buy into Meg's house and then they'll build the wing. This, they have concluded, is the only way that is entirely fair to each of them. Remembering that she has agreed to this plan with Joanna, doubt dizzies Meg. From the first day she claimed this house, for the first time in her life, land has been hers and hers alone.

Year after year in these woods, this cabin, Meg has been secure: the house, the land, the trees, the birds, all hers. No one to fear losing. No one to appease. She has invited her friends, her lovers, her children and grandchildren to come visit her in her own space.

Twice one of the children came for a long stay to recoup (once Liz and the children after the divorce; once Jimmy with a broken leg). Most recently Shannon and the boys. What if one of the children is again in need? Joanna and Meg have agreed that this house is for two women and two women only: clear space in which to work and love.

The kids are grown, she admonishes herself. They don't need to be here and you have work to do and don't need anyone to put a stop to that. They are all safe now. They don't need this safe space now.

Funny, she thinks, lovers have come and gone, but the thought of letting anyone buy into this house never occurred to her before. Once burned, twice shy, Meg thinks, remembering that she and her first lover had co-owned a house and they had ended up splitting up, forced to sell that house after Tim died in Vietnam. Years later Rosalyn had perched here in this house with Meg like a beautiful egret on its southern flight, finding a satisfying place to halt for the summer, then migrating away again in response to an inner necessity all her own. Meg stayed in the house, saddened, alone, but anchored on her own land.

As the months passed Meg and Joanna have discussed building a studio onto the house and the need for more living space. It became clear that they needed to work out an equitable financial arrangement. Gradually they shifted from pipe dreams to concrete ideas, from ideas to a plan that included sales contracts and deeds. Preparing to go together to a lawyer to change the deed to her home was different than whispering "I love you" in the night.

***

That night Meg has a dream:

*She is driving a car, pulling a boat on a trailer behind it. She is on her usual road to the beach but there is snow on the road and ice. At the top of the hill Meg realizes that the brakes will not work on the ice. The weight of the boat drives the car forward and although she brakes to slow the car down, the speed steadily increases. Meg is half enjoying what is like a wild, out of control sleigh ride, sailing across the snow and half terrified: there will be a crash and she herself will die.*

Waking, Meg tries to think about Joanna, her laughter, her loving arms, the brightness that will come when they can be together every day, but there is an abyss along her path, a panic at being on its verge. My land is no longer my domain, she thinks; what am I forfeiting?

***

The darkening of a light is silent in the night, soft as the passing of the moon behind dark clouds. Meg turns in yet another intense dream, comes awake aware of something altered, as though a corner of the room has gone askew. Moving only her head she looks from one wall to the other, across the ceiling, listening to the crickets in their unceasing rounds. Car lights strafe the ceiling, and she hears the tires' nearly inaudible crunch on dirt and weeds at the street's edge and the rise and fall of an engine as the car slides away into the night like a crocodile easing itself back into the swamp.

Swinging her legs over the edge of the bed, Meg sits a moment, gauging the time and place. Not a dream. Not the past of the cartons she's been sorting. The face of the electric clock next to the bed is dark. Through the top pane of the window she can see a few stars in the spaces between the highest branches of the oaks. She stands and looks out the lower pane of the same window, looks down at the driveway where the lamppost stands, where its light should be shining, splashing a brightness on the bushes and tree trunks, laying a familiar glow along the driveway, marking a safe pathway to the locked back door. Nothing. She cannot see the lamppost. There is no moonlight. She can sense more than see the thick presence of the trees now in full leaf.

Meg walks through the house to the light switch by the deck, knowing it will not work, knowing he has come again, the intruder who means her harm. She fingers the switch, waits a long breath's worth of time, and flips it gently up and down. The night remains its quiet ordinary self. The darkness hovers inside the house and all around the yard, falling like blackened snow from the sky above, covering the tops of trees, sifting down through the leafy branches of the oak, through the needles of the pine, to obscure the outline of each stone, woodpile, bush and garbage can, and in the open spaces along the drive and underneath the trees, to pile high in ever deepening darkened drifts that hide all that has been so long known and familiar to Meg's eye.

"Oh, Joanna, love, some 'Isle of Innisfree'! What are you getting yourself into?"

# CHAPTER FIFTEEN

"It's the perfect time to put this house on the market!" Flo Swenson, the real estate agent, waves her arm, silver bracelet flashing in the sunlight, at the yard. "Just look!"

Shasta daisies, foxgloves and a multitude of roses are in full bloom in the gardens that border the lawn in the backyard. Even the grass is decent. Joanna mowed it the day before in preparation for this visit. "So what happens now?"

"Let me do a quick walk-through and then I have some papers for you to sign."

This feels unreal to Joanna. She rests her hand against the spruce Aunt Frances helped her plant twenty-five years before which now towers beside the house, shading Emily's bedroom. Why would I sell this house? That would be insane, she thinks, her glance lingering on the wooden marker she carved for the graves of their beloved dogs and cats, that barely show now for the ivy that has overrun them.

Joanna leads Flo into the family room from the patio. "What a nice room this is," Flo says, "with the fireplace and the glass doors to that beautiful backyard. Are you the gardener?"

Joanna nods. Flo manages her sales enthusiasm well. Because she's genuine, Joanna thinks. That's why I picked her. She's an honest woman.

"We don't want to price it unreasonably high. It would stay on the market too long and eventually we'd have to drop it way down and you'd get robbed in the end. Let's be real. It's a fine house with a beautiful yard—on a street of fine houses. It doesn't have anything special going for it, you know? The location's not particularly great, it hasn't been painted recently, the basement's not finished. The taxes aren't that high. That's a plus. You have two bathrooms, thank God. And a little powder room on the first floor."

"What a beautiful table!" Flo runs her hand over the polished oak. "Family heirloom?"

Joanna laughs. "No, actually we got it at a yard sale when we were first married. It is beautiful though, isn't it?"

Flo glances around the kitchen without further comment. Suddenly it feels old and worn to Joanna. The appliances are ancient. The bar that runs down the center that has been so useful to her divides the eating area, filled by three high stools and the chairs and table, from the cooking area, which she's always thought was comfortably large—abruptly the whole room seems fractured, awkward, even small. Twice the size of Meg's, Joanna retorts. You couldn't even put a stool to sit on in that dark little galley. What am I getting into?

Flo has moved on to the living room which is a large room with windows on three sides. The piano stands against the inside wall. A sofa, chairs and a coffee table leave space to move around. This room has a history of faculty parties, church dinners for the homeless, meetings of the women's art group, and more recently, monthly meetings of lesbian groups, some political and some social. Joanna stands, seeing the gatherings, like pageants frozen in place, as scrim beyond scrim lifts, to reveal year before year. The clink of glasses, the swirl of women's voices, laughter, obscures Flo. Good thing I've had enough of that, Joanna thinks. You couldn't wedge any of those meetings into Meg's house.

The walls are covered with prints and drawings. Flo, in her tailored beige slacks, pastel blouse, spiraling silver earrings, turns to Joanna with a smile. "The work is wonderful. Do take down this one and the two at the end, though, before we show the house."

Joanna is jolted out of her reverie. She doesn't understand and then she does. Nudes go. Lesbian goes. Feminist goes? No way, she thinks, but does not say it out loud to Flo. Instead she takes a pad from the pocket of her slacks and makes herself a note as Flo says, "Some family will be lucky to get it. If it's still here in October, it won't go until next spring, I guarantee you. So we sell it this summer."

After Flo has checked out the four bedrooms upstairs, they sit at the kitchen table. Flo spreads out papers for Joanna to sign, explains that she will need a key, asks if she can show it when Joanna is at work, tells her she will always call ahead.

Joanna signs and as she does so feels the floor dropping under her, as in a whirling ride at a carnival, leaving her with her back against the wall, arms flung wide, at the mercy of centrifugal force. Flo shakes her hand, puts the papers in her briefcase, and goes out through the front door. It is, Joanna thinks, like intentionally scheduling mayhem for yourself.

Joanna automatically pulls off her slacks and blouse and grabs her jeans and work shirt. She stops in the kitchen to make herself a thick ham and cheese sandwich, then sits at the kitchen table where she starts sketching on a napkin as she eats and without really deciding to, picks up a sketching pad and settles on the back porch. Nude women. A lake. Summer maple trees. Rippled water. That one brushing that child's hair, the way it was at her aunt's farm.

The music of their voices was like the songs of varied birds. One was her aunt, her words the tolling of an offshore buoy. One was her mother, her voice a hushed wind among willows. Her own was a shout as she dove into the lake.

The women walked from the cabin to the shore every day to bathe, their laughter rising over them like the morning mist lifting from the invisible surface of the cool, calm lake. It was for Joanna the best hour of the long summer day. For that time she entirely belonged. Shafts of sunlight struck through the fir and pine to sparkle on the ripples spreading out from her quick strokes as she glided over and under the smooth clear surface exchanging calls with her cousins like the loons with one another far out across the lake.

\*\*\*

What Joanna wants to do is to forget the gallery opening and go downstairs to start work on a plate. This will be her last etching in Oregon. The heavy steel press will have to be disassembled for the move. It is ten feet by four and weighs two thousand pounds. She has already spoken with Vernon Matthews, the man who built it. He will come to take it apart for her. She will ask Greta to videotape the whole process. The videotape, along with the written instructions of Mr. Matthews, will enable someone in New York to put it back together.

Joanna can better envision the house being packed up and abandoned than she can the press being broken into parts. For twenty-five years she has worked here in this dark basement at this press, rolling out print after print. Might as well take the waters of the Sound away from Meg, she thinks, as take this press away from me. What if they can't get it back together right?

After the gallery opening, over hamburgers and beer, sitting in a booth at a local diner, Greta confronts Joanna. "Now tell me, please. Exactly what's going on?"

Joanna munches on her food and pretends not to understand. "Hmm?"

"Come off it, Joanna! Realtor? You're selling your house?"

"You knew that."

"We knew you were thinking about it! And then what?" Greta glowers at her. "I swear, you're like the first little pig, marching off with a bandana tied on a stick stuck over your shoulder, to build a house of straw."

"I'm moving to New York."

"You're moving in with Meg?" Greta takes out a cigarette and offers one to Joanna who takes it.

Joanna pulls out her lighter from her pocket, leans across the table to light Greta's and then sits back to light her own before she speaks. "That's right."

"And what happens when you two have a fight and break up? You coming back to reclaim your house? You gonna kick out the people you sell it to?" Greta orders another round of beers.

Joanna shakes her head, pushes her glass away toward Greta, then decides to drink it since it's there.

"Your track record's not that good, kid. You need a little insurance, like a room of your own, you know."

Joanna watches the disintegrating foam on the beer crumbling into itself. She rotates hers, admiring the way the amber fluid filters the light from the lamp on the wall in their booth. "I'm buying into Meg's house, Greta. We'll be fifty-fifty owners. Then together we're building on a wing." Greta sips her beer, studying Joanna. "I'm going to have a big, wonderful studio. The whole first story of the wing will be my studio. With windows all around. Light, Greta, light."

"Meg's willing to do that?"

"Umhm. The second story will be our bedroom. A big room with a bookcase at one end. My desk and a file or two. A little study in the corner. Just like my study in my house here."

"Is Meg rich?"

Joanna laughs and takes a swallow of her beer. "I guess not! But she's solvent. She has a teacher's pension and social security."

Greta tips up her glass. "Good luck, kid! Here's to you!" Her eyes are not persuaded.

"I'll be okay, Greta! Don't worry."

"You've got a lawyer? An accountant?"

"You know what? In fact, I have!"

Leaving the diner, the two women hug good night. "You know it's just that I love you, kiddo. You know that, Joanna, don't you?"

"I know that. Now you drive carefully, you hear? Say hi to Marlene."

Driving home, feeling a buzz from the second beer, Joanna knows she'll call Meg and that she'll be okay as soon as she hears her voice. "But Aunt Frances," she says, blowing smoke into the night, "I wish you were here to tell me that it really is all okay."

\*\*\*

The opening over with at the gallery, the realtor in charge of the house, Joanna flies to New York for one last weekend visit, to talk to the contractor Meg has lined up.

Young and eager, the contractor walks the yard with them while they explain what they have in mind. He promises to save all the trees but one. They go inside. He admires Joanna's prints which Meg has bought and hung around the house. "I like Van Gogh, myself," he says. He agrees to start building in October. He leaves them with an estimate and his phone number, saying to call when Joanna has arrived in New York to stay.

# CHAPTER SIXTEEN

Turning her head to check her turquoise earrings, Joanna smiles. She's dressing for a party. For a gala. For a celebration. Meg is giving a reading from her novel at the women's bookstore. Joanna loves to hear Meg read, her voice melodic and quietly intense. Meg comes up beside her and they turn into one another's arms and kiss. "Don't start up now," Joanna says, laughing.

"We have time," Meg answers, eyes twinkling, "don't we?" raising one eyebrow.

"No, we don't. Here, your collar's twisted. Hold still." Joanna smoothes the black collar of the multicolored jacket, then steps back to inspect. Meg, five feet five, is slightly shorter than Joanna. We each, Joanna thinks, carry our weight well. A little more than we should, but never mind. An interesting face, Meg's, not beautiful, but her lips are full, her eyes intelligent, their expression changing constantly. That face is never dull. Framed by curly brown hair flecked with gray, that face will wear well, emitting warmth and humor.

"It's okay with you if I read the new poems at the end?" Meg's voice is quiet now, entirely serious.

"It's your reading. Read anything you want." Joanna tries not to think about the private love poems Meg has written for her going forth into the public air.

"No. I won't read them if you'd rather I didn't. These are your friends. This is your town. And they're…"

"It's fine. I'll blush of course. But I'll sit in back!" Joanna laughs.

"The hell you will. You won't, will—"

Joanna teases, "Wait and see."

Meg reconsiders. "If you want to, you can."

"Hey, let's go. Can't keep your fans waiting, you know."

They arrive early at the small women's bookstore on the edge of town. "I once went to a reading in a Manhattan bookstore for a good writer; there were only six people in the audience and that included the women who owned the store and the two of us!" Meg smiles. "So don't worry if no one comes."

"It's hard to know," Joanna answers as they go inside. She introduces Meg to Sharon, who owns the store. Three or four women are browsing at the shelves. Chairs set in rows are vacant.

Suddenly Joanna feels as if she is the hostess and will be the one to blame if the room is not filled with attentive listeners. A list shapes up in her head of all the women she might have called. Or she should have given a party at her house and invited everyone. People come if there's a party afterward. Thinking of all the things she's failed to do to ensure a crowd, Joanna turns to the shelves, finds a new novel she wants to read and settles into it, leaving Sharon to show Meg around while they all wait for an audience to arrive.

Meg starts her reading with passages from her only lesbian novel, written twenty years before, published under a pseudonym because she was still teaching in a public school. Hearing laughter, seeing smiles, Meg knows the reading is going well. The room is packed. Meg allows herself to glance around the room, recognizing Joanna's closest friends with whom she has had dinner once or twice. Only women are there. Not only lesbian though, Meg thinks.

Shifting from those excerpts to an unpublished short story, Meg concentrates on the manuscript itself, noting a rough paragraph, a piece that needs to be fleshed in. She goes from that to a one-page excerpt about Tim. She always includes something from that book. Like a scrim between the audience and herself the Vietnam War flickers and is gone, heat lightning from a forgotten decade, silent and unreal, the thunder so distant as to be out of range.

Meg holds the poetry in her hand. "Ordinarily I only read poetry in private," she says, smiling. "But tonight is special. Because so many of you are her friends, I want to read a few poems that I've written for Joanna." Meg glances at Joanna who is sitting with Greta, Marlene and Hildy in the second row from the front. Meg does not dare let her glance linger to savor the beauty that is Joanna's face, the radiance that is her smile.

A pleased murmur traverses the room. Meg reads. She has chosen a set of seven. Halfway through the fourth, Meg is aware that it is as though she and Joanna are standing together before this gathering this night. She continues to read:

"The spell my lover casts/ with lips and hands/ is like the spray of crystal light/ that falls in shining rays/ to pierce the clouds/ below the sun in flight/ and when my lover's voice/ speaks love to me/ I take a long ecstatic fall/ a trusting dive/ into the deepest quarry pool/ with agate sides/ that resonate with light./ Like the slow soaring moon/ in a deep and quiet sky/ her voice compels:/ I cannot speak nor move/ but stay in silence/ like to the winter calm/ when falling snow/ mutes every tree and stone/ deep in the windless wood/ the wonder of her voice/ imprinting me/ with beauty/ pure/as what she carves in bone./ And sometimes her spell/ falls like a sea worn stone/ to plumb my heart/ I have forever known/ the deep tones that it knells./ The one by whom the spell is thrown/ and the one to whom its beauty's known/ we are together then/ and melded so:/ nor shall my lover nor myself/ ever be alone again/ such is the spell my lover casts/ luminous beneath the moon."

The applause is warm and enthusiastic. Joanna walks up to Meg and in front of everyone they embrace, long and joyously. The room is filled with smiles. The Mendelssohn wedding march might well be blasting as they walk, arm in arm, among the gathering. It is clear to all that they have joined their lives and clear to them that everyone there assembled gives their blessing.

# PART III

# CHAPTER SEVENTEEN

"My God, I can't stand to sort another drawer," Joanna mutters, and upends the empty sideboard drawer above the wastebasket, thumping its bottom to jar out all the dust. She slides it back into the bureau and pulls out the next drawer down. This one is full of old family photographs. Seeing four-year-old Miranda and three-year-old Emily wading in the frothy edges of the surf while Will, a quieter older six, sits watching them, shovel and bucket in his hands, Joanna smiles with delight and pockets that one in her flannel shirt. She riffles through several batches, held together by rubber bands. Kids in action, she muses, like those old Big Little books that you could flip through to see the Lone Ranger and Tonto galloping away. I guess we threw all those away: Tiny Tim, Tarzan.

Joanna pulls an empty carton across the carpet and quickly shifts the stacks of snapshots into it. Now and then she pulls one out to keep. Just before the carton is full, Joanna finds a party snapshot of Walter at the piano, stretching up one hand toward his glass of bourbon, his cigarette held in the corner of his mouth, lips taut in that required smile, eyebrows quirked, eyes veiled. A wave of revulsion passes through Joanna. Like a kick to her solar plexus she has a vivid flashback to that night:

She was lying in their bed. She had been reading.

"It has nothing to do with you, Joanna." Walter, emanating the smell of bourbon that masked the smell of sex, stood beside the bed, changing into his pajamas; having just come home at four a.m., he was speaking through the Wagner he had set blasting through the house.

Swirling downward in the vortex of his self-righteous voice, Joanna screamed at him, "*But I'm your wife! I AM your WIFE.* I am the one you constantly betray. That has to do with me!"

He seemed to shrink, become smaller than she knew he physically was.

"I tell you it has nothing whatever to do with you, Joanna. That's all I'm going to say."

The children then were like little puppies, nuzzling at Joanna the way puppies seek the teats. They tumbled among their toys. Joanna sat among them, snuggling, savoring their innocence, their smell, the way she did the apple blossoms in the spring, burying her nose in them, rumpling their downy hair.

There was no divorce for ten more years.

***

It's the regularly scheduled meeting night of their women artists' group. The crowd of women are due at Joanna's at seven o'clock.

Walking toward the door after a dinner out with Hildy, Joanna hopes the buyers of her house will soon leave so the meeting can proceed in peace. This is the last meeting for which Joanna will be responsible. She falters at the thought. Every day now she finds herself knowing that something familiar will not be happening for her in Oregon again. The leaves are beginning to fall from the maples and walking through them her breath catches: autumn being the season of relinquishment, this being her last autumn here. Hour by hour she is distanced from the places that she knows, the people that she loves, as though the parts of Portland, one by one, are being shelved and coated with shellac, leaving them in view but no longer in her hands.

"SURPRISE! SURPRISE! SURPRISE!"

Voices explode around her like fireworks. Joanna buckles with the shock. There are smiling faces all around and all the voices go silent and then avalanche into "Happy Birthday." Joanna sits on the nearest chair, laughing uncontrollably as tears roll down her cheeks.

Though it's her birthday, the cards make it quite clear that it's going away gifts everyone has brought. A traveling kit with a note hoping she returns sometime to visit; a map of New York with a gift certificate for L.L. Bean; the *Collected Eudora Welty* with a note saying, "Now that you're going off like a kid to college, here's something to read on those homesick nights!"

Reading that one, Joanna winces. There were a lot of bad nights in college and the desperate loneliness of those nights curls up around her like smoke from a forgotten ashtray. Not homesick, God knows, but lonely, not knowing how to find whatever it was she did not know how to name that would bring her happiness. Joanna turns to the woman who wrote it, a clerk at the bookstore who does pottery, whose husband is a superintendent of highways, and says, laughing, "Elaine—you don't understand. I won't be lonesome!" and for a flicker of a moment doubting, thinking, why am I leaving everyone I know?

Joanna lights a cigarette and draws in deeply. Why would I do that, to go to a strange land to live among strangers? The dark doubt darts through the room like a bat confused by the bright lights and out into the night as Joanna goes on speaking to the bewildered Elaine, "I'm going to be living with a Eudora Welty. She's a writer and her name is Meg!" Joanna blushes and realizes that Elaine may never have been in a face-to-face out loud conversation with a lesbian before, or not one in which Elaine couldn't pretend they were both straight.

Spoiled by hanging out with Greta and Marlene, I am, Joanna thinks. And the lesbian singing group. Straight women make everything so hard, she thinks. Actually odd to have any of them at my own birthday party. Except, of course, for an old friend like Hildy. For a moment Joanna remembers the long-ago academic parties in this very room: pedantic men, half drunk, pontificating to little clusters of inattentive colleagues; women in fancy dresses wearing expensive jewelry; everyone holding a cigarette, blowing smoke in thoughtful pauses in their conversation; half-hearted flirting. Walter cruising, masking his restlessness with bourbon. Herself drinking, chain smoking, having provided the obligatory cocktails, gourmet dinner with well chosen wine, the after dinner assortment of brandy and liqueurs, wandering the rooms, waiting it out, wishing they'd go away.

Cursing herself for ever having started, Joanna resolutely continues to explain. "We'll share everything, Elaine, just like you and Stewart do." Well, not just like, Joanna thinks with an inner smile.

"But where did you meet this woman, this Meg?"

Joanna is considering how to end this conversation when Greta marches in carrying a huge birthday cake which she sets before Joanna as a great cluster of long familiar, warmly smiling women gather close. And all of us in jeans, Joanna thinks, laughing to herself, as they burst into a lusty singing of "Happy birthday, dear Joanna, happy birthday to you!"

Joanna bends to blow the candles out, wishing that she and Meg will—will—will be happy, she ends the thought, expelling air through her pursed lips. "Those homesick nights" runs through her head as Elaine watches her from across the room like the thirteenth fairy at Sleeping Beauty's party. Someone snaps a picture of her cutting the cake and in the startling glare of the flashbulb, the ring Meg gave her glints on Joanna's finger, and she knows to a certainty that all will yet be well, that the debris of her past life will fall away like chaff from threshed wheat in the bright sunlight of those fields by the eastern shore.

# CHAPTER EIGHTEEN

Joanna has a preliminary sketch of the wing folded in her book. At lunchtime, sitting on the balcony of the store where she always sits to read, she unfolds it, doodles in a garden. Some lilies there, and there some tulips. Those lines are the studio, those the bedroom. Penciling in a garden, Joanna knows there may be trees in that area or a laurel or rhododendron to block flowers. She continues anyhow. Somehow, she thinks, she must make this all seem real.

Joanna goes to the closing on her house in two weeks. Then Meg will fly west and she and Meg will drive east, car packed to the gills. Joanna breaks into a sweat trying to keep hold of the order of it all, trying to believe she can get everything done in time.

Meanwhile, her pencil moves lightly over the page. What, she thinks, if none of it is real? The legalities are so foreign to her life that they only add to the unreality of it all: strange documents with language that is hard to understand; huge checks changing hands; taxes and titles and certificates of occupancy and deeds and notes; as though she is suddenly required to work incomprehensible calculus, and though the lawyers and the accountants explain it all to her, Joanna still feels like she's taking some exam that she has not studied for.

Her glance takes in the shelves and tables in the university bookstore where she's worked for twenty years. This is real. She knows every cranny, every book by cover and has read so many books that the manager teases her, saying she must come in every night to read the ones she's missed. Robert Kennedy's face catches her eye from a biographical section near her on her left. That wonderful crooked smile of his always breaks her heart.

The morning after he died, the kids had already left for nursery school and Walter had gone to meet a class before anyone turned on the TV. Then Joanna, with her coffee and cigarette, sat to relax, held out her hand with the remote, and, intending only to catch the weather for the day, clicked.

She was sucked into the video screen the way people are by the music that they hear through their headphones. The familiar world was no longer there. Except for her hand that moved the cigarette down to the ashtray from time to time to tap the ashes off or to bring another from the pack to replace the one that she had just ground out, without looking, each time her fingers started to burn, Joanna did not move for hours.

John Kennedy. Medgar Evers. Malcolm X. Martin Luther King. Robert Kennedy. The little girls in Sunday school in Montgomery. The three boys in Mississippi. And Robert Kennedy was dead.

This is not the way the world is, Joanna thought. This screen before me is not the real world. I could turn it off and I will have a living room again with books and a sofa and drapes that I have sewn that hang by windows that look out on an ordinary street where the kids ride by on their bicycles and the mailman walks slowly on his route.

I can turn this off. This is an unreal film. Like *1984*. Like the Orson Welles broadcast of the *War of the Worlds* in 1938. I can turn it off and go into my kitchen and bake bread. Yes. I will turn it off and bake. I will take my hand away from this bizarre object that distorts the world. She stared at the small black remote that rested like a melanoma on her hand.

My hands will be purified in flour like my mother's and my grandmother's before her and the good smell of baking bread will fill the house when the kids and Walter come back home. We'll eat it while it's warm, tearing off chunks.

Melting in my mouth like the wafer in communion, it will be, Joanna thought, and began to cry, choking out clotted sobs, staring at the unrelenting film that showed again and again, like the home movie some proud father shot with his new camcorder, if such a machine went mad, spewing foot after foot of film to ricochet all over the backyard, tangling in the daffodils, gagging the dog, malfunctioning so that every image on it is reflecting back sunlight from Robert's crooked laugh where he lies fallen, surprised as his brothers were, in the unreal world where the family goes out to play football on the lawn on Thanksgiving Day, where the boys fall, each in turn clutching the ball, rolling in the leaves, laughing a triumphant laugh, where Robert Kennedy, third son, lies dead.

Joanna gets up now and walks through the store, walks down the street, lighting her cigarette as she goes. Autumn is for her the heavy season, presaging death: her mother, John Kennedy, Robert Kennedy, her beloved Lily, the flowers in the gardens, the sky-launched maple leaves.

She wishes she were walking the paths in her own yard. Her hands want to be pulling an occasional weed, breaking off dead blossoms on the roses, stroking the grave marker she has carved for Lily and Gluck, her beloved dogs, and Sesame, her cat. Like the pall of the darkened rain-soaked autumn leaves beneath her feet, loss settles around her.

After work Joanna goes to the cemetery. "Aunt Frances," she says, lying full length on the ground beneath the maple, "I'm scared as hell. I can't even remember when I've been this scared."

***

The day arrives. Joanna picks Meg up from the airport. They hug. Joanna drives to a motel. The movers have already cleared out everything that was left in the house and the closing is scheduled for the next afternoon. After that, they will have dinner with Greta and Marlene and Hildy and be on their way east at dawn the following day.

Although Meg takes her in her arms, standing in the motel room, Joanna cannot respond. For a frantic moment, she feels as though she's on an escalator, going up, and has lost her footing. They are drawing near the top and she will fall, her shoestring sucked into the unforgiving crack where the stairs mysteriously go flat and disappear. She will lie there, being crippled, waiting for someone somewhere to throw a switch that stops the machinery of the stairs.

"It's okay, darling. I love you. Do you want to go by the house, walk in the garden?"

Joanna nods. "Yes. And go by the cemetery where Aunt Frances is. I'd like you to go there once with me."

They go first to the cemetery where they sit while Joanna tells Meg stories about her aunt and the summer visits to her farm. Joanna weeds around the headstone and lays a stone on it and they go back to the car in silence and drive over to the house.

"Let's not go in. It's eerie with nothing there. I just wanted to be in the yard once more."

They walk through the backyard where the roses have gone now and the leaves are falling. Meg stops by the wooden marker Joanna had once carved for the graves of pets. "Take this with you, Joanna."

Joanna looks surprised and then smiles at Meg. "Should I?"

"Of course. You can put it in a flower garden by our house. The new people won't even want it here."

Joanna lifts the beautifully carved board, brushes off the mossy loam that has adhered, and puts it in the backseat of the car. "I'll buy some plastic to wrap it in and it'll fit in the trunk."

Driving away from the house, Joanna feels her loneliness diminish and reaches over to hold Meg's hand a minute. "Thank you for that," she says, and finds she is back with Meg, has found her footing once again: this is the woman she loves and this woman, Meg, loves her.

***

Headed for New York, with maps and the thermos full of ice and apple juice, the familiar requirements of travel lock Joanna into their routine. Fall is the right time to make the trip, they congratulate themselves. The Cascades and the Rockies are beautiful, the weather magnificent, tourism at a low, and no risk of blizzards anywhere along the way. They drive long days and stay at the cheapest motels they can find in the AAA book.

The mountains of Montana, the day-long open spaces, the center of the nation marked by Fargo and the bridge across the Mississippi, the sudden rich green of the dairy states, the forests unimaginable after the plains, vanish behind them until they are in the populated east and counting down the miles to New York City. Joanna is nervous about getting from New Jersey to Long Island.

"Want me to drive?" Meg offers.

"No, you're not used to the car—and you're not used to shifting gears."

"This is true. But I learned on a stick shift and you don't much forget, you know."

"You might forget a little in the middle of the George Washington Bridge and a little forgetting might be a big problem in the wrong place at the wrong time!"

"You have a point."

\*\*\*

They pull into the driveway late in the day on the fourth day of the trip. The moving van is due in two more days. Meg looks up to see the lights have been turned on by Liz. Thank God, she thinks, they're working.

"Looks like a good motel. Think they have a vacancy?" Joanna grins at Meg.

"They do. I called. Welcome home," Meg says, giving Joanna a kiss under the trees before she unlocks the door.

**PART IV**

# CHAPTER NINETEEN

Joanna rises first. The sky is clear, the air crisp. It's a bright October day. Sleepily and automatically, Joanna heads for the kitchen, knowing even as she crosses through the living room that there is something skewed about the day. Ready to sit on the deck with the *Times* and her cigarette, holding out her cup to pour the coffee into it, she identifies the problem before her hand touches the handle of the automatic coffeemaker. There is no smell of coffee in the air.

She stays her hand, puzzled. Did I forget to set the timer? The usually glowing light is dark. She checks the cord; it is plugged in. She clicks the kitchen light switch but it does not go on. Meg's dark little alley kitchen closes in on her like dusk. The coffee grounds sit in the filter, high and dry as desert sands, untouched by water.

She can hear Meg moving about in the bathroom. "Meg!" she calls. "The power is off!"

"I noticed," Meg says calmly, coming into the kitchen. "I need to make a phone call. Then I'll talk to you about it."

"What talk? This is a New York special event?"

"Go have a cigarette. I'll be right out."

***

After she has called the police and the electrician, Meg sits on the deck with Joanna. "I've been having some trouble with the lamppost by the driveway."

Joanna walks to the railing, her back to Meg, and stares down as she listens.

"One night last winter someone rearranged the wires in that post to cause a short circuit and that made the whole house short out."

Joanna spins toward her. "Someone rearranged the wires! *My God! What are you talking about?*"

"That was December and January. I thought he'd stopped."

Joanna, her back against the rail, is staring at Meg in disbelief.

"But he did it again this summer. I've talked to the police about it. They can't figure it out." It sounds entirely different to Meg now that she's putting words to each incident for Joanna.

"Figure what out?"

"Figure out why anyone would do that." Meg wants to dodge Joanna's growing wrath. She wonders if she can get away to dig out her little butane camp burner to boil water. "I'll go make you a cup of coffee," she says, standing up and turning toward the door, "and me some tea."

"*Maybe not. Maybe you're going to explain to me what the hell you're talking about.*"

Meg studies the angry woman by the rail of the deck. Joanna is running her hand through her short gray hair. She's wearing a light purple sweatshirt over her pajamas and tapping a cigarette against the rail. *Who is this raging stranger?* "Look. It's happened a few times. The police are working on it."

"*My God!* I can't believe you kept this all a secret. You didn't think I had a right to know?"

"Now it has happened again so I'm telling you about it."

"*Now! After* I've moved three thousand miles to live in this house with you!" They look at one another in alarm. They've never had a fight before. "Oh damn!" Joanna paces back and forth by the deck rail, looking down the driveway.

Meg edges toward the door to the sunroom, saying, "I'm going to make breakfast."

Joanna stays alone at the deck rail with another cigarette, staring at the driveway, seeing the yard extend out from the lamppost as though the post is the axis of a whirling top and the trees and shrubs, the house itself, the deck on which she stands, all spin around and around with the post leering out from its fixed point in the center. Even to walk there now is hazardous. She turns to go back into the house and stops herself, exiled by Meg's astonishing deceit.

***

"So what's this? Breakfast with law enforcement?" Joanna gives a scathing glance at the tray of bread and jam, cheese and oranges that Meg is carrying out to the deck.

Meg sets the tray down on the deck table without comment. She has used her little butane burner to make Joanna a cup of coffee and herself a cup of tea, which she had already brought out. She studies Joanna a minute before she speaks. "Help yourself," she says, setting a plate and knife on Joanna's side of the table.

"No way," Joanna says. "You may be used to this, but I am not."

Meg picks up the front page of the *Times* and lays it down again. "The police won't be here right away." Thank God the sun is out, Meg thinks. It would be awful if we were trapped inside without the lights, when Joanna's this mad at me.

Joanna aims the words, staccato, at Meg: "Exactly what is happening? Tell me again."

"Someone comes in the night and messes up the wires in that lamppost. It shorts out and all the lights go out. I've called the electrician. The second time it happened, I also called the police."

*"You didn't even call the police the first time it happened? For God's sake, why not?"*

Meg looks toward the neighbor's yard and says, "Can we talk quietly?"

Joanna looks surprised as though she hadn't known she was shouting, pauses a moment and nods. In her usual voice, she asks, with growing incredulity, "Why not?"

"I thought it was just kids." And why hadn't she told Joanna from the very beginning? They were on the phone for hours, telling each other everything else about their lives.

"Did you call the police while he was here last night?"

"I was asleep while he was here."

"In the night they might have caught him!"

"I try, Joanna." Meg turns to sarcasm, adding, "Maybe if it happens again you can handle it better."

"I'll call the minute the fucking lights go out. That's for sure!"

***

Joanna walks back and forth by the railing until the police car comes up the driveway. She watches the detective get out, sees him glance around the yard, past the lamppost into the woods, before he comes to the back door. Meg leans over the railing, smiles down at him, calls, "Come on in. The door's open."

My God! Joanna thinks, how could Meg have left the door unlocked just after the intruder has been here? She is still rerunning in her mind the events that Meg has recounted. Some unknown man has been coming into their yard to tinker with the wires in the lamppost. They have no power today because of the short circuit this occasioned. This happened again and again before Joanna moved to New York. Meg had never told her. This is the part that snags Joanna's mind, leaves a series of jagged tears along each thought. He'd come last winter and he'd come in the summer. Twice in the summer. Now this is October and he's been here again, this very night, while they slept. This house that looks so serene and safe is a danger zone. And Meg has kept that secret from Joanna. Her thinking is like skating on thin ice: every time she tries a thought, it is as though one foot drops into the icy waters underneath the ice, and she must haul it up again and try to gain footing on the cracked and crumbling surface of her life.

The policeman smiles, stopping at the top of the stairs, looking for a way to walk through the sunroom which is filled with Joanna's cartons and furniture.

"Come on out," Meg calls from the deck.

"Detective Orenstein," Meg says, "my friend, Joanna. She's just moved here from Oregon." Meg laughs. "Everything isn't quite unpacked yet."

"It takes a while, doesn't it? Welcome to New York."

Joanna nods at him, forcing herself to smile. Joanna feels like an outsider as Meg and the policeman run through an account of the night's events. He's known the whole scenario all along, she thinks, offering him a cigarette which he refuses, and I wasn't even told.

***

Why are you feeling so guilty, Meg asks herself as she follows the detective out, stopping at the lamppost where he stands, studying the surrounding woods, looking for tracks in the leaves on the driveway.

I just didn't want Joanna to have one more thing to worry about, she answers herself, as Detective Orenstein's car disappears down the road. She couldn't have helped solve it when she was still in Oregon.

Meg continues to stand with her hand against the cool metal of the post. Suddenly losing her focus, Meg finds herself staring vacantly into the surrounding space as she challenges herself: or were you afraid it would scare her out?

Joanna leans on the deck rail as the police car backs out of the driveway and disappears. She studies the scene below. Everything in Oregon had been achieved on schedule. She had found the right machinist to disassemble the press; Greta videotaped the process; she has the tape and the step-by-step instructions for reassembling it. She'd boxed her books, tapes, prints, some carefully chosen dishes and kitchen paraphernalia, clothing and miscellaneous furniture, leaving many things behind, knowing Meg's house was small, glad to pare down to certain treasured things and what she needed for her studio. The movers had arrived on time and transported everything smoothly to New York.

Meg had warned her that her boxes and furniture would be jammed in everywhere. Joanna knew that until the wing was built there would be no way for her to unpack her boxes, set up her press, place the pieces of furniture she had brought along. But nothing had prepared her for the impact of the total disarray. The first day after the movers had delivered all her things she felt as though she'd stepped on slippery bark in a logjam. She'd raced through the house, squeezing through the narrow space in the sunroom between her bureau and her files. In the living room carton after carton filled every inch, leaving barely room to walk or sit. In shock, she'd laughed and asked for a glass of wine to take out on the deck.

Since then Joanna's spent some time every day reading on the deck, cigarette in hand, whenever the weather has allowed. Only in the evening does she settle in the living room, diverting herself with the TV, her breathing shallow in the cramped space. Now, this night, this day, a sinister fog has infiltrated the whole house and yard, its tendrils entering every crevice, every open space, making it hard to take in even a shallow breath, veiling every vista and worst of all, creating a scrim that irrevocably separates Meg and herself.

I could call Greta, she thinks. To tell her what? That some unknown creep is tampering with our lights? Maybe not. Oh, maybe not. I can vault down and walk around the yard without going through the clutter of the house or crossing paths with Meg. As she starts to go inside, Meg is coming out, carrying another cup of coffee. "No thanks," Joanna says, ignoring Meg's attempted smile, and threads her way through the sunroom, down the stairs and out into the yard.

Joanna strides down the driveway to the lamppost underneath the evergreens. The globe that encases the lightbulb has a flat and pale look in broad daylight, unlike its reassuring glow in the dark of night. Joanna leans her hand against the iron post, jerks it back as though hit by a live wire, thinking, who knows what's been done? She starts to open the box at the base of the post and stops. Leave that for the electrician to do, she thinks, whenever he gets here. I'll watch though. Want to see what the bastard did. And how to fix it.

Joanna walks back past the house to the untouched woods beyond. She stands there, surveying the land where the wing will stand. Some laurel and some rhododendron have to go, she sees, and one or two young dogwoods. Possibly that pine though she knows Meg is hoping not. The wing will be the same width as the present house, but Joanna can't quite gauge how far out it will extend. She never likes to go back inside the house where the clutter makes her nauseous. But now, as though to match the Halloween jack-o-lanterns in the yard next door, their own house has been transformed overnight into a house of horrors; she can't think where to step, how to thread her way in any direction through the frightening debris.

*** 

That night, at three a.m., Joanna wakes abruptly to an unexpected movement next to her and for an instant thinks Shadow has jumped onto the bed. Shadow, she remembers, is far away, sleeping on Hildy's bed. Not Shadow, Meg. Not jumped, turned. Joanna shrugs at her own bewilderment. She goes to pee. Returning, she stops to look out the window, checking to be sure the lamppost light is on. She is stark awake. Looking out into the dark night she listens to Meg's breathing next to her, listens to the wind in the unfamiliar trees outside their room. Listens for footsteps on the long driveway.

At home in Oregon it was a well-lit street and the house was set back a scant twenty feet. There were footsteps on the sidewalk occasionally and cars passing in the night but they were not coming to her house. Here the driveway is so long, the street so far away, that nearly every audible sound comes from their own yard, is something with which they need to be concerned. Would I even hear his footsteps by the lamp? she wonders as she stares out at the light.

Damn Meg for not telling me! Damn her anyway! As though if she had been told, the man would not exist. Oh, I don't mean that, she thinks, I mean I can't entirely trust Meg after all. I thought I could. I suppose she really didn't want to worry me. She really didn't want to scare me is what she means. Joanna ponders the lamppost, a small lighthouse in the darkened woods, its beam a muted signal to guide uncertain travelers in the night. What a fiendish idea to tinker with the wiring. She'd watched the electrician as he fixed it. Then, after he left, she'd opened up the hood and studied it. She could fix it herself, she knew. If need be.

I could get a pellet gun and shoot him from this very window. Or from the deck. And get shot back? God, what a mess! And the builder isn't answering our calls. The wing is back to being nothing but cheap talk! I might as well have moved to Belfast and joined the IRA. I'd be dodging around those crooked little cobblestone streets instead of squeezing from room to room here, living out of boxes with no room to even sit down with a pad to sketch!

And what else has Meg not told me?

Joanna lies down again, moving slowly so as not to awaken Meg. She lies on her back, staring up at the ceiling, waiting for it to be spattered by headlights. She is so wide awake that she can hear the far-off ghostly whistle of the New York train coming into Port Jefferson three miles away. She is so wide awake she can see in the moonlight a moth fluttering against the window pane, hear Meg's breath come and go, come and go, slow and easy, one to her own two.

Joanna lies in the strange bed in the strange room with the strange smell of fear in her nostrils, the strange sweat of fear in her palms. And she sleeps like a baby, this woman by my side, she thinks, leaving me here, alone. Alone. I've moved three thousand miles to be scared and alone. Oh shit! Wasn't that a brilliant thing to do! Joanna closes her eyes and lies rigid and apart as she listens to the moth's tiny noisiness at the window and tries to hear beyond it the stealthy approaching steps of an unknown man.

# CHAPTER TWENTY

During Joanna's quick trip to New York in January, Poplin, the builder they had met, had sat at the table in the sunroom with Meg looking at Joanna's sketches: a studio on the ground floor, a large bedroom for them on the second floor, with a bath and a corner space that Joanna will use for her study. He nodded and estimated costs. He walked the yard with Meg while he measured and paced it off. He didn't think they needed an architect, he said, and sent Meg with Joanna's sketches to an engineer who drew up plans which Meg shipped on to Joanna. They had talked about it during their phone calls at night; they agreed to Poplin's projected costs, and he said to call him when Joanna had completed her move east and he would definitely work the wing into his autumn schedule. Joanna runs by her memory of him: young and friendly, he admired Joanna's prints which Meg had bought on her second visit to Oregon, asked about Meg's novel, told them that he himself liked Picasso and Van Gogh.

Joanna dials. The secretary says Mr. Poplin has been exceedingly busy and takes Joanna's name and number once again. Joanna goes on the deck to have a cigarette in the only open space. At dinner these days their conversation is strained. They discuss the problem of Drew Poplin. "I won't get any work done for two years at this rate," Joanna says, pouring herself another glass of wine.

"I know," Meg says apologetically, as though somehow this as well as the wire cutter are all her fault. "I'm going to send a certified letter to Poplin tomorrow."

"What good will that do?"

"If he signs for it we'll know he's not a figment of our imagination and also that he is in this country!" Meg laughs but Joanna does not smile.

Restless without her studio, waiting for the builder, Joanna works furiously in the yard. Reluctantly Meg leaves her desk and goes out to help, carting piles of fallen vines and ivy out to the street. When she has almost caught up with Joanna she sees that the porch is under attack. Click, click, click, the vines are severed. Joanna hauls each tangled mass down, disengaging the tentacles from the gutter, ripping them off the posts that support the porch's roof. What has been a porch enclosed by a canopy of green, dark and wild, becomes naked weathered boards, open to the sun. Meg says nothing, resolutely carrying load after load of fallen greens out to the street, but she feels oddly invaded by Joanna's energetic and "improving" presence.

Drew Poplin does not call back. Joanna calls the Better Business Bureau which does not have negative reports on him. His mailing address is a post office box. They can't locate his office though he seems to have a phone in Mineola, a two-hour drive away.

"We'd go there just to find an answering service," Joanna expostulates.

"I can't believe he's just dumped us!"

"If the construction had started in October, the way he promised, the studio would be up and running by the end of winter. At this rate I'll be lucky to ever get back to work!" Joanna grinds out her cigarette with a hard twist of her fingers.

They send one last letter, certified again, citing his commitment, the lost work time Joanna is enduring, asking for the courtesy of a reply. The post office sends back the receipt, signed, signifying that he did indeed receive the letter but he neither calls nor writes.

"Okay, let's find a new builder!"

"Where do we start?"

\*\*\*

"Did you give him any money?" Liz asks.

"No. It was all handshakes and words."

"That's good then. Builders are notorious for pulling disappearing acts. At least he didn't rob you. I have a client who does roofing. Let me ask him if he knows an honest builder."

"I'm going to ask around. Someone might know."

"Good. Keep calm, Mom."

"I am but Joanna's getting frantic."

***

Meg is working on her novel in the cramped corner of the bedroom. Pausing to ponder a new chapter, she watches Joanna out the window. Joanna is working in the wooded section of the front yard, "liberating the dogwoods from those blasted vines." She is wearing jeans, a blue work shirt, and the brown leather gloves which Meg bought for her when they were at a gardening store the day before. In her seven years in the house, Meg's only yard work has been to gather and chop kindling and to saw up small fallen trees and branches to burn in the fireplace.

Joanna is cutting and pulling down the vines that wrap around and around the trunks of the dogwood, suffocating them as they go. Meg has never noticed them before. As Joanna tears one down with a triumphant shout, Meg quiets her anxiety at this invasion of the woods. She recognizes that the trees almost visibly breathe better once freed of the choking vines.

A few days later Joanna starts work on the paths. Meg has always only clipped her way down the center of the paths enough to make narrow trails like the ones through the woods when she was a child. Joanna has the shears in hand and is clearing a wide swath up the slope around the house. Meg, feeling obliged to share in the work, goes out to help haul away the trash.

"Not too much!" she says, wanting Joanna to stop, feeling as though her land is under attack.

Joanna laughs, raising one arm to wipe away her sweat. "I'm only clearing the width of the original trail. There's a beautiful slate path under there."

Meg sees that Joanna is pushing back the earth and the ivy that has overgrown the stone. The edge of the path is delineated by a carefully placed line of rocks that Meg has never seen before. The widened path looks raw to Meg, in need of the healing green that has lain over it.

***

Meg goes back to working on her novel. From the desk she watches Joanna with her rake and shears. Disappearing on the far side of the huge rhododendrons, Joanna opens up the second walkway, from the porch down to the street. Meg knew that a path was there but it has always been totally overgrown. On one side it is lined with azaleas, which Meg has only glimpsed from her work desk. Joanna clips back the ivy and other vines and clears off the dirt, revealing wide stone steps. Secretly alarmed at the rigorous tearing out of growing plants, Meg requires of herself that she imagine the spring when it will be lovely to see the azaleas blazing all along the side of the wide slate stairway to the road.

After calling around for weeks, Meg makes an appointment with Robert Canio. Meg runs from the phone to the deck where the stepladder stands by the rail.

"Hey, up there!" Meg calls up to Joanna who is on the roof, scooping out November leaves from the gutters.

"What's up?" Joanna leans over to talk to Meg.

"Ooh! Be careful!"

"Don't mother-hen me, my friend." Joanna has been enjoying the open space on the roof. "No clutter up here," she mutters, making her way from one side to the other, balancing thoughtfully as she moves up the shingled slope.

"We may have our builder. Coming tomorrow morning at dawn. Liz's friends have worked with him."

"You think he's an apparition like Drew Poplin or knows how to drive a hammer?"

"We can hope." Meg smiles up at Joanna, thinking how handsome she is, standing against the backdrop of the trees and sky. "I'd be scared up there!" she says.

"It's not a high-pitched roof, you know!" Joanna smiles down at her. "I'll go finish."

"Let me take a picture of you on the roof before you come down," Meg says and goes to get her camera.

# CHAPTER TWENTY-ONE

The wine with dinner sets Meg off, not to think new thoughts, but to tell Joanna what she has been thinking, letting it ripple off her tongue like a little waterfall that grows in the cascading, until, after dinner, it crashes, cresting in a great flood of words. "Look—I'm sorry I didn't tell you sooner about the wire cutter. I've apologized in every way I know. Are you going to stay mad forever?"

Meg looks across the table at Joanna who has stayed distant, entrenched in anger like an unrelenting winter freeze. Anyone else, Meg thinks, would have exploded and then made up with tears and hugs that led to kissing that led to long hours in bed. But Joanna is simply not available. She might as well still be in Oregon. No, Meg amends her thought, when she was in Oregon she was full of warmth and now she's locked in cold, like a river barely flowing under the thick white winter cover that won't give or crack till spring.

Joanna shakes her head. "I don't blame you, Meg. You had a lot to handle."

Meg repeats what she has said a dozen times before. "It was because you had so much on your mind. I didn't think it made sense to give you one more thing...something you couldn't possibly do anything about...one more anxiety in an anxious time..." Meg wonders if she's had enough wine to skew her logic but doesn't think that could be true. "I wasn't trying to mislead you. I didn't want to burden you, that's all. It felt to me like it was up to me to deal with this situation. It's me the wire cutter doesn't like. It's my problem, not yours."

"You were wrong though, weren't you? It's my problem, all right. People say you should always watch out when you buy a house, check for a leaky roof. This is the leaky roof, Meg. You know it is." Joanna stands and begins to clear the table.

Meg feels assaulted by this allusion to deceit. She reels a moment before responding. "We've gotten through a lot, Joanna. This whole thing wasn't easy for you. Well, it wasn't easy for me, either." She notes that Joanna does a slight double take at that. "We're not business partners. We're lovers. A mistake is a mistake. It's not like I'm the accountant and I've embezzled the firm's money. I'm your lover and I want to make love again."

"Talking certainly doesn't make me feel like making love," Joanna says in her flat angry tone.

"I know that. But if we don't talk about it, we won't find our way."

"Okay. We've talked about it," Joanna says, going to the kitchen to start to clean up. "Now let it go."

Meg can't stop herself from following Joanna to the kitchen where she leans on the counter, challenging her further. "What puzzles me is that we had such wonderful lovemaking in Oregon. So what is this? One strike and I'm out? Nobody's perfect, Joanna. I love you and yes! I wanted you to move in with me. Maybe I was scared to tell you about the wire cutter. Maybe I was scared you wouldn't move to New York." Meg pauses, having gone farther than she had intended. She waits to be reassured, wanting Joanna's arms around her, wanting to hear Joanna's deep voice telling her that she loves her too, that loving Meg makes it all worth doing.

"And maybe I wouldn't have," Joanna says, clanging dishes into the drainer.

In spite of herself, Meg throws out one more leaden question, "Don't you miss it too?" The wine in Meg makes her want to talk on and on. The stone wall that is Joanna's face halts her tongue. She requires herself to leave the room, to put the garbage cans at the road for the next morning's pickup, and take a walk.

The roads in the neighborhood wind and intersect in unexpected ways. There aren't any streetlights. This night Meg is careful to go right at every corner, knowing that will bring her back to her own house even if she is not noticing her path. Meg has always loved this country quiet and this country dark. She walks at a steady clip, up slopes and down, reflecting in the quiet privacy of the night.

Give Joanna time. It's not a tragedy. She's here. I'm here. We love each other. We need to get the wing built. We can't get any real work done until that's done. Coming down her own street, Meg feels the last of her anger drift away. A disappointment, like the first ache of arthritis, has settled in her bones, but I can handle that, she thinks, I can.

Back in the house, Meg automatically goes through the basement to unload the dryer, carries the clothes upstairs to the bedroom, takes a shower and returns to the living room where she says a noncommittal, "Hi," to Joanna and turns to do her yoga exercises while they watch the dolphins on the nature channel.

Joanna goes out to have a cigarette on the porch. "My God," she says, coming back into the living room, as she steps over Meg, lying scrunched between the crammed in cartons and the fireplace, "You don't even have room to swing your leg over!" Sitting down, watching Meg, Joanna laughs harshly as Meg bumps the TV with her foot. "It is chaos—pure chaos—you don't even see it but I can't live this way—bumping around waiting for the lights to all go out! And you want to know why I don't feel like making love? Look around!"

Meg pulls herself up from the sheet she uses for an exercise mat and stands, facing Joanna. She knows Joanna must feel assaulted by her verbiage. She herself feels abandoned by her lover. "I miss you, you know. I love you and I miss you, Joanna."

Meg takes a half-step, hoping Joanna will take her in her arms. Instead, Joanna shrugs, saying in a gentler, resigned voice, "I can't make love while that man is lurking just outside our window."

Stalemate. They stare at one another for a minute and then move for comfort into the warmth of a friendly hug. "I miss you too," Joanna says, a white flag of truce.

\*\*\*

A compact, older man, with a quiet sense of humor, Robert Canio walks the yard with them, then sits at their table, checks out their blueprints, says he thinks it will work out and that he will return with a contract. He is back in two days with a detailed contract and a promise to begin work in a few weeks. In late December. It happens, he says, that he has just finished a job and could fit this in. It would cost much more than Poplin's estimate. They figure out ways to come up with the extra money. "That might be why Poplin disappeared," Robert says, with his shy smile. "He may have been too embarrassed to tell you."

"Can you build in the bad weather?"

"Sure. In Long Island. Not everywhere." He smiles at them again, reassuringly. "It'll be okay."

They both like Robert from day one. On another day he comes with a tall man named Max to study the lay of the land. The cabin, as Meg calls her house, sits on a slope so the front porch is level with the ground but the back sunroom and deck are a full level up among the branches of the dogwood. The wing is to be added to the side of the house, beyond the sunroom and the little guest room. The land slopes there but not as sharply as under the present structure so the studio will be entirely above ground although it will be adjacent to the old basement.

"Max sees no problems," Robert says. "We'll start next week."

***

Meg moves from dream toward door before the knocking has quite stopped. She grabs her bathrobe on the run and notes the time: two a.m.

Joanna is bolt awake with a "What the fuck!"

"I'll look from the deck before I open any doors."

Meg knows what she will see below before she stands by the deck rail looking down. Shannon stands expectantly, smiling up at her. "Hi, Grams," she says.

"Well, Shannon," Meg answers, looking down the driveway to make sure there is no car there under the trees with a strange or drunken man in it. There is no car.

"Could I come in?" Shannon asks. "I know it's late."

"Just a minute," Meg says. She goes back through the sunroom, calls to Joanna, "It's just Shannon. Go back to sleep."

"Yeah, right!" Joanna turns on the lamp and picks up her book from the bedside stand.

Meg closes the bedroom door and goes down to let Shannon in, miserably knowing that Joanna will be stark awake for hours, and that for Joanna, missing her sleep will ruin the whole next day.

Shannon at twenty-two looks younger. She has long wavy hair and is wearing tight jeans and a bright green blouse. She stumbles up the stairs and into the kitchen.

"Mind if I have something to eat?" she asks as she opens the refrigerator door.

"Go ahead," Meg answers quietly in a deliberate voice, sizing up the situation. Shannon hauls out some bread and cheese, slathers mayonnaise on the bread, dribbling it all over the counter, and begins to eat. Watching her, Meg feels a mix of fondness and disgust for the drunken girl.

"Thanks, Grams. I'm sorry. You were asleep already, weren't you? I'll bet it's late."

Fear lashes up at Meg. "Who's with the kids, Shannon?"

"What time?"

"Two o'clock. Who's with the kids?"

"Oh God! Two! I really didn't know that. I'm really sorry. This guy and I were just having fun. We hung out for a while in his truck. He didn't want to drive me all the way home though. The kids? The kids are fine. I've got this really good sitter now. She's such a good kid, Grams. You'd really like her. No, she doesn't party. Not this one. But her parents don't like her to sleep over. My car's at home but I... Could you...I guess you couldn't..."

"What, Shannon?"

"You couldn't take me over there and drive her home, could you? I mean, I can't, you know." A laugh rumbles out of Shannon, long and cheerful.

Meg nods silently.

"Would you do that? That's terrific. I mean that's really noble, Grams. Dylan wants to see you, you know."

"I can't see him in the middle of the night, Shannon. But we'll talk about this tomorrow. Okay. I'll go put on my clothes."

Meg goes into their bedroom, pulls on her jeans and a shirt. Joanna is still reading.

"What's up?"

"I'm giving Shannon a ride home," Meg says, skipping the rest.

"She could walk."

"It's five miles, Joanna and it's the middle of the night. Besides, her sitter needs a ride home."

"Oh, sure. Pick up the paper boy too on your way back. It's time for him to start his route."

"I'm sorry, darling. Try to sleep."

"Yeah, I'll just turn over and dream the night away."

"Grams?" Shannon's voice edges cautiously toward their room from the living room.

"I'm coming, Shannon. Get in my car."

"See you later," Meg says and closes the door behind her, knowing a kiss or a smile toward Joanna would just make it worse.

Two hours later, after checking on the kids, paying the sitter and driving her home, Meg comes quietly back into the bedroom. Joanna is asleep, book splayed open next to her, lamp still on.

# CHAPTER TWENTY-TWO

The bulldozer comes at eight o'clock one bright morning in December. Meg hears the truck in front of the house and leaps up and into her jeans and shirt. Joanna, who usually moves gradually, first to her coffee and cigarettes while reading the *Times*, then to a shower and only then to breakfast and conversation, skips all that and pulls on her own jeans.

Outside, they see Max driving his small Caterpillar down from the trailer. He waves to them, parks it, and comes over to them. A tall, muscular man with a beard and light blue eyes, he smiles, saying, "Good morning, ladies. Are you ready for this?"

Thank God, Joanna thinks, it's going to happen. All the words are finally finished. It is going to be real.

Meg surveys the expanse of earth and shrubs and the machine that waits to shovel it up. She tries to envision the new home that will rise there but sees instead the familiar serenity about to be destroyed. Grow up, she silently admonishes herself.

***

Coming home with her arms full of groceries Meg stops halfway up the stairs to enjoy the rich aroma of bread still warm from the oven, to hold it that exact distance from her, as it was when she was six coming in from the first grade to find her mother baking, her father working in the garden by the creek, her brothers not due home for hours.

Joanna has commandeered the kitchen. Garrison Keillor's voice is on the radio. Meg sets down the groceries and laughs with delight, seeing that Joanna has made not only braided loaves, but goddess loaves. They will later be decorated more but they already have the form, the raisin eyes, the trailing hair flung back in waves of golden dough. They are meant as holiday gifts for their friends. Joanna, flour up to her elbows, laughs out loud at Meg's approval, as Meg gives her a hug.

***

Later, sitting at her desk looking out across the open porch, Meg realizes that she has become entirely accustomed to the differences Joanna has generated in the yard. Actually, she thinks, smiling, I even truly like it. With the vines gone from the porch, with the blue woodbox Rosalyn once gave Meg newly painted exactly its original blue, with two chairs that had been past use repaired and painted blue and white to match, the porch stands open to sunlight, a welcoming space in which Joanna sits to read and smoke when the weather allows, where Meg often joins her, where guests can sit in comfort, looking out into the woods.

The phone interrupts Meg's reverie. It's Miranda, in Oxford. "Hold on! I'll get your mom!" Meg runs to the kitchen, calling, "Hey, Joanna! It's Miranda!"

Joanna, wiping her floury hands on a paper towel first, goes to the phone. Meg goes to do a load of laundry, leaving Joanna in peace to talk with her oldest daughter. Coming back up from the basement, she sees Joanna's off the phone and back at the kitchen counter. "So how're things in England now that December's there?"

Joanna laughs at the reference to a line of Browning's. "Fine. She's going on a trip to Rome during winter break. And she's going with a friend named Chet. Apparently they've been together ever since summer." Joanna gives Meg an ironic smile with upraised eyebrows and hands lifted for a moment in mock despair.

"Great."

"Yes. I'm glad. But leave it to Miranda not to tell me for six months." There's an edge of hurt in Joanna's voice.

"Hey, you want to know about not telling?" Meg thinks of a story to lighten the moment for Joanna. "My good son, Jimmy, called me up one day about four years ago. Becky was already born, so—yeah, about four years ago—and said, 'By the way, Mom, I'm converting.'" Meg laughs with delight.

"Converting? To?"

"Judaism. Deborah's Jewish. So now they're all Jewish!"

Joanna stops short of turning the mound of dough on the counter. "Did you know he'd been thinking about that?"

"Nope. He'd never mentioned it before."

Joanna looks at her, perplexed. "How'd you react to that?"

"I thought it was a fine idea. I grew up without any religion. If I had to pick something I'd be a Jew or an Episcopalian."

Joanna hoots. "Big range!"

"My father's family was Episcopalian. My Aunt Elizabeth once said to me, 'If you ever decide to join a church, I think you'd like the Episcopal Church.' I do like the stands they take on social issues."

"Like the Democrats?"

Meg nods. "Umhm."

Joanna asks quietly, "Did you ever go to church?"

"When I was about fourteen I checked out the churches that my friends went to. I decided that God was love and truth and beauty. You know. But I never have believed in a God who controls events like earthquakes, wars, children getting hurt. And I get claustro when it comes to sitting through an actual church service."

Joanna begins to knead the dough. She doesn't comment. It would be odd, she thinks, to grow up without knowing who you were. She knows she is Christian as surely as she knows she is a woman. Doubtfully, she asks, "Your mother was Jewish?"

Meg laughs. "No. She wasn't much of anything. She'd been Lutheran as a kid but not later. I went with her two or three times and that was enough."

Joanna looks at her intently. "So where did the Judaism come from?"

"College. I took a course in the history of religion."

Joanna looks at her shyly. "I guess that leaves out Christ and the resurrection, hmm?" They have never talked about this before.

Meg wants to tread softly here. She softens her voice. "You know I'm no true believer." Or a believer at all, she thinks, but hesitates.

It feels harsh to say that to Joanna. As she would not have said it to Rosalyn. It feels like it would to stomp on a field of daffodils that they had planted just as they were flowering in the spring. She shies away. "I just meant to say I think it's great that Jimmy's kids will have a good community to grow up in."

"You still have time to convert!"

"Maybe not me." Meg smiles. Leaving the kitchen to get back to her desk, she adds, "That all got started because I was thinking that kids can really surprise us in a phone call! That's good about Miranda though. She's been lonesome, I'll bet."

"I'm glad for her," Joanna says.

"The fresh bread sure smells good," Meg says, hanging on the doorway a moment before leaving the kitchen.

Joanna continues kneading the dough, pushing it down, kneading it again, keeping her thoughts to herself.

That night, Joanna dreams.

*The wing has been completed. The press is assembled. Joanna is trying to set a newly etched plate in place. She is having trouble moving in the narrow space between the wall and the press and as she twists, trying to put down the heavy plate, she realizes she is in the aisle of her old church. Flustered, she thinks she should not be wearing her heavy printmaking apron. She should be in a satin tux, she thinks, as she hears Meg's voice saying, "in sickness and in health." She doesn't want to hurt Meg's feelings on this day. She thinks she will start to sing, standing beside Meg, instead of repeating vows. The first words of "Amazing Grace" rise in her throat. She strains to keep from setting the plate down, knowing the altar cannot hold its weight.*

Joanna wakes up in a sweat, hearing Meg's voice receding, vow after vow.

\*\*\*

Like the drone of Max's bulldozer when he's pushing the ground around, Meg and Joanna can almost hear the vibrations of the truce they keep about the wire cutter. They leave the lamppost light on at night. Each of them checks on it when she gets up to pee at two or three a.m. They do not talk about it. There was no disturbance in November nor so far in December and it's almost Christmas now.

At three a.m. they head for the bathroom simultaneously; they both start laughing. "After you," and "After you," they giggle. Coming back to bed again, Joanna stops at the window to look down the driveway. "It's like the buzz bombs in England during World War II. You never heard them coming. We never know which night he'll strike. New York's infamous night crawler…" And they both laugh grimly before they go back to sleep.

***

Waking, Meg turns toward Joanna for a morning hug. She rubs Joanna's back, as every morning, every night. Joanna arches contentedly under her moving hands. Moving her hands up and down Joanna's back, Meg feels herself fill with desire that rolls through her body like long ocean waves, mounting and almost cresting. This does not resonate in Joanna. They rise into the day without making love.

# CHAPTER TWENTY-THREE

"There's no room!" Joanna expostulates, laughing.

"I don't care!" Meg responds with a smile. "We have to have a big Christmas tree."

By moving a chair from the living room to the guest room and putting the TV where the chair had been, tight against the stacks of cartons in the living room, they clear a space in front of the window next to the fireplace. They go to the garden store in Rocky Point and choose a fir that will just brush the ceiling.

"Ready, set, go!" Laughing, they haul it up the trail around the house and through the front door into the living room.

"And you want people here for Christmas? Where do you intend to stack them?"

"We'll send them outside as soon as they've eaten! We'll go to the beach!" Meg is surveying the actual space and laughing.

"Right. We can build a snowman at the beach!"

Meg takes the stepladder from the basement to the front yard and sets it by a little cedar by the driveway. She finds the two strands of outdoor lights and carrying them, the outdoor extension cords, a roll of electrical tape, and the scissors with which to cut it, she goes out to hang the lights.

\*\*\*

Meg has put a two-pound box of chocolates under the tree for Joanna and a chocolate apple and orange. After a fruitless search of local bookstores, she has ordered a beautiful Odd Nerdrum book from an art store in Manhattan; it was delivered the day before. Meg knows Joanna won't be expecting that. They're going to the city to see an exhibit of his work in January. He is one of the few contemporary artists who fascinate Joanna. Meg knows just how Joanna's face will light up when she sees the book. It will be that special glow that she gets when she sees otters in a river. Meg has also found a cue for her in the billiards store in Huntington. These things are already wrapped and hidden in the bedroom closet, waiting to be put underneath the tree on Christmas Eve.

When she has put the food away, Meg carries the other bags from the car into the bedroom. She got candles and replacement bulbs for the outdoor and indoor tree lights, peanuts, chocolate Santas for each kid, candy canes for the kids' stockings, bubbles, little cars for the boys, jewelry for Karen, and other stocking stuffers. Must call Liz to tell her I found that LEGO set that Jonathan wanted, she thinks.

Meg's oldest friend, Jeanette, is coming out on Christmas morning. Liz will bring Justin for the first time and Shannon and the boys will come. They will all come for the tree around noon and stay for turkey dinner in the late afternoon.

"You're sure there're enough presents?" Joanna is teasing her.

"I think so." Meg laughs. She knows she always gets the kids a lot of things but she chooses carefully and she figures they grow up quickly. It will be different later when the magic is gone and it's become an ordinary holiday.

Meg checks out the array of unfamiliar ornaments that Joanna has added to the angel Meg's aunt hammered out of tin, her mother's wax angel flying near the tinfoil star, the blown egg ornaments Jeanette made for her thirty years ago, the silver deer, the carved wooden Santa, and the little golden trumpets from her first Christmas with Franklin, now forty-five years ago, when their world was wonderfully new and still untarnished.

Joanna has brought beautiful glass prisms that shatter ordinary sunlight into brilliant colors that splash around the room, a delicately fashioned ornament marked with a J that her mother made for her when she was four, a few very old ornaments from Sweden, a cluster of Mexican animal figures that were sent to her from California, a beautiful angel Miranda sent from Cambridge, and an arching dolphin Emily carved for her when she was in high school.

When they have turned off the TV and the lights to go to bed, they stay a minute to enjoy the tree in the quiet, darkened room. Joanna's arm is around Meg's waist. "It's always beautiful," Meg says.

"And so it is."

"Merry Christmas, love!"

"Merry Christmas!" Joanna tightens her hold on Meg as she kisses her.

\*\*\*

Christmas Day is bright and clear. By two o'clock the smell of roasting turkey has replaced that of cedar and cinnamon. The bright debris from unwrapped gifts is scattered around the living room where the kids were wedged in between cartons and the tree. The adults stayed in doorways and out on the porch. The day is mild and the kids are now playing outside, on the deck or in the yard, with their new toys.

"Beach anyone?" Liz has a Frisbee in her hand and is going from room to room.

"Absolutely!" Her friend, Justin, who has become a constant presence in her life, helps her gather up the kids. "Bring your cars. You can make roads in the sand," Justin calls out to Dylan who doesn't want to leave his new garage.

"I'll pass," Shannon says. "I want to watch *Miracle on 34th Street.* Okay?"

"Oh, come on," Meg says, thinking it would be better for Shannon to run around the beach than sit alone in the house where there are bottles of wine, which they will have with dinner. "It'll be uneven for Frisbee," Meg says, persuasively, but Shannon shakes her head and settles in her chair.

There is no way to require her to move, Meg thinks, and loads the car with the three boys and Joanna while Liz and Justin take Jeanette and Karen in Justin's van. Joanna joins the Frisbee game while Jeanette and Meg walk short distances, visiting, and watching Mack and Jonathan run around together for a while before joining Dylan, who is making a network of roadways in the sand. Jonathan adds a lake and canals and Mack makes bridges over the canals.

***

Much later Meg realizes it is four thirty and she has to be home to get the dinner ready. Jeanette and Meg drive back together. "I'll do the salad if you like," Jeanette offers, as they go into the house.

Going up the stairs and entering the kitchen, Meg checks the oven. "The turkey's almost done. I'll do the potatoes and the vegetables."

"Want me to set the table, Grams?"

"In a little while, Shannon. Thank you. That'll be great." Meg is in the back end of the kitchen, unloading salad ingredients, vegetables, cans of olives and cranberry sauce, cheeses, from the refrigerator. When she's finished, she goes to the other end of the small galley to figure out the order of preparations that are needed. Shannon is leaning in the doorway, watching. Meg smells the alcohol before she checks her out.

"Was the movie good?" Jeanette is asking, unaware.

"Very good," Shannon answers. "I'd say it's always very good. I've seen it every year since I was little. Have you?"

"I've seen it. It wasn't even there when I was little!" Jeanette laughs her pealing holiday laugh and it fills the kitchen for a minute.

Meg tries to find a way through the coming hours. Like trying to thread a needle with too small an eye, she holds up one possibility after another within her mind. No more alcohol and Shannon will be okay. Even as she thinks that, Shannon quietly edges out of sight, through the sunroom to the stairs and down and out. She's got a bottle stashed in her car, Meg thinks. She'll fall asleep and sleep it off. I'll keep the kids here. Where? Jeanette's in the guest room. I'll drive them all home after dinner. She'll conk out. And who will take care of Dylan? Mack will. And reluctantly, not wanting to know what she knows she already knows, adds, Mack always does.

"We may have a small problem," Meg says to Jeanette who is running water at the sink, washing the lettuce and tomatoes.

"What's that?" Jeanette asks, turning off the water.

***

In the melee of everyone's return, dinner preparations are completed. Liz, Justin, Shannon and Karen continue playing Frisbee in the street. Jonathan and Mack are chasing through the woods with their new weaponry. Dylan is driving little cars around the deck.

Joanna is resting with her book and a cigarette on the deck, keeping an eye on Dylan, while Jeanette and Meg finish in the kitchen.

"Hey, everyone," Jeanette calls from the deck. "Wash up for turkey dinner!"

Once everyone is squeezed in around the table and platters and bowls are being passed, Meg checks and sees that Shannon is both flushed and talkative but no one else will notice it, she thinks, in the general hubbub of passing food and eating.

"Can we have ice cream, Granny Meg?" Dylan, with his mouth full, and his fork loaded with mashed potatoes and gravy suspended in mid-air, looks up to the laughter of the grown-ups.

"After while, sweetheart," Meg replies.

At the far end of the long table Justin, who grew up in Brooklyn, is talking theater with Jeanette and Liz. Joanna is laughing about something Jeanette just said.

"Cranberries, please," Karen says, and Shannon lifts up the glass bowl in which the crimson sauce is shimmering in the candlelight. As she hands it across the table to Karen, Shannon's arm knocks over one of the candles which burns her as it falls. Shannon drops the bowl which hits the turkey platter, spattering gobs of cranberry red and splinters and chunks of glass across the linen tablecloth. The fallen candle has landed on a greasy paper napkin next to Mack which now bursts into flame.

"Christ, Shannon, watch it!" Liz yells simultaneously, leaping up.

"*Oh fuck, fuck, fuck!*" Shannon shouts.

Meg and Joanna are close enough to act and with the quick instincts of mothering, Joanna lifts the turkey platter and slams it down to suffocate the flames with a shouted "Dammit, Shannon!" as Meg grabs Dylan in one arm and Mack in the other, hauling them away from the site of the fire.

"Wow!" Karen says, standing to survey the debris littering the table.

"Karen," Liz says, with authority, speaking clearly over the uproar, "you and Jonathan take Mack and Dylan out on the deck while we get this all cleaned up."

"Grams, I'm really sorry. I thought Karen had hold of the bowl," Shannon is saying.

"I didn't have it yet, Granny Meg," Karen says, quietly emphatic, sliding past the chairs and around Meg to the deck. "Come on Dylan, let's play cars."

With the children gone, the adults start to cart away all the plates and silverware, glasses, and every serving bowl and platter that could even possibly have been splattered with flying glass. "I guess we have to clear the whole table to take the cloth off," Meg says.

"I'll help," Shannon says.

"I don't think so, Shannon," Liz says.

"Shannon, why don't you just go outside and have a cigarette," Meg says.

Shannon looks back and forth between them, shrugs, and follows the others down the stairs and out.

"Mom?" Liz says.

"Later," Meg says, giving a new tablecloth to Liz.

***

By dinner time on the twenty-sixth the house has become its ordinary, quiet self. "It was fun to see everybody but it's nice to be just us again," Joanna says, sitting down.

Lighting the candles on the table, serving the leftover turkey dinner, Meg leans down to kiss Joanna. "You can say that again," she says.

Joanna, laughing, starts, "It was fun…" and they both laugh.

After they have eaten, Meg asks, "Would you like to have a little after dinner wine in the bedroom?"

"The company is really gone? Every one of them?"

"Umhm. Scout's honor."

"Then that sounds good. Bring your new book along, why don't you?"

They go into the bedroom where they take off their clothes. Joanna lies down in her pajamas. Meg puts on a transparent pastel blue nightgown. She brings into bed with her the photographic study of lesbian lovers that Joanna had hidden under her pillow Christmas Eve. They sit up in bed and look together at various couples, kissing and stroking one another, or simply smiling and holding hands. Some are fully clothed and some are nude.

"That is a beautiful photograph," Joanna says, admiring a barely visible woman behind a white curtain that is blowing in the wind.

"Umhm," Meg agrees, "it is. Thank you for the book."

"You really like it?"

"I really like it." Meg closes the book and lays it down beside the bed and turns out the bright lamp, leaving only the soft light that comes through the doorway from a lamp in the living room. "But right now, we've read enough, haven't we?"

"Yes, we have." Joanna slides down in the bed, and moves one hand up and down Meg's thigh while she kisses her.

Meg makes a welcoming sound as she opens her lips to Joanna and curves her whole body against Joanna's.

# CHAPTER TWENTY-FOUR

Meg closes the door to the bedroom while she phones Angie. Halfway through the ringing she knows she should have gone to Shannon first. "Merry Christmas, Angie!"

"Merry Christmas, Mom! I tried to get through on Christmas Day but there was just no way!"

"So tell me what's new with you." Meg is buying time before the tough part starts.

"We're getting ready for that expedition to the Aleutians. I can't wait! But we've still got months of work to do before we head out. I'm working round the clock but it's great work, Mom!" Angie's voice is strong and eager. Meg can see her, as she was in high school, crouching, ready for the sprint.

"Angie, can we talk for a while?"

"Sure."

The silence leaves it to Meg to break into the crystal that is Angie's work, within which she thrives on the intensity of the light, unaware, Meg thinks, of the more mundane levels of ordinary lives.

"It's Shannon."

"She's had an accident." Angie's voice is flat with fact. She's waiting to be told that Shannon's dead.

"No. No, she's not hurt." Meg instantly regrets the shaft of fear she'd flung like a javelin to strike Angie sitting in her cabin so far away. She wants to say, "Work well, Happy New Year!" and hang up. There is a sharp pain in her hand from her grip on the receiver. Arthritis in that thumb, she thinks parenthetically, and deliberately loosens her hold. Tell her! she admonishes herself and speaks. "Shannon's in trouble."

"What kind of trouble?" Angie's voice is scientific now, probing for information. Meg envisions her bending over an otter, washed ashore, examining it for oil on its fur, seeking the cause of its death, needing to know.

Meg settles in to give the data. "She's drinking way too much, Angie. Drinking and driving. It's only a matter of time…"

The silence sits then between them, as inevitably closing as the gap between lightning and thunder. They are both counting silently, gauging distance and consequent hazard, seeing the two little boys in a mangled car.

"Oh God, Mom." Angie's voice catapults into the room with Meg. "Get her to AA."

"You need to back me up."

"I'll call her right now."

"No, you call her tomorrow night. I'm going to drive over and talk to her now. Okay?"

"Absolutely."

***

Meg tries out various verbal routes on her drive to Shannon's house. Once she's there, sitting at the all purpose card table across from Shannon, smelling the incessant stench of stale beer, Meg throws away all her elaborate approaches. "Go to AA, Shannon."

"No way, Grams. I can handle my own life."

The boys are in their bedroom. Meg wonders if they're asleep. Too quiet, she thinks. No help for that. "You wrecked Christmas dinner, Shannon. But that's nothing. You drink even when you're driving. You're going to get killed."

"I go slow, you know. I know these roads inside out. I wouldn't hurt anybody. I've never in my life hurt a fly, Grams."

"If you don't stop, you will. You'll kill somebody." Meg waves her hand at the bedroom.

"No way!"

Meg stands, glances into the boys' room, sees Mack, sleeping with his arm flung out across the laser gun he got for Christmas. "You'd never forgive yourself for that."

Shannon blanches and jumps up from the table. She walks around the room without speaking. She opens and shuts the refrigerator door without taking anything out of it. She turns back to confront Meg. "You and Joanna drink. You know you do!"

"We drink wine with dinner, Shannon, and I don't drink too much and if I did, I wouldn't drive! Don't wait until it's too late, Shannon."

"Lighten up, Grams. I'll be careful, I really will." Her face is a mix of shame and defensiveness. Meg wants to give her a big hug but restrains herself.

Remembering their long talks when Shannon first came down from Alaska, Meg says, "Shannon, you stopped partying once before for the good of the kids. You told me so. You can do it again. It'll help if you go to AA. You're entitled to some help this time. Go to AA."

*** 

Back at home Joanna's already in bed reading. Meg takes a shower, lays her heating pad in place and clicks it on, picks up the novel she's been reading and lies down. For a few minutes she holds the book, closed, on her chest, savoring the gradual warming of her back, the relief of simply lying still. "Don't know why I'm so tired," she says.

Joanna, beside her, picking up her book, laughs. "No, I can't imagine. So did you get through to her?"

"I dunno. I tried." Meg doesn't say anything more. They have an agreement to keep troublesome conversations for daytime.

Joanna continues to read, adjusting her own heating pad. "The heat does help!" She smiles her concession.

"Umhm," Meg answers, pleased. Funny about the sweet familiar comfort of the heating pad, Meg thinks—one of the quirks of getting older, these secret little pleasures. In the beginning of time on the farm it was the iron, warmed by the fireplace on winter nights and wrapped in newspapers that comforted her feet and warmed her bed. When Joanna first arrived in New York, Meg gave her a heating pad, and Joanna, after much protest, tried it, and found it truly eased the chronic pain in her lower back.

"I'm fading," Joanna says. "Ready to turn out the light?"

# CHAPTER TWENTY-FIVE

Joanna stands with Meg at the window in the sunroom, watching Max maneuver his hydraulic lift to swing and lower the massive concrete circles that comprise the septic tank.

"Once this system is in, you'll be set for good," he'd said the day before, adding with a laconic smile, "it'll outlast us all."

His Caterpillar slips on the wet clay in the pile he has unearthed. Joanna gasps but Max rights the machine and goes on working. "I don't see how he does that," she says.

"Scary, isn't it?"

"I'm off to the post office and the hardware store," Joanna says, giving Meg a quick sideways kiss going down the stairs. "We have a date for pool at four o'clock, right?"

"Right! See you later." Meg stays at the window, as Max slides about on the uneven ground. He has lifted the two huge circular blocks of the septic tank out of the hole again and swung them over to rest on the top of the cesspool blocks, which are rectangular. He is digging the hole deeper and deeper, trying to get through the layer of clay before placing the tank for good. Meg wants to go do her morning chores but stays at the window. The same phenomenon, she thinks, as calling Jimmy or Liz when there is a storm, as though checking on them keeps them safe. She watches Max as the wheels shift and slide on the slippery earth, as though her turning away will endanger him.

Below the window where Meg stands, Joanna has stopped to watch, ducking her head out of the wind to light her cigarette, standing under the bare dogwood tree, smoke curling up around her head. In her many-colored jacket, gloved, wearing a winter cap, flicking ashes to the ground, she reminds Meg of Ingrid Bergman in some war film, waiting to meet a fellow member of the Underground. A quick thrill of desire flickers through Meg's body. Max lifts his hand in greeting and continues his work, like a rider in a rodeo.

His "It'll outlast us all," echoes in Meg's head as she studies the huge cement blocks.

Expires in the year 2003. Meg's new driver's license is stamped with that. Eerie. In the classroom she used to say sometimes, "You will all live to see this change…" referring to racism or sexism or some other aspect of society. "You watch and see."

One day a student looked up at her and said, "What about you? Won't you see changes too?"

Meg laughed. "Yes. But you'll live far into the new century, you know. I won't."

Mortality flickered through the classroom the way a fluorescent light does when it's burning out—for a second the students startled, ducked their heads, blinked against the transient and discordant glare.

Staring at the gigantic cylinders of cement, incongruous in the woods, Meg thinks of pyramids in the desert, mummies within. She thinks of a lottery jar with spinning chips within, each chip a numbered year. 2003. 2010. 2015. "I'll stop smoking when I get to New York!" Joanna had promised. Meg hadn't thought she would; hadn't thought she could in a time of such upheaval. Maybe when the wing is finished, Meg thinks, maybe then.

Seeing Max swinging one of the great weights over the hole to lower it down, watching chain and concrete, man and machine, Meg envisions Joanna twirling away from her, swung out from earth by the line to an oxygen tank. "Damn the cigarettes!" Meg says and turns from the window and goes to change the linen, do the laundry, make sure there's money in her wallet for pizza on the way home from pool.

\*\*\*

Once in her car Joanna feels the comfort of being in her own space at last. The house is Meg's. Although her own things crowd every room, although some of her own clothing hangs in the closet, Joanna does not yet feel at home. Because of the crowding, she thinks, which generates a sense of chaos in every room, she feels continually out of sync. In the car the space is familiar, entirely hers, under her own control. A comfort, she thinks, smiling, like mashed potatoes and gravy are comfort food.

She zips off to the post office and on to the hardware store. The man and woman who own the store are her first friendly acquaintances in New York. From her first visit there, they have been smiling and helpful, and by now greet her with a comfortable ease that pleases her, "How're you today and what can we do for you?"

She finds a new drain stopper for the kitchen sink and a doorstop packet to put up in the sunroom where the deck door bangs. This reminds her that there is a hole in the plaster on that wall, now hidden by one of her own prints that Meg had hung there. She consults the clerk and chooses the putty he recommends.

***

Meg is on the deck tethering balloons to the rail on Saturday afternoon when the phone rings. She runs into the sunroom, holding a red balloon by the string, to answer. It's Shannon.

"Grams, we have a problem. Here's the story. Like I told you, my car's in the garage, and Pam's husband took their car to work and so she can't drive Jerry and us over. I'm sorry but could you pick us up and then we'll pick up the cake?"

Meg checks her watch. "Okay, Shannon, but have the kids ready—"

Meg stops long enough to write a note which she tapes on the back door. She grabs her purse and keys and runs into the bedroom where Joanna is doing letters on e-mail.

"I'm off to fetch Shannon and the kids."

"I thought they had a ride."

"It fell through. I left Liz a note in case she beats us back. She's dropping Karen and Jonathan off on her way to an appointment."

"Leave it to Shannon," Joanna says laconically.

"Sounds like it's not her fault—whatever—we can't have a birthday party without the birthday boy!"

"No, can't do that." Joanna gives her a weak smile and Meg is off, grabbing three balloons as she goes.

Dylan and Mack and another little boy who, Meg thinks, must be Jerry, are running around their landlord's patchy lawn shooting each other with squirt guns when Meg drives up. They run to give her hugs and she gives each of them a balloon on a string. "Happy Birthday, Mack!"

Meg starts to knock on the door as Mack throws it open and runs into the kitchen. Shannon and her friend, Pam, are sitting at the table. Meg smells the beer and thinks, oh, shit! before she sees the cans. Quietly, she says, "Hi."

"You're here already!" Shannon grabs each of the boys by an arm. "Clean shirt time, men!"

"And we're off and away!" Meg adds, knowing that Liz will have dropped the kids off at the house long before they get back home. She stifles her anger at Shannon's beer and goes to help Dylan change his shirt.

Later Meg and Shannon shepherd the kids through a suitcase relay race in the long driveway, musical chairs on pillows on the deck, the birthday cake and ice cream at the table in the sunroom, while Mack opens his presents, and they go out again to shoot the little squirt guns that they got as favors. Mack is wearing his new space helmet and shooting with a super large squirt gun that Jonathan fiercely covets.

Liz should be arriving at any moment to take Karen and Jonathan home and Meg intends to ask her if she'll give Pam and her son, Jerry, a ride. Meg is deliberately keeping herself from panic, assuming the kids will be gone in time. "In time" means before Shannon loses it and ruins Mack's party. Meg is listening carefully to the laughter from the deck where Pam and Shannon have settled with their beer. Shannon's voice is rising and their laughter is pealing like the tolling of cracked bells.

"Here, kids, catch!" Meg looks up to see Shannon untying the balloons from the railing of the deck and bopping them down toward the kids in the driveway below. They run to catch them as they fall and Shannon, unable to untie them fast enough, begins to rip the remainder free.

Dylan stands in the driveway just under the deck, holding up his hands. "Here, Mommy, here. I want a green one. Green!"

Shannon leans over, holding down a green one still attached to the rail. "Here, sweetie, catch!" As she smacks it down toward Dylan, it pops. Dylan begins to cry, party fatigue suddenly immersing him in grief as he gathers up the shreds of green and the long string. Shannon retreats into the house, calling back, "Never mind, Dylan, I'll get you a big green balloon on the way home. Big, Dylan, real big."

When everyone except Shannon, Mack and Dylan has left, Meg collects the gifts, balloons and cake to put them in the trunk of her car. "Let's go," she says and they pile into the car.

It's not until they have made the trip, stopping en route for the big green balloon that Shannon has promised Dylan, and unloaded everything into their apartment, that Meg realizes that she can't leave the kids with Shannon who is barely able to navigate the walk from the car to her doorway. "Go to sleep, Shannon," Meg says in a low voice laced with anger.

"I'm hungry, Grams," Shannon slurs. "I'll just have some soup." She finds a can of Campbell's tomato and cranks it open. She grabs a spoon and starts eating from the can, spilling down her blouse as she does so.

"I'm taking the kids back with me for the night," Meg says, surprised to hear her own voice, its certitude.

"That's really sweet of you," Shannon says, smiling a crooked smile, "but the party was long enough. Really."

"I'll bring them back in the morning."

"Okay. Good. Like your green balloon, Dylan? Want some soup, Grams?"

Dylan nods, clutching the balloon to his stomach, chocolate markings on his face and shirt.

"Mom," Mack says, "I can stay and take care of you."

Meg's voice almost falters but it does not. Good thing Liz's not seeing this, she thinks. "She's okay, Mack. We'll just go get a pizza and a video and let her go to sleep. Grab your pajamas and find Dylan's for me and we'll have a birthday sleepover at Granny Meg's house. Okay?"

***

"This won't work, you know." Joanna, lying in bed, looks up from her book.

Meg, having put the kids to bed, pulling on her pajamas, answers softly, "I know. I just need time to think."

"You'd better think fast or you'll be the proud mother of two boys."

Meg laughs. "No, no. I'll call Angie again tomorrow and we'll figure out what to do."

"Angie's in Alaska. The kids are in my house."

"Our house," Meg corrects her with a wry smile.

"Our house. And they can't stay. You do know that, don't you?"

Meg flinches at the acerbic tone in Joanna's voice. She nods, voice stuck in her throat, as she lies down. "Don't you?" Joanna asks again.

"Sure. I do know that," Meg says and picks up her own book to read.

# CHAPTER TWENTY-SIX

Max works alone from eight in the morning until after dark, day after day. He's buried the septic tank and the cesspool. The ground above them lies raw, a fallow winter field in the center of the woods. He's finished clearing away the brush and trees where the wing will stand. He has dug trenches for the footings. This morning the cement truck is pulling up the muddy slope that he has cleared to make a rough path in from the street. Joanna and Meg watch from the sunroom window. "Cement trucks always look like toys to me," Meg says. "Boys and their toys."

"I hope this particular toy doesn't tip over." Joanna laughs uneasily and turns away to the table where she is repairing the cord on a bedroom lamp.

Meg continues to lean on the sill. To her left and behind her, at one of the many other sunroom windows, cardinals, sparrows and bluejays take turns at the window feeder. If she stays perfectly still, though she is less than three feet away, they aren't startled, keep on lighting there. The men adjust the spout from the truck so the cement will spill exactly where they want it. "Come see, Joanna!" Meg calls and Joanna runs to stand with her, looking down at the event.

The cement flows from the truck down the trough into the narrow trenches, lined with boards. Max pushes it toward the end of the ditch with a long-handled shovel. "He's certainly got a lot of strength," Joanna says, admiringly. At sixty-two, she feels new limits now when she is digging in the yard or pruning; her back kicks up and she gets tired in a way she never used to do. "You know how hard it is to do that?"

Meg nods. Though it looks like he's executing slow movements in ballet, Meg knows Max is doing heavy work. As the cement is shoved along, then smoothed and stroked, the concept of the wing moves from the blueprint in her mind into the concrete outline there below them that has replaced a section of the woods on that side of the cabin.

Joanna goes back to the lamp cord. "I saw a notice at the library about a new tai chi place. I'm going to check it out tomorrow morning. A woman in our group said he is a master."

"I hope so. From what you say, the one you've got is definitely not!" Meg continues to stare down, watching every movement of the pageant below. Now that the giant concrete septic system has been successfully buried and the border of the wing etched in wood, Meg feels more peaceful about the invasion of the woods. She can see that the construction takes up only a small part of the land. The woods surround the house just as they always have.

Joanna plugs in the lamp she has just repaired. "Voila!" She waves at the bright light triumphantly. "I'm off on errands. I'll pick up a video for us. Have you seen *Desert Hearts?*"

"Sure but let's do it again. Do you know *Liana?*"

"I could see it again though."

"*Celluloid Closet?*"

"I missed that. I'll look for it. Okay! C'mon. I'm going to ask Max what's next." Joanna leads down the stairs, lighting a cigarette the moment she's out the door.

The cement mixer has gone. Max is carefully smoothing the gray surface within the frames. Joanna stands chatting with him while Meg walks out where the truck was standing to look at the house from that side. Then they walk together around the perimeter of the footing, climb over to stand where the floor will be. The two long sides of the footing connect with the side wall of the old house which still stands as it did before but looks odd, with the outer log siding no longer an outside surface but about to be enclosed within. It already seems inappropriate, like clothing inside out, Meg thinks.

"About time you had a studio with lots of light!"

Meg knows Joanna is ready to work, knows it's hard to stay suspended for so many months. From the first time Meg saw Joanna's work, she has known the depth of her mind, the amazing grace of hand and eye that generate the work in all its strength and mystery and beauty. As though she is alive only to create the beautiful, Joanna works on wood, bone and etching plates with a fierce simplicity. Meg holds her in awe when she thinks about her work. "You'll be working here soon now, soon!" Meg smiles at Joanna.

"Not soon enough! But yes, I know. I do know that!" Joanna laughs impatiently. Somewhere in her mind, like a flash of moving light reflected in a pane of glass, an image glows. Not yet, she thinks, and turns to go on her errands.

***

That night when they get into bed, Joanna is still caught in a glow from the progress of the studio. She pulls Meg to her in a sudden surge of desire. Meg, surprised and delighted, responds with a long, deep kiss and they make love with quick, sharp pleasure before falling asleep, arms stretched out at their sides toward one another, still holding hands.

Lying awake that night, Meg tries to lie still so as not to awaken Joanna who has gone straight to sleep. Joanna coughs, turns over, sleeps comfortably again. The cough automatically evokes anxiety in Meg. Anxiety is like a file in Meg's computer that contains Joanna and her smoking, Shannon and her drinking. Sprung alert, eventually Meg turns on the light and very quietly picks up her novel. The book in hand, like the heating pad, is another comfort, she thinks, as she opens it to read, purposefully abdicating her anxieties for the ongoing delight of a story to grab onto at bedtime, a towline into sleep.

***

Hours later, having fallen asleep over her book, Meg snaps awake with a familiar fear cramping her mind like a charley horse might her leg. She is sure the wires have been cut. Her book is still lying by her side and the room is dark although she had not turned off the lamp.

Carefully she establishes for herself which room she's in, which way she's facing in the bed. Not in a dream, she senses, more than thinks; this is in the real world although the edge of danger makes it seem unreal. Carefully she stands, gauging the depth of Joanna's sleep. No need to wake Joanna up just to have her scared, she thinks.

Meg steps quietly through the living room and kitchen and into the sunroom to the light switch by the deck where a hollow flick confirms what she already knows. She stays there long enough to be sure the driveway is empty of prowlers, the street of any stranger's car. Then she quietly returns to their bedroom.

Joanna is peaceful when she sleeps, like a child, Meg thinks protectively, standing by the bedside. Time enough in the morning for her to know. The familiar scenario will proceed: an angry Joanna, a makeshift breakfast, the police. Time enough then for Meg to admit that the wire cutter has not given up, that he is still lurking in their lives. Joanna will accuse her of not doing enough about this present danger and, Meg acknowledges reluctantly to herself, she will be right. Meg is elaborately careful with every movement so as not to awaken Joanna, wanting to postpone that confrontation.

# CHAPTER TWENTY-SEVEN

Meg stands at her watching post at the sunroom window. It's been raining a cold drizzle all this afternoon and now, at five o'clock, it's also dark and colder. Max is hammering on the last frame for what will be the walls of the studio. "He must be damned cold," Meg says.

"He says the concrete is coming in the morning. He has to be ready."

"Should we give him dinner? Or send out brandy in a canister around a St. Bernard's neck?"

Joanna laughs and comes to stand with Meg. "It's weird...putting up walls before the floor." The floor, Max has explained, comes last, after the roof to protect it from the weather.

"He's wonderful to get this done before the worst cold comes. If the ground freezes now, it won't stop the building."

"You don't think so?"

"No. That's why he's been working such long days."

They've watched him push earth around even in the dark, the headlights of the Caterpillar flashing in the window like a flashlight in someone's wildly thrashing hand signaling distress. But when they ask him if he wants coffee, if he shouldn't stop, if he's okay, he always laughs his surprised laugh and nods. "Oh, yes, thanks, I'm fine, just want to finish this up before I quit."

"Think he's married?" Joanna asks.

"He is. No kids though."

"How do you know that?"

"He told me so."

Joanna is bewildered by Meg's chronic conversational intimacy with strangers who often tell her all about their lives. Joanna thinks it's close to inappropriate, being herself intensely private, but seeing Meg's smiling face, she smiles back. After dinner, as Joanna clears up, Meg goes back to the window where Max works on in the rain and darkness until the frames are firmly locked in place and braced.

***

Meg wakes at three a.m. to see Joanna standing at the window of the bedroom. She is standing the way she sleeps, quietly, steadily, as though she may not move for hours.

"Hello?" Meg speaks softly, not to startle her.

"Oh, hi." Joanna's voice is strained.

"What's up?"

"I can't sleep, Meg. I don't know how you sleep."

Meg sits up, recognizing that Joanna is wide awake and probably has been for a long time. "Did something happen?"

"Not this very minute. Not yet tonight. But any minute, right? This is no way to live!"

"Come back to bed. I'll rub your back."

Joanna looks down at her and then again back out the window. Meg goes to stand beside her. The lamppost stands as usual by the driveway, casting its ordinary light, and nothing in their view of trees and shrubs, stars and moon, gives any slightest hint that fear should be rippling through the room. "Christ! That's no answer, Meg!"

"It's the best I've got right now. C'mon." Meg takes her hand and leads her back to bed. Joanna lies in the center of the bed so Meg can straddle her. Meg strokes and kneads and Joanna begins to relax. "In California the desert winds used to blow for days and days. They were called Santa Anas and they made their own kind of noise…something between a whistle and a moan—and they drove some people crazy."

"Not you, though, right? I can't help it, Meg. Most people couldn't sleep, never knowing when this maniac is going to attack!"

"We'll catch him," Meg says, "now go to sleep." She swings over into her side of the bed and stretches out.

"Thank you for the backrub."

"You're welcome."

"Meg! You have to do something about this."

Meg waits, tensed against whatever may be about to follow.

After a silence, Joanna goes on. "You can't just lie back and take it, Meg. You have to go to the high school and look at the yearbooks. Every kid has his picture in there, right?"

"Right." Meg has trouble enunciating the single word.

"Start with the most recent and work your way back. See if you can find some kid who would have it in for you—a kid you failed or a skinhead or just some really sick kid. That's what you have to do! They're after you, not me. The most likely suspect would be a kid."

"Okay, Joanna. Okay." A heaviness congeals around Meg's body like raw cold. Somewhere around two hundred and fifty kids a day for twenty years would be some five thousand kids' faces to check out. On suspicion. And how, Meg thinks, do you propose to catch him and how long do you think that it might take? And how much of our time, my time. Subtract that from my writing time and what do I have left? After Joanna falls asleep, Meg lies, listening to her breathing, listening out the window for any quiet arrival of a car, any unusual crackling of a branch, her eyes open, watching for the bat-like swoop of headlights on the ceiling or the sudden darkening of the barely discernible glow against the window ledge that the protective globe of light below casts through the night.

***

"How can the truck get high enough to pour the cement into the frames?" Meg asks.

Joanna stands beside her, watching the huge truck bumble up the muddy slope that Max has scraped into some sort of road. The light of early morning glints on the truck's tumbling sides. Joanna studies the high frames and the whirling mixer. "I do not know," she says, "but I'm a true believer! Max knows!" She goes into the bedroom to use e-mail. That is her link to all the friends she left in Oregon as well as her kids.

The truck rocks and slides but does not tip and comes to an unsteady halt. The two men maneuver the truck's funnel and spout into place, connecting with Max's trough. Max stands on a scaffold board that runs around the entire interior of the frames and guides the end of the spout. The thick gray cement flows like a muddy river, flooding down into the frames. Along the top there are boards to interrupt the flow every ten feet or so.

Leaning out the open window from which they have removed the screen so they can talk with Max at will, Meg calls down to him, "How does the cement get under those boards?"

"You want windows in the studio?" Max smiles at her silliness.

Meg blushes. "Yes!" Laughing, she stays at the window, watching, thinking she shouldn't bother him again. But driven to know, she asks: "What if it snows? Will the cement dry?"

"Oh sure." Max looks like a kid in his pullover snow cap as he smiles up at her from the scaffolding below. "It will be fine. Only a bad freeze would make us trouble and then we just put in some antifreeze. But it's not going to be that cold this week. We lucked out on the weather."

"Thanks for working so late last night!"

"I had to be ready for this fellow today!" He waves toward the driver of the truck. "Now Robert will bring the crew on Monday." He turns back to his work.

Meg had not known that. Excitement ripples through her like a wind. "Hey, Joanna! The whole crew will come on Monday!" she shouts over her shoulder to Joanna, then realizes Joanna isn't in the sunroom and can't hear anything she says. Meg closes the window and goes into the bedroom to give Joanna a bear hug. "Max says that Robert and the carpenters are coming in on Monday! This here building's going up, up up!"

"I guess! I'm through here if you want to get to work. I'll leave it on. I'm going out to get that big branch off the path in front." Joanna pulls on her jacket and work gloves.

"You going to use the chain saw?"

"No way! And neither are you!"

Meg starts to bridle. She got the chain saw to cut up a fallen tree after a storm just before Joanna came. She used it a few times and then it seized. She'd put it aside, thinking it needed to be checked and oiled, and not trusting her own competency, thought Joanna could do that. Instead Joanna has announced that chain saws are too dangerous and they should get rid of it.

Meg feels a current of resentment circle through herself and starts to say, *Don't give me any orders!* but thinks better of it. She says, "You really think we shouldn't use it, don't you?"

"That's right. Greta tried one once and nearly lost her hand."

"Okay, okay. I yield."

Joanna nods, smiling. "Good," she says, and her voice and something about the way she walks back to the sunroom in her work clothes sends a surge of desire through Meg's body so that she follows her to snag her for a kiss. "Not now!" Joanna laughs, pointing out the window.

Meg glances out at Max and says, "Let's give Max the chain saw! We should do something for him—he's worked so hard—and he'd like that."

"What a good idea!"

By noon both the cement truck and Max have gone. The weekend is stormy and Meg and Joanna stay in, welcoming some quiet, private time. Sunday morning Joanna suggests they return to bed. "May be our last private hour for a long time!"

Sunday afternoon the weather lightens up. Meg and Joanna go out together to explore. Meg takes snapshots of Joanna in her studio, saying, "I was holding my breath until the concrete work was finished. Are you going to carve your initials in the wall?"

"Too late for that!" Joanna laughs. "And it's really freezing out here," she says, heading for the back door.

"I'll be right in."

Going through the open space that will be the doorway, Meg turns back to check out the room one last admiring time. Her arm grazes the raw cement and she is smashed by a sharp gray vision of another wall.

Timothy Franklin Palladio.

Among the immeasurably long rows of names etched in the stone his name was singularly bare, naked in the sunlight, glowing as though carved on a great slab of stone on the ocean floor caught by a beam of sunlight striking like a laser through the depths; or his, uniquely his, the way his gangly printed signature stood in large uneven letters at the bottom of his blazing red, yellow, blue paintings in kindergarten; or secretly his, as squiggled in black ink on his first hardball and the bat that went with it; or past enduring, his, at the bottom of a hand drawn card for her birthday, sent from Vietnam.

Meg had crumpled then, right to the sidewalk, between an old Black man with a cane and three teenagers with Coke cans in their hands and cigarettes in their mouths. She came around quickly to find Rosalyn on the cement beside her, holding her in her arms. Gradually Meg allowed the scene to come back into focus. Tim was dead, now as he had always been since the day she was first told, now as every night since then, drifting just beyond her dreams, the ghost beyond the cycling boy with tennis racquet about to collide with the oil truck, beyond the hooded skydiver who is plunging without a chute, beyond the notes of the guitar drifting without words above the hands of a boy in jeans and a denim shirt who sits with his head turned away from her so she cannot see his face though she can hear the music that he makes. His name was there, among the names of other boys who had somewhere mothers whose nightmares still ranged the nighttime air of quiet suburban homes, still shrieked like fingernails down the blackboard in the space beyond remembering, in the wordless shapeless pit of emptiness that lay beneath what they did remember of their dreams as they rose with the first light to stoke the kitchen stove on the Mississippi farm or walk their grandchildren to school in the inner city of Newark or Detroit.

This was the Vietnam Wall in Washington D.C. Meg forced her mind to know. One more place to leave my son's memory, to let go. One more moment to let the clock hands pass, the calendar relinquish. Whoever it was who first said, "He's history," knew how it felt, she thought, not yet able to even slightly curve her lips in the bitterest of smiles.

"Okay."

"You're ready?"

Meg nodded and started to rise. Rosalyn on one side and the old Black man on the other held out their hands to her and she took both, Rosalyn's for support and the old man's in recognition of his own mourning—"My two grandsons," he said, pointing to their names. "Two," as though the number was their name, as though the single word indicted the powers that make war. "They weren't but boys."

Meg nodded, said, "My son," her hand moving toward the wall, her fingers extended like Michelangelo's Adam with his arm lifted toward God, waiting for life to enter, and as her fingers touched the hard stone wall, her body flinched, a frigid cold shivering through her every nerve and bone.

Now Meg leaves the studio to walk once all the way around the old house, which looks just like itself from the other side, and back around the concrete walls, darkening with twilight, with their great windows that gape into the roofless space that will be the studio. Meg steps inside again and stands for a long moment staring at the bare cement, its gray darkened almost to black. I still miss Rosalyn, she thinks, remembering how it was Rosalyn who held her all that long night, warming her against that irrevocable cold, crying with her before they slept.

Always the same unbelievable surprise. Her father there at the table for supper and the next morning when the oatmeal mush was sputtering in the kettle on the woodstove, when the cows waited to be milked, when the school bus came on time, her father was gone, leaving nothing but his jacket hanging on a hook underneath his farmer's hat and the kerosene lantern set carefully in its place on the back porch, casting no light. She had gone out into the woods where there was a fir tree so freshly felled by her father that the sap on the stump still quivered liquid silver in the sunlight; she had stood, fingers tracing the circling of the pitch, and understood that her father was forever gone.

"Oh Tim, good night," she says, touching the wall as she walks out through the doorless opening, walks under the trees to the door of the old house, goes in and up the stairs into the bright light and the slight drift of smoke from the fire Joanna's started in the fireplace.

# CHAPTER TWENTY-EIGHT

Joanna wakes to the sound of trucks pulling into the newly cleared space that will be a driveway to the studio when all is done. Used to the sound of Max's truck, she turns over peacefully, then, remembering that Max is gone and the crew is coming, snaps wide awake in pure alarm.

Joanna wants to shout, "Men on the land!" in a great voice but figures Meg might not think it funny, especially since the "night crawler" has neither disappeared nor been caught. Besides, Robert, the builder, and his crew might hear. Better to start off the first day in a friendlier mode, she thinks with a tiny ironic smile, as she walks into the sunroom where the builder is sitting with a cup of coffee and the blueprints, talking quietly with Meg. Through the window Joanna sees the other men carrying great sheets of plywood up from their truck.

The men are tramping in with ladders and boards, power saws and tool boxes, lunch buckets and water bottles. They stack various boxes of nails and miscellaneous items in the original basement, where they set up a big compressor for their power tools, then run their heavy extension cords from the sockets in the basement through a hole Max hacked in the connecting wall. Later they will cut through a doorway there, connecting the new studio with the old basement.

It's a halfway indoors place, like a tree fort, Joanna thinks, surveying the bare concrete enclosure. We have the concrete walls with holes for doors and windows, but no roof and no floor. The dirt floor reminds her of the hovels she has seen in documentaries of poor families in cities everywhere who have assembled sheets of cardboard and metal against the rain and snow, who sleep outdoors on the frozen ground, pretending that their crooked canopies keep out the rivulets that trickle across their floor turning dirt to mud, imagining that their cardboard siding is an insulated wall that shuts out the cold.

Back inside Meg has decided not to use the word processor for fear that the power tools will cause a break in power followed by a surge that will wipe out work. She is instead heading out the door to do the week's grocery shopping. Guiltily Joanna is glad. Overwhelmed by the presence of so many workers she craves solitude.

Joanna washes up the morning dishes and goes to the living room. Meg's stereo is accessible against one wall and a box of tapes is in the corner of the bedroom/study where they sleep. Glancing over at the word processor wedged into the corner beyond the bed, Joanna can't imagine how Meg gets any work done at all. She puts on a tape and goes in search of a sketching pad and her kit of charcoal pencils. She can't find either one although she remembers seeing the pad somewhere in this house or was it on a stack of cartons in the old house waiting for the movers?

It's somewhere, Joanna thinks, going down to look angrily around the cellar. Meg's Ping-Pong table is loaded with screens and other items for the wing. The men's compressor is roaring by the door. Cartons are everywhere holding Joanna's work, her clothing, what kitchen things she brought. Boxes and pieces of furniture are wedged everywhere. And where would I work? she challenges herself. There's not enough room to throw dice anywhere in this fucking house.

So go out where there is space. It's cold out there. Go to one of the thousands of malls? Go driving and get lost? Get on e-mail and complain to Greta? Can't—Meg doesn't want the machine turned on. Oh fuck! And this is only January. I'll lose it before summer comes.

At one o'clock Joanna leaves for the new tai chi class. She finds the house without difficulty. The class she had been attending for two months was more like an exercise class than the tai chi she did in Oregon. Once inside, once this small group has assembled and the master, a man in his thirties, she would guess, has begun, she knows she has found what she was looking for. Her arms and legs move as his do, her breathing is familiar and not forced. She watches the strength and grace of his body and feels her own body emulate its very way of being. Tears sting her eyes. She had not even known how desolate it made her to do without the beauty of this silent fellowship.

***

Joanna lies in the queen-sized bed, wedged between the writing desk and the closet, her book gripped in her hands. Meg is turning out the lights and locking up. Joanna starts each day with a book, her pot of coffee and her cigarettes. She returns to the book intermittently for a few minutes or for hours at a time, depending on her need as the day goes on. The book waits, ready to give solace, exacting nothing in return. At night it's as safe and comforting as the door to her own home used to be. Leaving the outside world, Joanna relaxes into the world the writer presents to her, a gift, entirely and secretly hers. Warmed by an overwhelming sense of coming home, Joanna begins to drowse.

Joanna knows Meg changes into pajamas and crawls into bed with her. Joanna knows Meg is a waking woman who wants to kiss and to be kissed and to go on making love late into the night. "Sorry, I'm so tired," Joanna mumbles against Meg's cheek. She struggles to revive herself and manages, "I went to the new tai chi today. The master is absolutely wonderful!"

"That's great, Joanna." There's a silence then as Joanna slides into sleep. "I love you," Meg adds.

Joanna shapes the words, "I love you too," but she is too lightweight to speak in words that can be clearly heard and instead drifts away, *is become a flat tin woman shape dangling in the wind outside Meg's house.*

# CHAPTER TWENTY-NINE

There are two windows in the wall opposite the deck end of the sunroom. One will be replaced by a doorway into the second story of the wing. Because the wing abuts only five feet of the sunroom, the other window will remain. Meg stands by that window, looking out at the workers' scene as she does several times every day.

The crew has erected studs around the inside of the studio walls and they are now hammering up the joists that will support the second story. The sheets of plywood flooring are stacked, ready to be laid. It looks to Meg like a magic act, building a floor across the air like that. Maybe by tonight, she thinks, we can crawl out this window and stand there under the stars in what will be our bedroom.

Joanna comes to stand next to her at the window. "I don't see how everything will fit in there," she says nervously, eyeing the open space. "The oak desk will fill this whole corner, you know," and she points down at the blueprint in her hand.

"Everything will fit just fine." Meg smiles reassuringly.

"I don't see how. Bureau, TV, two chairs, bedside stands, files…"

It is still surprising to Meg that they are financially equal partners in the building of the wing which will include the studio on the ground floor and a bedroom on the second floor which they will share. Contrary to her instinct to calm Joanna's anxiety, Meg decides this is the moment to bring up her own space requirements and adds, "I don't need anything except my bureau."

Meg can feel Joanna stiffen with surprise. She has carefully plotted in her own things and not anything of Meg's. After a moment Joanna nods without commenting and Meg knows her anxiety has escalated. Meg also knows she must claim some space in that room for herself if it is in reality to be their bedroom. She doesn't want to be sleeping there, making love there, feeling as though she is Joanna's guest in Joanna's space.

Meg, quietly startled, recognizes fear swirling in her stomach. Better now or you never will, she admonishes herself and speaks. "I'll need closet space too, you know." Joanna nods, again silently.

\*\*\*

Before going in to work on her novel, Meg stands on the deck a few minutes, watching the jays at the sunroom's window feeder, looking down the driveway and around the yard. Deciduous trees are winter bare and much of the ground cover has lost its leaves. Ivy spreads out around the house and triumphantly soars up numerous trunks; the rhododendron's leaves hang tightened against the cold but still keep their deep determined green. Meg leans on the rail and smiles. Now that Joanna has found tai chi and the chorus, she will be meeting other women, doing other things she likes to do, and feeling less homesick as the weeks go by. Watching her get in her car and back out of the driveway, Meg's focus is snagged by the lamppost.

A silent symbol of alarm, it stands inert and hazardous, like the little flags that mark lawns that have been treated with pesticide to warn off children and grass-chewing dogs. The neighborhood is quiet, filled with small lawns and many trees. There are neither streetlights nor sidewalks along the narrow, winding asphalt streets which are crowded by rhododendron and laurel. Like the rare siren that sometimes invades the quiet of their woods, snaking through the foliage like a strobe light, the unimposing lamppost stands, conveying fear.

Meg leans on the railing of the deck, hearing behind her the good hammering of the crew. Why? she wonders. As though a fungus has blighted the beauty of the woods, the menace of the wire cutter lurks in the familiar scene. Who? Joanna's words lodge like a neon accusation in her mind: "You can't just lie back and take it, Meg."

\*\*\*

Driving the road to the high school, Meg thinks the car knows the way and all she has to do is let it turn this way and that while she keeps her foot on the gas pedal. You should have done this a year ago, she thinks. I didn't think it would keep on happening, she responds.

Entering the building Meg feels so out of place she expects someone to stop her on the spot. The building is still the friendly, open school in which she taught. There are no guards at the doors and students move freely along the halls. My God, they are so young, she thinks. Meg goes down the hall and goes up the stairs to Guidance without incident. She looks for a familiar name on the little cubicles where counselors work. Finding one at last, she knocks softly on the open door. The young man looks up, draws a blank, and then smiles in recognition. "Hey, Ms. McKenna!" he says, with a big smile. "Whatcha doin' in these parts?"

She goes in, smiling, and as he waves her to a chair, sits down. "How goes it, Ken?"

"Same old, same old," he says. He tells her who's retired from the English Department, which she already knows, and how they've top-loaded classes, thirty to a class, and cut out electives that didn't draw their thirty. Meg thinks his office is smaller than it used to be, thinks the building is smaller than it was when she was there. When he stops talking and waits for her to answer, she knows he's asked her what she's doing there.

"I'm looking for a student, I guess." He laughs. "I'm looking for a bad guy, Ken." Now he looks surprised. Not easy to explain, she thinks. "Somebody is making me trouble."

"Not you! Not a kid!"

"I don't know who. Do you have a minute?"

He checks his watch. "I have ten minutes."

"Okay." She gives him the story.

"Does he do everybody's lights, up and down the street?" Ken grins. He's thinking mischief, she knows.

"No, it's odd, Ken. It's only mine. And it's not even once a month. But it's beginning to be a little scary. I thought maybe I could look through yearbooks?"

He looks at her blankly. "Look for what?"

"See if I can jog my memory. One theory is that it's an ex-student who is out to get me."

"Not you! I never knew a student who hated you, Meg!"

She laughs. "Well, somebody is making trouble, Ken. Somebody is!"

Not until she's seated in an empty cubicle confronting a stack of yearbooks on the desk before her does it occur to Meg that she didn't come out to Ken. Not a word. Would it matter? Maybe—maybe not. Seeing old friends in the faculty photographs in the first yearbook she opens, she thinks, call Ruth tonight and Ryan. See what they remember. She begins to turn the pages, one by one. An hour later, when Ken suggests she might be more comfortable doing this at home, she immediately agrees. Driving home with twenty yearbooks in the backseat, Meg is already sucked into a time tunnel. It's the names, even more than the faces, that trigger events for her.

*** 

Meg and Joanna are perched at the table in the sunroom like bluejays at the feeder. Joanna sits facing the deck, her back to her wedged in furniture. In the early dark of the winter she is already listening for the intruder down the driveway. Conversation is deliberately set in motion by one or the other, as though in front of a scrim, behind which a man is crouching, hands manipulating wires, about to bring down total darkness on their table, leaving only the candles' glow to calm their fear.

"Any luck at school today?"

"I brought home twenty yearbooks to prowl through!" Meg reaches behind her to show Joanna one. "Here, have a look."

"They're so young!" Joanna turns to the faculty photos. "And look at you! Pretty cute you were!"

A car turns into the driveway, its headlights glancing off the window behind Meg. Alarmed, Joanna jumps up. Meg follows her to the railing and even in the dark can recognize Shannon's car.

"It's just Shannon," she says, leaning on the rail, watching the kids come tumbling out. "Hi, Dylan! Hi, Mack!"

"We just came by for a minute," Shannon calls up to them.

I'll bet she needs to borrow food money, Meg thinks, going to let them in. They go trooping up the stairs, the boys' boots thumping as they go. Meg leaves them with milk and cookies at the table while she and Shannon go into the living room to talk.

"Twenty bucks? I hate to ask but I get paid on Friday and we're out of milk and bread. You know how it is." Shannon speaks softly.

"Twenty bucks." Meg takes two bills from her purse and walks over to hand one to Shannon, standing close to her for a minute to see if she can smell alcohol in the air. She can't. "Here's an extra ten for ice cream."

"Thanks a lot."

"Hey, how's AA going?"

Shannon puts the bills in her jeans pocket and turns away. "Good. Yeah, really good. My sponsor's a neat woman. You'd like her, Grams."

"That's great, Shannon."

As they start to go, Dylan holds up his mittened arms for a big hug.

"They're pretty cute, you have to admit," Meg says to Joanna as the car pulls out.

"Cute and smart and wonderful and not mine!" Joanna stares off into the night. "I remember being alone at the laundromat with three under four and laundry to carry!"

"Now that's a scene! Next time we'll join a kibbutz, right?"

***

Watching Meg fall so easily into mothering with the two little boys, Joanna wants only to escape. She goes to the deck to read so long as there is light. But late at night, hearing Meg on the phone with Liz, resenting the time stolen from their time together, even if she is busy elsewhere, occasionally, to her astonishment, she feels a stab of envy, like a lightning streak, as suddenly come as that and as suddenly gone.

How did those tumbling little ones of her own get severed so completely from her life? That's not what I meant to do, Joanna thinks, standing at the rail on the deck, cigarette in hand. Desperate for time to work, she knows she ran from them. Ran, she thinks, shaking off their clinging hands, twisting away from their whining voices, their angry yelling teenage accusations. Ran, drinking as I went, running from Walter, running from the constant demands of three, never one, never only two, but always three joined together like in a Rubik's Cube, escaping one to be confronted by two others, always three, three, three. And now we almost never call up to say hello, not I need, you should, why don't you? Just hello.

Joanna draws the smoke in deeply.

***

"Hey, let's go look at our bedroom."

They take turns climbing up on a chair so they can edge out backward through the sunroom window that will later be the doorway. Then they are standing on the newly put-down flooring of the second story. There are no sides yet to this space. It's flat and open to the air. They stand as in a meadow on a mountaintop. It makes Meg dizzy and she takes Joanna's hand, partly to steady them, partly in a surge of love.

The stars glitter through the treetops. The moon begins to rise. They stand under the open sky as in a field where they will sleep, with the smell of raw lumber all around them mixing with growing pine and cedar and the sharp clear ambiance of an unexpected snow.

"Will snow bother them?"

"No. But it may not start until they've got it roofed."

Balanced in the center of the sky, with branches over them—oak etched in sharp dark lines, pine and cedar moving in the wind, so that shadows drift down moonlight and stars shine and disappear and shine again—Meg and Joanna draw together for a quiet kiss.

# CHAPTER THIRTY

"Maybe I should join Al-Anon."

Joanna looks up as she sets down her glass of wine. "Great."

Meg forces a laugh. "You could come too."

"My favorite thing: meetings. Especially meetings where everyone talks of nothing but alcohol."

"Don't say I didn't offer."

Joanna takes a swallow of wine and adds, "Shannon and her kids are becoming the center of your life."

"That's absurd! I…"

Joanna slashes accusingly into her sentence. "I wasn't prepared for Shannon. You should have told me."

"I did tell you." Meg remembers writing and rewriting that letter, warning Joanna that Shannon was in trouble, naming alcohol as the problem, hoping the situation wouldn't frighten Joanna away.

"Not clearly enough. I had no idea!"

Meg studies Joanna's angry face. "It's not that catastrophic, you know. They don't live with us."

"You don't even know. You're always thinking about her—giving her money, taxiing, baby-sitting—I thought we'd live in a clear space—we talked about that—about the 'Lake Isle of Innisfree'…" Joanna's lament trails off reflectively.

"Everyone has some kind of problem," Meg mutters, thinking that won't wash with Joanna.

"It took me years to be free to do my work—I want to do my work, not babysit."

"Do I ever ask you to babysit?"

Deliberately they change the topic, speak of the rain, the sparrows at the window feeder, the news. Meg thinks, it's always like this—neither of us wants a fight. Usually I'm the one who goes on talking until I lose it. This time I'll keep quiet. She wishes Joanna had more compassion for Shannon, was less judgmental but she answers herself back, Joanna had to deal with an alcoholic brother and an alcoholic husband for twenty years. No wonder she doesn't ever want to be near another alcoholic.

"Half the world is cold and hungry. We are so lucky here." Meg points to a newspaper's front page picture of street people in Manhattan.

"It's okay. You don't have to feel guilty."

"I don't feel guilty. Just lucky. But it is all out of kilter. The rich get richer and the poor get poorer and not enough people care."

"I do care, you know. You don't think I do because I want to be left alone to do my work. But I didn't come this far to have my hands tied, my work time forfeited, for an addict, Meg. You may have to do that, but I don't."

"I get work done," Meg says defensively. She knows she gets much less work done than Joanna, much less than she would like to do. "It's the 'angel within' that Virginia Woolf said you have to kill. I have more trouble with that than you do. But Shannon is, after all, my granddaughter."

"As if I didn't know that."

"Besides, what's life about if not helping people some of the time?"

"Some of the time is one thing." Joanna sets down her fork and says, "But sometimes I think you should just live alone."

Meg stares at the stranger across the table. Speak for yourself, she thinks, in a silent rage. The piece of bread she's chewing seems too much to swallow and after she succeeds, she takes a long drink of wine. Then she stands up and leaves the table. "I'm going for a walk," she says. "I'll be back."

"What I mean is that you don't have time for a relationship."

"I know what you mean. I'm more available than you are, Joanna," Meg throws back over her shoulder and she's gone.

\*\*\*

The neighborhood is early evening quiet. Three boys go by on bikes, coasting down the slope. Don and Cyndy, the young couple who live next door are walking their big old black Labrador, Jake. Cyndy smiles and Meg starts to wave and keep on walking but stops instead.

"Hi," she says, inviting conversation.

"Hi. That storm held off, hmm?"

Meg puts down her hand to pet the Lab. "Yeah, it did. We're glad."

"How's that going?" The young man tips his head toward the wing.

"Fine. I did want to ask a favor of you, though." Both of them look surprised. They only see one another occasionally, just to wave when shoveling snow or raking leaves. "We're having a problem." Meg describes the wire cutting events.

"That's really weird!" Cyndy says.

"So I wondered—if you ever see a strange car parked in front of your house—if you ever see its license plate, would you tell us? I didn't ask before because he always comes in the middle of the night—but if you were walking Jake late—maybe?"

"Sure. Absolutely." Don nods vigorously. Jake tugs the leash and they walk on.

Meg walks quickly in the opposite direction, thinking about Joanna. She's such a private person, and she's never lived with a woman in the same house before, year after year. She's weekended back and forth or gone away on trips and had stolen hours in between. Erotically exciting, Meg thinks, more than daily opportunities must be. Still, not fair to blame me for saving Mack and Dylan. Mean-spirited of her.

By the time it's getting seriously dark, Meg has stomped it off. Damn it! I do love her, crazy woman, she thinks, and goes quietly back into the house.

"I'm home again," Meg says, going into the living room.

"Shannon called," Joanna says. "Wants you to call her back."

"You set that up!" Meg says, with a half-laugh. "It was a trap."

"Actually not," Joanna answers, turning back to the nature channel. "Look! Do you know about meerkats?" Meg goes to look. Seeing the strange animals stretching and peering about, guarding their homes, both women smile and the coldness is gone, replaced by their common delight.

"I'll call Shannon. And I'm going to make some night crawler calls tonight."

Meg leaves Joanna with the meerkats while she calls her teaching colleague, Ruth, who has moved to Florida. Ruth remembers a boy named Blake. "Remember, Meg? They had to white out his Heil! in the senior picture!"

"I remember."

She remembered Ruth and herself standing together, leaning on the balcony railing in the high school commons, looking down, as Blake, a tall, broad-shouldered boy, walked down the stairs below them with a friend. Their heads were shaved. They wore flight jackets and Doc Marten boots. They had swastikas on their belts. They were in Meg's afternoon class.

"You know, Meg, they remind me of Hitler Youth." Ruth's voice was strained.

"I know. They went into the city to bash Blacks and gays. They wrote about it."

"He throws pennies at me when I walk by him. They think Jews are cheap, you understand."

Meg nodded grimly. "I've seen the pennies fly. There's a bunch of them who do that but you can't catch them in the act. I've been trying to change these guys for two years, Ruth."

Blake was always polite, entirely calm, and certain of his Nazi line. Meg turned to share a glance with Ruth, whose parents died at Auschwitz. Ruth's face was ashen. Knuckles white, her hands had gripped the rail of the balcony.

"He's the most likely one," Ruth says now.

"Could be. If you think of anybody else, would you let me know?"

Meg also calls Ryan, who is now in Florida as well. He remembers Jimmy Tomkins of the "Are you a lezzie" story but nothing otherwise. "I'll come up and hide in the bushes all night," he says, giggling at the thought.

"Okay. You do that."

"Hey, couldn't you set up a camera like in the bank?"

"He only comes once in a blue moon. What, run a camcorder around the clock for forty days while waiting?" They both laugh. "If you think of someone, let me know. And what's new in Florida?"

***

It's midnight. They're reading in bed. Joanna lays her book down on the bedside stand, turns out her light. "That's as long as I can stay awake," she says.

Meg closes her book, clicks out her lamp, and turns toward Joanna. As she nestles there, smelling the familiar warmth, feeling Joanna's welcoming arm that pulls her close, Meg thinks, forget the words, this is what it's all about, just snuggle in.

Joanna murmurs, "Could you scratch my back? Up high in the center." Meg obeys, smiling to herself. "Thank you," Joanna says. "That feels so good. Too bad you don't like to have your own back scratched!"

"To each her own." Meg lets her hand slide soothingly up and down Joanna's back as Joanna slides toward sleep. Joanna's breathing slows, thickening toward a light snore. "You'd better turn over—you're falling asleep."

Joanna retrieves her own arm from underneath Meg and turns away, adjusting the pillow she uses for her knees. "Love you," she says, fading out again.

"Love you, too," Meg answers, feeling her whole body savor the sleepy closeness that they share.

After a few minutes Joanna stretches out and Meg slides away a bit so that she can extend her arm to rub Joanna's back again. With long slow strokes she eases the pain that has crouched there all day. She continues moving her hand up and down, up and down, until Joanna's breathing deepens into steady sleep.

***

On the ferry, headed north for an exhibit in upstate New York, Joanna sits on deck, a museum catalogue in her hands, smiling up at Meg. Pavel Tchelitchev is an old favorite of hers and they are off for a two-day holiday to see a special showing of his work.

"We should get away more often!" Meg says, smiling down at her, thinking how radiant Joanna looks.

"We should!"

They drive through prosperous Connecticut communities, taking back roads when they can. "Which way do you think Katonah might be?" Meg asks at an unmarked fork.

"There's no clue. Nits!"

"You check out the right; I'll take the left, okay?"

Joanna, laughing, ponders the map. "Hard to say."

They follow one branch which eventually takes them into a small town which is not named on the map. "It's gas station time," Meg says, pulling in to a Texaco.

The young man at the pump knows very little English and smiles and nods, pointing to the garage. The old man in the garage waves away the map and points down the highway, back the way they've come. "Turn back at the fork," he says. "Just make a U-turn."

Laughing together they head back. "As long as you get us there before closing time!" Joanna says.

"Guaranteed."

The museum is a small, beautiful building in the countryside. There are almost no visitors in the three rooms. Joanna checks it all out and then settles in front of her favorite painting: *Hide and Seek.* Meg wanders from room to room, returning to stand beside Joanna, pondering the hidden children and the highly visible children, the darkness, the gnarled branches and great and secretive roots where they disappear into the ground. They spend the whole afternoon looking at the painting, talking about the sexual clues that come to mind as the imagery emerges.

"It's not a cheerful painting. I guess I didn't realize when I first saw it how dark it is. I was at the Art Students' League and saw it at the Modern. And that was more than forty years ago!"

They leave the gallery and go to their motel. "I'm glad we decided not to crowd it into one day," Joanna says. "Thank you for doing this!"

"You're welcome," Meg says, smiling, thinking how beautiful Joanna truly is, knowing it shows more when she's free of the anxieties that bother her at home.

They eat in a diner and watch TV in the motel. The next morning, after the free coffee and doughnuts, Joanna beckons Meg back into bed. "Checkout isn't until twelve," she says.

"Thank God for small favors," Meg says, smiling, going into her arms.

# CHAPTER THIRTY-ONE

On the run for the phone Meg notes the time on the bedside clock. It's two a.m. Joanna is already rearing up, saying, "For God's sake! Tell her not to call at night!"

"Shannon! Where are you?"

"Listen, Grams, I'm really sorry to bother you but I'm having a little trouble and I need to ask a favor. I wouldn't call—I know it's late—I know you were asleep—and I'm sorry. It won't happen again. It's just—"

"Shannon!" Meg interrupts her. "Where are you?"

"It's the kids, Grams. They're home. They're safe—don't worry. They're safe."

"And where are you?"

"They're keeping me overnight. Could you go over to the apartment and get the kids?"

"Are you in jail?"

"Bingo!"

"You got a DWI?" Sounds so much better than "you were drunk," Meg thinks with a wry smile.

"Yeah. Yeah, I did."

Meg sees it in a flash. The kids are home alone and Shannon is locked up. The kids are home alone sends a chill through Meg. "What happened? You never leave them home alone."

"I have to go, Grams."

"I'll go get the kids, Shannon," Meg says quickly, before the line goes dead, and adds, "Don't worry," but thinks Shannon didn't hear her say the last two words.

"You're not going anywhere this time of night!" Joanna stands in the doorway in her pajama top.

"I have to. Shannon left the kids home alone."

"And where might she be?"

"In jail."

"Oh terrific! They should just keep her there. Except then we'd have the kids for good!"

"I don't know what happened. She never leaves the kids alone."

"That you know of!"

"No, she doesn't, Joanna. Well, I won't bring them here. I'll just go sleep in Shannon's bed and take them to school in the morning."

"Oh, is that all you'll do?"

"Go back to sleep." Meg quickly pulls on her jeans and shirt and grabs her purse. "See you tomorrow. Sorry about this." She bends to kiss Joanna who is now sitting on the bed.

Joanna does not respond. She picks up her book and lies down to read. As Meg leaves the room and heads downstairs and out, Joanna relents and calls after her, "Be careful, Meg."

Meg calls back, "Don't worry—I'm awake."

Driving from her house to Shannon's place on the back road that is midnight quiet, Meg fights down her fear. What if there were a fire? What if Mack woke up from a nightmare and he and Dylan found out that Shannon wasn't there? She drives faster with an inarticulate feeling of desperation.

The boys are sound asleep in their room. Meg walks quietly around the two-room apartment. There are empty bottles everywhere and a smell of beer drifts through the air. The empty glass on the kitchen table with water melted from ice cubes, Meg surmises, sniffing it, was something stronger. Meg settles on the sofa and reads, trying to sleep, but on the level underneath the novel's content she is seeing the wreckage of a car with two small bodies in it. She gets up and walks around again, makes herself a cup of herb tea, sits to read. She turns out the light and thinks of ways to compel Shannon to go to rehab. She checks her watch. Four a.m. The kids will be up at seven. She'll take them to school and then she'll go post bail for Shannon in the morning court and drive her to wherever she parked the car last night so she can drive it home. And then she'll explain what happened. And then, Meg thinks, as though it is an old established fact, I'll take her car keys away from her to keep Mack and Dylan safe. Then Meg falls asleep.

***

"I only went to the convenience store for milk, Grams," Shannon says contritely.

"Shannon, you didn't go for milk. You went for beer. You ran out of liquor and you went for beer."

"I was only gone a minute."

"You left the boys alone and you were gone for hours, Shannon. I'm taking your keys. You may be going to AA but you haven't stopped drinking. You need emergency help, Shannon."

"I'm calling my sponsor as soon as you leave," Shannon says, drinking her third glass of orange juice. "Thanks for watching the kids."

"Talk to her about rehab. I think there are some day programs, part-time programs so you can go on working. Find out. I'll babysit whenever necessary." Shannon nods automatically. Meg picks up the key ring from the table and drops it in her purse.

Shannon jumps up and grabs the purse and tries to pull it from Meg's hand. Meg twists away with a burst of anger. *"NO! I'm taking them."*

Meg runs out the door. She turns back at the corner of the house and calls back, "When do you usually pick Dylan up?" Shannon does not answer. "I'll pick him up at four. That's about right. You call your sponsor." Meg goes on to her car and drives back home.

***

In the morning Joanna reads until ten in her current mystery. The crew has been hammering since eight and she feels awkward sitting any longer with her coffee, book and cigarettes. She's tired; she had trouble getting back to sleep after Meg left in the night. Reluctantly closing the book, she showers, dresses, and makes herself a morning meal of ham and eggs. Meg has not returned yet from her overnight at Shannon's and Joanna is smoldering with rage.

When Meg does arrive, she's carrying bags of groceries which she sets down in the kitchen while she goes back for more. Joanna's back chronically hurts too much to help but it makes her feel useless and guilty to watch Meg carrying things. Sometimes she says, "I wish I could help. Thank you for doing that." She goes out on the deck now to have a cigarette, standing by the rail, watching as Meg totes in load after load. They eat simply but Meg makes sure there is always a big reserve "in case we get a storm sometime!"

When she's put the food away, Meg comes out on deck. "They've got a lot of boards out there. What do you think happens next?"

"Dunno." Joanna wants to shout at her about Shannon but she does not start.

Meg, as if activated by the very thought of the crew's activity, walks back in and over to the window and stands looking out. "I could just stand here all day watching." She laughs.

Joanna checks the thermometer on the deck. "It's just under forty. Their hands must get cold."

"They're not wearing gloves?"

"Can't. Too hard to use the tools."

Automatically Joanna looks beyond the rail down the driveway to check the lamppost as though it too has mercury rising or falling, and numbers to read that measure this day's risk. What can I do? Joanna thinks. Where can I go? The last of her toast and eggs sticks in her throat as she recognizes, as she does every day, that there is nowhere yet to go, nothing yet to do. Not until spring when everything is finished will she be able to go to the studio and get to work. Her hands want to be at work so much that her muscles hurt with waiting. I'll go to the library again, she thinks, and to the hardware store for some corner shields for the bathtub.

Driving down the street Joanna is in full flight. She feels her tension ease as she nears the library. Two years of waiting to be with Meg, she thinks, and now I race away from her like a startled pheasant rising from the thicket. Not Meg, she argues with herself. The everything in abeyance of it all. Nowhere to work. Nowhere to quietly relax. Men hammering and sawing everywhere. Not a square foot of order. Barely room to sit, let alone to breathe. Disorder doesn't come near describing it. The wire cutter loose in our own woods in the night. Never knowing when Shannon will arrive nor what state she will be in. Or call, demanding that Meg find a way to rescue her. Pure chaos.

Parking at the library Joanna chooses the space closest to the entrance. Walking on concrete aggravates her sciatica. For a minute she sits in her car, keys in hand, staring at the blue lettering of the sign that designates the space next to hers as reserved for the handicapped.

Blueprints.

Her father at his workbench in the cellar had a whole file of blueprints. There under the dim bare lightbulb that hung on a chain above his bench he constantly refined and redefined the house that he intended to build for them someday. He'd already bought the lot. Sometimes on Sunday after church they drove over to check it out and he paced off the living room, made notes about the line the setting sun must take, going down. Back at their house while her mother made the Sunday dinner he was painstakingly adapting the blueprints hour after hour, sitting hunched at the bench in the basement.

Dinners were not conversational. Her father asked and answered, interrupting his pontificating with questions meant to elicit answers he had already formulated. Laying down her fork and waiting for a pause, her mother spoke, putting a pleasant fact before them, like laying a napkin, folded, by each fork. "Aunt Emma called. Arthur's wedding will be on a Saturday after all. That will make it easier for traveling."

"I suppose we have to go." Her father chewed his meat while speaking, swallowed, continued on. "That girl strikes me as somewhat too interested in her own plans. Where will they live?"

"I think they're buying a house outside Los Angeles."

"That's a terrible place to live. He should work until he can get a transfer and then move north. The San Francisco area is better. They shouldn't buy right off like that. They'll lose when they sell. You have to hold on to a house at least ten years to make it pay. You understand," looking at Peter, "that buying a home is entering the commercial market. People make a mistake, thinking of it as a private, one-time thing. It isn't. It's for most people their biggest venture into business. So you should think about it like that. Here you are, without much capital, taking the same risk that other investors take. So you should think about resale possibilities. Will it sell? Will you be able to see a gain? How long would you have to hold it to see that gain? Would it be advantageous to rent until the market shifts?"

Joanna thought of the Monopoly board and how Peter always beat her, piling up his money in huge stacks, laughing at her when she couldn't pay the fine for landing once too often on Boardwalk which was always his. I'll never buy a house, she thought. I'll live at the beach. I'll rent a cabin on the shore and hunt for shells.

"Being a landlord, if the property is small enough so handling it wouldn't be a problem, can bring in a steady income through the years."

Joanna studied the Hummel girl on the sideboard. Was she picnicking in the sunshine in a field of daisies? Were there butterflies in the field?

Her father went on, "Even renting with an option to buy can sometimes be an answer. That sometimes cuts the Gordian knot. Joanna, do you know what that phrase means?"

Joanna remembered the illustration in the book of myths in the school library. She saw the flash of sunlight on the sword as it descended severing the rope. "Yes. In Greece there was a king named Gordius. His wagon was tied to the yoke—I don't know if it was oxen or horses pulling the wagon—with a rope that had gotten snarled. No one could untie the knot. It was called a Gordian knot. The oracle said whoever untied it would rule Asia." She took a breath before going on and Peter leapt in.

"Alexander sliced it in half!"

Joanna sent him an angry glance. Whenever he knew anything she knew he interrupted her but whenever she was in trouble, not knowing something that he knew, he didn't help her out, but sat with a snide grin waiting until it was clear that she had failed before he spoke.

"In this case then, what is the Gordian knot?"

Joanna looked at him blankly. Monopoly boards and houses twirl through her mind. Her mother rose. "Please help me clear, Joanna," she interjected. "If you are finished?" She looked toward their father.

"Almost. Joanna?"

"Whether to rent or buy." Joanna said this calmly, with a touch of finality, figuring it may pacify him although she couldn't take it very far if he wanted her to elaborate. She started to rise, extended her hand toward her father's plate.

He spoke, but turned to Peter as he did so, dismissing Joanna with a nod. "Many people pay rent for far too long. You want to start to build up equity as early as you can."

Joanna gratefully lifted his plate and retreated to the kitchen, thankful to be able to move, most thankful to leave the inexorable pedantic drone of her father's voice.

# CHAPTER THIRTY-TWO

Meg drives Dylan home from day care. When she gets to the house Mack is already there. Listening to his story of the food fight at lunch, sitting at the table opposite Shannon, Meg is uncertain what comes next. Mack calls his friend Jerry and goes out to ride his bike with him. Dylan tags along. "Thanks for babysitting last night, Grams," Shannon says. "Want a Coke?"

Meg shakes her head. "So what do you intend to do?"

Shannon carries her Coke to the window to look out. With her back to Meg, she answers, "I have to go to AA meetings and I have to pay a fine."

"Good. But what do you intend to do about your drinking?"

"I said I'll keep on going to AA."

Not so much evasive as in denial, Meg thinks. "Shannon, you were driving when you were drunk! Think about it!"

Shannon swings around. "I'll handle it, okay?"

"If it weren't for Mack and Dylan, I'd be out of here, Shannon." Well, Meg thinks, that's certainly not true. "Actually that's not true.

You're my grandkid, remember. I don't want you to get hurt. Or to hurt anybody else!"

"I won't drive when I'm drunk. I promise." Shannon sighs, checks her watch, and goes to the refrigerator for another Coke.

"Where's your car?"

"I can walk over."

"Where?"

"A few blocks from here, really."

"I'm not sure I should give you back your keys."

Shannon whirls from the refrigerator toward Meg. "They're *my* keys!"

Fear trickles through Meg's body. I've stayed too long, pushed too far, Meg thinks, and stumbles on for one last shot. "This is about the kids, Shannon."

*"Give me my fucking keys and leave me alone. You think I'd hurt the boys?"*

Meg feels herself shifting around inside her skin like a boxer feinting in the ring. She wants to throw the keys on the table and run. She wants to keep the keys and run. She realizes that the running is what she wants to do. She stands up. "Did you call your sponsor?"

"Yes. For your information, I did call my sponsor!" Shannon's controlled words come through gritted teeth, rising to be a shout.

This is just Shannon, Meg admonishes herself. You're not afraid of Shannon. She starts to leave. "Don't just go to meetings because the judge said to. Go for real." Shannon is standing by the table, holding out her hand, waiting for the keys. Meg takes the key ring from her purse and lays it on the table.

Shannon picks up the keys and puts them in her jeans pocket. "I'm going to get my car."

"Right. Take care, you hear?"

"Food fights, Grams, do you believe it?" Shannon says, laughing, as they go out the door. "My mom told me they had them when she was in school."

"Shannon…" Meg turns toward her own car and turns back again, watching Shannon ease herself away, knowing this is all just words. Shannon doesn't for one minute intend to give up alcohol. Shannon looks at her over her shoulder but keeps on walking.

"Do the ninety days and ninety meetings," Meg says, thinking despairingly, it's words in the wind.

"Yeah, right! I have a job, you know. I work! And now I jog!" Lifting her hand in a wave, in a few quick steps Shannon is half a block away.

Meg gets in her car and realizes as she drives away that the knotted terror in her stomach is unsnarling itself, minute by minute, and she can breathe in even breaths again.

***

That night Meg gets a call from Shannon's sponsor, a woman named Claudia. "She'll sign herself into a residential rehab if you'll keep the boys."

Meg hears her own triumphant cry of "All right!" and even as she hears it, she's caught in her own whiplash. She'll have to tell Joanna that they're keeping the boys awhile. "How long do you think she'll be there?"

"You can't predict. It took me three months."

"When does she go in?"

"Tomorrow, if you can be ready."

"Sure. Great."

"She'll send the boys off to school and day care and you'll pick them up in the afternoon. I'll drive her to the facility and make sure she gets signed in and all. You have my phone if you need to call me."

"Yes, thank you."

Meg decides to tell Joanna later on the deck where Joanna goes for her after dinner cigarettes. Meanwhile Meg goes by the police station to check with the anti-bias section.

"Anything new?" she asks Detective Orenstein with whom she is by now very comfortable.

He shakes his head. "You?"

"I'm working my way through yearbooks from the high school but I'm not finding much."

"You know, I really doubt it has anything to do with school. With all due respect, they've forgotten you by now." He grins.

"Right. You been having any hate crimes in this area?"

"None to speak of. Two neighbors had a fight and one sprayed the other's windows with red paint. It said 'Nigger get out' but in fact the guy was just roaring drunk and mad."

"It's racist though. What happened to him?"

"A fine and he has to do some community service."

"Any anti-gay stuff?"

"Nothing heavy. A couple of bar fights."

"You have any record of a kid named Jimmy Tomkins or one named Blake Mueller?"

"Record like what?"

"I don't know. If they were sent to prison, would you have them in the computer?"

"I could look. You have reason to suspect one of them?"

"Yeah. Based on what they were like in school, I do."

"Let's check just for the hell of it." He leaves her and comes back after ten minutes. "Jimmy Tomkins went up-state for dealing drugs about three years ago. Blake Mueller doesn't have a record."

\*\*\*

"I have to tell you something," Meg says, sitting down across from Joanna on the deck, wishing she could skip the rest.

Joanna, resigned, looks at her. "Shoot."

"I have to keep the boys awhile."

"Surprise!"

"It's good though. Shannon has agreed to go into rehab."

"Whoopee!"

"No, this is really good, Joanna."

"Let it go, Meg. You'll do what you have to do. Pretty soon the studio will be up and running and I'll be out of the way. I need a place to work. This all makes me crazy." Joanna goes to clean up the kitchen.

As Meg walks through, on her way to the guest room to make sure the bed is freshly made, towels are laid out, space is cleared for the toys and clothing, Joanna looks up from the sink and asks, "How long would you guess?"

"I don't know. It might be more than a month."

"Well, spring is coming. You can take them to the beach!"

\*\*\*

That night they all crawl through the window and stand together where their bedroom will be. "Amazing, hmm?" Meg says. The graceful symmetry of the open structure against the darkening winter sky takes her breath away. "I'd like it to stay exactly this way awhile—it's so beautiful."

Joanna peers intently at the room's dimensions. "The bed will take so much room I don't see how we can fit the bureaus in."

"Why is this hole here?" Mack asks, shimmying over on his tummy, leaning his head over a yawning cutout in the floor.

"That's where the bathroom will be," Joanna tells him. "And they can't put the floor there until they get the bathtub up."

"How will they get it up?"

"I think they'll lift it up through that hole, Mack."

Dylan is studying the toy red car he carries with him all the time. He starts to push it up along the side of a stud. Meg does not let go of his hand.

"Hey, Mack, look up," Meg says, lying down on her back right next to him, smelling the rich pine of the raw floorboards and studs, staring up at the sky. Bare oak and green pine branches move in the wind above the rafters. "If you look carefully you can see the very first star come out."

"There's one," Mack says. "And there's another."

"Keep watching. There'll be a lot of them in a few minutes."

Mack lies close beside Meg on one side, Dylan on the other. It is as though they are on a raft drifting quietly between western river banks. A ragged V of geese that winter in Long Island fly over high above the trees in the last light. Mack's hand grips Meg's to point upward as if to speak would break the mystery of the moment.

# CHAPTER THIRTY-THREE

After lunch, Meg stands at the window watching for a while. The men are kneeling on the open floor, sawing two-by-fours into sections, nailing the boards to studs. The whole of the open space where Meg and Joanna have walked at night is covered now with lumber, saws, hammers and nail carriers. Meg shivers as Robert stands, goes to the edge, where he leans over to check on a joint, measuring, straightening, hammering. The men seem unaware that they are working on an unfenced plateau in the middle of the sky.

Meg walks back through the house, stopping in the living room to lay a fire. Carrying in the wood, readying the kindling, is Meg's favorite chore.

As a child Meg had read in *Wuthering Heights* about people coming in out of the stormy night, how welcome the house was, a refuge from the cold, a haven from the dangers on the highway. For her the opposite was true. Inside the house there was no air to breathe, and outside the house, the woods still held her father, as though he were still there, just beyond the nearest cedar, moving the crosscut saw back and forth to fell a giant fir, so that the wind carried the even scraping music of the saw, just out of earshot, to her across the meadow or on trails through the woods.

Joanna likes to watch TV in the evening. First Meg does yoga exercises. "Oh, look. Bobby Dylan!" Joanna says, smiling. "We met him at Iowa. What a good fellow he was!"

"I never listened to Dylan."

"How could you miss him?"

"Franklin didn't like him."

"But what about you?"

"I never argued."

"That's so unlike you."

"Unlike me now." Meg is uncomfortable in this conversation. "I missed a lot of things. Especially music. The kids were on to some of it. But Franklin wouldn't have their kind of music around."

Joanna has turned her full attention from the TV to Meg, her disbelief showing in her face.

"You know, from the beginning I thought he knew music and I didn't." Meg remembers accepting Franklin's rulings on the greatness of Beethoven, the elitism of Mozart, the magnificence of Wagner, the inconsequentiality of the Beatles and Bob Dylan. Meg continues her stretches. "It was my own fault." Meg stops stretching and turns to face Joanna. "I guess I thought wives supported their husbands…if he didn't want us to socialize with someone, we didn't; if he wanted to change his job, we moved again. We certainly never fought." And I numbed my own mind in deference to his, she thinks.

Joanna laughs, interrupting her. "Walter and I fought all the time. I mean *ALL* the time—"

"Well, we didn't. Not until Tim and Vietnam. Then I went into therapy and worked on everything and came out a feminist with my own mind and, I might add, my own BODY!"

Joanna smiles. "And a lively body it is, my dear!"

Starting to stretch again, Meg says, "It's like Rip Van Winkle—with twenty years vanished—twenty years when I was wrapped in some kind of noncombative self-inflicted acquiescent cotton—a kind of self-chosen retardation!"

"Not no more, you ain't!" Joanna leans over to poke her in the ribs, then smiles and says, "You know what Robert said today?" Meg shakes her head.

"I told him we're not going to put any curtains in the bedroom so we can enjoy the trees and sky outside. He was quiet for a minute, thinking about that. Then he said, '*My* wife wouldn't let me do that,' and we smiled at each other. He really understands about us, doesn't he?"

"Umhm, he does." Meg smiles at Joanna. "And he likes us too!"

"We are sure lucky to have found him."

***

The next day Meg is stomping around the yard looking for branches the February winds took down; she checks out the two jays by the woodpile, the woodpecker working his way up and down the broken off oak next to the house. That hurricane was almost twenty years ago, she thinks. Once Meg could think of each twenty-year span as a passing period in her life...always as passages that led her on. Childhood, parenting, teaching. When love relationships faltered and were lost, there was always the next cycle in which to try again. We two women are building this space for ourselves for this next cycle, she thinks with a smile. This present span of twenty years is my last turn, she thinks, watching a cardinal in quick flight—as quick, as brief, as beautiful as that! Knowing she does not truly believe for one minute even that time itself will ever abandon her, that she must ever forfeit life, that the cardinal might flash scarlet through rhododendron leaves without her witnessing.

All those earlier times are still inside me, she thinks. I wandered on the soft cedar loam of the deep woods when I was young, walked where I thought only deer hooves and moccasins had stepped before. Close to my father I explored, safe as I am now about to wander with Joanna, on the farm of my childhood that is now become the wooded yard around my present home.

Above, Meg notes an unusual silence and then a sound she does not recognize. She backs off from the concrete wall of the studio so she can see what is happening above her and then instantly pulls her little camera out of her pocket and lifts it to snap and snap and snap. They are lifting up the frame that is the outer wall of the upstairs room. Two men hold it up while Robert nails on supports. Then they move back to lift the southeastern wall. It rises like the wing of some great straight-boned bird starting its flight into the sky. Last, great smiles on their faces, they lift the final side, hammering, hammering, until every board is steadied by another, every side held up by every other.

Meg has never seen a house raised before. She had not comprehended that the crew was actually building walls. Looking up she can barely breathe. The frames rise against the green and brown of trees, the blue and cloud-white of the sky, like a new species of trunk and branch, a man-made phylum destined to exist devoid of leaves and even chlorophyll, static in shape and size, and yet somehow alive. "Our home in which to love, our place in which to work," she whispers, "this space we build in which to soar."

# CHAPTER THIRTY-FOUR

Joanna sits in the window seat on the plane to Boston, reading her Laurie R. King mystery. She glances nervously out from time to time at the dark storm through which they fly. She doesn't like flying any time but especially in winter she avoids it when she can. She agreed to come to this opening because Miranda, who runs this gallery, is wonderfully enthusiastic about her work and has included four pieces in this show.

"And now that you're in New York!" Miranda had exclaimed, as though Long Island were Cambridge and the gallery just down the road.

Oh Lord, Joanna thought, she'll be wanting me to travel all the time! "You know I like to stay home and work!" she answered.

"I know you do! And we're all glad you do because then we get all those wonderful new prints! But right now is the perfect time to come because your studio isn't up and running yet, is it?"

"No, it's not!" Joanna laughed. Miranda had cornered her. "I'll come, I'll come."

Nothing about the trip does she like. Not the crowds. Not the travel. Not the gallery talk-talk-talk. Still, if she has to attend a show, this is the best time. Nothing but chaos in Meg's house right now. "Our house," she corrects herself. Doesn't feel like our house, she retorts. Feels like I left my house in Oregon and am nowhere. Adrift without a place to work. The night crawler, crouched and clipping, flashes through her mind. Oh give it up, she chides herself. This is what I wanted. Meg. And a new studio. Yes, it is, idiot. Just hang on. It will all be fine. Joanna starts to read again and almost immediately begins to doze.

Waking, Joanna reaches for a cigarette, takes it out, breathes easier for its weight against her fingertips, puts it back, knowing where she is, knowing she can't actually close her lips on it, light it and inhale until she's off the plane. She looks down at her book, opens it to read. The familiar print reassures her. She reads slowly at first, letting the words shape themselves in her mind one by one, then opening herself to the flow of sentences, and then gratefully disappearing into the action of the scene where she remains until they have landed and taxied to the gate.

***

Surrounded by the rapid-fire chatter of the slightly drunk, avoiding the pretentious posturing of a pair of men in intense conversation as they lean close to a print, Joanna makes her way across the crowded carpet of the gallery. The improvised bar is two small tables set together, draped with a linen cloth, on which there is an array of hor d'oeuvres and soft drinks. Joanna cringes at the plastic cups stacked by the soda. The wineglasses however are truly glass and gratefully she pours herself some chardonnay from one of the cluster of bottles, empties her glass in three deliberate swallows, savoring the warmth as it drops into her like one of the decorative silver spirals that spin in the rising currents of warm air above the table. She refills her glass, ready to wander off again across the room.

Turning away from the table Joanna sees herself from the side and for a millisecond admires the lines, the scarlet markings on the silver jacket against the tight black slacks, the quiet elegance of the silver and turquoise earrings—the style of that woman—before realizing it is herself. Did it right, I did, she allows herself to think, with a slight smile.

"Joanna! How wonderful to see you!" Miranda, the gallery owner, gives her a good, warm hug. "Come meet someone who is starting a veritable collection of your work. I have to go put out more food! It's a good crowd! But first, here—"

Blushing, Joanna is introduced to a young woman with long dark hair, wearing long silver earrings and silver bracelets. No ring, Joanna notes and thinks, and that no longer matters now that I've found Meg.

"It's a real privilege to meet you," the young woman says. "And this—" pointing to Joanna's most recent print, walking over to stand in front of it— "this is extraordinary. Your work is so beautiful. I know lots of artists who do powerful pieces but to have the strength and the beauty in one work! And you have that every time!" She stops, looking somewhat embarrassed. "I'm sorry. You must hear this all the time. But it's such an honor to meet you."

Joanna shakes her head. "Thank you. No, I don't hear that very often!" She laughs. "There's a lot of silence to be heard, you know."

"Oh, I know."

"Are you an artist?"

"No. I'm on the faculty at Boston University."

Young to be a professor, Joanna thinks. "In the art department?"

"Oh no! I'm in history. Art is my private love, is all!"

"That's wonderful!" And your private private love? Joanna wonders. "Lived up here long?"

"Ten years. My partner is in the English department." The young woman has a flicker of anxiety as she lets the pronoun come into the light. "She's been here a long time. I came up from New York to be with her."

Joanna smiles broadly. "I just moved to New York to be with my lover. She's lived on Long Island for a long time!"

They both laugh with relieved delight. "That's wonderful. And where did you move from? Let's get some wine!"

***

Settling into her seat for the return flight, Joanna feels celebratory. She spent the night after the show with Miranda and her longtime partner, Hillary, in their new home in Newton. No lack of money there, she noted. Hillary is a tax lawyer. They had a pleasant dinner, catching up on one another's lives, and Joanna went to sleep early, tired from the long day. In the morning Miranda dropped her at the airport on her way to the gallery.

Joanna opens her book immediately and reads through take-off. Once they are safely in the air, she looks out the window. Today there is no storm and though she is still skittish about flying it's better to be headed home than out into the anxiety of the opening. The clear blue sky holds no alarm for her. Good to be going back to Meg after a breather, she thinks, and smiles as she considers what that means. I'm going home, she thinks, I'm going home to Meg.

# CHAPTER THIRTY-FIVE

After Mack has caught the school bus, Meg drops Dylan off at day care and goes to Shannon's apartment. She begins with the refrigerator. Half-melted popsicles and half-used TV dinners are mixed with unused hamburger and half-empty ice cream cartons in the freezer. Jars of applesauce with fuzz growing on top, rotten heads of lettuce and mildewed cucumbers from the drawer, and everything on the lower shelves goes straight into the garbage. How many times have I cleaned up a fridge before moving? Meg wonders.

This is, however, the first time Meg has dealt with pools of beer under the drawers and beer cans and bottles, empty, half-empty, shoved, stacked, dropped, everywhere. There are nearly empty wine bottles on the top shelf and in the very back of a lower shelf there is a half-full fifth of Seagram's lying on its side, hidden behind two stale loaves of sandwich bread spilling their hardened crusts along the shelf. She scrapes and scrubs until the muck is gone, and leaves a pan of baking soda to remove the last vestiges of the stench.

Meg sits on the back step in the sun. The back door hangs uneasily on its hinges, its once white paint shredded and peeling, leaving blotches of rain-streaked gray. The frames of the screens on the two windows are bent and there are holes in the rusty wire. The backyard consists of a rectangle of dirt with grass clumps here and there and a broken swing set. She can see where Mack has scraped flat spaces on which to stand his soldiers and there is still a red dump truck and a green steam shovel that Dylan was using by a pile of dirt.

***

At the house, the phone rings. Hoping for an Oregon voice, Joanna picks it up.

Mistaking her voice for Meg's, Shannon starts right in. "This place rots, Grams. It absolutely rots. And it's largely your fault that I'm here. I should've stayed in Ketchikan. You're not a criminal there just because you like a beer after work. If you weren't so—"

Joanna wedges in at last to say, "This is Joanna, Shannon. Your grandmother is out. I'll tell her you called," and she hangs up. Joanna writes a note for Meg: *Shannon called again.*

***

The next day Meg borrows Joanna's small radio so she can play classical music while she works. She cleans the stove in Shannon's place, scraping and scrubbing until it is like new. She empties out the kitchen cupboards, saving only unopened cans of soup, pitching the sticky jars of jam, the peanut butter jar left open on the shelf. She finishes just in time to go to meet Mack's bus.

The next day Meg stands in the center of the kitchen/living room at the apartment, immobilized by the debris that is stacked everywhere. The boys were sleeping on a single bed in the little bedroom. There are two bureaus wedged in between the bed and the wall, stuffed with clothes, Shannon's and theirs, clean and dirty, intermingled in every drawer. Shannon was sleeping on a filthy sofa that almost fills the living room. There is a shaky drop-leaf table, the leaf hanging crooked because one of the two hinges has been broken. There are four rickety straight back chairs, one of which has lost its back. There is a TV that works and a tape deck that doesn't, a filthy toaster oven and an automatic coffeepot. In the bedroom there is a cheap mirror on one wall and there are Beatles' posters everywhere. Meg sits at the table with a paper and pen. "You can do it," she says out loud. "Just take it one thing at a time." When the list is finished, she stands up and continues.

Meg locates the boys' clothes, pulling shirts out from under the sofa and little shorts from among the toys, piling them into pillowcases, taking them home to wash. At home, after they are clean, Meg separates them again, putting Mack's in the top two drawers of the bureau in the small guest room, and Dylan's in the bottom drawers.

Day after day Meg works in the apartment. She gathers Shannon's clothing, washes and dries it, and stores it in cartons in the garage at Liz's. She packs miscellaneous shampoos, cosmetics, jewelry, in a carton. There is one carton of books and papers, CDs and tapes. She fills two cartons with the toys and books she thinks the boys would most like to have. The other children's things she packs to store at Liz's.

She calls Shannon to ask if she wants her to bring by some of her clothing. "Never mind, Grams," Shannon says. "I'm not going to be here very long!"

Meg hesitates but can't help saying, "Give yourself time, Shannon. Everyone says it does take time. Don't—"

"Just shut up, why don't you?"

Meg wants to end on a friendly note. "The boys are fine," she says.

"Nothing about this is fine, okay?"

There's a clunk in Meg's ear as the line goes dead.

***

Several nights later Meg sits at the table, adding, dividing. The boys are asleep. Joanna is watching a mystery on TV. Finally Meg closes her account book, sets aside the little calculator, turns off the lamp and goes to join Joanna. She waits for an ad and then says, "I want to talk to you about the kids."

"Yes?"

It's like walking into the Sound on a cold October day. There's no way that won't be hard but once started she always makes herself go in. "I talked to a counselor today. They're thinking it will take Shannon months, not weeks."

Joanna doesn't speak but her lips tighten and the look in her eyes backs off.

"I can keep the boys here and feed them and get them a few clothes. But I really can't pay rent on an empty apartment."

"Shannon *can't* move in here when she's discharged!" Joanna's voice is laced with angry fear.

"No, of course not." Meg laughs her defensive laugh. "And Angie will help me come up with her first month's rent and the security when she gets out. What I'm saying is that I want to close down their old apartment in the meantime."

"What if Shannon can't get a job? You're going to carry all three?"

"No, no. Don't worry. She will get a job once she's sober. She's bright and quick. She'll probably start with some temp agency and move on from there."

The mystery starts up again and Joanna pays attention to it, then says, in an aside to Meg, "And the furniture?"

"She hasn't much. I think Liz has room for it in her garage."

Snapping off the TV, Joanna walks out of the room, pulling her pack of Virginia Slims out of her jeans pocket as she goes. "Whatever," she says.

Meg follows her to the deck. Joanna sits at the table, lights her cigarette, inhales. As the smoke trails up into the breeze and away, Meg sees Joanna disappear into another space, no longer close enough to kiss, to hold. "It's not a terrible thing, Joanna," Meg says, but her words fall flat into the space Joanna has already gone through, leaving an emptiness behind. "Joanna?"

"You'll do what you have to do, Meg. I'll manage."

"I'll talk to Shannon about it then." Meg walks away, turns back to add, "And I hope we'll do better than just manage—both of us!" But as she speaks, Meg knows Joanna is not hearing anything but the wind in the trees, not feeling anything but the silent comfort of the cigarette smoke within.

***

It's Joanna who goes to pee at five a.m. The bathroom light won't work. She comes back to phone, whispering, "Meg! He's here. I'm calling the police."

Meg jumps up and takes the two steps to the window. Outside it is just beginning to be light. The lamppost is dark. "He's not here now!" she says.

"I'm calling the police."

"He's not here now—look—no car, no man. No light."

"I'm calling anyhow."

Meg starts to restrain Joanna, but thinks better of it and turns away. Joanna gives her name and address and tries to explain the situation.

Meg pulls on her jeans and blouse, checks the boys who are sprawled asleep in the guest room, and goes out on the deck. The driveway stretches peacefully toward the street. The light in the lamppost will not go on. Back in the kitchen Meg turns to heat up the teakettle and curses, remembering that there is no current anywhere.

"They're coming right over," Joanna says, flushed, standing by the kitchen doorway, naked.

"You may answer the door," Meg grins, "exactly as you are."

\*\*\*

In about thirty minutes the police come, lights flashing in the driveway, but without a siren. "At least they let the neighbors sleep," Meg says, as they both go out to meet them.

"Actually it's the electrician that you need," the older policeman says, with a wry smile, shining his flashlight on the lamppost.

Joanna looks into the woods as though the perpetrator might still be hiding there. "I thought you might catch him as he left."

"We didn't see anyone anywhere around here. You think it's a neighbor kid?"

Clueless, this one, Meg thinks, answering him. "No, Detective Orenstein doesn't think that's it."

"You want us to look around before we go?"

"Thank you, that's a good idea," Joanna says politely, knowing only Meg will know it's a sarcastic answer.

"Glad to do that," the younger says, gallantly.

"Thanks again," Meg says, heading for the house.

\*\*\*

Joanna starts to turn on the coffeemaker, then remembers that they have no current. "Damn! Oh damn, damn damn!"

"Here. Let's use the camp stove." Meg rummages on a back kitchen shelf and pulls out her little one flame butane burner. "It'll heat up water anyhow. You'll have to settle for instant coffee though." She balances the teakettle carefully on the burner.

Joanna goes out on the deck, leans on the railing looking out, and lights a cigarette. Morning light is shafting through the trees. Meg follows her. "I don't suppose you could go back to sleep?"

"Absolutely not."

"I could," Meg says wistfully.

"Go ahead."

"Actually can't. The crew will be here in half an hour and Mack has a bus to catch."

"I wish you could figure out who's doing this."

"Me too."

"How's the yearbook search going?"

Meg shakes her head. "I don't think it's a kid." She goes back in to pour Joanna's coffee and her own tea. Bringing Joanna her coffee, Meg says thoughtfully, "Unless it's the skinheads, all grown up—but that was years ago—those kids wouldn't even remember me."

"Would they remember your anti-bias club?"

Meg smiles. "They might remember that."

"So tell the police."

"I told you that I did. I also told Detective Orenstein about Blake, but he doesn't have a record. This stuff is more fun when it's in your mystery books, isn't it?" Meg remembers Joanna's fear in the night and adds, "I'm sorry about all this, Joanna. I'm really sorry."

"It's okay, Meg. We'll catch the bastard yet."

"All right," Meg capitulates. "I'll go prowl the yearbooks some more. If anyone saw me carry that stack out they must have thought I'm having a pretty sad time of it!"

Joanna laughs. "You can say you're feeling nostalgic in retirement."

Meg giggles. "Want to come with me?"

"Sure. I could point out the type you're yearning for!"

Meg starts to laugh. "Right! The one with no hair and horns!"

"I'll say to the new principal, 'You don't mind, do you, if we do a short incantation? And 'Round about the cauldron go—'"

"'Double, double, toil and trouble—'"

"'With eye of newt!'"

"'And toe of frog—'"

Joanna's laughter escalates and does not stop as Meg joins her and the two of them bend over on the deck, their laughter tumbling down like ivy, spilling over between the rails.

Dylan stands at the sunroom door, watching them laugh. "Is Mommy coming to get me today?" he asks.

Meg shakes her head and goes to give him a morning hug and fix his cereal. "Or would you rather have a muffin?" she asks, as Robert's truck rattles up in the front of the house and the day begins.

# CHAPTER THIRTY-SIX

"They did it!"

"Did what?"

"Got the roof on and the walls up before a single drop of rain or flake of snow hit the open floor!"

"So now we can have a blizzard."

Meg pours their five o'clock glasses of wine, delivers one to Joanna and lifts hers high. "I'll drink to that!"

Joanna clinks her glass on Meg's and walks over to the connecting window. "C'mon! Let's go see." Meg holds both glasses while Joanna opens the window, climbs up on the chair they've parked there and crawls through. She reaches back to take the glasses while Meg follows her through the opening.

"Where are the kids?" Joanna blocks her path.

"Liz took them away for an overnight with Jonathan."

"Oh, blessings on you Liz!" Joanna smiles and walks out across the plywood.

Their treetop space under the open sky has been transformed into a room. The sun has already set and the vacant window frames let in only dim swaths of a twilight glow. Meg walks to the window and leans out, studying the long scaffolding the men have been standing on all day as they hammered up the outer siding. It dizzies her to think of walking out there, far above the ground. She pulls back into the safety of the inner space.

Joanna goes to the window frame and swings one leg out, "Shall I play Tarzan?"

"Don't you dare!" Meg grabs her arm and tugs her back into the room where, laughing, they embrace. They stroll up and down, checking the views out of each yawning window frame, which are sharply delineated now that the walls are solid and block out sections of the yard, now that the roof closes out the sky. The windows are just under four feet by four feet and look out on trees the way the windows in the sunroom do. When they have admired every angle, shivering in the cold evening wind, their glasses empty, they head back toward the kitchen.

Meg extends her arm to stop Joanna as she starts to climb through the window opening to the sunroom. She pulls her close and tries to give her a long, inviting kiss. Joanna breaks away, shaking her head, saying, "Not now, Meg—I really need my dinner."

Angrily Meg turns away to climb through the window. As she puts her foot down on the sunroom floor, she turns back to take their glasses from Joanna. "I know you don't like to talk about it, but—"

Joanna stops halfway through the window, knowing what's coming, a vacuum sucking her in. She wants to back out of the window frame and slam the window shut. She wants to stay out there, with a book and a cigarette and a glass of wine. Alone.

Meg is revving up her rational voice. Like an ice-encrusted snowdrift that's been slowly softening until the noon sun lays its rays across it, first glazing it, then turning every sparkle into a drop of water, causing the whole drift to lose its shape, to dissolve into a slowly softening crash—like that snowdrift, a part of Meg has been silent day after day. Like the sunlight the wine, their closeness, the joy of the new room, have prompted her to speak.

"I keep trying to figure out what's wrong," Meg says, walking through the sunroom to the kitchen. "Sometimes I think you just don't want to make love anymore."

Joanna makes a demurring noise in her throat.

Meg goes on without stopping. "You don't want to very often, Joanna." She pauses ever so slightly as though wanting Joanna to interrupt with some passionate disclaimer and goes on. "When you first got here I thought we'd have a honeymoon and maybe that pressured you—maybe I was dumb. I know it's hard for you with all the changes you're making and all the disarray here—"

Joanna looks down to avoid Meg's puzzled face studying her.

Meg again waits for her to speak and then goes on, "I keep thinking this is the same you and the same me and you like making love and I like making love and—" Meg pours the wine, gives Joanna her glass, lifts her glass to touch Joanna's in a toast and with an awkward smile, says, "To us, to love?"

"To us, to love," Joanna answers, her smile nicked by her embarrassment.

Meg stumbles on, the more insistently articulate for her doubt. "When we were visiting back and forth, we made love all the time. And it was wonderful! Remember?"

Joanna smiles and nods.

"So what's wrong then? I think you still love me. I know that I love you." Remembering their trip to Katonah, that morning in the motel room, she adds, "We can't go on trips all the time." Meg opens the refrigerator, takes out a head of lettuce, hamburger buns, frozen vegetarian patties, cheese. She sets these things on the counter, turns to look at Joanna.

"I do love you," Joanna says, looking away, wanting this conversation not to happen, having nothing to say, not wanting to hear the lines repeated. She knows what's coming, word for word, hears it sing-songing through her head: I never had this problem with my other lovers.

Other lovers. Other lovers. The words strike Joanna's flesh as though she has become a drum. Damn those other lovers. She wants to snap back, *So why did you leave those perfect lovers if they were so damned perfect?*

Meg is droning on. "I know your experience has been different than mine. I know you've never lived with anyone before."

Never lived with anyone? "Only twenty years!"

Joanna is splayed by a sudden sense of Walter, a palpable presence in the room. Walter, first glimpsed on a tennis court, first known as a graduate student, once a friendly and to be trusted pal, then an arrogant and betraying chameleon, one minute laughing with the kids, the next too drunk to have a conversation, one night tumbling Joanna in bed, the next night sneaking home in the middle of the night in an alcoholic haze laced with some pornographic guilt, fresh from a liaison with some stranger, leering at her as though they'd heard a dirty joke and he finds her too righteous to allow herself to laugh, as though the cold confusion in the room comes from her recalcitrance, not from his duplicity.

"I mean you haven't lived with a woman before—not full time." Meg is not pausing to wait for Joanna's rebuttal. She is delivering her tedious, well thought out speech. Joanna is glad. It means she doesn't have to rake the shoals of her own mind for words. She can take the speech the way she'd take a beating.

"What puzzles me so much is that it wasn't like this before. I mean, I'm not comparing you to other women. I'm comparing you to how you were before. You've changed."

Bedlam, Joanna thinks dryly, just might affect a person.

Meg pours a little olive oil in the pan, adds the onions she has sliced and two patties. She pours a dash of hot oil on Joanna's patty, a little soy sauce on both, and sprinkles them with garlic powder. She covers the pan and turns back to wash the lettuce and a tomato.

"I know it's been hard for you, all the confusion, having your things in cartons, not having anywhere to work." Meg spins the lettuce dry and starts chopping the tomato on the cutting board. Trying to be fair, Meg adds, "And the night crawler and Shannon do make it hard."

Joanna wants to scream and run away but there is nowhere to go. She takes slow steps away from Meg. "I'm going out on the porch for a few minutes," she says. They both know she needs a cigarette but she doesn't like to say it.

"Okay," Meg says. Her face crumples. Joanna flinches and heads for the porch.

"Don't you miss it?" Meg throws after her. Her voice trails off as Joanna opens the front door and enters the cold night air with infinite relief, leaving the words behind her like a flow of lava finally outrun.

Joanna settles with her book and cigarettes in the chair she painted blue one fine day last fall. She smiles ruefully, remembering her jaunty and determined work as, like a cat marking its territory, she proceeded to prune and clear, to fix and paint, after she moved to New York.

Joanna knows that sometime later Meg will make a reference to her earlier speech. It will be short: "It's just because I love you—you know that?" or "I think it will just take you time to get used to everything, that's all." And then, having reached some unilateral resolution that contents her, Meg will shut up and turn to the night's video. She won't be a dark mass of suppressed rage or snipe at Joanna all night long. She'll be her usual self. There's that. Once she's said her piece she doesn't point back to the text incessantly.

She remembers: In the car on the way home from church, her father says, as he does every Sunday afternoon, "There's Abner Mueller cutting back his hedge again. That man should go to church."

Joanna knows that Abner Mueller lives with a woman who is not his wife. Her mother has explained to her that they are both divorced but one divorce hasn't gone through yet. Joanna has an image of a tunnel, a kind of underpass below their street, where divorces roll through on wheelbarrows, and of one stuck under there, of Abner Mueller waiting to push it on through and out into the light so her father will stop complaining.

As Joanna turns back to her book, she is aware of their dilemma around sex. They are meeting infrequently in bed. It's getting worse. Meg's bed is wedged between her word processor where she writes and her closet. It reminds Joanna of the years when Walter was in graduate school and she was working to pay their bills, her art supplies packed away as they are here.

The apartment had been small and Walter's books and papers, coffee cups and beer cans, were everywhere, on every surface, on every square foot of floor. Their bed was not exempt. A bookcase, filled with seventeenth century poetry, was being used for a headboard. He kept a clipboard on the floor beside him at all times in case he thought of a note for his dissertation, which was on "The Interstices of the Ephemeral, the Literal, and the Transcendent in Metaphor in the Work of Robert Herrick."

"Want to die a little?" he said with an expectant smile, wanting sex.

Joanna laughed at the allusion to the metaphysical poets, and followed him, allowing him to do whatever occurred to him, hoping her own body would respond, as they fumbled together toward his orgasm in the bed where literary journals were crammed between the headboard and the mattress.

Desire seems to flow in Meg like a mountain river running to the sea: walk up to it, hold out your cupped hands, or lie down beside it and immerse your face to drink its pure clear waters. Joanna immediately loved this about Meg as she had about Rebecca in P-Town long before. During the first week Joanna was with Meg there were moments in the night when she turned toward Meg to make love to Rebecca and only if Meg spoke in her own voice did Joanna fully take in the time and place and know that Meg's breasts and thighs offered to her so naturally were not Rebecca's breasts and thighs, that the amazing flow of intensity, the flowering of orgasms, was happening in Oregon and not in Provincetown more than twenty years ago.

Joanna breathes deeply, her fingers delivering the small white cylinder to her famished self. How can I be her lover in this fucking chaos between an alcoholic kid and a maniac in the driveway? I can't enter her old lovers' bed like a marriage bed crammed in next to her papers and her books. This thought crosses Joanna's mind like a meteor, out of sight before she entirely recognizes it.

The cardinal that is at the feeder chirps and its mate takes flight. For just a second tears rise in Joanna's eyes. She takes off her glasses, gives her eyes one quick rub with the back of her other hand, puts her glasses on again and reads on steadily, smoke rising in a swirl past the short gray hair the winter wind stirs constantly on her quietly bent head.

"Suppertime," Meg calls.

***

While Meg is showering, Joanna thinks, so we have a night without the boys, and Meg wants attention. So okay. Yeah, she thinks. I'll fool her. I'll be on deck all right! She stands up, and turning off the TV, goes into the bedroom. She rummages in the closet and then in a carton on the floor of the closet. She grins and pulls out a heavy brown tool belt. She puts on the denim shirt Meg gave to her for Christmas and buckles the tool belt on over it. She stands in front of the long narrow mirror hanging by the door. Seeing her image, looking like a telephone worker ready to climb a pole, she laughs out loud.

When Meg comes into the room in her nightgown, Joanna is standing with her head tipped slightly up, hands on hips, pelvis thrust forward, with the tool belt snug against her waist. "Hey, woman! How's about a kiss?"

Meg does a double take and starts to laugh. "I don't even believe you!" she says, and then adds, raising one eyebrow, "Would you like me to put on lipstick before the kiss?"

Laughing, they tumble down together, pulling off one another's clothes.

# CHAPTER THIRTY-SEVEN

"Shannon, it would save a lot of money to just close down that apart—"

"Absolutely not, Grams! How long do you think I'll be in here anyhow?"

"I don't know, Shannon."

"Don't even think about that!"

Meg stands in silence by the phone after their conversation and then follows Joanna out onto the deck.

"I was afraid that this would happen." Joanna says as she leans against the railing, looking out down the driveway, and lights a cigarette. "What about the boys' father?"

"Shannon doesn't even know where he is."

"Liz?"

"Oh Joanna, Liz's got her hands full—and they're not her kids!"

"Not mine, either. And not yours, I might add. You'll go bankrupt."

"No, I'll give her a week to get used to the idea. I'm sorry about all this. But it won't be long and the kids are sweet—"

"Right," Joanna says with sarcasm. "And I'll see you after they leave—" She turns from the railing to face Meg. "It will be long—it'll be three or four months—rehab takes a very long time! If it works!" Joanna inhales deeply. "I guess it wouldn't help if I refused."

"I have to do it, Joanna. Her drinking puts the kids in danger. And I can't let them go to foster care—I can't." Meg watches the bluejay scolding on the limb of the dogwood.

"But you can sabotage my work space, compromise my living space, not to mention eliminating our sex life. I'm trapped here, you know. I could just forbid it. It's my house, you know."

"It's our house, Joanna." Knowing it's only rhetoric, Meg says, "I could go live in their apartment, I suppose. Want that?"

Joanna sizes Meg up carefully, smoke wafting in and out of her mouth, spiraling around her head. Then, as though she is a draft horse harnessed to pull a heavy load, she very slowly shakes her head. "No. I don't. Keep them here."

\*\*\*

The nude model is a young man. God, he's beautifully proportioned, Joanna thinks, edging her chair and easel closer before she begins to work. She has found a life drawing group. These two hours are her most joyous time of every week. While she works with her charcoal and her pencil, she is entirely consumed by her determination to make happen on the paper what nature has made happen in the flesh. Around her other artists work, chatter, curse. Unaware, Joanna keeps her focus. Each hidden bone, its contours hinted by the shaded skin, each muscle and tendon lifting the flesh in gently rolling waves, each curving shadow, compel her attention. Her hand accomplishes as her eyes survey. Nothing beyond this moment contains meaning.

\*\*\*

Meg goes into automatic mothering as though she'd never left it. Sitting on the bed, leafing through Mack's huge *Mammals of the World*, his current favorite at bedtime, reading him whatever sections he selects, reading Dr. Seuss books to Dylan after that, Meg feels herself within the order of the children's world. There is a certainty in her actions with them, as she feeds, escorts, clothes, puts to sleep. Their conversations flow like songs once daily sung, long put aside; knowing them by heart, she takes a quiet pleasure in singing them again. Tucking them in now, nudging Dylan's bear, Mack's manatee, snug against their arms, kissing each boy, saying goodnight, she leaves the room the way she'd leave a finished poem in the long-ago time when she still wrote poetry, savoring each line the way it lay, letting the words resound once more in her mind.

\*\*\*

A week later, Joanna is sitting on the deck, reading and smoking before dinner. Meg goes to join her. "Want to check out the upstairs room?"

"Sure."

They are just leaving the deck when the phone rings. It's Shannon's sponsor Claudia's Brooklyn voice. "She's left the facility."

Hearing the resignation in her voice, Meg knows neither of them is surprised. "Oh damn!"

"The kids are there with you?"

"Sure."

"She's likely to turn up after partying. Don't let her drive with them."

"Okay." Meg lets herself be talked through what may come.

"It's a cycle," Claudia says. "Give her a week or two. Let her find out that she can't leave the stuff alone. That's better than our telling her that she's not ready to be out yet."

Smart woman, Meg thinks. And how do we get her back in again? She doesn't ask out loud, knowing she knows some of the answers but isn't ready yet to spell her way through, still needs a script and will wait for Claudia to help put it in her hands.

\*\*\*

Getting Mack out for the bus the next morning, getting groceries on the way back from dropping Dylan off at day care, Meg is watching for Shannon's orange Chevy in her mirror and on the side streets as she drives. She expects it to be parked in her driveway when she pulls in. Only the builder's truck is in the street and when she hears another car approaching and looks up, it's only a pickup which parks behind the builder. A young man gets out and begins to march in and out of the wing, unloading big puffy squares of insulation. It begins to be an indoor house now, Meg thinks, the upstairs like a tree house but closed in and snug, the studio still hard to count as indoors because of its dirt floor. Should I call Shannon? Is she out drinking at a bar? Will she come, drunk, to get the boys and if so, what will I do?

***

Shannon does come at five o'clock while the boys are watching cartoons in the living room. Meg hears the Chevy in the driveway and goes out on the deck to call down hello. Shannon looks up with a grin. "Hi. I brought us pizza. Okay?"

"So come on in."

She comes up and into the kitchen. "I'm working again. I'll drop them off and arrange the bus change on my way to work in the morning." Shannon sets the pizza boxes on the kitchen counter, talking fast, before Meg has a chance to speak.

The boys have heard Shannon's voice. Dylan comes tumbling through the doorway, grabbing for her legs. Noting that she's sober and has a carton of Coke, not beer, in her hand, Meg nods. "Sounds like a plan."

Mack calls, "Hi, Mom." Mack's mad at her, Meg thinks.

Shannon walks, swinging Dylan, who has planted himself on her feet, in front of her, into the living room. "Brought'cha pizza," Shannon says to Mack.

"Big deal," Mack says.

"Mad, huh?"

"You didn't tell us you were going anywhere."

"I'm sorry, Mack."

"Mommy," Dylan asks, still standing on her shoes, "are you back home?"

"Yeah, kiddo, I'm home. Now who's for pizza?"

After they've eaten, Shannon says, "Get your jackets, fellows. And your pajamas and your bear and manatee and whatever you need for school, Mack. I'll need to borrow sheets and towels, Grams. And I'll come over tomorrow after work to get some of their clothes, okay?" She goes into the bedroom to pack up their things.

Meg knows there's no point in arguing. She figures she'll take a deep breath and hold it for as long as it takes. "Sure. And whatever else you need."

As Shannon's car pulls out of the driveway, Joanna shakes her head.

"I know," Meg says. "But let's enjoy an all-adult evening anyhow."

***

"It would help to have more space in the kitchen," Joanna says thoughtfully, after breakfast.

"We could put cupboards up along this corner wall," Meg answers.

"Do you think Shannon will stay sober?"

"She's gonna try."

"So let's go to Home Depot and see what we can find."

They range up and down the aisles where Joanna finds an additional medicine cabinet for the old bathroom and cheap shelving for the basement so they can store extra canned goods and paper towels, toilet paper, napkins, freeing the small kitchen cupboards of their overflow. "I can put those up myself," she says. They also find disassembled cabinets for the kitchen wall. "We'll need a carpenter to hang these for us though."

"Let's ask Robert. Maybe one of the crew would do it."

The next day, when the men have gathered in the studio for lunch, Meg leaves the bills she's working on spread out on the table and goes to see what's happened in the upstairs section of the wing. The tub and toilet are in place and the walls are already halfway lined with thick, puffy panels of insulation. Meg goes to find Joanna who is pounding up shelves in the basement.

"Oh, God, it's going to be wonderful to have more space!"

"Thank you for doing that!" Meg says, realizing yet again how claustrophobic the crowded jumble in the house makes Joanna feel. "They've put in the plumbing in the bathroom—have you looked?"

"No!" Joanna leaps up and they go back, through the window, to check it out. "What's that?" Joanna lets out a yelp, pointing to the toilet.

Meg looks again and sees a strange concrete block set around the base of the bowl. She hadn't noticed it before. "I don't know," she says, appeasingly, feeling somehow responsible.

"Well, it's got to be changed!"

Meg's stomach knots at the outrage in Joanna's voice. "Talk to Robert about it," she says.

Joanna is off, back through the window, and down the stairs, out and around to where the workers are sitting with their sandwiches. Meg goes back to the table and continues writing checks. Her body tenses over the tenor of the conversation taking place below. After a while Joanna returns. "We'll have to get tile."

"Tile?"

"Instead of linoleum for the bathroom floor. If we use linoleum they have to mount the toilet bowl on that ugly block. That's code. It has to do with structural damage from water on the floor. But no one ever told us that. Come look at it again!"

Meg follows Joanna and they stand, studying the odd base of the toilet bowl. "Not too attractive, hmm?" Meg says, apologetically.

"I'd say so! Okay with you if we get tile? It'll cost more but we can't live with this!" Joanna knows Meg will agree but she waits for an answer.

"Sure. Tile is fine." Meg knows Robert won't like to rip up this block but she can see there's no other way to go. Joanna hates the ugly block. Meg realizes she hadn't thought about the bathroom floor. She herself doesn't like linoleum. Originally Joanna had chosen it to save money and she'd concurred. Now Meg doesn't like to inconvenience Robert and knows if she were handling this alone she wouldn't insist that they make the change. "They won't like to take the toilet out and put it back again but there's no way around it, I guess."

"I guess not! I'll ask where we go to get the tile."

"The plumber will have to cut the pipes again when he reconnects the toilet."

"So he'll have to deal with that. This looks like the toilet in a public restroom at Jones Beach!"

It does. Meg laughs. She is simultaneously concerned about the builder's reaction to ripping out the block and relieved that Joanna has fought the issue through so that they will be spared the ugliness of the rough chunk of concrete.

# CHAPTER THIRTY-EIGHT

Hearing the familiar squeaking of the mail truck, Meg walks to the end of the driveway to take letters from the box. As though mud has sloshed against the post, purple paint has been sprayed up and down the post and all over the metal box. Staring at it, thinking it's not Halloween—Meg sees the blurred words, DIE DYKES, scrawled across the side where she and Joanna have spelled out their names with little square stick-on tags from the hardware store.

"Goddammit," Meg mutters and heads for the garage where she finds an old rag and a can of turpentine. She forgets to get gloves and the turpentine stings her fingers as she scrubs fiercely at the paint, first smearing it to blot out the words, then working to get off the paint.

The swastikas, she remembered, had been carved into the desk. Meg found the custodian and asked him to sand them off. The boy who sat there didn't deny he did it. "I just like its shape is all. I don't even know what it means."

He knew all right, she thought. The next day she spent the whole class time on symbols and their meanings, respect and hate. He sat quietly, his attentive seriousness concealing a cocky smirk.

What the hell was his name? When the box is fairly clean, Meg gauges the amount of time it would take to do the post if turpentine will even work on wood and decides to do that another time—when she will remember to wear gloves. Putting the rag and turpentine away, she thinks she won't tell Joanna. It'll just scare her more, she thinks. You have to tell her, she answers back. Not today though. She scrubs her hands and muses, with a wry smile, that Joanna will ask about the smell of turpentine. Then you will have to tell.

***

While Joanna is out at the post office, Meg calls Detective Orenstein. "Now do you believe me that the wire cutter is committing a hate crime?"

"How do you prove the same guy did it?"

Meg's astonishment keeps her silent for a moment and then they share a bemused laugh before they go on with the conversation.

"Actually it may be good." The detective chuckles. "He may get careless. He needed some kind of light to paint the mailbox and it's out in the open—right? Not hidden up the driveway. Have you alerted your neighbors?"

"The ones next door. I guess I should talk to the rest of them." Which won't be such an easy thing, Meg thinks. Easier than telling Joanna about the mailbox—I'll tell the neighbors about the wire cutter instead. And that's enough.

***

"We could take turns standing guard," Sue says, passing the bread around the table. Everyone laughs uncomfortably.

"I don't do guns," Mary says, "and neither does Fern."

Fern, a tall, heavy therapist, with short, wavy gray hair, gives her a playfully defiant look. "Says who?"

Meg laughs. "I do begin to see why women buy guns."

"Petey had a rifle." Sue's new partner, Yvonne, a slender blonde with shoulder length, wavy hair, says this quietly.

A waiting silence goes around the dinner table. Meg, to break it, says in a mock therapeutic tone, "Want to tell us more about that,

Yvonne?" We're in a strange domain, she thinks, checking to see if anyone needs more chicken. The words we have don't fit.

"It was in West Virginia. I went there to teach art in a country school. Petey was teachin' there. About the third year Petey and I rented a house together on the side of a mountain. It was rugged country. Absolutely beautiful."

Sue has told Meg and Joanna that Yvonne's lover, Petey, died of cancer ten years ago. Meg has never before heard Yvonne talk about her. Yvonne's voice softens when she says her name.

"There was a trailer camp pretty nearby. You could hear them partyin' whenever you drove down the road at night. Sometimes they'd come chargin' up our road in their pickups, yellin' and all." Yvonne glances around the table, lifts her glass to take the last sip of her wine. Meg leans forward to refill her glass.

"So they started parkin' at the end of our road. It was a dead-end and they'd line up three or four of their vehicles and stand around, drinkin' and carryin' on. Petey figured there might be a problem so she came home one night with a rifle and a box of ammo, and she put a sardine tin in the fork of a birch out front and started practicin'. She'd been in the WAAC's before she started teaching, you know."

Her Georgia-softened voice goes on. "One evening after supper we hear a pickup clangin' by and then another and another. Pretty soon we hear 'em shoutin' and laughin' and the noise keeps gettin' closer. They're comin' up our driveway. Lucky starts barkin' and whinin' to go out. Petey doesn't even look out the window. She just picks up her rifle, which she keeps loaded in the corner of the kitchen, and walks out the door. 'No,' she says to Lucky, 'stay! Keep her inside,' she says to me, and closes the door on her way out."

Everyone at the table is listening intently. Sue puts her arm on the back of Yvonne's chair, and Meg knows she wants to give her a hug but has to wait for the story to be finished.

"I run over to the window. I'm so scared I'm shiverin'. There're five or six rednecks stragglin' up the driveway. The one in the lead's a six-footer with a Bud in his hand. 'Hi, honey,' he yells, and they all keep walkin' toward the house, drinkin' as they come. 'Wantuh party tonight?'

"'No, thank you, sir,' Petey says.

"'C'mon, let's have a little fun. We'll treat, won't we, fellas?' They all guffaw and nod and they all keep on walkin'.

"Petey just stands there, right off the porch, between them and the house, and they keep comin'. I think if I call the sheriff he can't get there for a good half hour and that's only if he thinks there's any need which he likely won't.

"Petey says, in a clear, low voice, but loud enough that I can hear her, even though her back's to me in the house, 'I'm askin' you all to go back home now. We're teachers down in town and we don't want trouble.'

"And I'm thinkin' they're way too drunk to care, and I watch 'em gettin' closer and closer to her. Then the first guy throws his beer can high and wide into the woods and laughs a really ugly laugh and kinda lunges in her direction.

"Petey lifts her gun and points it right past him at her old sardine can. She fires and hits the can: *PING!* Her rifle holds eight shots. 'Now leave,' she says. 'I'm not foolin'. I'm just politely askin' you all to take your beer and your pickups and go do your partyin' somewhere else.' And she fires another shot that went *PING!* on the sardine can again and then she swings the barrel over a bit and points it right at him.

"The guy stops dead in his tracks and stares at Petey. It's like he's never even seen her standin' there before. He takes a long, slow look. She doesn't waver in the slightest. I can see her shoulder with the rifle snuggled right against it and she's steady as a rock.

"I was shiverin' and sweatin' at the same time."

Sue nods. "Been there, done that," she says softly.

Sue served in Vietnam and got a medal for evacuating babies from an orphanage under fire. Meg has read about it in a manuscript Sue is working on. Meg sends Sue the slightest smile in acknowledgment.

"I was so scared," Yvonne says, quietly, to Sue. Then she remembers the rest of the women at the table and goes on.

"They all stop and look at Petey and look back at the can on the birch branch. They look bewildered, like they don't know whether to be mad or what. Then one of them guffaws and yells, 'Yuh gonna let the cunt get away with that?' and they all start up with the hoots, yellin' at him to take care of Petey, eggin' him on.

"He lets out a 'Fuck you, bitch!' and takes two steps toward Petey.

"She sends a shot that rips right through his jacket. He freezes and looks down.

"'Next time it's you, not your mackinaw,' she says.

"He takes hold of the bottom of his jacket with his right hand and pulls it out from his body, studyin' what must be a hole right through it. He shakes his head. 'Okay, fellows,' he says. 'I guess these dykes ain't in the mood to party.' And he turns around with a funny kind of hootin' laugh and they all turn around together like they're marchin' in a platoon and they walk back to their trucks, laughin' louder and louder, so that it sounds like they're comin' closer but they're not.

"Petey waits until the first truck revs up and guns off and then she carefully reloads her gun and comes back inside the house, sets it back in the corner of the kitchen, pats Lucky a few times, and takes me in her arms for a real good hug."

There's a long silence at the table. Mary has tears in her eyes and Meg thinks probably everyone else does too.

"To Petey," Sue says, lifting her glass.

"To Petey," everyone echoes and the candlelight glints on the glasses as they click against one another.

They spend the evening around the table in the sunroom since there is not room in the living room for everyone to sit around the fireplace, as Meg likes her company to do when it's cool. They have wandered through the house, admiring again Joanna's prints that Meg has had hanging for a year, and some have seen for the first time the beautifully carved bench and chair and assorted carved bone pendants that Joanna brought with her. They gathered back at the table for coffee and dessert.

Joanna suddenly leaps up to check out the driveway from the deck. Everyone goes silent, watching her, listening themselves. She comes back in, closes the door. "I hate it! I'm always hearing branches crackle or a car go by and I think it's him again!"

"Sure," Mary says. "My God! I'd never sleep!"

"I don't!" Joanna says, half-laughing.

Sue stands, squaring back her shoulders, looking like she's still in the military. "I'm good at guard duty! Hup! Two! Three! Four!"

Everyone laughs as Yvonne says, "At ease, Sarge!"

Sue grins and circles back to her question earlier in the evening. "Seriously, would you like us to take turns sleeping over?"

Meg and Joanna both shake their heads. "Thanks, but we're fine," Meg says. "Really. We just call nine-one-one."

"We know it by heart," Joanna says, and their ongoing laughter rises in bursts like puffs of smoke, drifting up through the still bare branches of the oaks.

# CHAPTER THIRTY-NINE

As though in a film she's seen before, Meg answers the phone and hears Shannon's not-quite-sober voice asking her to pick up the boys after school and keep them for the night. It's less than a full month since Shannon signed out of rehab and took back the boys.

"Where are you?"

"I have to work late, Grams. I hate to bother you, but could you just get Dylan from day care? Mack's bus takes him home. But he's locked up. No key. Okay?"

"Shannon." Meg's need to keep the boys safe overrides all else. "Yes, I'll get the boys but where—"

Before she can go on to question Shannon further, Shannon has said, "Thanks," and hung up.

Meg leaves a note for Joanna who is out on errands, looks in the refrigerator, decides on pizza, checks her watch and heads for the apartment to meet Mack. She gets there before the bus has dropped him off and uses the key Shannon gave her long ago to unlock the door. She sits at the table, where there are jars of peanut butter and strawberry jam beside an open loaf of bread. Observing the disarray: clothing scattered here and there on the floor, dirty paper plates and glasses everywhere, the sink unusable because of the piled up cups and silverware sitting in stale dishwater, and beer bottles scattered around, Meg goes to check out the refrigerator. Feeling uncomfortable about spying, she sees cheese, butter, sliced ham, pickles and behind the cartons of milk and orange juice, a bottle of gin. Two half-empty six-packs of Bud fill the bottom shelf. Hearing the bus squeak to a stop, Meg closes the refrigerator and goes to meet Mack at the door.

"Hi, Mack! How about pizza and a sleepover?"

Mack nods with a half-smile. "Where's Mommy?"

"I think she had to work late."

He shares her disbelief but doesn't say so. Together they pack up his manatee, Dylan's teddy bear, and clean school clothes for the morning. "Toothbrushes," Mack says.

"You have some at my house," Meg reminds him, groping for Dylan's pajamas in the jumbled bedding.

"Oh, right."

"Let's go get Dylan."

Outside the day care center, Meg swings Dylan around three times before helping him into the car and strapping the safety belt.

I'm a polar bear with two little cubs to snuggle again, Meg thinks. Now how do we get their mother to hibernate until she's well? And Joanna will not be pleased!

The boys have had their baths but aren't in bed yet when Shannon calls. This time she is clearly drunk. "Need a ride, Gramsokay?" she slurs.

"Where are you?"

"Where'shis place?"

Meg can hear her asking and trying to repeat the name and street address. "Are you in Commack, Shannon? On Jericho in Commack?"

"Gimme a ride? My car's at my house, Grams. We can go get it."

"But what's the name of the bar?"

Shannon finally tells her.

"I have to go find her, Joanna. Will you watch the kids?"

"Why go?"

"Oh, come on. She'll get hurt out there."

Joanna considers for a moment. "I guess I will," she says.

"Thanks. I don't know how long I'll be."

***

Meg finds Shannon sitting, smoking, on some concrete steps that lead into the bar. Meg pulls up beside the curb and honks. A man in a parked car ahead of Meg's is beckoning Shannon to join him. Shannon's laughing and shaking her head at him. He holds a beer out his window toward her and she stands up, taking a few steps in his direction, as Meg gets out of her car and calls, "Shannon!"

Shannon looks back and forth between them. "You've got beer at home," Meg says instinctively. "C'mon. Let's go."

"Stop at the 7-Eleven, Grams, please," Shannon says, getting into the car, opening her purse and counting change.

"Umhm," Meg says, willing to say anything to get her in the car, driving away, thankful to be safely on the road with her.

"I need a cup of coffee."

"I'd like to get you home, Shannon."

"C'mon, Grams, 7-Eleven." She points ahead.

"We can stop at McDonald's."

"No."

"Shannon, you don't need a beer right now."

"Then just let me out, okay?" Shannon starts to open the door.

"Shannon. Stop it!" Meg hits her door lock button. "Okay, I'll stop at the 7-Eleven."

Shannon disappears into the store. Meg studies the beer ads plastered to the windows. She hadn't realized six-packs were so cheap; anyone with ten bucks could get drunk. She sees Shannon approach the counter, six-pack in hand, pay and come back to the car. The minute she sits down she pops open a can and takes a long, quick drink.

Meg says nothing. She backs her car out of the parking place and heads for Shannon's. Meg recognizes that she can't have a sensible conversation with Shannon. All she can do is get her safely to her apartment. Then I'll go home and figure out what next, she thinks. I'll call her sponsor. Claudia might know what to do. Meanwhile, just watch the road and mumble "umm" now and then while Shannon tells stories about the people in the bar.

\*\*\*

"Want popcorn?"

The two boys look up at her and nod. Joanna looks around the little kitchen for a popper and gives up. She takes out a deep pan with a lid, the corn oil, the can of popcorn from the shelf, the butter and the salt, knowing the boys are watching every move.

"She's making it," Mack tells Dylan.

Joanna realizes they have never seen that done. "Yes," she says, smiling. "You can watch but stay back. Sometimes the oil spatters."

When the oil is hot, she pours the popcorn in. The sizzling noise gradually escalates and the kids slide away from it through the door into the sunroom. When the popping starts the boys come back into the kitchen, puzzling.

"It'll be ready soon. I'll let you put the butter on."

When the popping stops, Joanna carries the pan to the table in the sunroom and pours it out into a big bowl. She hands the small pan of melted butter to Mack and the saltshaker to Dylan. "Climb up on the chairs and do the job," she says.

They sit in the living room watching the gorillas on the Discovery Channel while they're eating it. "Can I have a drink?" Mack asks.

He thinks there might not be any in the house, Joanna thinks, going to get glasses and the big bottle of apple juice. "Here you go," she says, pouring, thinking, Shannon should be shot.

*\*\**

When Meg comes in the boys are asleep already. Meg sees the popcorn remnants on the kitchen counter, smells the popcorn in the air. "That was nice of you," she says, smiling at Joanna.

"It's none of it their fault," Joanna says, going out to sit on the deck.

Meg finds the number of Shannon's AA sponsor in her address book under Shannon's name.

Claudia's voice is Brooklyn warm and tough. "With Shannon, it's the kids…"

"And?"

"Everyone has something that matters most. With Shannon, it's the kids. Sometimes it's people's jobs—then the boss says, 'Do rehab or you're fired. No more airplanes for you to fly.'" Claudia laughs, pauses. Meg can hear her lighting a cigarette and breathing it in before she speaks again. "Let's call the Child Protective bunch."

"Shannon would never hurt the kids! She's a wonderful mother—" Meg blurts out.

"—Yeah! When she's sober." Claudia gives a curt laugh. "She doesn't want to give up on the kids. Let's use that to bully her into rehab."

"How does that work?" Meg asks, and listens, keeps herself from arguing, holds back from diving in to rescue Shannon, knows that would be a phony save.

Feeling a vague vertigo, Meg goes to find Joanna on the deck. "I think I have to blackmail Shannon into staying in rehab," Meg says, half-sure.

"How so?"

"By threatening to let the Child Protective Agency take the boys."

"Can you do it?" Joanna shakes a cigarette out of the pack, slowly lights it, looking reflectively at Meg.

Meg stops herself from snapping back an answer and then says softly, "I don't know."

"Why don't you call Sarah?"

"Too late."

"Not in California, it's not."

Meg hesitates. She keeps in close touch with Sarah, her old therapist, but not usually to ask her advice. "I'll think about it," she says, and goes to take a shower.

With the hot water soothing her tired bones, she runs through the whole event. Sarah will say to be tough. Sarah will say to cave in now will mean she will have not only Mack and Dylan, but a drunken Shannon on her doorstep all the time, and she will lose Joanna, who did not move across the country to deal with all that shit. Okay, Meg thinks, so can I stand firm with Shannon, can I threaten her with losing the kids? I couldn't ever really let them go to foster homes. I couldn't, Sarah.

After the shower Meg forces herself to dial Sarah. It's only seven o'clock there, she thinks. Sarah herself answers. "So call in the marines, sweetheart. Get someone from Child Protective Services to be there with you."

"But I don't want them to take the kids."

"Don't tell Shannon that. Don't sabotage this, Meg. I know how hard this is for you. But you and Joanna have a right to have a life."

"What if the social worker won't let me have the kids back?"

"Oh, Meg! Any judge will send them home with you. But get Shannon inside the rehab first."

Meg is quiet. She feels her resistance pulling her back. She doesn't want to call Child Protective Services. She absolutely does not want to do that. She wishes she had not called Sarah. She feels herself nodding to Sarah as she extricates herself from the phone call. "So how are things with you in the sunshine..."

"Meg," Sarah interrupts her. "You don't have to be afraid of doing this. The kids are entitled to a good mother. Shannon is entitled to help in fighting her addiction. And you're entitled to have a life with Joanna."

"I know," Meg mumbles. She wishes they were in the same room. The phone line stays silent for a while. This is an old story between Sarah and herself. Finally Meg breaks the silence. "It feels like I should rescue Shannon, not lose her."

"Right. But this *is* the way to rescue Shannon. It *feels* to you like you are abandoning her. You *are* pulling away. You *are separating* from her. That's true. And that feels wrong. But this time you can't trust your feeling. This time you have to enable her to stand on her own two feet and decide to choose sobriety. Separately from you. You'll get her back again later but she will be independent, like Angie, like Liz. Trust her, Meg, give her a chance."

Meg goes out on the deck to think it through. She wishes there were others to circle in with her. She's mad at Joanna for being so separate. Then she remembers that Joanna hasn't even been in her life that long and that Shannon is not hers in any way. Can't expect her to adopt that kind of trouble. She made the boys popcorn, didn't she? Meg smiles at that. I'll call Angie. I'll call Liz. But I can't ask Liz to be in on this.

***

"It's time for a confrontation, Angie. Any chance you could join us by phone?"

"We're leaving at dawn for this fieldwork in the Aleutians, Mom. This is what we've been getting ready for! This is IT!"

Meg sees Angie in a furry hooded jacket ducking her head into the thick spray of snow kicked up by her dogsled team as they pull her across the glacier. Incongruously, Angie says, "I can send you some money to help feed the kids. I'll send you a check tonight."

"You take care. Stay safe."

"I will. So you will call the Child Protective Service? Don't hesitate, Mom. It's the only leverage you've got. Use it."

"I will, Angie. It's hard is all."

"I wish I could be of more help, Mom. I really do."

"I know you do."

And I don't blame you for being far away, Meg thinks, remembering. Angie and Tim were always a pair, tuned in on one another as though they were twins. When Tim died in Vietnam, Angie bolted; like a hurt animal, she ran away to gnaw her wound alone, to let the ice and snow cauterize the gash. In time she generated a new life in Alaska, the farthest place she could find, where there were mountains and blizzards, cliffs and forests, and no abandoned bicycle leaning unused in the garage to scrape her heart raw day after day.

"Angie, do be careful, hear?"

"Hey, Mom, don't worry. My ice floes are safer than your freeways!"

They both laugh. Hanging up, Meg feels better for having Angie's blessing for this assault on Shannon. Still, numbers would help, she thinks. Shannon needs to be bombarded by voices from all sides. Too bad there's not an employer who knows the score and cares. My voice is too reasonable. I don't know how to threaten. Okay. There's Claudia. There's me. I will call Liz.

Back on the porch, trying to figure out the logistics of confronting Shannon—at her apartment? Where? Meg hears the phone and runs in to answer, thinking it might be Claudia again.

It's Shannon using her one phone call from the precinct. She must have driven out after I left her, Meg thinks. She says that Meg can come bail her out in the morning in the courthouse in Hauppauge. The pay phone cuts her off but Meg knows Shannon will be confident that Meg will be there, ready to sign, ready to rescue.

"On condition that you go to rehab right now!" Meg starts to practice her speech, relieved Shannon will be locked up, under guard. It will feel safer to give her an ultimatum there. Ashamed of her own cowardice, Meg goes into the kitchen to wait for Claudia to call back to give her a name and number, to help her set things up.

The phone has awakened Mack who comes out for a drink of milk and a cookie. Meg gets it for him. He smiles at Meg as he sits at the table. Big brown eyes. So like Angie. Meg smiles back and like a grace note interposing grief: so like Tim.

***

This is surreal, Meg thinks, as she walks up the long courthouse stairway. The flag is blowing in the April wind. At least the kids are in school, Meg thinks, realizing that she is already thinking like a mother from the minute she wakes up. Around her lawyers dressed for court with their briefcases in hand march up the steps. Kids in sagging jeans lean against the outer wall, smoking, drinking Cokes. Worried women, like herself, walk slowly up the steps.

At the top of the stairway a thin blonde in a maroon dress, wearing dangling silver earrings, bright lipstick and carefully applied mascara, grinds out a cigarette beneath her high heeled shoe, and waves. Meg keeps on walking until she hears Claudia's voice call, "Hey, Grams!" and realizes who she is. Not the motherly woman Meg had envisioned as Shannon's sponsor but a sharply dressed young woman who could be Shannon's older sister.

Laughing, Meg says, "Oh, hi! I didn't recognize you!"

Claudia laughs back. "No problem! I'd know you anywhere!" Together they walk through the revolving doors into the giant lobby.

"You got hold of Madeline at Child Protective Services?" Claudia asks.

"Yes." Meg looks around the lobby, spots a young Black woman with extended scarlet fingernails and a leather jacket, thinking she must actually be more than the eighteen she seems, coming toward them from the door into the courtrooms where they'd agreed to meet.

"Madeline Smith," she says, holding out her hand. "You're Meg?"

As Meg says hello to her, Liz comes into the hall and joins them. "Can we talk with Shannon before she's in the courtroom?" Meg asks.

"I'll ask the bailiff," Madeline says.

Is Madeline somehow in charge of these proceedings, Meg wonders, as she, Liz and Claudia follow her into the courtroom where the rows are half-filled with people waiting to bail out their parents, children, spouses. There is some subdued conversation. Meg sits in a seat by the door, watching as the social worker leans over the bailiff's desk. They are both young, Black, competent-looking women. They look across the room at Meg, nod to one another, and Madeline motions to Meg to come with her.

The guard lets the four of them come inside the door on the left, unlocking it for them to enter and locking it again behind. They go down a hall and into a little conference room. Shannon is brought in, looking like Shannon only not. Meg studies her. Something about her is like an imitation. Perhaps it is her smile, her liveliness, stamped with fatigue and a kind of elusive despair, Meg thinks, as though the place itself costumes and so disguises her by putting her on its stage.

"Hi, sweetheart," Meg says with a big smile, giving her a hug.

"Oh Grams, this is a mess, isn't it?"

Meg watches her check out the others. When she sees Liz, Shannon is surprised. "Hey, Liz," she says.

"Hi, Shannon," Liz answers, smiling. It's her forced smile though, Meg notes. What do you expect? She's entitled to be mad at Shannon.

"Grams has a proposition for you, Shannon," Claudia says quietly, pre-empting Madeline who was obviously about to speak.

"You're bailing me out, right?"

Meg wants to reassure her instantly, rout the terror that is in her eyes. She pushes her palms against the wall behind her and keeps still. Claudia rescues her.

"She'll bail you out, kiddo, but after you tell the judge you're ready to be taken to rehab."

"*Go back to that fricking place? No way.*"

There's warmth in Claudia's voice but there's an impatient edge along with it. "It's the only way, Shannon. C'mon! You know that yourself."

"Look, Claudia, I'll do the ninety meetings in ninety days, okay? I know I blew it. I'll be serious about it this time."

"It's too late for that route."

Shannon's glance is taking in the room, the window too high up to use for a way out, Meg, Liz, Claudia, the guard just outside the door. She ignores the young social worker with the bright red nails.

"Look, I'll sign a contract. Ninety in ninety. And if I don't do it, you can lock me up yourself!" She smiles whimsically at Claudia as if they are co-conspirators.

Meg wants to yield to the offer but knows better. She adds her voice to Claudia's. "You have to go back and stay this time, Shannon."

Shannon gives them all a defiant glance, intending to win by a new capitulation: "So I'll just serve the fucking ten days or whatever the damned judge gives me!"

"It's not that simple, Shannon." Madeline opens her briefcase the way a judge pounds a gavel. "We have the authority to remove your children from your care."

"Who are you?" Shannon explodes.

"I'm Madeline Smith. I'm here from Children's Protective Services. If you don't choose to rehabilitate yourself, we have a court order to remove—" She looks down at her paper for the names— "Mack and Dylan—"

"*NO FUCKING WAY YOU DO!*" Shannon leaps out of her chair in rage.

The guard in the hall opens the door and steps inside. Claudia grabs Shannon's shoulder, pushing her down into the chair. "Let's talk this through."

"Aren't Mack and Dylan at your house, Grams?" Shannon turns the frightened eyes of a cornered animal to Meg.

For the first time there is a silence. It works its way around the room like dust motes in the dim light. "Yes," Meg says, "and they're—" But before she can go on to reassure Shannon, which she knows she shouldn't do, Claudia interrupts.

"And they can stay there *IF* you go back to rehab and stay and do it right this time. It's the kids that matter, Shannon. You know that." There's a rock-bottom sureness in Claudia's voice. She understands Shannon, Meg thinks, loves the good-hearted tough kid that's done right by Mack and Dylan until now.

Shannon is staring at Claudia.

Claudia puts her hand lightly on Shannon's arm. "Don't quit on them."

"Right," Liz says quietly, almost to herself.

"Yes, we'll allow that," Madeline says.

Shannon is silent, examining the trap. She crosses her arms in front of her, runs her fingers up and down her upper arms as though tracing a pattern of bruises. Her body is clenched forward as she thinks, her eyes turning again to the one narrow window high up in the wall, gauging the world she can glimpse beyond the smoke-stained pane.

Claudia studies Shannon. "This is for real, you know. It's your chance, Shannon. Why not take it. For Mack and Dylan and for yourself." It's not a question she poses. It's a fact.

"And if I go back? If a few days is all I can stand in there?"

"I'll take the kids." Madeline speaks to Meg, sending a contemptuous look toward Shannon.

"No way!" Shannon's hands clench into fists, her eyes flash rage.

"Oh, yes!" Madeline faces Shannon now, waving papers in her face. "You got yourself three DWIs and you've been fired for drinking. You can't keep those little guys safe."

Meg sees the disbelief in Shannon's eyes as she takes in the legal nature of the papers in the young woman's hands. She sends an incredulous, accusing look toward Meg. "You'd let them?"

Claudia speaks, quietly. "Last night in that cell you knew you were in deep trouble, Shannon. *YOU KNEW THAT WHEN YOU WOKE UP IN THAT CELL.* I've been there, Shannon. I know what you knew at three a.m."

"It's not up to your grandmother, Shannon. It's up to you." The authority in Madeline's voice doesn't match her nails, Meg thinks.

The silence wanders again, like bird shadows flickering through the room. Shannon's glance darts from floor to ceiling, wall to wall, person to person, avoiding Meg's eyes, searching for a secret panel, for a way to escape. Again examining the trap, Meg thinks, like a fox beginning to chew off its captured foot to make an escape back to its lair.

"Time's up," the young woman says.

It's the right thing to do, but it's like riding to hounds. That's what this is like, Meg thinks, watching Shannon, treed, mumble, "Okay, okay," and glaze her face with a mask of nonchalance as the guard takes her away.

Madeline Smith closes up her briefcase, nods, says, "Good luck," and leaves.

Claudia says, "Hang in there, Meg."

Liz gives Meg a long, warm hug. The three women walk out together, and down the courthouse steps. "Keep in touch," Claudia says, lighting a cigarette.

"Thank you," Meg and Liz both say.

"She's gonna come out right side up," Claudia says, walking away with a wave.

Meg forces her attention to shift to Liz. "Karen and Jonathan okay?"

"Absolutely. Karen spent all day Saturday at the animal hospital with Justin. She got to bandage a collie's leg!"

Meg smiles. "That's great. Justin's a real find, hmm?"

Liz nods. "Yup! He is that. I've gotta run, Mom. Don't worry. I think this is gonna work. Shannon looked like she began to see the light."

"Thanks for coming down. Take care." They hug and walk to their separate cars.

***

"Are we sleeping over, Granny Meg?" Mack's eyes flash more knowledge than any six-year-old's ever should, Meg thinks, nodding as she picks him up at the bus stop in front of the apartment. "Where's Mom?"

Meg feels a sharp guilt, as though she's abandoned Mack and Dylan by taking away their mother and abandoned Shannon by forcing her to sign into rehab where she will be kept behind locked doors. "She's gone away for a while, Mack."

"Is she dead?"

"No! No! Darling, she's not dead." Meg stifles startled laughter. "She's gone to a very safe place. They're going to help her get well."

"She's sick?"

"Yes, in a way. But she's going to be fine, just fine. Let's have a snack and then let's go get Dylan and go by the library. We'll get a video on the way back home."

***

Meg puts the sleeping bag on the floor next to the twin bed in the guest room. "Mack's up here and Dylan's down there!" she says, tossing Mack's manatee on the bed, Dylan's teddy bear below.

"I want the sleeping bag!" Mack says.

"You can take turns. Tomorrow night. Okay?"

"How many nights are we staying?" Dylan crunches his teddy bear against his chest and cocks his head at Meg.

"A lot!" Meg says, smiling. "Lots of good times at the beach and yummy pizza, hmm, Mack?"

Mack nods, not persuaded.

# CHAPTER FORTY

Joanna comes in from tai chi just as Meg is about to leave to drop Dylan off at day care. Joanna is glowing from the exercise and the cold air afterward. "I'll see you later," Meg says. "I'm going food shopping and stuff—want anything?"

"Check the bread, will you? And the peanut butter!"

Mack lives on peanut butter sandwiches which Joanna also often has for lunch. Meg knows Joanna notices whenever the boys affect her and Meg's habits, especially if they run out of some standard household item. "It's on the list," she says.

Joanna lifts her sketching pad up from behind a carton. "Want to see what I did this week?"

Meg hesitates, knowing that Dylan will be late if she delays.

"Sure," she says.

"You don't have to," Joanna says, noting her hesitation.

"Of course I want to. I'll be ready in a minute, Dylan."

Meg leans over Joanna's shoulder as she opens her sketching pad on the table in the sunroom. She sees drawings of a young woman that make her gasp. "Beautiful!"

Joanna cocks her head to one side. "They're good, aren't they?"

"Umhm. They're wonderful!"

"She's a fine model. She knows how to hold the pose, you know."

Meg doesn't know. She is amazed every time she sees something new. Now that Joanna's going to the weekly drawing session Meg is seeing a whole new aspect of her work. "God, you're something else!" she says.

"The head's too small," Joanna says critically.

"Looks good to me."

"No, it's not. But the arms are right. And the breasts. See that curve." She points to a light line from the armpit to the breast. "Isn't that lovely?"

Dylan walks through and out onto the deck. He throws his bear and his giraffe over the railing and pulls himself up on his toes to look for them below. "I'd better go," Meg says, feeling as if she's leaving too soon.

"Okay." Joanna closes the sketching pad.

Meg thinks Joanna feels slighted. "Thanks for showing me."

"Well, sure."

\*\*\*

Joanna is watching Robert hammer up Sheetrock over the insulation in the bedroom. The room is shrinking before her eyes.

"Seems to get smaller, doesn't it?" he says, nodding sympathetically. "But once it gets painted it'll get bigger again." He grins. "What color are you going to use?"

"An off-white."

"That'll look good. You still want to do it all yourself?"

"Yes!"

Joanna's body throbs with eagerness. She's like a runner at the line, already crouching, ready to charge forward at the gun. She can feel the brush in her hand, smell the paint.

"Well, it won't be long now. The spackler will be in here sometime next week."

"That's great!"

Reluctantly Joanna leaves him to his work. She walks around the outside of the house, looking up for buds. The day is dark and cold. A storm is gathering. She sees that no one is working in the studio and stands in its doorway. Squares of wallboard lie in stacks. The unfinished door openings through the cement walls make it cave-like. She steps through the doorway onto the cement Max poured recently. Should have carved initials when it was wet, she thinks. Too late now.

The room abruptly fills with all that is not there. As though the vacant door frames lacking doors reflect in their nonexistent glass her Oregon friends, Joanna imagines Greta lighting up a cigarette and blowing smoke rings which drift upward toward the exposed insulation above their heads. A circle of women are pouring wine into paper cups and Hildy, smiling, is holding out her arms to Joanna for an embrace. In and out among their legs her own beloved Penny runs, a streak of eager russet warmth. *I'll stop by to see Aunt Frances after work* flickers through Joanna's mind like a rush of honeysuckle sweetness from the summer vine by her aunt's house.

Joanna shakes her head. Gone. Aunt Frances is dead. Penny is dead. And every single friend I have on earth is in Oregon where I cannot go. And they won't move here.

Here is where the wire cutter comes, crawling in the night like a mole in its tunnel, not needing any light, to gnaw away the tulip bulbs. And here is where Meg has become a full-time babysitter in our own house. Joanna takes out a pack of Virginia Slims, shakes one out and lights it, pulling in the nicotine as deeply as she can, holding it as long.

\*\*\*

She looks out at the rhododendron leaves that have recently unsheathed themselves from their winter mode and the bare gray branches of the oaks. The earth movers and the cement truck have left the ground churned up in deep ruts of hardened mud. A war zone. And in this moment the studio itself looks to Joanna like an abandoned shed in some bombed out factory.

Caught in her bleak isolation, Joanna leans against the wall, smoking, waiting to find a way to move her body on.

\*\*\*

Joanna parks in the empty lot behind the church. She lights a cigarette and smokes it slowly as she walks from the car to the front door. She stands on the doorstep until the cigarette burns down, then grinds it out in the concrete ashtray anchored to the porch. Entering the narthex she takes a deep breath, struck by the familiarity, and walks through the adjoining doors into the sanctuary itself. There she stops, her hands resting on the back of the last pew, looking up at the stained glass windows where the sun is heightening the colors. Tears fill her eyes. She makes the sign of the cross and kneels in the last pew. The church is empty. She bows her head to pray. After the Lord's Prayer she stops, looks up again, seeing the altar. Behind that is the choir loft and seeing that, Joanna's throat seizes. For twenty years she had sung in the Oregon choir. Singing on Sunday had a radiance all its own. This choir loft stands silent, empty of her friends, without the hymns soaring forth, without her own voice mounting up to heaven.

During the marriage Joanna was a pillar of the church, giving readings during services, providing her home for potluck dinners, cooking for the homeless, welcoming visiting clergy for carefully crafted cuisine. And most important to her, singing in the choir. But since the divorce, in her burst of lesbian fellowship, she had moved from the patriarchy of the church to women's groups.

The resident priest enters from a side door and approaches her. "Welcome," he says, holding out his hand.

"I'm visiting from Oregon," Joanna says, wondering why she puts it that way to him.

He rambles on but she is not listening to the words. She is lost in a foreign land, hearing a language not her own. The silence of the empty choir loft, the slightly different odor of the wooden pews, the diminishing glow of the sunlight on the glass above, fasten her loneliness within, tightening her throat.

"You've come a long way," he says, smiling. "If you decide to stay, we have a number of senior groups that you might enjoy. I'll ask my deacon, who is a woman of your age, to call you if you leave your number." He is smiling again, Joanna realizes.

"Thank you," she says, turning away from him, "have a good day," and she takes herself out the door to the narthex and out to the world outside, taking out a cigarette as she goes and lighting it immediately. Breathing in deeply she walks toward her car, feeling without thought as she turns the key that nothing but this car, this cigarette, has come with her from home to be with her now.

# CHAPTER FORTY-ONE

On the phone with her, Meg can tell that Shannon has hauled herself up above the bedrock of her rage. Mack and Dylan matter more. Meg recognizes that it's for the boys that Shannon is back on ordinary ground, sliding on the clay, kicking at the stones, but making a path that will lead her back to them and that will keep them safe with Meg until that time.

"Then I'll call a mover and we'll store the bed, bureaus and the TV with Liz," Meg tells her. "The sofa and the table and the chairs aren't usable; I'll just leave them at the curb with the garbage. Is that okay with you?"

Shannon's voice is friendly. "Sure. I'll get new ones at the thrift store when I get out."

"Right. And this way you can get your deposit back and use it on a new apartment when you're ready."

"Thanks, Grams. Is Dylan still home? I'll say hi if he is."

"Yeah. We're about to leave. Hey, Dylan, your mom's on the phone."

Dylan runs to say hello and Meg says to Joanna, "It's wonderful to see Shannon working so hard. She's going to come out of rehab in good shape."

"She's done enough damage!" Joanna says, not looking up.

Meg doesn't answer.

\*\*\*

Joanna watches as Meg leaves to drive Dylan to day care. The boys in the house have made the oxygen level drop so that Joanna cannot breathe. She pours her last cup of coffee and sits at the table, enjoying the brief time of solitude. No one home, she thinks with a slight, defiant smile. I'll smoke inside.

Time has been frozen in place since she came as though her arrival signaled the beginning of a long winter freeze. Sitting with her coffee, Joanna is groping for something to give shape to the hours. The chorus practices once a week and standing among the women as they sing, Joanna feels at home. She is deeply comforted as her voice joins the others in songs that are entirely hers, clear and known. Time and space are filled with their beautiful resonance. Her isolation begins to drift away but returns every morning that she has neither tai chi nor drawing nor chorus practice to look forward to.

She goes to see what's happening in the wing. Joanna leans against the wall, watching the spackler work. He is quick and steady and she admires his economy of movement as he makes his way along the bedroom wall, dipping his brush in the can and adroitly covering the tape, smoothing the surface. In the center of the floor two rackety electric space heaters, their long extension cords connecting them to basement sockets in the old part of the house, clank a little warmth into the chill air.

"It's cold in here," the spackler says.

"Yes. The pipes are in. I don't know why the heat isn't on yet."

"Right. Well, I'm leaving in about an hour. I don't like to work in this damp cold."

"I don't blame you."

Joanna leaves him and walks back through the old part of the house, squeezing through the narrow spaces and out the front door where she lights her cigarette and walks slowly around the house. The regular work crew did not come this day. The plumber is due back later. Joanna cocks her head as she looks up at the old house roof and gutters, noting paint-worn patches and one board at the roof line that looks like it's rotting out.

"You should have an engineer check out the house before you buy into it," her accountant had told her.

"No, I wouldn't do that."

The accountant smiled and shook her head. "Money and love don't mix, you know."

"Meg is different."

With a what-can-you-do-that's-none-of-my-business look, she had added, "Well, she does sound wonderful. I hope you're happy there."

Joanna grinds out her cigarette and takes the stub to the garbage can. In early April, with the oak and dogwood, birch and maple all still bare, the yard looks untended, ragged and desolate. She walks slowly back to the front door. She has to write a check for another twenty thousand for the builder this week.

The wing seems frozen in a spin of incompletion. Everything there is almost done—the walls are waiting for the spackler to finish before they can be painted; the outer siding isn't on; Max is coming back someday soon to pour a very small patio by the studio door and to stucco the outside of the studio walls which meanwhile are barren concrete, flat and gray; the wing is without heat; everything everywhere is cold, dark and chaotic.

Sitting at the table, Joanna writes the big check for the builder. Checking her balance, it is as though all the money she received from the sale of her house in Portland swirls in a toilet bowl and is being sucked down, while she stands with her hands on the two sides of the bowl, the way one does after vomiting, watching the water disappear downward, leaving her with nothing but vertigo as she stares at her checkbook. Never in her life has she written out such checks. It is as though she's losing at Monopoly as she always lost to Peter.

I could have bought a whole house outside Portland instead, she thinks. A little house, just for myself, with a studio in it. I could have bought a little place and built on a studio right there in Oregon where everybody is. Now the money has come and gone. Gone. And I am alone in this fucking chaos.

Meg is off with Dylan. In a flashing vision, Joanna sees Meg sitting by the boys' bed, reading to them, and at the beach with Liz's clan or at the court with Shannon. All mine are a day's flight away. Hers are here. And that leaves me out again, again, again. Joanna whirls through a dismal cloud of images of herself at the edge of the crowd, at a high school dance, at a football game, in the college dorm as the girls giggle on about their dates, while she herself folds in within herself like a beautiful orange day lily closing up at night, dark in her center, unreachable and untouched, bound by the tight pressure of the fragile petals that enclose her in an inner silence.

"What the fuck have I done?" Joanna lights another cigarette. No one here yet. I'll smoke it right here at the table and to hell with it.

"Quit feeling sorry for yourself, you fool!" What, then? she thinks, inhaling deeply. And the answer comes, like the return of a familiar song, momentarily forgotten but entirely known by heart, and more, like the answer to a prayer she has been in too great need to pray, an answer she receives by grace: *I'll carve.*

I'll find my fucking toolbox if it takes all day. Cigarette between her lips, Joanna goes from the sunroom to the basement and begins methodically to search. After half an hour she locates the tool box and takes it to the living room. There she gets out her favorite knife and finds a piece of cedar. The smooth handle in her hand, its movement against the wood, soothe her like a magic balm. By the time Meg returns, the house is filled with music and Joanna is sitting by the fireplace, peacefully carving, turning the cedar into something half woman and half spoon—a kitchen mermaid, a woman once called a similar piece in a moment of awed recognition.

"You found your tools!" Meg says with a great smile, bending over to give her a light kiss. "Now you look like yourself again!" She pauses and then adds, reluctantly, but with determination, "I'm going to go do it."

"Do what?"

"Talk to the neighbors about the night crawler. Want to come along?"

Joanna thoughtfully shakes her head. "No. You go ahead. They all know you."

\*\*\*

Meg starts with Don and Cyndy's house next door because she's already talked to them which, she thinks, will make it easier. Jake barks and races from window to window when she knocks but no one comes to the door. I'll come back tonight, she thinks, and goes across the street to the old people's house. Mr. and Mrs. Young. Meg has given them homemade cookies for Christmas every year since she moved in and they give her fresh cut zinnias from their yard every summer. Today he is outside, starting to clean up the grounds. Meg sees that he is white-haired and bent, moving more slowly than she remembers from the year before.

Meg smiles. "I have to talk to you both about something," she says.

Inside the living room, he motions her to sit, and Meg settles on the flowered sofa. He sits in a big rocker by the window. He calls to his wife in a loud voice, "Agnes! We've got company!"

Agnes comes in, all smiles, leans down to kiss Meg's cheek, and sits in an overstuffed chair beside the sofa. "Will you have a cup of coffee, dear?"

"No, thanks," Meg says, wondering why she's never been in this house before nor they in hers. "We're having a problem," Meg says, "and I wanted you to know."

Their heads turn toward her like weathervanes in an uncertain wind. "Someone doesn't like me. He poured paint all over my mailbox." That's not the complete story, Meg thinks.

"On Halloween?" Agnes asks.

"No, not on Halloween. He comes in the night, about once a month, and cuts the wires in my driveway lamppost so all my electricity goes out."

"Oh my!" Agnes puts her hand across her mouth.

Her husband—what is his name, Meg wonders—hasn't quite heard what she has said. Agnes turns and speaks clearly in the direction of his hearing aid. She repeats what Meg has said.

"Mighty troublesome, that," he says, nodding slowly. "Short circuits are bad news. Need me to take a look at it, I could."

"Oh, thank you! No, I have an electrician who comes and fixes it."

"You don't live alone," Agnes says to Meg, in a matter-of-fact way.

"No. My friend, Joanna, lives with me."

"You say somebody keeps doing this?" he asks, nodding thoughtfully. "Whole block or just your house?"

"Just our house."

"Why's the fella doing this? You flunked him out?"

His name is Ed, Meg thinks. Ed and Agnes. I've heard that said around the neighborhood sometime. Meg laughs. "I don't think so. I don't know who it is."

Agnes smiles at her. "Sure you don't want a cup of coffee?"

"No thanks. I have to go." They'd like some company, Meg thinks, surprised. She's seen their grandchildren and great-grandchildren come and go. Old as the hills, they are, she'd told Joanna. So are we, Meg thinks, smiling to herself.

"So how can we help you?"

"I just wanted you to know that someone is coming around here making trouble."

"Why you?" Ed looks at her carefully, as though to see what he's missed, eating her cookies every year, handing her flowers.

"We're lesbian." Meg can't believe she said that. She's never told anyone in the neighborhood. Not in so many words. They all know she lives alone and they've all seen her women friends come and go. This summer she told them Joanna was moving here to live with her and that they were building on the wing for Joanna's studio.

"That's no one's business but your own," Agnes says.

"What'd she say?" Ed asks.

"She says they're lesbians. Women who would rather live with women than with men, you know. I said that's no one's business but their own." Ed nods and says nothing more.

"Well, I thought the neighbors ought to know someone's up to no good in the night."

Agnes shakes her head. "Some people don't have enough to do. You tell those kids with the big Lab next door to you?"

"Cyndy and Don? Yes, I did." But you didn't really come out to them, Meg thinks. "Well, thank you."

"Sure you don't want anything? I've got juice. Next month we'll need iced tea again, won't we?" Agnes laughs, as though the passing seasons are a familiar joke.

"You'll have to come see Joanna's studio when it's finished," Meg says. Ed and Agnes nod and smile and Meg leaves, hearing their voices take up with one another in familiar cadences as soon as their door is closed.

***

How easy can it get? Meg thinks, going to knock on the O'Neill's door. They have a troop of kids, one about Mack's age, and Mack has already found his way to their street hockey games. He asked the other night if he could get Rollerblades. Meg thinks he is too young but said she'd think about it.

"Hi," Sharon says, opening the door, a baby on her shoulder.

"Hi. Is this a bad time? I need to talk a minute."

"Come on in. I have to nurse Ezekiel and can use some company. I get bored, sitting there so long." They sit in the kitchen. "Coffee?"

"No thanks. Beautiful baby," Meg says, smiling. "You must really have your hands full right now."

The baby begins to fuss. Sharon lifts her blouse and snuggles him against her. "Yeah, I guess. Mostly it's just I'm sleepy all the time!" She laughs.

"Oh, I remember!" There's a pause and Meg remembers what she's doing there. "Well, we're having a problem, Sharon. I wanted you to know."

"Let's hear it."

"Some creep is coming around at night and messing up our lamppost by the driveway. That makes our lights go out. All of them."

"Oh my!" Sharon looks confused. "But why would anyone do that?"

"Because I'm lesbian?"

The baby's sucking sounds abruptly fill up the kitchen. Sharon's face is flushed. She pulls her blouse over her breast a bit and looks around the kitchen, as though to reassure herself that the children aren't in sight. "Oh," she says, "I see."

"Joanna's divorced. Her kids are all grown up. One's in school in Maine. Going to be a doctor. One's in California. The other one's in England, going to Cambridge." Why are you rattling on? Meg asks herself and knows the answer but does not stop. "My kids are all grown up too. So it makes sense for us to live together."

Sharon checks her watch, looks at the door, checks her watch again.

Meg goes on, "Joanna is an artist. You should come see her studio when it's finished." She stops. None of this will help, she thinks. It's the word. Sharon has probably never been in the room with A Lesbian before. Not that she knew about.

"Do the children know?"

"No. We thought it would just scare them."

"They're living with you now?"

"For a few months, I think. Their mother's in rehab." That should finish this off, Meg thinks. Out of the frying pan into the fire.

"Oh, I'm sorry."

Sharon looks down at the baby and then back at her watch. The numerals must be reassuring, Meg thinks. Something you can count on.

"I just thought you should know. Whoever this is person is, he's not a good neighbor!" Meg laughs ruefully.

Sharon is not even smiling. "I meant do the children know about you and Joanna? I don't want mine to know."

Meg watches the baby's hand as he opens and shuts his fingers against his mother's breast. Her own breasts shiver inwardly in the old response, ready to flow. "I nursed my four children, too," she says. And knows it will do no good. Sharon's face has changed, shut down against her, as surely as if she'd spun the chair around to face the other way. "No," Meg says, reflectively, "I guess Mack and Dylan don't know that."

"You'll have to excuse me," Sharon says, "but Ben's bus is due any minute now. I'll tell my husband about the problems tonight."

"Thank you," Meg says, knowing Sharon means all the problems and that they will talk after the kids are safely asleep, knowing Sharon wants her out of there before Ben comes in for lunch. "I'll let myself out," Meg says. Should I end with a question about street hockey? Would that help? "Mack wants Rollerblades—do you think it's safe for them to Rollerblade around here—I mean the asphalt isn't smooth and level like concrete—and they're so young?"

Sharon considers for a minute. "I think it's okay. You might want him to wear a helmet if it worries you. Tommy won't wear his but I wish he would." For a minute everything is recognizable again: Meg is a grandmother, a little too old to handle a six-year-old, but still in the same league with Sharon, still speaking the same mothers-on-the-block language that gets them through the long hours of child-care, the loneliness of being the only adult while the cartoons blast and it's a crisis when you run out of milk or one kid takes apart the other's LEGO racing car.

"Right. Take care," Meg says, and thinks, as she goes out and closes the door behind her, she'll tell Tommy and Ben that it's okay to play with Mack and Dylan outside in the summer but not to come inside our house when the weather is bad. Meg envisions Sharon's concerned voice as she counsels her sons, without explaining why, advising them not to accept cookies from Meg's hands, not to get into Meg's car for rides to school, and not to go inside Joanna's studio to see the big press where she makes her prints.

# CHAPTER FORTY-TWO

With a lot of laughter, Joanna poses with her cue stick for a snapshot before they leave for the pool hall. Liz has agreed to keep the boys overnight on Wednesdays until the tournament is over.

"It's really good of Liz to do this on a school night!" Meg says, as they drive away from dropping Mack and Dylan off.

"Yes, but when you have tournament level pros in your family, what can you do?"

They're still giggling when they enter the pool hall. "Yo! Lauren! Are you ready?" Joanna asks the young woman behind the counter. She's in charge when her boyfriend, Mark, isn't there. "Absolutely!" Lauren grins. "Scared, but ready!"

The draw is posted on the wall behind the counter. They study it, note the name of their opponents in the first round. "Are Cheryl and Maxine here yet?" Meg asks.

"No. Can you go warm up at tables six and seven? I'll send them over when they come in." Lauren hands each of them a tray of balls and chalk. "Maxine is really good, Joanna."

"You might not come in first," Meg says, laughing, as they go to the appointed tables.

"You think not?" Joanna gives her a look of mock disappointment.

They warm up for ten minutes before the others come. Then the serious play begins. The first to win six is the winner and they will play round robin with a new opponent each Wednesday night.

Joanna's opponent, Maxine, wins, five to three, by midnight. Meg is still playing. "What's the score?" Joanna asks as they rack up for another game.

"Four to five," Meg says, smiling.

"I'm going to go sit down," Joanna says, ruefully rubbing her back.

Cheryl breaks but doesn't pocket any balls. Meg gets the solid blue down and misses her next shot. Cheryl shoots much faster than Meg does. Meg studies the table longer, plans ahead. Cheryl, she thinks, is a better player, all in all. At twelve thirty, Cheryl sinks the eight ball, winning her sixth game. Smiling, Meg congratulates her and goes to find Joanna.

Driving home they chatter about their good shots and their opponents. "Her boyfriend was watching! I think that threw her off at first, but she got over it."

"I should have had that first game. The balls were a setup but I missed a really easy shot and she almost ran the table!"

Joanna leans back and lights a cigarette. For a few minutes the car is quiet, then Joanna says, "You never did tell me how it went with the neighborhood."

"I'll tell you over breakfast."

"That bad?"

"No, no." Meg knows now that if she doesn't share those conversations, Joanna will think some catastrophe took place. As though she's downshifting, Meg leaves her playful mood and slides into a sober account of the exchanges. "First I went next door but Cyndy and Don weren't home and Jake didn't let me in. He just barked when I told him."

Joanna laughs obligingly but waits for the real story. "So then I went to the old folks—who didn't seem so old to me once I went inside their house."

"As in, the older we get the younger they get?"

"Right. So I told them. Ed was cute. He offered to come take a look—but I think he was glad when I said we had an electrician!" They laugh. "They must have already figured me out. They weren't surprised and they'd help if they could. They're plain friendly is all."

"And Sharon of the street hockey gang?"

By now they're in their own neighborhood. For the first time since she's lived there, Meg feels a wave of estrangement as she turns onto their own street, as though she doesn't know her way, isn't sure where to slow for the turn into their own driveway, has to double-check the angle of the turn. Parking behind Joanna's car, as always, she feels a slowly twisting pang, as though, she thinks, as though I'm—what? Homesick, that's what. I feel the way you do when you're far away from home. "Sharon is not enlightened, shall we say."

"Jesus talk?"

"No. Just don't tell the children."

"Oh that one."

"I think I kind of scared her, actually. She may not know a single lesbian."

"That she knows of."

"That she knows of."

"Hey, I'm hungry. That kind of play deserves a snack!"

"We can eat and hoot and holler! The kids aren't sleeping here tonight!"

They go inside where Joanna makes herself a ham sandwich and Meg gets a bowl of frozen yogurt. Sitting in the living room with their food, they try to revive the fun of the pool hall, but their laughter is edged with disappointment at Sharon's rebuke. "So exactly what did she say?"

Meg repeats, as accurately as she can, Sharon's every comment. "Okay," Joanna says. "Win some, lose some. I'm a tired athlete. Let's go to sleep!"

***

Fear curls through the house like smoke. Meg smells it when she gets up to pee in the middle of the night later in the week. It's as though Joanna, lying stock still, is sneaking a secret cigarette but there is no tiny glow just above the bed. Meg knows Joanna is not asleep. She knows she listens: hears the far-off train whistle in Port Jefferson, three miles away, when mysteriously it finds its way to their very bed; hears the raccoons as they prowl through the underbrush to clatter at the garbage can; hears the neighbor kids down two houses park their car and go quietly inside their house at three a.m.

"Maybe you'd like to work with a therapist a little?" Meg asks tentatively at breakfast.

"Maybe not too!" Joanna snorts. "I'd like to catch the bastard!"

"Me too," Meg says, feeling guilty that although she wakes

frequently in the night she does sleep sometimes when Joanna can't, that she goes about her work and life without the terror that's nipping sharply, incessantly at Joanna's heels. For her it is a dull and muted fear that drones like the roar of heavy trucks on a hidden highway just within earshot.

Telling their friends does not help. Each friend responds with her own story—threats by phone, hang-ups, their friend who was beaten up outside a bar, press accounts of the two lesbians who were murdered while camping in the west, the TV interview of the two in Mississippi who live with constant menacing because they're turning their farm into a refuge for battered women. Being among a crowd of lesbians who have encountered threats only heightens their own anxiety. Stories about Matthew Shepard's murder and the murder of other gay men fill the *Times* often enough to ruin breakfast once a week.

When the boys are playing in the yard, Meg finds herself posted at the Mac which sits by the window in the bedroom. Meg can scan the driveway constantly. Not that the night crawler, as they now call the wire cutter, has ever struck in the daytime.

At night Meg finds herself guarding the boys' room, checking their sleeping forms often, and attuned to awaken at any noise they make, leaping up if one of them gets up to pee to go tuck him in again. Meg wakes three or four times every night for no reason and gets up each time to prowl the house quietly in the dark, looking out each window, especially looking out their bedroom window at the driveway or the sunroom window from which the whole driveway can be seen stretching to the street if the moon is full. When it's turned on, as it is right now, the globe in the lamppost casts a circle of soft light and glints gently on the sides of their two cars. If there is no moon and the lamp is not on, she can't make out the outlines of the cars and the driveway is a darkened path she scarcely can discern.

*\*\*\**

It is false dawn. Like an orange moonlight today, Meg thinks, looking out the eastern living room window at the pale light above the trees, almost but not quite beginning to delineate the highest branches. Passing the boys' room, she peers in, seeing Mack on the sleeping bag on the floor, Dylan's smaller form curled up on the bed, both only barely visible by the slight glimmer of the nightlight plugged into a socket near the floor.

She goes through the dark kitchen to the sunroom and stands at the window that opens on the deck and beyond, along the driveway where the pale glow of the lamppost begins to be diminished by the sun's first hint of light. Meg stares through the semidarkness and abruptly freezes, one hand against the window frame on each side of the pane. Her flesh shivers from within, oddly, as with a fever chill.

Dreamlike, outside of time, the scene exists:

There is movement by a fallen garbage can. Not a natural animal rhythm. Grotesque. Not the lazy possum. Not the quick raccoon. Surreal. A man is kneeling by the lamppost, his hands working at the wiring in the box, like a penitent saying the rosary within the gentle circle of lamplight.

And then the world goes darker.

Meg's body is jolted into rigidity. Her eyelids snap shut. As though she has been seared by an explosion, flashes of light careen like shooting stars within her lids.

Her feet sensibly take charge. She backs away from the window carefully. She turns and bewildered, moving as though newly blinded, makes her way, knowing the steps by heart, back through the kitchen, through the living room, to the bedroom/study where she begins again to fully function. "Shhh, Joanna, shhhh," she whispers.

Joanna startles upright but does not speak.

"I'm calling the police," Meg whispers. "He's in the driveway now."

Joanna automatically reaches toward the light.

"No, no light." Meg says in a stage whisper.

"Call nine-one-one!" Joanna says, leaping up. "The fucker!"

"That's what I'm doing." Meg dials. Her stomach clenches as she speaks softly but clearly into the telephone. This desk sergeant recognizes the situation as soon as she identifies Detective Orenstein as the one in charge—it's like telling the emergency room who your doctor is—flashes through her mind as she gives him her address.

"On our way," he says. "Don't turn on any lights until we're there."

"Thank you," Meg says. "No, we won't. We haven't." She hangs up, thinking: we can't.

Joanna is sitting on the edge of the bed. "I have to pee!" she says with a nervous laugh.

"Pee, but don't flush," Meg whispers. "I'm going into the sunroom to watch him out that window. It's still too dark for him to see me from outside."

"Wait for me," Joanna says, going into the bathroom.

When she comes out again, Joanna follows behind Meg, as they carefully feel their way through the dark house. When they get to the sunroom window, Meg looks out, afraid he will be gone, fearing she got something wrong when she told the police.

He is there. Crouching by the lamppost, he is just putting back the cover of the little box that hides the wires. He always leaves it as he finds it, making the act more ominous for being hidden in the ordinary appearance of the post and lamp.

Meg can make him out by daylight now. The early morning light is sharpening, slipping like yellow flames around the trunks of trees, widening to show the spaces underneath the firs and cedars that stand around the lamp. He is there, having two hands now, having a dark jacket, faceless, his back to her, having a shaved head: Skinhead! Meg's whole body jolts again as though he has arranged the wires to send an errant current through her flesh.

Meg stands as though compressed, like a child doubled up, hiding in a small projection cage. Closed within this space too tight for her, she will in a moment be choking without air. The projector throws off heat as it bombards screen after screen—above her, below her, to her left, to her right, and dead ahead—with image after shifting image of skinheads: Blake at school, sunlight glinting on his swastika ring as he gestures while speaking in favor of the Klan in her own English class, while his skinhead friends applaud; the skinhead who shot the Denver commentator, being interviewed on TV; a newspaper photograph of the Black mailman the skinhead in Ohio shot; seeing the front pillars at the school covered with swastikas as she went to work one day; seeing on TV the children in nursery school in California running, crying, as a skinhead strafes the playground, seeing the five-year-old fall, dead among the swings.

As if waking from a nightmare, Meg forces herself to focus on the table beside her that she knows, running her fingers back and forth along its surface, as though she is rock climbing, sliding her hands carefully along a ledge, looking for a foothold, looking for a way to climb up and out of the nightmare of murder and mayhem where she has been watching skinheads with cold dead eyes sitting in her classroom waiting her out. She puts out her hand to take Joanna's hand and finds Joanna is not there.

\*\*\*

What then? Dream before nightmare? No, outside the window she can see the deck, the cars below, the form still kneeling at the lamppost. She is awake, was awake when she first saw him, when she called the police. How long ago was that? How long was she spinning in that waking nightmare, that knot of fear? It was like a nightmare in the night, that deep, that powerful, that real. She has no way to measure it by waking clock time.

Quietly Meg goes to check the boys and find Joanna. Thankfully, she sees Mack and Dylan are asleep, in that deep early morning sleep from which she often has to wake them to get them off to school. Meg steps closer for a moment, and barely able to see the features of their faces, she stares down in silence, moved to tears. "They look so innocent," people always say of sleeping children as though innocence is a color that can infuse form.

Carefully, she steps quietly from their room and goes to look for Joanna. Joanna is not in the house.

Meg stands again by the table, looking out. And then she sees the shadow by the car and knows that what she sees has to be Joanna drifting very slowly down the driveway, moving toward the enemy, and Meg's body clutches in disbelieving fear.

Around the two figures the trees gather the morning light as though they are the same familiar cedar, dogwood, oak taking on the particularities of their usual shapes at dawn. Meg hears the cardinals' quick waking calls, sharp and sweet. She sees Joanna moving like a stalking cat. She sees the wire cutter stand, like any worker rising from his task, stretch and bend down for his tool kit.

Like a shot ringing out there is a flash of light. Then a few seconds in which a bluejay screams out his alarm. Then another small explosion of fiery light. Like sparklers flaring up and fizzing out into the darkness once again. One more. Meg does not immediately understand.

***

Joanna turns to run but has delayed too long. By the second flash the man is moving and by the third he is so close to her that she can smell an odd mix of beer and aftershave as his arm lashes out at her and then she's falling backwards, knows she'll hit the ground, can't catch herself, can't hang on to the camera that he snatches from her grip, can't dodge his foot that collides with her knee first and then, as he snarls like a rabid beast, "*Oh no, you don't, you fucking dyke!*" kicks with incredible force into her thigh and again, into her side, before he turns and runs into the woods.

"Oh damn, damn, damn!" Joanna mumbles, as Meg comes running from the house to kneel beside her. "The bastard got the camera! Oh, Meg! I thought I'd scare him off!"

# PART V

# CHAPTER FORTY-THREE

The police come without a siren, the patrol car gliding into the driveway like a great whale sliding ashore, flesh against sand, silently beaching itself at dawn. Joanna and Meg watch from the ground where Meg holds Joanna in her arms, as the night crawler runs away, contorting like a hooked sea creature of the deep, writhing through reeds. In the deeper darkness of the woods, like an apparition, he twists and disappears. Policemen emerge from their car. Meg and Joanna point after the wire cutter. The two, with arms lifted—my God, Meg realizes: GUNS!—thrash through the underbrush, giving chase.

"They should go around," Joanna says, "head him off at the street."

*They don't know the lay of the land*, Meg thinks she might say if she could make her mouth form words, make her breath come and go again. "Are you okay?" she succeeds in asking, helping Joanna stand.

"The bastard kicked me."

"Come on, come inside." Meg tries to help her walk but Joanna pulls away from her encircling arm and limps toward the back door.

As they go up the stairs to the sunroom, Meg has a desperate need to know that the boys are safe. Joanna goes to the window to look out across the deck. Meg ducks away for a quick glance at the sleeping boys then goes back to check out Joanna's injuries.

"He didn't know there's poison ivy in there," Joanna says, with a wry half-laugh.

The policemen come back after half an hour. They didn't catch him but when they got through the woods and came out on the street at the far corner of the lot, they saw a dark blue sedan pull away half a block down and take a right, disappearing at the bottom of the slope. "There was no way we could get back to our car in time to pursue him," the younger of the two states in an official voice.

"I'm real sorry, folks," the older fellow says. "Did he hurt you, ma'am?"

Joanna shakes her head. "He knocked me down and kicked the hell out of me. He also stole my camera."

"Do you want an ambulance?"

Joanna looks at them in surprise. "No, thanks. I just want that creep in jail."

"At least we can write him up for assault this time," the policeman says, with a smile. "That's more than criminal mischief!"

\*\*\*

Later that morning, after the kids have gone to school, Detective Orenstein calls to say that he wants to see them. Meg and Joanna go down to the precinct.

"Now we know he's not a kid, we have some candidates. You got a good look?"

"Enough to see that he's over forty-five and bald," Joanna answers.

"Skinhead?" Meg asks.

"Maybe, maybe just gone bald! Usually the skins are younger," the detective says. He turns to Joanna and asks, "Think you'd recognize him?"

"Yes, I think I would."

"Then we have a few photos for you to look at. You feel like getting a start today?"

Joanna nods.

"You look too," he says to Meg. "But mostly I want you to think about it—this guy has some reason to pick on you. Keep on thinking about what you've done. In the neighborhood. Even at school though that's probably ancient history. At these workshops you do. Wherever.

He knows you so probably you might know him too. Ask around. See if anybody's been bad-mouthing you. Okay?"

Sitting beside Meg, studying face after glowering face, Joanna absentmindedly touches her tender knee. Her back hurts from the fall when he pushed her down. Her side hurts but she can breathe without any stabbing pain. His other kick hit her thigh where there was already a spreading purple bruise which she saw when she used the bathroom before they left the house. I should be cleaning out flower beds in Oregon, not memorizing the glowering faces of rapists and killers in New York, she thinks.

"Here's Joe Friendly for you," Joanna says, pointing to a fiercely scowling, younger man. "But he's got too much hair!"

Meg laughs with her.

"At least I can still laugh," Joanna adds, nudging Meg. "Proves my ribs aren't broken."

***

For Meg it is as though their house has been engulfed by dark floodwaters. She has read in the papers, heard on the news, about hate crimes and vandalism. Somehow it had seemed that her house was on high ground, vulnerable to an occasional nor'easter when the wind might lash down a few weak branches but not susceptible to rising water in a flood. Now it stands swamped.

Meg struggles to surface, to focus on the task at hand. Some of these men look familiar but she knows it's because they remind her of characters in dramas on TV. Focus, she tells herself. Focus. The detective is asking questions she must answer. Later, she thinks, she can bail out the basement, make sense of it all.

***

Once the boys have gone to sleep, Meg walks over to Don and Cyndy's house. This time Don comes to the door and asks her in. Jake starts to bark and then jumps on her, wagging his tail. She sits on a chair in the living room, petting the dog, as Cyndy comes in from the kitchen.

One of them is sitting on her right, one on her left; Meg turns her head back and forth as she speaks. "I told you about this guy that's messing up the lamppost?" They nod.

"He came again last night—actually it was this morning, about four o'clock." Meg has the odd feeling of being at a microphone, broadcasting to the neighborhood. "Joanna sneaked down the stairs and around our cars which we'd parked in the driveway, and snapped his picture. But he grabbed the camera, knocked her down and kicked her, and ran away."

"Oh God!" Cyndy exclaims, flinching as though she herself has been hit.

"The police came but he'd gotten away. Just watch for his car, will you? It's a dark blue sedan."

Don glances at Cyndy and frowns, saying thoughtfully, "You be careful, Cyn. You look before you unlock your car, coming home. She works the nightshift sometimes, you know," he says, turning to Meg. His voice changes. "Why's he after you, Meg?" he asks point-blank. "We've been thinking about it. It's just your house he hits, right? Nobody else's?"

Meg nods. "As far as I know, it's just our house."

"So what's the story?"

"I'm lesbian, you know." Meg looks down at Jake and continues to stroke his head. She waits for the air to thicken.

"So?" Cyndy says.

"We figured you were," Don says.

Meg looks up, smiling. It's okay, then. "So somebody hates lesbians, I guess. I have no idea who it might be."

"Why do you think it's because you're lesbian? It could just be some crazy guy."

"He painted 'Die Dykes' on our mailbox."

The room goes quiet then. Cyndy brings in cookies and they talk on a while.

When Meg leaves, Cyndy gives her a hug and Don says, "You call if you need help—even in the middle of the night, hear?"

***

Stretching in her first yoga exercise, Meg feels as though it is the first breath she has taken in all day. She stops and faces Joanna who is sitting with a newspaper in front of her. "My God, what a day! Is the Advil strong enough?"

Joanna nods. "So how are our neighbors to the west?"

"Great. Don said to call in the middle of the night if we need help. Both of them said we should have told them sooner."

"Why didn't you? Before I came, I mean?"

Meg hears the accusation in Joanna's voice. "I was always too busy teaching to get to know the neighbors much," she says, thinking that isn't adequate. "I used to leave home by seven every morning and I always tutored after school or gave a workshop or something so I didn't get home until after six at night. We waved when we saw each other—said hi when we were out raking leaves. Or shoveling snow! And that was it."

"Cora, next door, and Miriam down the block and I raised our kids together—it was like a co-op! Any time one of the kids so much as lost a tooth, everybody knew about it. Of course, I lived in that house for thirty years!" Joanna yearns for her Oregon neighborhood the way it was when the kids were little.

"Yeah. Well, I wasn't here any thirty years. Not ten even before you entered the scene. And my kids were all grown!"

An hour later, as Joanna lies down with a great sigh and picks up her book to read, Meg sits on the bed beside her, saying, "It's probably more complicated than that, though."

Joanna lays down her book. "What might the antecedent of 'it's' be?"

Meg laughs at Joanna's confusion and explains, "Not coming out to the neighborhood. I couldn't be out at school—so I guess I just wasn't out anywhere except to my best friends. Were you out to Cora and Miriam?"

"Cora had moved away before my divorce. And Miriam? She probably figured it out eventually. The kids were all grown up and she'd gone back to school and was director of the United Way and busy, busy, busy."

"So you weren't out in your neighborhood, either!" Meg swings into bed and makes herself comfortable under the blanket. She picks up her book from the nightstand and opens it to read, grateful for the restored light.

"But if someone had attacked me, I would have told the neighbors! Partly so they could be on guard!"

Meg nods. "Um. I guess I'm used to handling things on my own."

"I guess you are."

"And you're not?"

Joanna and Meg both laugh and turn to their books for a while. The heaviness of the long day lifts off and away as they read until their eyes start to close and the books are put down and the lights turned out. Meg turns into Joanna's arms, nuzzles against her breasts, and puts an arm around her to rub her back. "Side still hurt?"

"Yep."

"Bastard!"

Meg feels as though their daily balancing act between danger and safety has been sabotaged. The night crawler cut not only the wires in the lamppost but the invisible high wire on which they walk, leaving them holding their balancing poles as usual, but not knowing where to put their feet as they go step by step forward in their ordinary lives.

"Sleep well."

"You too. Love you."

"Love you, too."

Lying quietly they hear one another's even breathing, familiar and comforting, each hoping that the other can find a peaceful sleep, listening to the spring wind move gently through the evergreens in their own yard.

# CHAPTER FORTY-FOUR

Driving toward the high school on the familiar roads she used for twenty years, Meg hums, "The horse knows the way to carry the sleigh o'er the…" some kind of snow, she thinks, "white and drifting snow?" Leaves you free to think anyhow. Since Joanna was hurt, Meg has been on red alert. Meg rises every morning with a plan. Get the kids to school and then work to solve the case. Today it is to visit guidance at the school again to see if anyone there remembers anyone she has forgotten, any violent incident that could have left a student smoldering for years, to see if anyone is currently mounting a hate campaign against her for her antibias workshops.

Meg has put herself back in time in the neighborhood and considered everything that's ever happened there. Come up with nothing. Put herself back to open housing marches and worked forward through antiwar rallies all the way to gay pride parades: found lots of hostile yelling from the sidelines but nothing ever directed right at her. She keeps returning to the five thousand students. Who among them? Why? Why?

This time she has an appointment with the chair, a young man she has never met, who is wearing a dark suit with a maroon tie, whose hair is short and slightly graying, who looks like he's in a hurry to get to his next appointment. He stands and comes around his desk, ready to shake hands, saying, "I've always wanted to meet you, Meg. I've heard so much about you. Coffee?"

He walks over to the coffee machine and picks up a cup. Meg shakes her head, wondering what he's heard and from whom. "No thanks."

"Then what can we do for you today?" He sits back down behind his desk, lets his eyes stray to his calendar, looks up again and waits.

Meg says, "Someone is gunning for me and I don't know who it is."

He lets his surprise show only for a moment and then asks guardedly, "Is this school connected?"

"I don't know." Meg proceeds to summarize the wire cutter's actions. "He's clearly homophobic," she says, "But why pick on me?"

"But you're—aren't you—" His face flushes and he glances toward the door as if to make sure no one can overhear them.

Meg laughs again. "Oh, sure, I'm lesbian. But there are thousands of us in Suffolk County. Why is he after me? That's what the police want to know."

He looks down at his phone as if hoping it will ring. Then he looks up at Meg, his face under control again. "So you're here today?"

"I thought maybe someone around here has seen a scribbled hate sign—I don't even know—remembers some incident—heard rumors?" Meg feels like she's lost on the Internet, wandering from chat room to chat room, entirely out of place.

"Many of the faculty have retired since you left, Meg," he says, condescendingly. "But you could ask anyone who's around. Good luck. I hope you can put a stop to that harassment! I have a meeting now, I'm afraid. It's good to meet you after all I've heard."

"Thank you," Meg says, smiling, leaving the office, thinking the man is clueless but it is an odd mission she's here on.

Feeling awkward and out of place, Meg walks back down the long corridor where the counselors have their cubicles. She'd changed from her daily jeans into a pair of slacks and a decent blouse but she's still misplaced by style, by age, by demeanor. There's not a student of hers in the building, not a class for her to meet. Without them, she is an intruder.

Meg wants to bolt out of the building but holds herself back, reminding herself of Joanna's collision with the wire cutter. Until that night, he had been almost mythical to Meg—his actions a metaphor for bias. That night he became a specific man: dangerous and real. You're here to catch the man who kicked Joanna, she reminds herself.

"Hey, Ms. McKenna!" It's the warm voice of Maria Torres.

"Hey, Ms. Torres!" They hug and Maria waves her toward a chair. "I thought you'd retired?"

"No way! Actually next year they may force me out." A short, chubby woman in her late sixties with curly gray hair, wearing jeans and a blue shirt, Maria tips back her head in deep laughter. Then her voice softens to a friendly note. "So to what do we owe the honor of your visit?"

Meg tells her the whole story. Maria listens intently, doodling with her pencil on her message pad. When Meg gets to the night of the confrontation, Maria murmurs some indistinguishable curses under her breath. She lifts her pencil from the paper and says, softly, "It's a father, of course!"

"Father?" Meg drifts out to sea, staring at Maria who has walked over to close the door of the cubicle to give them privacy.

"An angry, angry father. Let's think of some!" Maria's eyes darken with intensity as her pencil scribbles names. "What was the name of the thin little dancer whose father beat her black and blue?"

Abruptly Meg comprehends. Not a student. Of course not a student. The FATHER of a student. That's who could never forgive her.

"Rebecca Wyeth!" Meg sees the beautiful child, graceful and lithe, curled down over her desk, writing accounts of his belt coming down on her, her long sleeves and net stockings hiding the bruises, the imprints of her father's gripping hands.

"And Heather O'Neill! Remember when her father locked her out after the school concert and she slept on their front porch in the snow?"

"And turned up here hungry and half frozen the next morning at seven o'clock?"

"She's okay, you know. She sent me a card from Africa—Peace Corps!"

The list is endless. "Remember the first time I brought a student to you!"

"Sure I do. It was after school—you said you had a hunch I shouldn't wait till morning to talk to him—sweet kid! Would have been dead by morning. I can't think of his name though."

"Jim something. A musician. Gay."

"Umhm. He's in California now—San Francisco, I think. He's teaching."

"Wonderful. Speaking of successes, I saw Rowena Mathews at a checkout counter a couple of years ago. She was in her last year of grad school. Remember when she was in my writing class and wrote a scene about sitting in the psychiatrist's office, having the fantasy of taking the razor to her wrist in the bathtub, and he told her she could leave the session early because she was quiet and didn't have anything to say?" Meg adds, "That was the only time I ever gave a student my phone number—said to call me any time, day or night. Rowena never needed to."

They reminisce for an hour, jotting down names and incidents. At last, Maria passes her list to Meg, saying, "I have to go to a meeting! It's good to see you, Meg! Otherwise things go okay?"

Meg nods. "And when the wing is finished, you and Mike must come see the studio and meet Joanna. How are your kids?"

"It's how are my grandkids now! Knock on wood. Everybody's fine. Usual bumps but fine! And yours?"

"Liz lives near me. Jimmy's in California and Angie never came back from Alaska."

"I remember." Maria gives Meg a strong hug, and Meg knows she really does remember. Tim and Maria's Bruce were buddies; Bruce had a heart condition that kept him from the draft. He nearly lost it when Tim was killed. Maria and Meg marched together, mourned together over students who were killed or wounded in Vietnam. "Remember when you got Dan Berrigan to read his poetry after school? And we had to use the gym and someone pulled the fire alarm?"

Driving home Meg can't wait to tell Joanna. *It's a father we're looking for.* Now and then she pulls over to the side of the road to jot down another name. "Barry Schultz." "Paula." "David Kroener!"

She remembers a day after school in her empty classroom. Ralph Kroener stood over her, refusing to sit down. "I want you to raise David's grade. He gets A's in English."

Meg smiled. "David is very bright. He would have had an A in this class too but he didn't do all the work. His first piece of writing was an excellent short story."

"Show that to me!"

"I'm sorry but I can't do that. The students' work is their own. If they want to show it to someone, they can."

"Look, Ms. McKenna, that's nonsense." He takes a step toward her, reaching out as though to take papers from her desk. "This is school. I'm his father. Show me David's work."

That's why he's here, Meg thought. He's worried about what David might have told about his life at home. "No, sir. I promised the students I wouldn't violate their privacy."

"What privacy? I'm his father, for God's sake!"

Meg knew she could not show his father the story David had written in which he narrated his father's chronic drunken rages, in which he threw furniture, slapped his mother around and beat David with a belt, accusing him of cutting classes or drinking beer. One night in a violent drunken rage he charged around the backyard, heaving chunks of firewood at David and his brother while they tried to get away, one of which nearly broke David's arm. His mother had called in the Child Protection Agency, separated from him twice, gotten an Order of Protection once, but he returned each time to live at home again. Child Protection visited but did not take the kids away.

After more discussion, Meg said, "Good night, Mr. Kroener," left her classroom and headed for the English office. Ralph Kroener was just behind her, briefcase in his hand. "I want his grade raised to a ninety-five. Do I make myself quite clear?"

Meg deliberately softened her tone. "This is only April. I told David that if he completes the missing work, I'll override his final average."

"No way! You will correct this *NOW!*" Ralph Kroener's hand lashed out to grip Meg's forearm.

Meg tried to take her arm out of his grasp but couldn't extricate herself. She gauged the distance to the English office, and twisting to one side of him, kept on walking while he still clenched her arm.

Ralph Kroener shifted to block her path again. His face contorted with rage, he snarled at her in a low sneering voice: "I can make big trouble for you, lady, big, big trouble!"

Using all her strength, Meg twisted free of his hold, dodged past his bulk. Close behind her, Ralph Kroener smacked his briefcase, shouting: "*There are things in here about you, Ms. McKenna, things that you don't want to come out! You had just better change that grade!*"

"No. If you want a conference with the chairman of my department, we can set one up."

Close behind her, he snarled at her back, "Oh, I'll do more than that. I'm going straight to the superintendent!"

Meg turned into the open office, passing the secretary's desk, heading for the table where several of her colleagues were in conversation. Ralph Kroener was right behind her, menacing her with the briefcase in his raised hand, his voice by now a full-fledged shout spewing garlic-saliva toward her face. *"You'd better think again! You had just better watch your step, Mssssss. McKenna—if you want to keep your job!"*

Meg's body recoiled as if during rape. In slow motion, the secretary put out her hand to pick up the phone. One of the male teachers rose from his chair, saying, "Is there a problem, Ms. McKenna?"

Ralph Kroener glanced around as though he hadn't seen the others until then. "You won't get away with this," he sneered in a voice suddenly curbed to a menacing whisper. "Don't think you will!" and he was gone.

At home, Meg tells Joanna what Maria Torres said. It's as though there's been a dark cloud hiding the sun and Meg has been searching for the culprit in that half-light for a year. Suddenly there is a beam of light. Meg knows that Maria is absolutely right. And she is sure that now the search will end.

"I don't even believe I didn't think of that!" Meg says, hitting herself on the side of the head. "Dumkoff! I'm calling Orenstein."

Meg calls to tell the detective she has a list of suspects.

That night, after the kids are in bed, Meg compiles a list to take to the precinct in the morning when Joanna is going anyhow to check on more mugshots. Men who might like to make me trouble: Ralph Kroener heads the list.

Meg had known the district would back her up on the boy's grade. Meg also knew that Kroener was out to get her fired for being lesbian. In the seventies there was neither a law nor a contractual clause to protect her. Two weeks later a colleague informed her that the board, in a closed session and by a narrow vote, had refused to fire two members of the faculty charged with homosexuality in spite of Ralph Kroener's documented allegations and furious demands.

# CHAPTER FORTY-FIVE

Joanna is standing on the two-by-six that the spackler left behind. Honoring a long-standing promise to her son, Jimmy, and his wife, Debbie, Meg has gone to California to help with their newborn baby and their other kids. Liz is keeping Mack and Dylan. Before she left, Meg helped Joanna hoist this plank up and across the stairwell so Joanna could reach to paint the ceiling and the stairwell walls. The rest of the wing, Joanna figures, she can reach by herself from the stepladder.

As though she is creating space itself, Joanna works with the suggestion of a smile on her lips. Every inch delights her. The smell of the fresh wood in the room is overcome by the smell of the fresh paint but she knows the wood smell will remain when the paint has dried and she will be living with the wood.

"You won't paint the wood?" Meg had asked. "I love it just as is."

Joanna cocked her head and studied the windowsills, the closet doors that comprise the wall adjacent to the old part of the house, the two built-in bookcases, the stairway banister. "Yes, we can leave the wood if you like." She was not sure. She had envisioned a pure sweep of white. "I wouldn't have painted the banister, of course," she said, laughing.

Now, as she paints, she lets the idea of the unpainted wood enter into her vision of the finished room, which has been in her mind like a potential print. The altered design lights like a skittish dove, staying longer every time. At first she was agreeing as a concession to Meg who rarely questions her choices in design. By now Joanna herself likes the notion, can see the way the wood will be against the white, bordering the windows. They have agreed that there will be no curtains, no blinds.

Besides the bathroom window, there are eight large windows that open toward an acre of trees, rhododendron, laurel. Boughs of dogwood fill the two windows in the small alcove where Joanna's desk will stand, as though they are deliberately growing there so she can work in the treetops. One window catches a tall pine whose branches barely miss the wall when they move in the wind. Two others face three giant oaks.

It takes two days to do the stairwell. When she's finished with the high ceiling above the stairs, Joanna slides the plank down so it's lying on the floor of the bedroom. She sets up the stepladder in the alcove which is at the outer corner of the room. She intends to paint her way across the length of the room so that she can do the doorway last. Standing in the center of the room, with open space on every side, Joanna's shoulders quietly relax and her lungs begin to fill. She can feel the oxygen going into her blood, coursing through her arteries, starting to restore every cell in her starved body. As though her body has been hunched into a small and cluttered cage since she first arrived in New York, every muscle is still howling, tightly cramped. She rises on tiptoe, arches down in a graceful bend, stretches up again and lets out a shout, extending her arms full length.

When Meg has been gone a week, Joanna's daughter, Emily, comes for her spring break from medical school. Joanna drives her around the block on her way back from the airport.

"What a beautiful part of the world!" Emily says.

"Isn't it? I had never thought of Long Island as country, had you?"

"No way. So much dogwood, Mom!"

"And before everything else there was a lot of forsythia. And we're home!" Joanna turns into the small parking area that is near the studio end of the house.

"This is IT?" Emily leaps out of the car and stands, staring at the house, which rises in the center of the acre, surrounded by blazing azaleas, dogwood, oak and evergreens. "Oh Mom! What a beautiful place! Where is the studio? Show me! Show me!" Like a gazelle, Joanna thinks, admiring her daughter's grace as she lifts her arms toward the trees. She's wearing jeans and a bright short-sleeved orange shirt. She has wavy blond hair and bright blue eyes, is lean and quick.

Laughing, they go into the wing first. Standing in the center of the unpainted studio as Emily twirls across it, clapping her hands and beaming, Joanna sees it as it will soon be—complete with her assembled press and work tables.

"Oh, Mom! It's so light!" Emily goes from one window to another, peering out into the wooded yard. "How could you have worked in the basement all those years?"

"Only thirty!" Joanna says, with a half-hearted laugh, "but who's counting?"

"You two have turned a cabin into a palace, haven't you?"

Joanna nods, smiling, and leads her on, up into the living room with the fireplace. "You'll sleep in there." Joanna gestures to the small guest room to the left of the living room, barely big enough for a bed and bureau, bookcase and chair, with Mack and Dylan's toys and books stacked everywhere. "And we sleep over here." Joanna crosses the living room to Meg's bedroom where there is not a foot of space anywhere, with the queen-sized bed between the built-in closet on one wall and the desks that hold the word processor and the printer on the other.

"Will this still be a bedroom?"

"No. This will be Meg's study. The upstairs part of the wing will be our bedroom."

Joanna puts out cheese and peanut butter, sprouts and good wheat bread, a bowl of fruit. She looks admiringly at Emily, so young at thirty and eager. "Now. Tell me about your year. And what gives for the summer?"

During the afternoon Joanna paints. At supper time they work together in the kitchen, laughing when they bump into one another, making spaghetti and salad, catching up on one another's news as they work and eat. After dinner, Emily makes several long phone calls and Joanna takes advantage of the moment to go out on the front porch for her after dinner smoke. She's reading a new book on Arctic mammals and halfway through her second cigarette when Emily comes out.

"I don't even believe you're still doing that, Mom," Emily says in a coldly even tone.

Joanna does not answer. She watches Emily as she runs back into the house, wonders what she's doing. She didn't have that much wine, she thinks, meaning she's not even high. Maybe she's gone to do e-mails.

"I want to show you something, Mom." Emily comes back out, a paperback textbook in her hand. She lays it on the wood box next to Joanna, open to a full page spread of lungs: lungs normal and lungs destroyed by smoking. Joanna glances at the pages and sees section headings glaring CANCER and EMPHYSEMA up at her. She sighs, grinds out the butt still in her hand.

"You know," Emily says, sitting down beside her, "at school the women have teach-ins about date-rape and all. I go. Half of them SMOKE! Even the medical school women! So they attack their own bodies, doom their own bodies, while they're learning to defend those same bodies from the attack of men. Go figure. Does that make sense to you?" Her voice cracks with intensity.

Joanna shakes her head. "No, Emily, it doesn't. You're right."

"So then?"

"I tried again last summer before I moved. Greta and I tried together. It didn't work."

"Oh, Mom! You're such a strong woman! How can you wimp out on this?"

"I thought I could stop when I got here. I even told Meg I would. But I couldn't. It's so chaotic, Emily. And then there's been a threat! I didn't want to worry you but…"

Joanna talks on, giving a monologue about the wire cutter. "And I haven't even told you about her granddaughter and her children. You know those toys in the room where you're sleeping?"

Emily listens but she is not smiling.

Joanna's voice finally winds down, turns iron, invoking her authority as parent, as hostess. "Let it go, Emily."

Emily turns and goes into the house. Joanna walks out and along the path around the house, snapping dead heads off one of the last daffodil stalks. "Damn the fuckers!" she mutters under her breath, shaking one more cigarette from the pack in her pocket, lighting it, and walking on farther so she can finish it before turning back to follow Emily into the house.

# CHAPTER FORTY-SIX

This baby on my shoulder is this baby on my shoulder is this baby on my shoulder, Meg thinks. Gertrude Stein with the rose had it right. Like the summer breeze in the lilacs, the strains of the cello through the trees, the softest waves against the sand, this baby on my shoulder. Exactly right. Exactly its own self.

Meg walks the room of her son's house in California and sings. The words to the lullabies return. She goes from "Hush little baby, don't you cry" to "Down in the valley," and though this little grandson David is only and entirely himself snuggled so beautifully warm against her neck, though it is Jimmy's wife, Debbie, who has just finished nursing, yet it is Meg's breasts that give that certain twinge she felt when she was about to nurse one of her own as she breathes in this baby's scent and sings and sings.

The body knows what it knows, she thinks. Some forty years ago, all the babies and the happy years with Franklin inside the nest, like squirrels, hidden, cherishing the private moments: "mowngower" Tim called the lawnmower—"dow" Liz said for cow. Tim would have been forty-four this year. He stays forever twenty in her mind: Wilfred Owen's gentle soldier. Owen himself dead in the first World War, caught in the same slow-motion khaki lines of bayoneting boys that trapped her father, young then, now dead more than fifty years.

The baby makes a sleepy noise and burrows slightly into her neck. Meg pats his back lightly and sings softly, "By yon bonnie banks and by yon bonnie braes, where the sun shines bright on Loch Lomond..." as she walks back and forth, looking out at the San Bernardino Mountains rising, dry and brown, at the edge of town. "But me and my true love will never meet again on the bonnie bonnie banks of Loch Lomond." Abruptly it is the ache of lost love that moves through her like a Santa Ana, blowing its dry heat over the mountains with its high persistent howl and she knows with a guilty surprise that it is Rosalyn she sings about, remembering not exactly Rosalyn herself in the time they were together but the deep lashing of her own grief as she relinquished her.

Long ago, she thinks, that was a long, long time ago and in another land. And eons before Joanna! Meg shifts to "Hello, young lovers da de da de da..." And wish Joanna was here, I do. I'll call her tonight and see how she and Emily are doing. She's painting that room right now, right this minute.

The image of Joanna transforming their bedroom in the wing, getting it ready for them to move in, fills her head. Once the wire cutter is caught and out of their lives, once Shannon has reclaimed her sons and they are left alone, Meg knows that Joanna's presence in their house will be a quiet daily joy. At that thought a peacefulness fills every cranny in her body. Meg savors the softness of the baby's head as she carefully tilts her own head so as to gently graze the baby's with her cheek.

Debbie, still with the beautiful afterglow of giving birth, comes in to check on them and Meg nods, saying quietly, "He's asleep but I couldn't put him down!"

\*\*\*

From my grandfather in the sleigh to my grandson in my arms, Meg thinks. This dizzies her and Meg braces herself for steadiness against the spin of mortality.

She can think about her grandfather and her father and her son and her grandson and be amazed at the incredible symmetry of that, feel even the strange sharing of time and space as though what is not possible does exist—the deaf old man with his palsied hand holding his slender pipe, is reading the note she writes to him about the butterflies in the orchard in 1938 even as she is rocking David, sleeping on her shoulder. Her own father walks beside her in the twilight down the hill toward the barn where he milks the cow while she watches even as she sits beside Jimmy in his car as he drives her from the airport to their house, eagerly telling her how beautiful the baby, David, is. The way the lantern casts its flickering light across the soft flank of the docile Jersey is the way the lights from passing cars splash in Jimmy's rearview mirror. The sleeping baby in her arms is distanced from her and yet is flesh of her flesh, his breathing as integral to her body as the breath that carries oxygen to her own heart; the delight in the eyes of the grandfather lifting his palsied hand to acknowledge the beauty of the butterflies is her own eyes' delight.

And yet even as Meg recognizes herself as the synapse itself, as the embodied point in time and space where the older generation kindles flesh into being and gives to her the power to ignite the next, even as she feels the presence of herself in the baby that is her own son's baby, and knows that her father's father more than a hundred years ago loved her father into being as she once loved Jimmy into being and as he has now loved David into being—even as her own life exemplifies time, being the linchpin both of the hundred years that ended with her own birth and the hundred that her birth began—as David's birth begins another hundred that will eventually exclude her from life itself—as he lives on beyond the hundred that her own death ends, Meg spins in wild confusion, glorying in the radiance of the last light of the sunset on the mountain, delighting in the absolute and wondrous beauty of the baby—but in no way ready to acknowledge the transience of her own life.

***

Once in flight, Meg checks her watch. Another two hours. Clouds drift above the plane, pure white against an intense blue. Meg looks down, studying the blue-green of forests, the cluster of houses that make up a farm town, the silver trickle that is a river through the valley.

The distance itself evokes thoughts of her mother and her grandmothers. On Meg's bureau there is a small circular frame within which there is a snapshot of herself, age three or so, with her father sitting on a log next to her, his arm around her, her arm resting on his knee. There is only one picture of her mother, that in the hallway, showing her standing stiffly at Meg's college graduation. And she has no memories of her grandmothers at all.

In the valley that was originally part of her grandparents' homestead there had been a small log cabin, built about 1880. My mother was born in that cabin, Meg thinks, before my grandfather built the house up on the hill. As she thinks about that valley, she remembers a falling down, abandoned cabin overgrown with vine maple somewhere off the old road—that had to have been it. She had never been taken there to see it up close.

Strange to think of my grandmother giving birth to my own mother in that cabin at the end of the wagon trail west before there were highways across the country, Meg muses, when they went to the post office and the general store in the horse-drawn carriage, when there were no airplanes in the sky but only abundant flocks of pheasant, quail, ducks, hawks, eagles. Meg is stabbed by an old wish to have known her grandmother, that woman watching the woods for deer, gathering wildflowers for the table. She died of the flu in 1918 while my father was in France, Meg thinks, before he'd even met my mother—in the same epidemic that took his mother and his uncle. We are historically connected, my grandmothers that I never knew and I, as I would stay connected with my grandchildren yet to be born even if this plane were to crash and I were to die today. But not in our body memories, not like my father and Tim and I and this little baby David.

My father in his uniform in the trenches in France stayed alive while his mother died in her own home. The counterpoint of that blazes across Meg's mind: I stayed alive in my kitchen in New York while Tim died in the tangled vines of Vietnam. Although she knows that Tim had been dead for weeks before the soldiers brought her confirmation of his death, it was their presence in her kitchen that marked it on her body, made her know it in her bones.

Meg sees again the absolute emptiness of the space around the plane that separates it from the limitless blue above, the measured green of the woods, the specific brown and white of farmhouses far below. Like a paper cut then, death can be, she thinks, that quick and unexpected, slicing generation from generation. Quiet and forever desolate like a high thin sheet of summer lightning across the sky without even thunder, without even rain.

Shuffling around in her seat, starting to gather her belongings for the landing, Meg realizes that she can still smell the baby smell of David on the collar of her shirt. Meg tips down her head to sniff it, smiling, remembering his head's softness against her neck, his fingers grasping one of hers. "Good to go, good to come home," she'll tell Joanna when she gives her a long hug and says hello.

# CHAPTER FORTY-SEVEN

Joanna, sitting in her beach chair, watches Emily start her run along the shore. Now she turns to wave and Joanna smiles and waves back as the tall lithe woman grows smaller in the distance. The sky is a sharp blue with streaks of cloud. The surface of the Sound is rumpled by a light wind from the north. Joanna watches a couple at the water's edge: the girl searches for flat stones which she hands to the boy who skips them while she stands still, admiring his skill. Wish the girl knew that she could do the skipping too, Joanna thinks, remembering herself at that age, equally unknowing.

Farther down the beach some children play. Their bright jackets lift in the wind. One has an orange beach hat on, another green overalls. Picasso's beach, Joanna thinks, seeing their arms and legs the way he drew them dancing along the Spanish shore. French shore?

The children are throwing rocks into the water; their laughter rising around them matches the spray out from shore where their rocks are splashing. Glancing up the shoreline to see if Emily is in sight, Joanna sees a twist of color, the sail of a windsurfer gliding by, and is back in France. Years after the divorce, the first year the kids were all away at college, Joanna took some of the money her father had left her and went to France to see Paris, the Riviera and Chartres. She went with a group of women and a guide who led them through the Louvre and along the Seine. She went with one of the women to the shore where they dined and swam, where she sketched for two days at the beach. Last, she went by herself on a day trip to Chartres.

Joanna spent many hours studying the stained glass portraits in the hundred and seventy-three windows in the cathedral. Finally she whispered the Lord's Prayer and moved to the center of the nave where she knelt in one of the last pews to pray. The sides of the cathedral rose up to heaven. She remembered looking up to the tops of the redwoods in California, feeling their ancient roots beneath her feet, seeing the sunlight shine through the green, so that the glowing sky seemed to support the branches as the branches supported the sky. The height of the nave was like that; it rose into the sky where the presence of God imbued the music of the choir with surreal beauty.

As though the air of the cathedral were a rich wine, Joanna took it in, and her whole body glowed. "'Beauty is truth,'" she whispered, "'that is all ye know on earth and all ye need to know.' I will go home and I will work all the days that I live to bring beauty into being."

***

"What a great place you have here, Meg!" Emily says. "Come see what Mom's done to the bedroom!"

"Just the first coat," Joanna says.

They troop through the sunroom to the bedroom. Sunlight is streaming through the eastern windows and the whole room glows.

"Brava! Brava!" Meg shouts. Joanna smiles. "It's magnificent! You did good!"

"It needs two more coats," Joanna says.

"It's beautiful," Meg says.

Walking back to the sunroom, Joanna catches Meg's arm and says softly, "You have to call Detective Orenstein back. It's not Kroener."

Meg has been free-falling into the spacious beauty of the room, the joy of seeing Joanna once again, the satisfaction of a trip well done, the comfort of being safely home for good. She is unexpectedly jerked back and hangs, strapped, suspended in midair over a crevasse.

"Kroener moved away years ago. He lives in Idaho, I think Orenstein said."

"Damn. I was so sure."

"Well, give Orenstein a call."

\*\*\*

Checking her calendar, Meg exclaims, "Oh God! I have a bias workshop coming up in Patchogue!"

Liz, who is bringing back Mack and Dylan, takes Meg aside to tell her Shannon is expecting them to come to the hospital for visitors day next Sunday.

"Did the kids talk to Shannon while I was gone?"

"Every night. She sounds good, Mom. Call her. Okay, we're off." Liz leans on the deck rail to summon her kids to the car.

After supper, Joanna and Meg are sitting on the deck when Mack comes running into the house, through the sunroom and into their bedroom. Dylan comes running after him shooting the water pistol as he goes.

Joanna says sharply, "Not in the house, Dylan!"

Meg goes after him and captures the gun. "Outside, please." Dylan begins to howl. "I'll give it back outside," Meg says.

"I want to go home!" Dylan yells suddenly. "Aunt Liz said we were going home."

Oh God, Meg thinks, he thought she was taking them back to Shannon today. "Not tonight, darling. Soon, though, soon. Now go swim in the tub!"

Once she gets them into bed, Meg goes to the phone. She thinks Shannon sounds good, steady and calm. "What time on Sunday?"

"Any time between one and four. How's two o'clock?"

"You've got it."

"You sound good, Shannon."

"I feel good, Grams."

# CHAPTER FORTY-EIGHT

The yard of the detox facility is like a corner of a park. There are oak trees with patches of worn lawn underneath them and sidewalks and a small playground. Shannon and the boys collide in a barrage of hugs and laughter. After that Meg takes Dylan over to the swing while Mack reads to his mother from a *Little Bear* book.

When he's had enough of the swing, Dylan runs over to Shannon. "Are you coming home?" he asks, climbing up on her lap.

"Not today," Shannon says. "But real soon."

"Okay," Dylan says, and heads for the climber.

It's Mack who hangs back, checking her out. "How long is soon?" he asks suspiciously.

Shannon gives him a serious look. "I think sometime in July," she says. "That's not a promise but I really think I'm coming in a few more weeks."

Mack nods, without smiling. "It's long," he says.

Meg isn't sure if he means the coming weeks will be long or the time she's been away has been long. Or if it matters. "We're planning a pizza party the day we bring you home," Meg says.

"Oh boy! That's great!" Shannon leans down to give Mack a hug as Meg goes over to lift Dylan up to hang on a higher bar. Mack comes after them to show off his own climbing and then both climb up the ladder to the enclosed circular slide. Shannon and Meg sit on a bench nearby.

"You know what, Grams?"

"It's a beautiful day?"

"Yup. But you know what? I've been on the run. I've always been on the run—I mean since I was about thirteen. I think I caught it from Mom."

Meg nods, smiling. "Could be."

"I know she ran from New York when she went to Alaska. She told me some about that. I grew up on peacenik music—leftover Beatles and Bob Dylan, Arlo Guthrie, Simon and Garfunkel—you know—and the kids I hung out with were into pot and beer, beer and pot."

Meg listens, remembering the way her own kids and their friends were in the sixties and the way some of her students were, all through the seventies and into the eighties.

"Like I always wished I'd been born in time for Woodstock, you know?"

"Umhm, I know."

"Look at this, Mom," Mack calls, back on the bars.

"I see you, Mack," Shannon answers. "I got pregnant on the run. It wasn't just their dad who wasn't ready. I wasn't either. He took off. I kept the boys but I kept on running—when I worked in the cannery—when I drove to New York."

Meg watches Mack carefully gauging his hand-over-hand progress along the bar. "Good, Mack," Meg calls to him.

Shannon checks her watch and calls out, "Five-minute warning, boys."

"Mommy. I want to swing," Dylan says, as he pops off the bottom of the slide.

"Okay. Get on. I'll come push you in one minute. This is the very first time I ever sat down without a beer in hand to think about myself—not about Mack and Dylan—about me. What I want. You know what I want, Grams?"

Meg tips her head sideways, listening.

"I want to be fifteen again and do it a different way."

Meg laughs appreciatively. "Don't we all? But okay, so what next?"

Shannon walks over toward the swing. "No guys for a while. Music. School. More music. No booze. No joints. I can work and go to night school. I want to learn to play the guitar. There're a lot of things I want to do and the booze just gets in the way. They're right. It just fucks you up."

"You've got it, Shannon." Meg flashes her a big smile. "And I'll get you a guitar for your birthday!"

"Okay, Dylan. Last turn on the swing."

After pushing Dylan for a few minutes, Shannon tells them, "It's time to go."

Dylan shakes his head and tightens his hold on the swing chains. "Come on, Dylan, give me a hug."

"No, no, no." As Shannon hugs Dylan, he begins to cry. "I'm staying," he announces.

"No, sweetheart, you can't."

"Can too."

"How about stopping at McDonald's on the way back home, Dylan," Meg interrupts, motioning to Shannon to go back inside. "Would you like a chocolate milkshake?"

Dylan considers Meg's question as Shannon hugs Mack and then heads toward the door. Mack walks down the sidewalk toward the car. "Beatcha to the car!" he yells.

Dylan jumps off the swing and runs after Mack, still crying, and trips on the grass at the sidewalk's edge, falling flat. He begins to howl. Meg waves to Shannon, who had started back inside, for her to keep on going. Meg opens the car doors and lifts Dylan up and in.

***

Driving to the church on the south shore where she has been invited to give her workshop, Meg knows there is a stiffness to her body that is not natural to her. She doesn't get stage fright. It's the wire cutter on her mind. Does he go to her workshops? They're announced in the newspaper. Was he at the last? Was he the guy who attacked her for not coming out at school? She tries to remember what he looked like but can't summon up any visual clues at all. Don't turn your back on them, she says to herself, and laughs. It's a church, not a classroom, she answers herself back. Equally hazardous to your health, mayhap. Watch out. Fine. I'll watch for bald men over forty!

At the church, as she takes them through the first part of the session, Meg finds the audience warm and interested. She starts the next part as usual: "One year we had skinheads who were harassing Jewish kids and faculty.

"We fought to stop any bullying of anyone in any minority group...I don't think the words 'gay' or 'lesbian' had ever been said out loud or printed in the school paper before!" Meg smiles and sees a number of people smile back at her. "And now lesbian and gay came over the loudspeaker in the announcements after the flag salute for a week once a month. The school got used to the idea that gays and lesbians had a right to the same respect as everyone else."

As she talks on, Meg tries to check out the whole room but she's distracted by questions and absorbed by her message. Only near the end, when the final round of questioning begins, does a well-dressed, baldheaded man in the back open his assault. "You personify deceit!" he says, standing and moving forward down the aisle to confront her. "You tell them it's all right to be gay while you conceal your own identity. You do that so you can take home the big check each month, right? You don't want to call it sin but you know that God-fearing people call it sin. We trust teachers. You use that power to convert children to your own perverted ways. Telling them there's nothing wrong with sin. Nothing wrong with stealing either, I suppose, or murder. You, Ms. McKenna, are a hypocrite!"

As he marches toward her, Meg struggles to understand his words. The church becomes the woods, the aisle the driveway. She waits for him to kneel at the lamppost. She waits for him to physically attack her as he did Joanna. It takes all her strength for Meg to stand perfectly still, forcing herself to translate his hatred into English, preparing an answer to give to the audience. Her body wants to run away. Her mind wants to find a phone and call the police. What could she prove? Nothing. He is in a public gathering, making a statement of his beliefs. On what charge? He's not in her driveway now.

Meg stands, listening, and she does not flinch.

"You should be ashamed! You aren't a teacher. You are a LESBIAN. And you are a LIAR. A LESBIAN IN DISGUISE! SHAME! SHAME!"

It is on the last "Shame" that the minister who invited Meg and the president of the local chapter of Parents and Friends of Gays and Lesbians close in on the bald-headed man. Meg sees the minister's hand grasp his arm, sees the president's hand on his shoulder. Surrounded, the bald-headed man stops shouting.

Meg speaks clearly, looking at the friendly crowd, not at the enemy. "No," she says, "I'm not. I am a lesbian. And I am a teacher. You forget about the separation of church and state. In a school in a democracy, everyone, including the faculty, has the right of privacy and the right to choose his or her own religious beliefs. Many denominations do not consider homosexuality a sin…"

Afterward, accepting the minister's apology, the reassurances of a cluster of embarrassed men and women, leaving the coffee hour early, walking to the parking lot, Meg can't remember what she said. Words and phrases whirl through her mind but his assault blacks out all else: A LESBIAN IN DISGUISE! SHAME! SHAME!

Should have called Detective Orenstein, she thinks, walking through the parking lot. For what? To cry? He couldn't get here in time even if he came. The night crawler would be gone. He's gone already. Or not. Feeling fear lash against her back, Meg looks around her at the shrubs, the trees, the shadows beyond. It's a big parking lot. There was a good-sized crowd. Here and there someone is slamming a car door and driving away. Station wagons. Vans. Compacts. In the dark she can't tell color. Her own red car looks black. Could she spot a dark blue sedan? No way.

Meg walks more slowly, looking at each car. But I can tell a truck from a sedan, she thinks, and stops in her tracks. She takes a pen and paper from her purse. Leaving out the trucks, vans, station wagons, RVs, she starts recording the license plates of every sedan. There aren't very many in the lot. The church has two floods high up on the back wall that cast enough light for Meg to read the numbers. She finishes copying them down and walks back to her own car. Footsteps anywhere near her make her shiver as though a February wind gusts through the softness of the summer evening to chill her skin.

Joanna will say I should have given her a call, she thinks, closing and locking her car door, looking around as she pulls out to see if any other car is following. All the way home along the familiar roads she's driven for thirty years, Meg feels oddly displaced, not certain of the turn, not accustomed to the lay of the land, wondering in stretches of the road that she has long known by heart, exactly where she is, which neighborhood comes next.

# CHAPTER FORTY-NINE

Once the car is settled in its place aboard the ferry, they go up the stairway and Joanna settles with her book in a chair in the stern, snug in a maroon sweatshirt. Liz has taken Mack and Dylan for the weekend so they could get away for Joanna's show.

They had vowed not to mention either the wire cutter or the boys on the trip and they have succeeded. Now they're coming home after the respite, more relaxed than they've been in a long time, Meg thinks. The day is clear and cool out on the water. "A beautiful day," Meg says.

"You'll wish you had a book." Joanna smiles up at Meg who is standing at the rail.

"I won't bother you," Meg says, laughing. "I'm going to walk."

It's partly, Meg knows, that Joanna's back needs to rest after the day of standing at the opening of her show in Boston and it's partly that she needs to be alone for a while after the crush of people. Much as Joanna likes Miranda and Hillary, the long dinner and late-night conversation left her in need of quiet space. Still, walking the length of the upper deck, enjoying the view of Connecticut close at hand and of the open Sound with Long Island not yet visible in the far blue distance, Meg is a shade surprised that Joanna is not at her side, that they are not holding hands, not leaning arm-in-arm against the rail.

Then she sees her. The woman with the short gray hair, wearing the dark blue denim jacket, with her hands tucked in her pockets, is/is not Rosalyn. Meg stops abruptly, as though instead of walking briskly she's gliding downhill on a bicycle, as though the wheel of that bike is suddenly twisted to a standstill by an iron spike jabbed between the spokes, throwing her against the rail. She grips that rail with both hands, thinking it cannot be Rosalyn, knowing that it is.

In that moment nothing has been forgotten. It has been years now since Meg thought about Rosalyn every day, and longer than that since her desperate yearning for her softened, and still longer since Meg was crumpled inside herself in grief, living in inner ash and rubble, like Pompeii after the eruption. Now for years she has slept without constant dreaming of Rosalyn, walked the city without wondering where Rosalyn is performing now, without turning her head at every marquee in case there is a mention of one of her forthcoming concerts. Today, walking this deck, Meg had forgotten every moment, every touch, every joyous meeting of their eyes.

Meg thinks, I could pretend I didn't see her. As she thinks this she is already turning toward Rosalyn. As she walks toward her, Meg thinks, I could walk the other way, go down to the lower deck and stand near Joanna, use her as a shield. As she nears Rosalyn, all thought is gone.

***

Rosalyn hears Meg's footsteps on the deck, senses her stopping next to her, and turns, casually, to see what stranger has approached. There is a fraction of a second as they recognize one another past any doubt and then a trapdoor opens into the past and they drop through.

In one another's arms they tighten their hold in an embrace that they do not know how to end as though the only way out is to fall to the deck to make love in the wind and sun. "Oh, Meg," Rosalyn says and at the sound of her voice Meg is drawn, like an apparition through a wall, back through all barriers of time and space. Meg knows only what she knew in the time they were together, knows that she belongs entirely to this woman that she loves.

They break out of one another's arms. *Hello, Rosalyn,* Meg thinks to say but there is no sound. Her lips do not shape the words, her lungs do not send up air. Meg thinks she is in a different century than when she walked this deck alone earlier on this voyage.

"Are you here alone?"

Still without her voice, Meg shakes her head.

Rosalyn's voice retreats before her eyes grow veiled. She speaks as though she is in France, her voice crossing the ocean on an archaic phone cable sunk beneath the sea, shaken by the winds, jolted by the currents. "We only have a minute then, *n'est ce pas?*"

Meg nods.

Meg watches Rosalyn become transformed. The warmth of her eyes in the moment of recognition cools. Her hands return to her jacket pockets. "So tell me. Are you happy?"

Again Meg nods, her throat closed in an obstinate refusal to reduce what she is feeling to mere words.

Rosalyn takes a step away as if to leave but she still speaks. "I'm off to a concert in Brooklyn. After that, Chicago. Do you have a new book out?"

"I'm working on one," Meg says, and notes that she can now speak. "Have you found someone?"

Rosalyn looks away, pointing to a sailboat coming out from shore. "Like that. I move along. I am okay."

"Could we write letters now and then?" Not to let go of this, Meg thinks in desperation, not to be lost forever to one another after this.

Rosalyn shakes her head. "No, love, we cannot."

Meg stares at the face before her and sees it age, sees that it is not the Rosalyn she remembers but a later one, an older one, a Rosalyn known to others but not known to her. As though she is in the audience and Rosalyn is on the stage, as though Meg is not sitting up front but in the balcony, looking far down, she sees only the outer shape of Rosalyn's body which is that of an older woman, only the distant contours of her face, not the eyes she loves, the mouth she wants to kiss.

We're older than we were, Meg thinks, hauling herself back into the present. She's seventy now.

"Years and years from now, we'll sit on the veranda rocking when students come to call," Rosalyn had once said, laughing, "two old women side by side, and they'll never know how the bed shakes in the night, how we make the earth move out from under us, even then!" They had laughed together, walking hand in hand.

She looks older now, Meg thinks. Her voice is no longer tender. Her eyes are withdrawn. But we could write. My God, she must need warmth from someone in her life. She can't go from one concert to the next on nothing but martinis and raw nerve. The audience will tell her that she plays magnificently but who is there to hold her in the night?

"Why can't we stay in touch? Just once a year even, Rosalyn?"

Rosalyn shakes her head. The ferry's whistle signals the approach of land.

"Just birthday cards with a scribbled note?"

The loudspeaker squawks out, "Will drivers please return to their vehicles."

Knowing all the answers now are no, Meg blunders on, "Do you want to stop to see the studio we're building and meet Joanna? Stay for supper?"

Rosalyn gives her a rueful smile and starts to walk away. Meg puts out her hand to catch her arm. "Do you want to just say hello? She's on the next deck—we'll walk right past her."

Rosalyn shakes her head. "Don't ask me to explain but it's better we don't write, *cherie*. Trust me, Meg. Silence is the only way." With a touch of anger, she pulls her arm away and walks along the deck beside the rail to the nearest stairway down.

Meg wants to say goodbye, wants to hold and be held again, wants to lie once more all night, lost in their love, wants to go out for drinks and meet and begin to talk and talk all night until she begins to know who this stranger on the ferry is and to have her begin to know who she, Meg, is in this present time. Joanna would be there too then, wouldn't she, she thinks, watching Rosalyn go down the stairs without looking back, seeing her gray hair, the familiar tilt of her head, and then not seeing her at all, seeing only a tall man who walks behind her and then is himself gone, both like figures in a distant diorama, set off in a museum case behind glass which is itself behind the rail that Meg grips.

Meg goes down the stairway to the deck where Joanna sits, lost in her book. "Hey, time to go below," Meg says, in what she hopes has become her own voice again.

Joanna closes her book, smiles, asks, "Did you have a good walk up there?"

Meg nods. "Saw seals," she says, and Joanna looks alert, then laughs as she adds, "And dolphins—three." I'll tell her in the car, she thinks, and walks down the stairs.

They're sitting in the car then, waiting for the ferry to slide into dock.

"Rosalyn is on board," Meg says, as though this is ordinary English, as though she is not herself wafting, become a transparent phantom wandering in and out of cars, searching for an insubstantial Rosalyn who must by now be seated in an actual car.

"Oh, is she?" Joanna jolts in place. "Is she making trouble for you? Shall I speak to her?" Joanna goes into her mode of mock combat.

"No, thank you," Meg forces herself to laugh. "I offered to introduce you."

"I'd rather not, you know."

"Don't worry. She's not coming over to the car."

"Good."

Meg turns the key in the ignition, drives carefully up the rackety, uneven gangplank to the dock, across the parking lot, onto the street, down the street to the light. She signals and turns toward home.

Somewhere behind her she knows that her spectral self lifts, rising on the wind like a kite, blowing higher and higher, flying in tandem with Rosalyn's ghost high over the waters that separate Long Island from Connecticut, New York from France.

# CHAPTER FIFTY

At the precinct Meg gives Detective Orenstein a description of the bald-headed man at the bias workshop. He has checked out the license plate numbers that she gave him by phone. "Here's a list of names. And you can scan the photos on the drivers' licenses. Not too clear, but good enough maybe."

Meg glances down the list and at the photos. Two women. Not them. That leaves half a dozen men. One is Black. That leaves five. Two are in their early twenties. That leaves three. Rosenblatt. Thompson. Dowling. None of the names ring any bells at all. The license photo of Rosenblatt shows an older man, with bushy white hair and a comfortable smile. Not him. The one of Thompson is possible except that he has a thin scattering of hair. Not much though. Could have worn off by now. Could be. Dowling is bald but doesn't look like the man at the bias meeting. Meg checks the mug shots of men arrested on various charges of burglary, DWIs, assault, rape, domestic violence. His face is not among them. Disappointed, Meg leaves, staring at the sheet with Dowling and Thompson on it.

"Could be one of these," she says over her shoulder.

"Good." The detective pats her shoulder. "Keep thinking about these two. This guy's fixated on you. He's getting back at you. Try to figure out for what!"

***

Meg watches for Don's RV to pull in next door and then goes over to catch him before he goes inside. "Hey, Don. I might have his license plate number. If you happen to see one of these two plates around here, let me know, okay?" Meg hands him a card with the two possibilities on it. She's also written the two names.

"How'd you get 'em?"

"I gave a workshop in Patchogue and this guy started ranting and raving at me—so I wrote down license numbers but I'm just guessing that one of them was his car!" Meg laughs. "As a private investigator, I'm new on the job."

Don laughs with her. "We'll sic Jake on him when we take him for our midnight walk."

"Thanks. That just might do it!"

"Seriously though, Cyndy and I were thinking. Does your phone work when he messes up the wires?"

"Yeah."

"If you called us the minute it happens, I could go right out with Jake and get his license. Nobody around here leaves their car in the street—they're all in the garage or at least the driveway."

"He comes in the middle of the night! I hate to wake you up!"

Don grins. "We'll get even sometime when the baby has us up. You can come over and walk the floor and let us sleep!"

Meg smiles broadly. "Baby? Oh, wonderful. When?"

"Late December."

"Congratulations!"

"Thanks. So do it. Call right away though!"

Meg studies him a minute. "Thanks. I will."

***

Meg's old teaching buddy, Ryan, is up from Florida for a weekend visit. Over six feet tall, with wavy brown hair and carefully casual jeans and shirt, sitting with his long legs stretched out, Ryan is having his after dinner cigarette on the deck with Joanna. Meg comes out, bringing coffee and cake.

"So tell me more about this menace in the night."

Meg says, "I can't remember any man named Dowling or Thompson. I keep trying. The wire cutter—if that man even was the wire cutter—may have left the church that night before I checked license plates so it may not really be either one of them."

"I think it's Thompson," Joanna says. "He looks right to me! But I didn't get as good a look as you did at the meeting."

"The pictures aren't very clear. And I'm not good at visual recall. It could have been Thompson at the meeting. But I can't remember ever knowing anybody with that name."

"Not a student—a student's father?" Ryan muses, blowing smoke away from Meg.

Meg nods. "If Maria's right, it's a parent. I got along with almost all the kids. Besides this is an older guy. So what Thompson kid did I ever have?"

Ryan sends a rich laugh across the deck. "Let's all hide in the woods all night. We'll wrap him up in a sheet and take him in!" Then he looks thoughtfully at Meg. "Remember the kid whose mom flushed her story down the toilet? What was her name?"

Meg remembers. She got an A because Meg had already read the story. It was about her parents' divorce and her own affair with a college boy. "Shirley something? Or maybe not?"

Joanna asks, "Why did she flush it?"

Meg and Ryan exchange a glance and recite in unison: "You don't tell your family business outside the house!" They all laugh.

"Meg always told her students to write about their own experiences," Ryan tells Joanna. "And they really learned how to write that way. It was amazing. Remember the story about the piano teacher who tried to seduce the girl during her music lesson?"

Meg has a vision of that girl's long dark hair as she bent over her desk, writing, writing. "Yes, I remember. She took him to court."

"Now there's a man who hates you!"

Meg nods, thoughtfully. "True. He moved away after the trial though."

The past has been stirred up in Meg's mind like a whirlpool and she stands at the railing, looking down into the darkness of the early summer woods, Ryan's familiar voice evoking another time and place as story after story works its way back into the present: the athlete who wrote about how he felt he fell short of everyone's expectations and was driving, drunk, thinking he might choose to crash his car into the canyon; the gentle girl who shielded her little brother from the violence of her drunken father, a principal in one of the district schools.

And the shy and brilliant girl who wrote and wrote, page after page in her bound blue journal, marked on the front, *Don't ever read any of this out loud,* about her attentive and loving father who took her to Disneyland, who sat on her bed and read her stories every night when she was little, until in the late spring when she wrote about the ways in which her father also taught her about sex. He had explained to her that in the same way she would later learn from him how to drive, she could first learn about the way boys' bodies were, and their needs, and how to satisfy those needs. Rachel. Rachel Thompson. *THOMPSON!* Meg grips the railing, dizziness swirling through her for a minute. Of course! She whirls from the railing and shouts at Ryan:

"It's *Thompson!* Incest. She was graduating and leaving home by the time she wrote about it for me." Only in that June had the truth emerged, scene after scene of early seduction and later entrapment, until Rachel was close to suicidal with self-loathing and despair. "I got her to a fine therapist—years later she sent me a long thank you letter. She'd graduated from college with honors and was off on a fellowship somewhere in the west. The bastard! The creep!"

"The night crawler!" Ryan adds.

"She actually wrote all that for you." It's more appreciation than a question from Joanna.

"Yes. The night crawler! She must have told him sometime that I knew. Or he saw her journal. Found it when she wasn't home. Yes! That's who it is! I'll call Detective Orenstein in the morning."

# CHAPTER FIFTY-ONE

The Tin Woodman, Meg thinks, driving the country road that leads to Smithtown and the MRI. I'll be costumed as the Tin Woodman and the little kids will throw their pebbles at my head. Ping ping ping.

Tin Woodman should do just fine. And in my mind I'll go to the old slue the day my father taught me how to float. I'll know his hands are under me and I can trust him not to let me sink. I must have been four that day. My brothers weren't there. The water was clear and still. It was a slow river really, not a slue, and we went down by the bridge just outside of town.

"One more thing," the technician says. "If you can, don't swallow. You'll hear the sounds—that's when we're taking pictures. Try not to swallow while you're hearing sounds. And this is the panic button. If you need to, just squeeze it and we'll pull you right out." He slides her inside the tube, head first.

Meg keeps her eyes lightly closed. Don't open them, she admonishes herself. You'll get claustro if you open them. Remember.

Tin Woodman. The sound comes at her like crowbars but small. I can handle this, she thinks. It's not like bombs. I don't explode. It doesn't hurt. It's only noise. Kids throwing their little rocks the way they do at the beach. Ping. Ping. The sound smashes more than that. It's more like being run at by a battering ram. But less than huge.

Stay at the river. Feel his hands holding you up. Stay there. Soft water flowing gently by. Blue sky. Woods interrupting the blue of the sky. Only a trail of blue between the edges of the branches blowing in the wind. Robins still there. And the hawks. And above the hawks? Eagles. Yes, eagles highest of all, gliding, soaring up again.

Lie back, relax. Breathe. Will the breathing affect the imaging? No.

Meg moves one foot ever so slightly, thinking it's been a long, long time now. Maybe an hour? She hadn't thought it would be so long. They're going to pull her out and give her an injection and then do this all over again. Panic slithers through her. I can't hold still that long. Not two hours. They said one hour.

She feels herself losing her hold on wakefulness. Hovering. Dropping. Hovering again. Try gliders. Three gliders towed by every plane. Yes. That's interesting. And parachutes. Hundreds. Yes. Thousands. Many, many parachutes opening against the blue and drifting down.

***

That night, in bed, Joanna folds Meg into her arms for their goodnight hug. Meg lets her face nuzzle against Joanna's chest, and with her face pressed just above her breasts, she thinks of a line from Gerard Manley Hopkins' "God's Grandeur" that refers to the depth of nature's freshness. Giggling, she quotes it to Joanna, adding, "I love the way you smell deep down."

Joanna smiles at the irreverent allusion. After a silence, she says, "I'm sorry you had to have the MRI. It must have been pretty awful."

"It wasn't terrifying, you know. I'm glad Ryan told me about it ahead of time. It helped me know how to be ready for it."

"Good."

"It was…oh…it was difficult. That's the word. It was difficult."

Joanna holds Meg close, her arm tightening protectively. "I love you," Joanna says.

"Love you too," Meg answers. The moon glows through the summer branches of the trees and the room is still.

\*\*\*

The surgery is scheduled for the following week. This means, Meg understands, that Dr. Chen, the surgeon to whom her own doctor sent her, is in a hurry. They have virtually ruled out infection. It could be cancer localized in the lymph node but that's highly improbable. It most likely is cancer carried to the lymph node from somewhere else, i.e. lymphoma. Meg understands this but only as medical speculation, not as something connected with herself.

So this is how it is to find out if you will die. Not if, she thinks, just what death's name might be and when, remembering Sarah saying, "Your body wears out in time. Then something goes. You just don't know what it'll be or exactly when." Sarah was saying that at eighty-five, though, Meg expostulates to herself. I'm sixty-six. I've still got work to do. You'll think that at eighty-five though too, she retorts, with a wry smile.

Meg likes the young woman surgeon. Brisk. Bright. With a clear and open intelligence in her eyes. Chinese? And a quick warm touch of her hand on Meg's arm as she left the consulting room. Most likely cancer then. Not AIDS like the young fellow next to her waiting for surgery. Not a sudden heart attack. Just looking up into the rearview mirror while backing up in the supermarket lot one day and seeing a small swelling on her neck. Putting up her hand to touch it idly, noting that it is, in fact, a lump. That simply, death can stroll into your life, she thinks, that casually on an ordinary day when you've just put the groceries in the trunk.

Cancer of the breast, which many of her friends have now survived, is at least in one locale, Meg thinks. Pure hell but hell confined to one town if the body is the nation, she thinks with an ironic smile. Lymphoma would be like cancer of the entire highway system; she envisions a map with the federal highways in red, opening off at cloverleaf after cloverleaf onto the state highways, which fork off onto county roads which branch onto streets which ultimately turn into private driveways where ordinary people park their cars and live. LIVE!

With a flick of a biopsy the map becomes the body and the lines become the lymph system carrying not the nation's cars and trucks hurtling through time and space at eighty miles an hour and finally slowing to ten to be parked in their own driveway so the driver can go in to hug and be hugged and to sit down to eat and talk, lie down to make love and laugh—but carrying instead an insidious and invisible load of cancer cells that flow everywhere, infiltrating every organ, every space, every muscle and tendon, imbuing every bone, every stretch of flesh with poison.

POISON.

Meg sees the skull and crossbones on the tiny bottle of dark red iodine they kept in the medicine cabinet when she was small. Lymphoma would mean only a few months left.

She remembers walking at the beach. The morning had been dark and stormy. By noon the rain let up and Meg figured she could have a walk before it darkened up again. Halfway down the beach, rocking in and out against the shore, the black thing was adrift.

Meg stopped, stared, went slowly on, approaching as though there is some doubt, as though there may be choices about what she will now find.

Work shoes. Still wearing a brimmed hat. Black coat. Not a jacket but neither is it a full length overcoat. Dark pants. Face down. Doing the dead man's float. Should I roll it over, Meg asked herself. Could there be life? But she was already running back along the beach, headed for a phone, knowing this was a man's body, a dead man's body, doing the dead man's float, sunken and waterlogged, washed ashore to waft in and out against the sand like any other log.

\*\*\*

Lying on the gurney, Meg orders herself: calm down, breathe deep, as in relax. This is easy. You just breathe and go to sleep and let Dr. Chen do the work. Meg starts deliberately breathing long, slow breaths. "Fourscore and seven years ago," she begins, and is not even to the "in a larger sense we cannot consecrate this ground—the brave men, living and dead, who struggled here have already..." when an orderly arrives to wheel her in.

The operating room seems loud. She sees among the array of metal and bright lights, where everything is speeded up a notch as in an action shot after a long still, parts of people and objects intersecting one another: a nurse's surgical cap pulled tight over her blond hair, a hanging intravenous bag, a tube, the cold flatness onto which she somehow helps them lift her own body, itself not quite connected to her anymore, the face of Dr. Chen smiling at her, the arm of the anesthetist reaching down to put a needle in her arm as Meg obediently counts backwards from twenty, wanting to smile back at Dr. Chen.

\*\*\*

Joanna goes into hiding in her book in the waiting room. Occasionally a random thought, like a stray bullet, grazes her and, terrified, she goes out for a cigarette or two. Lymphoma would not leave us any time, she thinks—not even a chance to be together in the new house. Not Meg, she thinks, not my lovely Meg. I just found her. That wouldn't be fair. She's so gentle, so good.

The last time she's out, checking her watch for the hundredth time, Joanna leans back against one of the pillars that line the long hospital patio, looks up at the clear July sky, and in silence, prays, *Please, God, not Meg. I'm not asking this for me. For her. For her children. For Mack and Dylan, Jonathan and Karen. Not Meg. For herself. Don't take her yet. Let her go on writing.* Joanna smiles a little crooked smile. *Let her go on swimming. Please, God. Amen.*

She walks back into the waiting room and as she ducks back into her book, she thinks, She doesn't even know yet how good I'll be to her. Joanna has a flash of the ferry as they left it, of Meg's flushed face as she told her about seeing Rosalyn aboard. But she's mine now, not hers. Mine. And I'll learn every way there is to make her happy. She'll forget her precious Rosalyn. She'll be glad it's me. Joanna reads again and waits.

***

It is the young resident who leans over Meg, smiling, as she awakens. "Not cancer," he says. They speak to one another for a moment and he leaves and Meg, dozing and waking, tries to remember if he was in a dream or in a waking time and what it was he said.

Joanna is waiting for her when they take her out of the recovery room.

"Did you see Dr. Chen?" Meg asks, knowing that is the point. Joanna nods, leaning down to hug her. "It's fine. It's not lymphoma. It's not cancer at all. It's not in the lymph node. The MRI was not clear. It's next to the lymph node. It's called…" She checks her notes and reads the unfamiliar word to Meg. "It's called a hemangioma and it's a harmless thing, kind of like a birthmark except it's down inside—you were born with it. It's nothing, Meg." Joanna touches Meg's hand with hers.

"And Dr. Chen knew not to remove it?" Meg feels the weight of her body lift as the facts arrive.

Joanna nods. "Dr. Chen knew what it was and knew just what to do with it. They biopsied it. You're fine."

"Here's to Dr. Chen!" Meg lifts an imaginary glass as the nurse starts filling in her discharge papers, saying, "Just sit here for an hour and then you may go home. Leave these at the office where you signed in."

A peaceful glaze of medical relief encloses Joanna and Meg. They look at magazines and chat. After an hour Meg stands up and starts to leave, papers in hand.

"Are you sure that you can walk?" the nurse asks her. "I can take you out in a wheelchair."

Meg checks out her legs, feels a little shaky, but less like falling than like taking flight. She reassures the nurse and she and Joanna, arm in arm, go down the hallway toward sunlight.

As they step out onto the sidewalk, Joanna says, pointing to a bench, "You sit here. I'll get the car."

"Okay, thanks."

"Look!" Joanna waves at the flowering plum trees, their purple blossoms stirring in the breeze, with the clear sky above. "Hopkins had it right about 'The Grandeur of God.'"

Meg smiles and nods appreciatively. As she hurries toward the parking garage, Joanna whispers, "And thank you, God. Oh, thank you."

# CHAPTER FIFTY-TWO

The plane circles down on a clear summer day. Mt. Hood is its unreal self, snow-capped and perfect. Any art teacher would say to rough it up to achieve a natural look. Far to the north Mt. Rainier reigns. The Cascades stretch from north to south and in the farthest northwestern distance the Olympics are only shadowy suggestions of the giants that they are. The Columbia curves serenely toward the sea. The only clouds are wisps of white off toward the Pacific.

Joanna knows it is uncommon luck to get Portland on a clear blue day. One year when her kids were small, sick with chickenpox and flu and colds in an unending stream of confining calamities, she had personally counted forty days and nights of rain here in Oregon. It was the constancy of the gray sky that got Joanna most, as though an unending bolt of soggy cotton unrolled at dawn across the sky, between the sun and earth, weighing the air down so that she felt there might not be any left to breathe by dark, so that she could not jump high enough to break through to blue, so that even if she were to launch a kite it would not find a way upward to the sky but would only drift beneath the fog-like canopy, bumping jerkily against its clotted floods of gray.

Is it unbearably beautiful here? she wonders, as the plane comes down over evergreens and little lakes and taxies to a stop. Or is it the contrast? That the immediate glory of this day is magnified by its surround of month after month of steady gray.

"How long since you've had a day like this?" she teases Greta who is there to pick her up.

"Every day for months!" Greta answers, hooting her laughter, giving her a long hard hug.

"Liar, liar, your pants are on fire!" Joanna retorts. "So tell me everything!"

Greta's voice conveys Joanna into the darkroom of the past two years and one by one lifts from the murky developing solution the Oregon friends Joanna left behind. Day after day each person's image comes sharply into focus. Day after day a void within Joanna becomes peopled once again. The show, in which Greta and Hildy and other friends had work, was one reason that Joanna came. To see room after room filled with sketches, paintings, sculptures by the artists among whom she has worked for many years, replenishes some desert in herself.

The party is at the end of the first week and by then Joanna has everyone back in their proper place inside her head, face by face, life by life. Joanna leans on the kitchen counter, chatting with the hostess, and the chorus of voices in the living room, on the patio, in the hallway, is like a chorale she has been yearning for: just those voices, blending in exactly that way, with that very laughter breaking out.

***

At Aunt Frances's grave the day before she leaves, Joanna sits for a long time, her back against the nearest maple, whose green leaves, some touched with russet and gold, are rustling above her in the wind. The cemetery lawn is adjacent to the churchyard, a protective green that encloses her in its safe and everlasting peace.

"I didn't know how much I'd been missing you," she says to Aunt Frances.

Two doves startle at her voice and lift up in a flutter to the safety of a lower branch. Joanna tips back her head to watch them move from limb to limb, as they call back and forth with their gentle song. Even their soft gray is brighter than the steady expanse of sky, its heaviness holding the rain that is about to fall.

"I didn't mean to leave you," Joanna whispers through her tears as the rain begins to fall in a steady drone. She gets into the car, parked by itself on the narrow driveway that winds among the graves, slams the door, lights a cigarette and inhales deeply. The rain pounds on the roof above her head, streams down the windows all around, encasing her in a darkening and desolate cave.

She remembers Laurel. The group of college seniors had interrupted their hike up the mountainside for lunch, perching on the rock ledges by the cascading river. Laurel, her roommate, whispered to her, "C'mon, I want to show you something." They followed a barely visible trail down and around the ledge, under it and out the other side, until suddenly they were surrounded on three sides by thunderous sheets of water.

"Don't be scared!" Laurel laughed and took her in her arms in mock protection.

Standing in Laurel's arms under the waterfalls, Joanna's whole body trembled.

"Wild, huh?"

Laurel's lips brushed hers and then she turned away and disappeared. Joanna could barely hear her footsteps running back to the trail, up the trail back to the ledge. Joanna stood alone, wanting with such intensity that she could not move. Wanting jolted through her like a prolonged streak of lightning, held suspended in midflight, infusing every cell in her body, locked there in fiery silence.

During the two years they roomed together Laurel teased her, dancing naked around the room, giggling with her until they crumpled to the floor, leaning their bodies in a tangled heap, coming in after dates to lie next to her, whispering the details of her date, sometimes stroking, kissing as she talked, as though their holding, kissing were casually integral to the recital.

Joanna stood shivering, alone. The roaring of the sun-drenched water that surrounded her imbued her flesh with a slow explosion of desire. Where Laurel's lips had touched, her own lips swelled. Where Laurel's body had stood with hers, Joanna's breasts, arms, dampened inner thighs, stood raw with need. It was an intense and immediate magnification of an old familiar keening of her flesh but she had never before known for what she mourned. She had known only the ache, only the wanting, unresolved.

Joanna stayed under the waterfalls until the others packed up and hiked on up the trail, calling out that she would follow in a little while. In the silence that followed their retreating laughter and fading footsteps she was able to force her body to leave the shimmering water cavern, to sit alone on a rock ledge and let the sun beat down on her until it seared her flesh. She sat there, alone, reading, until the others came back down the trail on their way out. By then the throbbing of desire, like a great pain, had diminished until she could manage it. She could walk again, as on an ankle sprained along the trail, that has been rested enough to allow the hiker to limp her way back home. Indeed, she told them she had turned her foot and has been resting it, confident that they would not know the difference, noting her pale face, her still shivery flesh, and should anyone care to listen, her wildly uneven heart.

The cigarette burning her fingers snaps her back. The rain beats on. Dreamlike, as though summoned by Aunt Frances, Joanna leaves the car and walks in the rain back up the hill. At the grave she stops and kneels on the now drenched lawn.

Although Joanna has answered questions about Meg, made proud speeches about the wing they're building, the studio ready to be up and running, ready for the press to be assembled, and has passed around radiant spring shots of the house and the blazing azaleas, of Meg and herself at the beach, in the privacy of her own secret mind Joanna has not thought about Meg since she left New York except to give her a perfunctory call to say that she had arrived safely and was lost in a whirl of socializing. Joanna has been so happy to regain what she has lost, to have what she has mourned, that Meg has been left in the distant past, as though she had existed before the Portland friends, before Aunt Frances's lake, on that dim plane of distant memory, and is not in the present in any way other than as a faded memory, a sepia snapshot carried in her wallet, worn thin and dull.

Now, on this hill, Joanna stands, leaning against the maple whose wide branches hold back most of the rain. "I wish you'd known Meg," Joanna says to Aunt Frances, recognizing as she says it the depth of the wish. "I wish she could know you."

It is as though she has brought Meg up the hill with her this time. Joanna feels the maple's bark against her back, marking the flesh of her body where she leans full weight upon it, the way the paper is imprinted forever by an image as she turns the roller. As though she herself has been waiting, the way the concepts of her work have been waiting for the press to be assembled—as though she couldn't envision herself with Meg until she could invest herself in the imagery of her first new print made in her new life, in her new studio, in the world that she and Meg have forged together, as though she has held her breath, been blank, unfilled within, waiting, waiting, knowing only what was missing and not what was newly there, she has felt a vacancy within, a vast and hidden shameful lack, a terrifying void.

"This is Meg, Aunt Frances," Joanna says gently, in the tone of the rain, and her body remembers Meg's body against hers as they danced together in the pool hall their first year. She remembers standing on the floor of the bedroom before there were walls or a roof, when they stood under the stars, as though in the wilds together. It is as though Meg's hand is now held in her own hand. "This is Meg, Aunt Frances, and I love her. You can let me go. I've found my way."

As though Aunt Frances's ghost moves up and away through the rain into the now birdless trees, merging with the gray of the streaming rain, Joanna feels her presence leave. A familiar sorrow starts up within Joanna but before she yields to it, Joanna lets herself know that Meg's presence is beside her. She is not alone.

Walking out from under the tree, Joanna lifts her head into the falling rain, tips her face up as she would to take communion. "You're blessing Meg and me, aren't you?" she asks gently.

Aunt Frances's house by the lake of her childhood whirls around her and away, as though to make room for her present house with Meg. "I've mourned enough, haven't I?" And like an incantation, memorized in her childhood, Joanna says out loud, not knowing where the words come from, "What is lost is never lost but mine forever so that what is found now may be truly found."

Joanna walks back down to the car as though waking from a long sleep. The rain streams down around her in a windy mist of gray which parts around her as she begins to run. "Wait up, Meg!" she calls out softly, "I'm coming home."

# CHAPTER FIFTY-THREE

"Grams, can I bunk with you for a few days?" Shannon asks on the phone.

"Of course you can."

"Are you sure?"

"Look, Joanna won't even be back from Oregon for another week. Good timing, Shannon!"

Meg takes the boys with her to pick up Shannon. "We'll have a pizza party tonight," she says.

"Mommy too," Dylan says.

"Mommy too," Meg says.

"But she's all well now, right?" Mack's voice has a tiny quiver in it.

Meg keeps her eyes on the road but speaks carefully to Mack. "Yes, Mack, she's all well now."

At the rehab center they find Shannon sitting cross-legged on the sidewalk beside her stacked belongings. Like a little kid coming home from camp, Meg thinks.

After the boys are asleep, Shannon reads the *Yankee Trader*, makes calls about apartments, and takes back her car keys. The next few days she is like a meteor, checking out apartments, answering want ads for jobs. Friday morning while the boys are in school she rents an apartment with money Meg is lending her. "We can't have occupancy until next Monday. Is it okay with you for me to bunk here till then?"

"Of course," Meg says. "I thought it would take longer to find a place."

"Could you babysit just three more days? I want to catch a meeting every night, and I want to start work tomorrow. It's a waitress job. I'll find a sitter at AA tonight."

Shannon is charged with energy. Watching her, Meg remembers a young Angie and sees Shannon as the lively, responsible woman she is working to become.

Shannon has Monday off. While the boys are at school, she moves their few belongings to the new apartment. Meg drives a load over and helps her set up a new bunk bed in the bedroom and a sofa bed in the small living room/kitchen space. The apartment is in the back of an old house but it's not the basement and there's a large yard with oaks and maples bordering a large lawn where the boys can play.

"Remember to call me for emergency babysitting."

Shannon nods and gives her a big hug. "Thanks, Grams. Don't worry about us. I'm going to be okay."

"You bet you are!" They smile at one another.

*** 

That afternoon, when she would usually be waiting for the bus to bring Mack home and go to pick up Dylan, Meg walks through the quiet house with a vague nostalgia, as though she's missing all her children that have ever come and gone. In a kind of time warp, for a flicker of a moment she knows that this house, this yard, as they now stand, are the perfect home for her own children, were they to be young right now. She sees in her memory moving van after moving van depositing their belongings in the house with the blue siding, the house with the hilly backyard with velvet ants in it, house after house through the years, Meg standing with a baby in her arms, watching the men carry the cartons into the newest house, trying to make this nest feel as warm and safe as the one they have just left, like squirrels running from one bunch of leaves piled in the branches to new bare limbs, racing up from the ground with orange leaves in their teeth to wedge them in the forked branch once again against the winter winds. Until the divorce in the thirteenth house.

A plane drones across the sky, an unusual sound filtering through the giant branches over the deck. Tomorrow Joanna will return. Check schedule. Drive to airport. Drive home with her.

Shannon and the kids are safely gone. Joanna is about to reappear. You can't move Tim and Angie, Jimmy and Liz as a baby, into this house. They will not be playing Robin Hood in these woods, perfect for that though these woods may be.

***

"Don't know what to do with yourself, do you?" Joanna comments, sorting her mail on her first day back.

"Not quite. I'm getting back to work. The manuscript is still there. Want to celebrate our newfound adult life with Chinese tonight?"

Joanna smiles. "Let's do that."

# CHAPTER FIFTY-FOUR

A young man lays the carpet on a Thursday evening. They open all the windows to let the chemical odors blow away. "We'll move in Saturday night," Meg says.

They walk back and forth, admiring. "I hate to move any furniture in even—it's such a beautiful clear space," Joanna says, laughing.

"We can sleep on the floor for the first month, if you like."

"Maybe not!"

\*\*\*

The open space of her study is around Meg like new water in which to swim. She walks back and forth, looking out the windows which seem to be wider, clearer, than before, and then goes to see what Joanna is doing in their new bedroom.

Joanna has put up a rack for her tapes by her desk and beside her bureau she has hung embroidery hoops with cloth stretched taut across them on which she is hanging her earrings. For a moment Meg feels betrayed. They have agreed not to hang any paintings or prints on the bedroom walls, letting the windows frame tree branches and sky instead. Joanna has marred the bareness of the walls. Meg censors her own reaction, recognizing Joanna's ordinary need, the usefulness of the tape rack, the fun of the bright earrings spattering the hoops of cloth.

"Would you like me to fix one for you?" Joanna asks, noting her attention to the hoops.

"Yes, thanks." Meg puts her arms around Joanna, craving a good hug. She can feel Joanna's muscles straining to get on with the tasks at hand. Reluctantly, Meg lets her go.

*** 

Lying in bed that night the moon rises directly above their heads, moving upward in the sky beyond the branches of the pine. They have intentionally centered their bed under the casement windows which divide in the center, opening to each side. They are wide open to let the night air flow through the room.

No one has ever lain in this space before. And in this bed only they have lain. This moonlight is falling for the first time into this room they have designed and entered, across this bed, to lay its glow against their naked arms and shoulders, to shine on their hair and faces, to show them one another's breasts, thighs, hands. They move together, the drift of their bodies and their cries as much a part of the natural night as the distant gliding of great winged owls and the mysterious gathering of wolves, their calls rising toward the stars.

# CHAPTER FIFTY-FIVE

"God, I hope they know what they're doing!"

Joanna takes boxes of doughnuts and goes to the studio where the men are assembling the press. They've got the base up and have stopped for a coffee break. Joanna's joy in being almost home free—to have the studio up and running after the long hiatus—is warped by her intense anxiety about the etching press. It's a complex machine, weighing two thousand pounds, and requiring delicate and exact balancing for it to work. She serves them coffee and doughnuts but can't eat herself.

The afternoon tumbles on. Joanna sits at her worktable, out of the way, and watches. Now and then she cautions, questions, comments. "Doesn't that piece have to be edged in first?"

They pay attention. The man in charge has set up a similar press once before and has studied the instructions that were sent from Oregon by the man who took the press apart for shipping. He moves faster than Joanna would like him to, but he knows what he is doing. He answers Joanna over his shoulder, "Yes, it does, but this part has to be aligned just right and be ready to be attached when we slide that in." His attention is on the section he's holding as he speaks to one of the men. "Hold it steady there."

As the last parts are adjusted, he turns to Joanna. "How about testing it for us?"

The vertigo gone, Joanna gets the pads, paper, an old etching plate. Setting it up, her hands are like the wings of a long grounded hawk. There is not the slightest hesitancy. This is her domain. Her hands glide here and there dampening the paper, inking the plate.

"Okay. Here goes." Her voice sings eagerness. She moves the heavy wheel and the roller turns. Joanna knows immediately that everything is right. They lean over to see the practice print emerge and a loud cheer goes up.

***

Every Tuesday they go to the pool hall. Joanna has barely left her studio since Saturday but she comes up to change her shirt and get her own cue stick.

"Good break!" Meg says, sizing up the spread, choosing her shot.

Watching Meg focus as she sizes up the table, bends to send the cue ball straight at the blue which drops in the corner pocket, smiles and walks around the table to take her second shot, Joanna feels a heavy haze lighten and lift off. As they play on, laughing and concentrating, Joanna knows an image is crystallizing, but it is not for a print. It is her original view of Meg, bright and lighthearted, intent, graceful and eager. The whole evening it works in her mind. She chooses her shots and shoots through the lens of that image and the longer it stays in her mind's eye, the more she herself smiles.

"You look so happy since the studio is up and running!" Meg says. "I love it!"

"I guess I am," Joanna says. *And is that why I'm seeing Meg this way again? She's the way she was the first day I met her at the airport and took her home.* By the time they leave the pool hall, Joanna knows. *I've been in a dark cloud since I got to New York and when I looked out through it I couldn't even see Meg's face. It was because I didn't have the studio. It wasn't her. It was me.*

*Now the studio is actually, beautifully mine—I am myself again! And I see Meg! She is herself again!*

***

Joanna works in her completed studio. The walls are a stunning white. The press is shining, ready to print. A deep sink stands next to a counter under a hood that houses a heavy fan. Her workbench is against one wall, her long table against another. Bright summer light floods in everywhere through the expanse of windows. She's tacked snapshots and photographs on a big piece of cork that she's hung on the wall between two windows.

The space itself seems about to lift up and away in the glory of its light. Daily Joanna enters it with disbelief that turns to peaceful joy as she sits at her carving table. There, hour after hour, waiting for the press to be assembled, she had scraped, ground, carved, polished bone until a pure and shining shape emerges—sometimes an animal, sometimes a Celtic design, sometimes simply beauty seized by bone.

Today she is starting a new print. The door is closed, the phone, as always, is turned off. In other parts of the house there are doors that open, phones that ring, work that will be interrupted. Here she is safe. Here she can work alone and none will enter.

When she read Virginia Woolf's edict to free yourself for your work in *A Room of One's Own* Joanna nodded fiercely and agreed. The children to whom she had already given birth were to be loved and nurtured but as they grew older they were given limits to observe to free their mother's time for work.

Work is like flight. It is as though she lifts up and away, leaving behind her all the chaos of people and their demands, eluding disorder and disharmony, finding clear space in which to generate the beauty she envisions. In her mind that beauty emerges gradually until she has only to focus on its point of emergence and she will forge the print that she intends. The work itself is precise and intricate. Joanna works with the care and exactitude of a master artisan.

Joanna draws her ideas from the knowledge gleaned from incessant reading and research and her dreams and musings. She knows exactly what it is that she must do. Concurrently she does not know exactly what will at length emerge. There are surprises and happy accidents. There is beauty hidden within beauty. As though along with the plates and acid, the room is filled with candlelight and a sacred presence, she works to enable images to come into being that speak of the mysterious wonder that is at the heart of the world as she first encountered it when she was a child. Since then she has lost patience with religious doctrines and the patriarchy of the church but never with the underlying premise of God at the heart of the universe and nature as an expression of God. An intellectual process helps her choose her imagery and give order to the print. She also yields to the intuitive and long after the print is finished makes discoveries of her own about what the print embodies, what unsuspected meanings it suggests, and in what ways its unrecognized origins have affected the movements of her hands, the flow of texture and the curve of line.

Joanna works with such a fierce and quiet concentration she barely hears Meg's knock. When she does recognize the intrusion she does not lift her head. For a millisecond she is in the dark of her old basement space, hunched over the pan of acid in which she has submerged the heavy plate.

Then she is back in this time and place and answering Meg's knock. "Come in," she calls in what she construes to be a friendly voice.

Meg walks in with the day's mail in her hand. "You heard from that gallery in California. I thought you'd like to know."

"Yes, thanks. Just leave it on my table, will you. And Meg, look!" Joanna holds up the pencil in her hand that so often trembles. "Steady as a rock when I'm in the studio!"

"That's amazing. And wonderful." Smiling, Meg leaves the studio.

Joanna bows her head to her work. After a moment she stops to light a cigarette, inhale deeply, and gaze out the window. Hours, days more, she thinks, not quite finishing the thought, meaning, time alone, to work, to be left unbothered. She lays the cigarette carefully in the ashtray, picks up her tool again, and returns to work. She drinks in the solitary work time like a desert wanderer who has finally found an oasis that is real. She has only barely begun to slake her thirst.

# CHAPTER FIFTY-SIX

In their bedroom in the wing, Meg and Joanna are far from the old driveway with the lamppost on it. There is a new two-car parking area where Joanna leaves her car in front of the studio. From the wing they cannot see the old driveway, cannot feel the darkness deepen when its light goes out.

Joanna is dreaming of a great blue heron lifting into flight. Meg is dreaming she is swimming in a calm mountain lake when a pack of hounds races through the underbrush on shore, baying and chasing their prey. Joanna wakes to the knowledge that it is Don and Cyndy's dog, Jake, that he is barking up a storm. She keeps her eyes closed, thinking it must be very early, that they're walking him before they go to work. Meg sits up, checks the travel alarm Joanna now keeps on her bedside stand which shows it to be two a.m. and thinks immediately that it is the wire cutter. She jumps up and runs through the house. There is no moonlight. Halfway across the sunroom she sees that the lamppost has gone dark.

Certain in herself that the night crawler is a known man, the same Thompson she hated so many years ago, Meg's fear has changed to rage. She snaps up the phone as she hears him running through the woods. Nine-one-one instantly responds. Jake's bark turns to a growl and she hears Don yelling, "Get 'im, boy! Get 'im!"

Meg goes out on the deck. Joanna, who had stopped to pull on jeans and a shirt, is with her by then. They stand by the rail, staring down into the darkness, waiting.

Everything happens in staccato. Barking. Growling. Yelling. Thrashing in the underbrush. Flashes that Joanna names immediately as "Don's camera!"

The police car comes with flashing lights, throwing beams through the woods, first from the long driveway and then around the corner where Thompson's car must be parked. Meg and Joanna run back through the living room to the front porch from which they can see down through the woods to the street. It is like watching *NYPD Blue*.

The man is cursing and kicking at the dog. The searchlights fasten on him like liquid lariats, lassoing him in his rage, roping him in his terror. The dog is jumping at him, growling.

A second police car turns into the long driveway and turns more lights into the woods. Now it is the darkness that surrounds the light. Meg and Joanna hold hands and watch as the men in uniforms, guns in their hands, close in on the night crawler. Handcuffs click. Don calls Jake off. The sweeping floodlights go dark again.

Around the neighborhood a few windows flare up. Don and Cyndy's porch light is on. Meg and Joanna stand in darkness, watching the neighbors brightening the night. They go back in to light the big hurricane candle they keep on the table, and using a flashlight, go down to the long driveway. They walk out, uncertain, toward the patrol car. A young policeman approaches them.

"You made the call, ma'am?"

"Yes."

"May I come in and take down your report?"

"Please do. We don't have any lights," Meg says.

"I guess that's what this is all about?" His voice sounds as though he's smiling but it's too dark to tell.

Using their flashlight they go up the stairs and sit at the table where he writes on his little pad by candlelight. Like poetry, Meg thinks, short lines in the woods at night, written by candlelight.

"I hope they lock him up!" Joanna says.

"His name is Thompson, right?"

"That's right, ma'am. You should call Detective Orenstein in the morning." He thinks a minute, then adds, "He'll come on duty at four in the afternoon."

When the police cars have gone back into the night, Don knocks at their door. "Got 'im!" he says with a grin.

"Hey, thank you!" Meg gives Don a hug.

"And thank you!" Joanna leans over to pet and hug Jake, who is back on leash, looking proud.

"Cyndy worked the nightshift so she came in real late, and I took Jake out so we wouldn't have to get up to walk him early. It worked out real well!"

"I'd offer you coffee but we can't make any!"

"Want to come over for a cup?"

"Oh, no thanks. You get some sleep. But thank you, thank you!"

When Don has left, Meg and Joanna sit on the deck in the candlelight for a while, letting themselves comprehend what has occurred. Joanna chain-smokes while they review it all. Then they go back to bed and lie holding one another, talking softly about this and that, until the excitement wafts away like smoke, and they sleep again, each hoping to retrieve her broken dream of the great blue heron, of the mountain lake.

*** 

"I don't even believe them!" Joanna throws over her shoulder as she pours everyone a glass of wine. They've just returned from the precinct. Sue and Yvonne have come by for pizza and to hear the story.

"Nervous? They think he made us nervous? Rape makes women nervous too!" Joanna is furious.

Meg sits at the table, trying to think what they should do. Meg feels disappointed, as though the long connection with the detective and the police has led nowhere in the end. "The case is solved but it doesn't feel like much has changed."

"So tell all!"

"I'd like him sent upstate," Joanna says. "Fined indeed!"

"It's harassment, criminal mischief and trespassing," Meg says. "He'll be sentenced by a judge, most likely be given a suspended sentence and fined."

Yvonne is angry. "A fine! How can that be? He assaulted Joanna!"

"Orenstein says Thompson will claim that was inadvertent, an accident in the dark," Meg says sarcastically.

"And what about hate crimes?" Sue sets the pizza on the table on the deck. Meg brings out plates and napkins.

Joanna answers angrily as she and Yvonne light cigarettes, "He says we'd be opening a can of worms. Publicity and all."

"And he would still just get fined," Meg adds. "Double, maybe," she laughs grimly.

Their silence is laced with the residue of months of fear and rage. Suddenly Sue says, "Get an Order of Protection!"

Meg nods. "Let's do it!"

"They never work!" Joanna explodes.

"The night crawler would go to jail if he trespasses again. You want him in jail, right?"

"You know they never—"

Sue interrupts. "They don't stop men from bashing their wives—but it might stop this guy. Thompson's sneaky, not violent. The bastard seduced his daughter—he didn't physically assault her."

"That could foul a kid up even more than a violent rape," Yvonne says, "but yeah—he's a coward, not the other kind of brute."

"And now he's scared!"

Unpersuaded, Joanna yields. "Okay, if that's all we can do, let's do it."

Meg says, "Then we could get Thompson locked up if he comes around ever again."

"Okay. We can do that." Joanna adds, "We should call the Lesbian Avengers. They'd know how to keep the man far hence."

***

Meg concentrates on her driving on the way to court. She doesn't like the speed of the Long Island Expressway but doesn't know how to find the courthouse from the back roads. Once there, they go through the metal detector; Joanna has to unload her pockets because her Swiss Army knife sets off the alarm. "You can pick that up on your way out," the guard says, smiling.

They fill in papers, are sent from one clerk to another, then go wait in the courtroom to which they are assigned. As in old Greyhound stations the odor of slept-in clothing and unwashed bodies hovers over the worn wood of the benches. The mix of languages and skin shades reminds Meg of city streets but here there is a heaviness in the bodies slumped on the benches, expecting nothing, that is the opposite of Manhattan's liveliness. She knows Joanna must need a cigarette but they have to stay to answer when they are called. Joanna brought a book but the bailiff shook his head at her. No reading is allowed in courtrooms.

In front of them a Black woman reprimands her adolescent son for taking out a cigarette. He says he wasn't going to light it, just hold it in his lips. She laughs and knocks it down. "Aw, don't do that!" he says, bending to pick it up and the bailiff, who is also Black, walks back to tell him to keep down the noise.

The bailiff calls Meg and Joanna forward. The judge asks what this is about. He ascertains that Thompson is not present. Meg tells the story.

"He's been shutting off your electric power?"

"Yes. And writing hate graffiti on our mailbox."

"You saw him doing this?"

"They arrested him while he was doing it," Meg says with satisfaction.

"Do you know this man?"

"Yes."

"A neighbor?"

"No. His daughter was in my class in high school some ten years ago."

The judge, an older, balding man, tips his head slightly to the side, pondering Meg and Joanna. "And he's been mad at her teacher ever since?"

"Apparently."

"Why would that be? Did you flunk her?"

"No, she was an excellent student."

"So then?"

"He wanted to read her journal and she refused to give it to him."

"You both refused to show him his daughter's schoolwork?"

"Yes."

"And why was that?"

"I told my students in creative writing classes that their work was private, and I promised them not to ever show it to anyone."

The judge raises an eyebrow and lifts his head from leaning on his arm. "Even their parents?"

"Yes."

"Why?" Now he's interested, Meg thinks.

"Students sixteen and seventeen years old often write stories about personal experiences that they don't want anyone to know about."

"Such as?"

Meg knows she's on thin ice. "It might be their grief over the death of a grandparent or about their parents' divorce. It might be about being in love or drinking." She wants to add "Or child abuse, beatings or incest," but she does not. What this child had written was not current abuse but a history of past abuse over many years. She was leaving for college and the abusive father would pay the tuition. It was not the time to call in the police. Meg believed that was for Rachel and a therapist to decide.

"Are there ever circumstances in which you would show their work to someone?"

"If their life were in danger or someone else were in danger. I told them all that in the beginning."

The judge seems satisfied with this and changes direction. "Do you remember what this girl wrote?"

"Yes." And now I'm in deep shit, Meg thinks.

"And what was that?"

"I'm not free to say," Meg says.

"And why not?"

"I can't break trust with her."

"Can you give me some idea what it might have been?"

There is a pause. The stenographer looks at Meg with real interest. "It was a personal problem. I urged her to go to a therapist for help and she did so. I can say that she wrote me later, after she graduated with honors from college, to thank me."

"And would your guess be that he eventually found out what she had written and blamed you for it?"

"That would be my guess."

"So he waits ten years and then he writes graffiti to say teacher is a witch?" The judge supports his head with his open hand, leaning on his elbow; he is smiling down at them. The judge likes us, Meg thinks. He likes these two older women, teachers under attack.

"No, Your Honor. The graffiti attacked my identity with obscenities."

"You're Jewish?"

Meg feels Joanna's tension. Their bodies are almost touching. No way back, Meg thinks, and says respectfully, "No, Your Honor, I'm lesbian."

The judge's face shifts. Not repulsion, Meg thinks, so much as disbelief. He studies them. "So why now?"

"I gave a workshop in Huntington last year on homophobia. I think he saw an article in the newspaper about that and found out where I live."

"Let me get this straight. You were his kid's teacher years ago. But he didn't harass you until now?"

Meg nods. The court stenographer looks at her expectantly and she remembers she must speak. "That's right, Your Honor."

"He held a grudge and waited to get even?"

Meg nods. "I don't think he knew where I lived until now."

"Did Mr. Thompson talk to you at the time you taught his daughter?"

"Yes, sir." Meg wonders if you are supposed to end every sentence with Your Honor and decides you're not.

"And?"

"He came to school and asked me for her journal. I refused to give it to him."

"Did he threaten you at that time?"

"Yes, Your Honor." Meg hadn't expected to go into all this. Her stomach tightens. She cannot find a way back. "He said he'd get me fired."

"For protecting her privacy?" He smiles at her. The judge is finding this an entertainment, Joanna thinks. How did I get here? She thinks of Kafka.

Meg shakes her head and says, "No, he threatened to out me as a lesbian."

"You said that you are lesbian?"

"Yes."

"So?"

Meg tries to be succinct. "I didn't make that known at school."

"And his threat?"

"To tell the school board."

"You'd lied to them?"

"No, Your Honor. No one had ever asked me."

"Don't ask, don't tell?" The judge smiles broadly.

Meg nods.

"Did he?"

"Sir?"

"Did he expose you?"

Interesting term for outing, Meg thinks, and pauses. "I think he may have behind the scenes."

"Could you have been fired for being gay?"

Meg nods. "Yes."

The judge looks from Meg to Joanna. "What do you do?"

"I'm a printmaker."

"Then your lifestyle doesn't interfere with your work?" The judge looks like he's about to go out for coffee with them and have a chat.

Suddenly he glances at his watch and at the bailiff and gets down to business. "So what is it you want protected? Your lamppost?"

"Your Honor," Joanna says, with fire, "this man trespassed, harassed us and subjected us to considerable inconvenience by short-circuiting our power. We were left without electricity, heat or hot water. But the more important thing is that he physically assaulted me. This all was a form of terrorism."

The judge nods, with a condescending smile. "Isn't that feminist rhetoric? Inconvenient, yes, I'd say. Adolescent anger, yes. Terrorism, no."

"Die dyke! is a threat. It was like being stalked." Joanna's face is flushed with rage.

"You two look like it would take a lot to intimidate you!"

"He came at night. We'd like an Order of Protection. He has no right to sneak onto our land at night to do us harm!"

"I'll grant you that. But if this is your worst trouble, we should all be so lucky." The judge glances meaningfully around the room. A young man in the front row grins up at him.

"The clerk will give you your Order of Protection."

"Thank you, Your Honor," Meg says, feeling tripped up halfway through the action, knowing Joanna is ready to kill.

They go to the clerk who sends them to another clerk in another room to get the actual Order of Protection documents. As they walk toward the back door of the courtroom they see a man in the last row of seats bend over as though to pick up something from the floor. He is keeping his head down and simultaneously they break step, somehow knowing that the man is Thompson. Meg senses Joanna's surge, like a panther about to leap. She grabs her arm and holds it fiercely. "You bastard!" Joanna hisses toward the man who lifts his head then, revealing a frightened face. He is wearing a dark suit and a wine-colored tie. He starts to rise as though to retreat out the other end of the row of seats but he stumbles trying to move along. "You contemptible bastard!" Joanna tugs away from Meg but there are several women between her and Thompson and her out-flung fist falls short of his face. Meg pulls on Joanna's other arm, taking a step toward the outer door. She hears the judge's gavel as she propels a resistant Joanna away and out. Once in the elevator Joanna takes out her pack of cigarettes and holds one ready to light as soon as they get outside.

"I'm going back to that other clerk to get the papers. You wait here, okay?" Meg hurries back in with a long glance first at Joanna who is inhaling deeply, her face still flushed, her hands still clenched.

# CHAPTER FIFTY-SEVEN

They stroke with almost no conversation. The Carmen River is narrow and shallow and the kayak moves easily under the overhanging branches. Joanna has the bow and guides them around the occasional boulder. Egrets and herons occasionally flash over and a pair of swans with seven cygnets watch them carefully as they glide by. For the first hours they move downriver they see no other human beings.

Then abruptly the river widens into a pond with a concrete dam across its farther side. Puzzled, they come to a stop. The young fellow who rented them the kayak had given them a map but there was no such notation on it. "We have to ford here," Joanna says.

"How?" Meg sizes up the height of the dam and of the riverbanks on either side. They cannot lift the kayak that high. Neither can they carry it all the way around the dam to put it back in the river.

"Good question, that." They look at one another and then begin to laugh. "Two lost old women camp out on the Carmen River. Found after several days they ask for food and strong drink."

Behind them at the other edge of the pond two swimmers surface. "Hey, they can do it for us!" Meg waves in their direction. "Let's paddle over to them."

"Need help?" the boy asks.

Meg sees his clothes are all on the shore. "Could you carry our kayak around for us?" Meg asks. "We'll paddle over there but we can't lift it out." She knows he can get his trunks on while their backs are turned.

The boy helps each of them ashore before he carries their kayak up and around and down into the river on the other side where they board it again and go on down the river. "Lucky he happened to be there," Joanna says. "No thanks to the nit who gave us the useless map!"

"Rescued by a pair of skinny-dipping kids," Meg says, laughing.

"I didn't notice that!" Joanna says, joining in the laughter.

Near the mouth of the river there is a shallow mooring where they go ashore. Together they manage to haul the kayak up on the beach.

They wait there for the boy who will load the kayak on a truck and give them a ride back to their parked car. This secluded spot is already touched with September's evening shadows but the open patch of sky beyond above the ocean is still an afternoon blue, glazed with purple and orange, ready to hold the last light for several hours.

Joanna takes Meg in her arms. "That was wonderful," she says. "The world is always beautiful, isn't it?"

Meg smiles, thinking how glad she is that she brought Joanna out here.

"And I love you." With a quick glance around, Joanna kisses Meg.

"I love you too," Meg answers, as she also does every night, letting it be the last thing they know together before they fall asleep.

***

On her birthday Joanna is in her studio working on a new print. A local gallery has included five of her pieces in a big show and she has received a lot of praise, including a good write-up in the paper. Another gallery has asked to see her work. Reluctantly she puts down her pencil and goes upstairs for lunch.

Meg is just taking a cake out of the oven.

"Okay if I fix myself a sandwich?"

Meg nods. "No one's coming till five. You can work till then."

They sit at the table on the deck to eat their lunch. "I used the tripod and camera already. It works like a charm. Thanks again."

"I'm glad."

Joanna goes to the rail while she has her cigarette. Cards have come from friends in Oregon. Emily has called.

With the night crawler met and conquered, the house has stopped turning around and around as though spun by a tornado and has settled comfortably into its own space. It is as though the land is posted: NO HUNTING NO TRESPASSING NO WIRE CUTTING OFFENDERS WILL BE PROSECUTED! Around them the green of summer has just begun to yield. A few leaves drift down.

Joanna smiles at Meg and waves her hands in an all-encompassing arc over the yard: driveway, lamppost, oaks and evergreens. *It is a safe and magic bower,* Joanna thinks. And says to Meg, "And now it *is* what you promised me."

Meg raises an eyebrow, waiting. *Joanna is radiant again,* she thinks, admiring her intensity and her beauty—*and as for the cigarette that is intrinsic to her artist-self,* "Que Sera Sera." *I cannot change the way I am, and she cannot change the way she is. And we love each other as we are. What will be, will be.*

"'*The Lake Isle of Innisfree.*'" Joanna says, still smiling. "Remember?"

Meg goes to stand beside her, putting her arm around her. "Happy birthday, Joanna. And yes, love, I do remember."